COVENT GARDEN
in the Snow
Jules Wake

A division of HarperCollins*Publishers*
www.harpercollins.co.uk

HarperImpulse an imprint of
HarperCollinsPublishers
The News Building
1 London Bridge Street
London SE1 9GF

www.harpercollins.co.uk

This paperback edition 2017

First published in Great Britain in ebook format by
HarperCollinsPublishers 2017

A catalogue record for this book
is available from the British Library

ISBN: 9780008221973

Typeset in Birka by Palimpsest Book Production Ltd,
Falkirk, Stirlingshire

Printed and bound in Great Britain

For my Mum, Di, the real make-up artist
and my children, Ellie & Matt, whose
love of theatre has been infectious.

Chapter 1

To: Felix@nutsmarketing.co.uk
From: Matilde@lmoc.co.uk
    URGENT – Possible loo roll crisis
    Working late tonight, pls record the Arsenal
game and don't forget loo rolls!!! Can you get some
when you go shopping tonight – and remember
no gummy bears or chocolate peanuts, we need
food we can actually cook with!
    And have you seen my book, *The Rosie Project*,
I've got a horrible feeling I might have left it on
the train.
    Tilly x

No! No! Stop! Despite knowing it was probably
completely hopeless, I stabbed at the keys on the
keyboard, bracelets clinking like maracas as I watched
the computer screen. It was the *Sorcerer's Apprentice*
all over again. With horrifying speed, the number of

emails leaving the outbox increased.

Five!

Then ten!

Twelve, eighteen, twenty-one, thirty-three.

'Oh hell.' This couldn't be happening. Emails with the title *Urgent – Possible loo roll crisis* which should have gone to Felix were busy whizzing off to goodness only knows where.

Jeanie, my boss, glanced up from the wig she was working on.

'What have you done now?' she asked, rolling her heavily kohl-lined eyes as she came over to stand behind me. 'Don't tell me, you've sent another email to Alison instead of Felix? Attached a picture of Dr Who instead of our leading man and sent it to the head of costume at La Scala?'

Give me a make-up palette, a couple of pencils and the right hair-piece, and with a deft touch of shading and brushing, I can transform a sixty-year-old granddad into an irresistible Lothario. Give me a computer and there's more chance of me splitting the atom in my own kitchen with an egg whisk.

I blame my biospheres; apparently, I have dodgy ones. Mobile phones give up the ghost on a regular basis and I can't wear a watch without it losing time. Me and technology are a disaster. I just don't have the patience. Even so, I thought *I'd* cracked email.

Unfortunately, once you've clicked that mouse, there's no going back. It's Pandora's Box all over again. And just like Pandora, how could I resist. After all, what's a girl, on the wrong side of twenty-nine, to do, when it's coming up to Christmas and her fiancé seems to be spending more time potting snooker balls than checking out her erogenous zones, and some random person sends her an attachment called 'Santa Baby'.

It sounded cute and harmless. When I opened the attachment up, it was even cuter still – a very handsome Santa danced across my screen to the tune of jingle bells before dropping his trousers to reveal a full moon of pert buns, flashing a very naughty grin over his shoulders. The moment I moved the cursor to try and close the picture, Santa started zinging about, bashing the edges of the screen with the speed of a demented bluebottle.

Although amusing at first, after the initial dancing, his frozen image didn't do much but ricochet off the sides of the screen as erratically as a pinball on speed. It was only when I tried to close the thing down that everything went haywire.

Now, as I watched the identical subject lines of the emails racing, like armed and dangerous carrier pigeons from the inbox, regarding the imminent loo roll crisis at home, I guessed something more sinister had been going on.

Flipping dip, the numbers in the outbox were still going up.

Fifty-six, sixty-nine…

Did I even *know* that many people?

The whirring from the hard-drive under the desk was getting louder and faster, with the intensity of a plane revving up. I didn't think kicking it was going to help. Any moment now it might take off.

Jeanie pointed one of her neat, shortly trimmed nails at the screen. 'It's six weeks until Christmas. What's *that*?'

'Santa baby apparently, except I can't get him to go away.'

She shook her head. 'You didn't open an attaché, did you?'

Now was not the time to correct her casual misuse of the English language.

'Who? Me?' I gave her a big smile and a shrug of my shoulders. 'Might have done. Oops.'

'What are you like, Tilly?'

The two of us stood there staring at the computer and I vaguely registered the squeak of the studio door.

'Only one thing for it.' I dived down onto my knees, bum high in the air and took the most obvious course of action.

I pulled the plug.

I heard a gasp from Jeanie.

'What?' I wiggled out, feeling my skirt riding up. 'It can't do it any harm, can it?'

There was silence and somehow, I just knew someone else was there. Someone else getting a bird's eye view of my favourite lilac silk and lace cami-knickers which were more lace than anything else, if you get my drift.

Still on all fours, I managed to manoeuvre around to find Mr drop-dead-gorgeous glaring down at me, although the expression on his face was decidedly Sir-seriously-pissed-off.

'Hi,' I squeaked like an over-sized guinea pig. My heart stuttered as I stared at him. Someone had been more than generous when handing out the good-looking genes.

'What the hell do you think you're doing?'

How bloody unfair. Even his voice – melted sodding chocolate with a very faint trace of an accent. Talk about being front of the queue for sex appeal. He must have snagged an entire birth year's quota.

Cool eyes studied me intently.

Oh God, he seriously expected an answer? Any moment now I'd start drooling. What the hell was wrong with me? I was a happily engaged woman for heaven's sake.

The thing was those green eyes, high cheekbones and the short dark hair sparked a dart of instant sexual attraction, sending my heart rate into intensive care levels. Lust at first sight. Nothing more. My libido sitting up and taking notice. After all, it wasn't as if my lady parts were getting an awful lot of attention at home at the moment. Yes, just lust.

I realised he was still waiting for an answer.

'I just thought it needed rebooting.' I plucked the phrase out of the air, knowing I'd heard Felix use it once or twice.

His eyes narrowed, his mouth tightened. I swallowed. Even scary, he looked damn attractive.

'Rebooting,' he spat the word with enough venom to strike down the entire make-up team.

I nodded with a hopeful smile.

He closed his eyes, a look of pain crossing his features. I could see tension in his jawline as if he were clenching his teeth really hard.

When he opened them, I leaned over and patted his arm. Getting stressed like that wasn't good for you. 'Hey, it's only a computer. It'll be fine. We don't use it that much anyway.'

Out of the corner of my eye I could see Jeanie shaking her head ever so slightly.

'Give me pen and paper any day.' I smiled encouragingly at him.

Jeanie looked horrified.

Green-eyes took in a strangled sort of breath but couldn't hide the slight twitch of his mouth as if he wanted to smile.

'Do you know who I am?'

I didn't but he seemed to expect I did. In that suit, which added to the overall heart-socking attractive package, (and I don't normally do corporate types), he didn't look as if he worked here. The fine wool jacket emphasised broad shoulders and the sharply creased trousers hinted at long lean legs. Visiting sponsor? Interview candidate? Contractor?

Then I spotted the staff badge tucked under his suit jacket. He must be new ... oh minims and crotchets. Sweet hallelujahs. The new guy. There'd been a department note circulated last week about the spanky new appointment to whizz up our computer systems. I'd filed it under irrelevant, i.e. straight in the bin. My heart plummeted stone-like and I stepped in front of the computer as if I could hide my recent misdemeanours.

'Mr Memo, I mean erm ... Mr er ... er.' *Could this get any worse?*

'Walker. Director of IT.' The way he said it, he might as well have said 'defender of the faith' or something else weighty.

'Right.'

'So, Miss, Mrs ...?'

Jeanie jumped in, 'This is Matilde Hunter. She's one of our team.' She'd pronounced it in the French way,

7

which I thought might be deliberate as if to suggest that English wasn't my first language, so how on earth could I possibly be trusted with a computer.

'And this is exactly what I was talking about in the management meeting,' he glared at Jeanie.

She nodded. 'And as I explained at the meeting, we don't have much call for computers up here. We're more hands on, if you know what I mean.'

'Rubbish. It's the twenty-first century. How do you manage your inventory?' He glanced around at the untidy room, over to the shelf with rows of head blocks, some with complete wigs, others pinned in grid patterns ready to start making a new one and others partially made. Like a rather odd rainbow, hair in every shade spilled from the shelf. From the white of yaks' hair used for seventeenth century Rococo wigs and the golden blonde of Brunhilde's tresses through to an intricate plaited Titian hairpiece and a dark black coronet of ringlets.

'Surely you need to keep track of how many wigs you've got and the materials you use.'

Jeanie and I both glanced over at the antiquated filing cabinet hiding the tattered card index system we used.

'Not only,' his eyes bored into mine, 'does this place need a thorough overhaul but you ...'

For the briefest of seconds something flashed in his eyes.

'... need to learn how to deal with a computer properly. You do not yank out the plug ... ever. You shut it down. You don't ...' There it was again, that little twitch of his mouth. 'Reboot it.' His face softened but we're talking degrees here. He still seemed pretty fearsome. 'Leave that to the experts please.'

'Okey-doke,' I said with a cheery smile. Thank goodness he hadn't walked in two minutes earlier, when all those emails were flying the nest. At least I'd got away with that much.

To: All Departments
Please join me in welcoming our first Director of IT, Mr M Walker, who joins us from a significant financial institution in the City.

    This is a new appointment for the London Metropolitan Opera Company. I therefore hope you will make him feel welcome and offer your co-operation as he gets to grips with our wonderful work here.

Julian Spencer
Chief Executive
London Metropolitan Opera Company

Chapter 2

After the cluttered mayhem of the wig room, the calm, clinical atmosphere of the make-up department was like stepping into an operating theatre.

Harsh white light from a bank of bulb-lit mirrors filled the room. Underneath them, a spotless white counter ran the full length of one wall, in front of which sat a row of cream leather swivel chairs as impressive as thrones awaiting royalty.

'Hey Pietro.' The imposing figure filling the plush chair with his broad shoulders and wide chest was waiting for me.

'Tilly, darling.' Under the dark bushy brows which contrasted sharply with his silver hair, his eyes glinted with merriment. On either side of him, the other opera singers chattered away together as they waited for their respective make-up artists to arrive.

'How are you today?' I fished out a black cape and draped it across the rich fabric of his heavily embellished costume. 'Did your granddaughter like the zoo?'

'She *loved it* darling.'

The words came out as 'lorved eet'. Despite all his years in England, he'd never lost his Italian accent and the exaggerated vowels always made me smile.

'Especially the snakes.' He shuddered dramatically and winked at me in the mirror. 'Revolting child. Next time we're going to Selfridges. To see Santa, that will be far more civilised.'

He didn't mean it, he positively doted on twelve-year-old Lottie and had even been into her school in Notting Hill to talk in assembly. Not something that many international superstars did in my experience.

Laying out my kit, I checked I had everything, not once but twice. It made me antsy if I had to break off half way through to go searching for a brown pencil or the right brush.

Yup, everything was where I wanted it to be. I looked at Pietro in the mirror. In front of him, on a wooden block, sat the long flowing wig which made the final transformation from favourite grandpa to Don Giovanni.

'How was your morning?'

'I had a run in with a virus, blinking thing,' I said shaking my head. 'Think I've spread it everywhere.'

'*What?*' Pietro's face filled with concern and his hand strayed to his throat in self-concern. His precious vocal chords could be rendered useless if he caught a nasty cold.

'No. No,' I laughed. 'Not a real one. A silly computer one.' I patted his arm quickly. Infecting anyone in a principal role, especially the world's most renowned baritone, was *Make-Up Artist's Cardinal Sin Number Three*. 'I'm germ free.' I waved my hands to reinforce my point.

As I carried on pencilling and shadowing his face, our conversation moved on with its usual easy flow as he related scurrilous tales about his arch-rival, an up and coming American singer, naughty, libellous gossip about one of his co-stars in a previous production and the difficulties of learning an aria for his next part.

Half an hour later, I put down my pencils and make-up palette.

'Thanks, wonderful girl.' Pietro stood and with a wicked grin admired himself in the brightly-lit mirror. 'God, I'm lovely.' He patted the outsize codpiece stuffed down his buckskin trousers. 'All ready to seduce my daily quota of virgins.'

'Oooh, Pietro, you are wicked,' sang Vince as he applied the finishing touches to the doe-eyes of one of said hapless virgins. A chorus of giggles erupted as Pietro strutted around the room thrusting out his pelvis. Even Jeanie, who liked the team to maintain an air of calm before a performance, managed a smile.

'Come here you.' Crooking a finger at him, I beckoned him back to his chair. 'There's no seducing anyone until

I've checked your wig again.' Running my fingers around his hairline, I gave the hairpiece a testing tug, this way and that. All snug. Perfect. *Cardinal Sin Number Two* was something coming adrift mid-performance. Jeanie's mantra had been drummed into all of us – you can draw blood as long as the wig stays in place.

'How does it feel?' I stood back, studying the fit. It looked fabulous on him. All the wigs were hand-made. Most were sent out to trusted pieceworkers but the principals' wigs were made in-house. I didn't want to think how many finger twitching hours this particular one had taken.

Pietro tossed the long hair back over his shoulder with a leonine-shake.

'It suits me I think. Perhaps I should keep it on when I go home.' He winked lasciviously. 'My wife would love it.'

'Beginners stage left please.' The tannoy burst into life, punching the muted quiet of the room with a spike of electricity. A sudden hush fell as everyone sobered, ready for that first step on stage. Now on count-down to curtain up, with the precision of a well-drilled army, the make-up team straightened, smoothed and stroked, giving each of their charges a final check to ready them for the vast audience out front, while the wardrobe team, like bridesmaids at a wedding, assessed, tugged and tucked.

Several floors down, two thousand people were taking

their expensive red velvet seats in eager anticipation of the evening's performance. The picture was so clear in my head; the excited hum of chattering voices, the Mexican Wave of up and down bobs as the audience squeezed past each other's knees and people peering down through their opera glasses at the orchestra in the pit, already seated and tuning up.

As we were about to leave the make-up room, crowding into the corridor to make the journey backstage, Pietro's hand suddenly shot to his chest. For a horrible moment, I thought he was having a heart attack, until he gave me a sheepish glance and fished out his mobile phone.

'Pietro!' I gasped. Mobiles were strictly forbidden backstage as they could interfere with some of the tech stuff. I'd never even seen him with one before.

His face darkened, lines of temper marking his mouth as he homed in on the caller ID.

'I have to take this,' he snapped and wheeled back into the empty make-up room, slamming the door.

'Shit! What do I do?' I hopped from one foot to the other, glancing from the closed door and back at Jeanie. This was uncharted territory. You don't argue with a star as big as Pietro but I had to make sure he was in the wings for curtain up. No excuses. No reprieves.

'Fuck,' said Jeanie looking at her watch. 'Go get him,' whispered Jeanie, shoving me toward the door, looking anxiously at the rest of the actors hovering in the corridor. 'Be firm. We'll go on down but make sure you're right behind us.'

I could clearly hear a tinny voice talking excitedly down the line but not the words. Not that I needed to. Pietro's face said it all.

'Porca Miseria!' The vehement words rattled around the room as he started to pace the floor, Italian expletives exploding from his mouth periodically.

Keeping a panicked eye on my watch, I deliberately walked into his path.

'Er Pi ...' His eyes flashed furiously at me and he shook his head, putting me in mind of an angry lion – one that would be quite happy to rip my head off there and then.

'They'd better not print a word! Not one single word you hear me,' he bellowed. Gone was avuncular grandpa. His anger permeated the room in shock waves. Standing so close, it felt as if I was holding a punch bag while Muhammad Ali practised his right hook.

I could feel sweat beading on my forehead. This was awful. I had to get him down to the wings.

The tinny voice started jabbering again like a rabid Dalek.

'I don't care about that!' Pietro took another turn at the end of the room and stopped – an angry bull about to charge. 'You stop it. Take out an injunction.' Menace hissed in his voice.

His gaze came to rest on me, the steel grey eyes glinting and my heart stalled for a minute. Hell, it was *The Godfather* all over again.

'You stop it! You're my agent Max. I don't want the story getting out.'

He listened and then turned puce. 'You wouldn't want your grandchildren to see pictures like that in the paper. Stop it. That's your job! Do it!' Pietro snapped the phone shut with a vicious clench of his hand.

'Merda', he spat, throwing the phone with such force onto the table that it flew across to the back wall and bounced onto the floor.

The sudden action stirred me. 'Pietro, I'm sorry but we have to go down. Now.' I was quite impressed with how calm I managed to sound. Inside, it felt as if there was a bat trying to beat its way out of my chest. I had to get him backstage.

'*Now*. You expect me to go on stage *now*?' His hand touched his throat and he stood there with his head thrown back.

'Yes,' I said, feeling as if I'd stepped off a cliff and desperately hoping I sounded firm. Oh crap, he couldn't not. Jeanie would kill me. She trusted me to get him there.

'My vocal chords are far too tense. I'm too upset.' He

started towards one of the chairs, every inch the prima donna.

I tentatively touched his arm. 'Not as upset as the audience, Pietro. Some of them may have waited years to see you. You can't disappoint them.'

He straightened. Narrowing his eyes, he nodded.

'Do it for them. Don't let,' I nodded to the phone discarded on the floor, 'them win.' I held open the door, standing back to let him through before following in his wake. He strode down the corridor, leaving me almost running to keep up. When he stopped suddenly, I cannoned into him. Whirling round, he grabbed my forearms in a tight grip and stared intently.

What now? With my arm clamped in his, I risked an agonised glance at my watch. Four minutes to curtain up.

'You love your job,' he fired at me. 'It's all you ever wanted to do?'

I nodded, thinking it could all be over if I didn't take charge of him. He knew how much I loved my job.

Pietro's hands gentled suddenly, his eyes filled with regret and something else.

'Like you, this is all I ever wanted to do. My father, a poor man, worked the fields. A farmer. His voice. Bellissimo. He would have been greater than me but he never had the lessons. I needed lessons. The money to pay for the best lessons.'

I nodded, trying to be patient and not let my agitation show – he'd told me this many times before.

His usually flawless English deserted him. 'Now… in … when a youth, I …' he stopped and then whispered the rest.

I couldn't help the gasp of surprise that whistled out next. Bloody hell!

The curtain went up two minutes late. The audience probably didn't notice but the production crew knew. Backstage there was a noticeably tense atmosphere. Jeanie nodded and mouthed. 'You OK?'

I held up crossed fingers and shook my head. Vince sidled over and gave me a quick hug.

'God that was awful,' I muttered into his ear. 'Really thought he was going to refuse to go on. He's really shaken up.'

Vince pulled a sympathetic face.

Thanks to the quick scales practice in the lift that I'd manage to coerce Pietro into doing, his voice settled quickly and soared in the theatre within the second bar. Hopefully the audience would forgive his quavery first few notes.

'What the fuck do you think you are playing at?' hissed a furious voice, pressing right up to me in the wings. Alison Kreufeld, Artistic Director and head honcho virtually had steam coming out of her ears.

'I ... I ...'

'That is fucking unforgivable. See me tomorrow. My office.' With that she turned her back and disappeared through the stage door. When I looked around all the crew were absorbed in looking down at the floor.

Nursing a large G and T, I sat at the kitchen table resting my forehead on the wooden top. What a day. I wanted to cry. Why did scary, super superior Artistic Director, Alison Kreufeld, always manage to catch me doing something stupid or getting something stratospherically wrong? Like the time, in a fit of enthusiasm, I thought I'd impress her by doing a series of hair designs for the corps de ballet in Swan Lake. Only I hadn't read her briefing notes properly. It was the Matthew Bourne all male production. She dined out on my stupidity for weeks.

And after a day like that I should have known better than to answer the phone. We still had a landline. Only three people used it. Felix's mum, my mum and my sister.

'Hello Tilly. It's Christelle.' I winced guiltily as I heard the carefully enunciated words, spoken as usual in her precise fussy way.

'Hi, Christelle,' I did my best to inject some enthusiasm into my tone. 'How are you? Has your cold gone?'

'Yes, thank you. It was several weeks ago, you know.' *Had it been that long?*

'Well, sometimes they linger,' I said, determined to keep the conversation afloat. 'How's work? Are you very busy?'

'Exceptionally. My caseload keeps growing. But I'm getting more and more of the high-profile stuff, which is a good sign.'

Idly, I straightened the photos on the mantelpiece. All of them were of me and Felix in various silly poses, accompanied by assorted friends. It struck me that in all of them, there was always someone else in tow. A day at the beach – Felix and five mates buried up to their necks in sand. Me and Felix and friends at Alton Towers. Felix and I, with three of his mates and their girlfriends, on the day he proposed.

'It's been an excellent week in chambers. We won an important case. Got a new clerk. Not terribly bright but I think he'll get there. You know how it is with these people.' She spoke, as always, in little staccato sentences.

'Sure.' I lied, feeling guilty. I had no more idea about what went on in my sister's world than she did about mine. She was a legal eagle, a high flyer with straight A's, a fabulous degree and apparently in the right chambers.

The second hand on my watch ticked its way around the face. Thirty seconds and we'd nearly exhausted our lines. Regret pinched at me. We had so little in common.

'Maman hasn't heard from you. It might be a good idea to call her. She won a bridge tournament. And Dad's put his back out again.'

Resentment replaced regret. I didn't need her reminding me. Mum was just as capable of calling me. Deliberately being flippant I said, 'Poor Dad, back to the chiropractor. Must be love, I swear he spends more time with her than with Mum. Not that I ...'

'Tilly!' Christelle's voice was sharp with reproof.

'Only joking,' I said. My poor sister was a chip off the old block. A sliver of ice.

'You'd better phone her.' Christelle's words were clipped with disapproval. 'Now, lunch? Can you do Wednesday? One-thirty?'

What would she say if I turned around and said, 'No, I can't'? Maybe she'd be secretly relieved. Our lunches were hardly fun, Chardonnay-fuelled, gossip fests.

'I think so ...' She was so well-organised she probably knew her schedule off by heart, even had appointments entered in her smart phone, whereas I wasn't even sure where my antiquated brick was now.

'Let me check. If it isn't, I'll let you know.'

'The usual Café Paul. One-thirty. See you then. Try Tilly, not to be late.'

Familiar Tiggerish thumps made me lift my head as Felix bounded up the stairs to our first-floor flat and then the front door crashed shut as he yelled, 'Missus, I'm home.'

'I could murder a beer,' he said as he burst into the kitchen. Pulling a bottle out of the fridge, he flicked off the top and took a long swallow without breaking a stride. He glanced at my glass. 'More gin vicar?' he asked.

'No, this was a large already,' I mumbled, toasting him with my half-full tumbler.

He dropped a brief kiss on my head and wriggled out of his favourite RAF style overcoat, tossing it over a chair, heedless when it slipped to the floor. Perching himself on the top of the kitchen counter, his legs swinging and bashing the cupboards, he studied my unhappy face.

I winced. The cupboard was already hanging from its hinges.

'What's the matter? You look like you swallowed a pound and shat a penny.'

'Crap day. Seriously crap. The crappest of the crappiest.'

'Tell Uncle Felix all about it.'

I shook my head, pulling a face. 'Urgh, Uncle Felix sounds well creepy. And this is bad.'

'Do we need Mojitos?' he asked teasingly.

'Not this time.' I sighed and took a slug of gin. 'I might not be able to afford Mojitos ever again.'

'That bad.' He pulled a face of mock horror.

Sometimes Felix just wore you down with his indefatigable refusal to be serious. I gave him a half-hearted smile because I couldn't not.

'Been a shocker of a day. Started with a virus. Then I got bollocked by the new IT man and then Pietro missed curtain up. And Alison,' I twisted my mouth in a bad-medicine taste expression, 'Kreufeld went ballistic and wants to see me tomorrow.' I covered my face with my hands, stretching my skin over my cheekbones. 'I just know she wants to get rid of me. And that freelance woman, Arabella Barnes, is desperate for a job.'

'Well, she can't do that because you're ace and Jeanie and Vince would put syrup of figs in this Arabella bird's coffee. Although personally I don't get it.' He shook his head and jumped to his feet. 'How do you put up with all that gruesome squawking?' Clutching his chest and holding out one hand, he launched into a horribly shrill falsetto vaguely reminiscent of *Bohemian Rhapsody*. 'Kill me now. I beg of you. Spare me from this awful music.'

In spite of myself I burst out laughing. 'You are awful. You should come, you might even enjoy it.'

He shook his head like a mutinous toddler.

'How do you know if you've never tried it?'

He pulled a face. 'That's what mothers say when they want kids to eat green stuff, like broccoli or cabbage or Brussels sprouts. If I ever have children, they can live on jelly and ice-cream if they want.'

'They'll get malnutrition,' I giggled.

'Yeah but they'll be the happiest kids on the block.' He took a long swallow of beer, almost downing the whole bottle in one and then smacked it down on the table.

'So, what have you done?'

I told him about the Santa baby image because quite frankly that seemed the least of my problems.

'Oh missus. You big numpty!' He jumped up, oblivious to the cupboard door which dropped another inch, and then gave me a fleeting hug before whirling over to the fridge to help himself to another beer. 'I wouldn't worry about it,' he grinned.

'People get those virus things all the time. It's no big deal. That's what you have virus protection for. It'll be fine. I think half the time, the IT bods just use the fear of a possible virus to frighten people, so that you think you need them.'

'Well we've got a new one. An IT Director. He's a bit of a stiff. He caught me yanking the plug out of the computer.'

'Director eh? Big title. I'm sure he's got more important things to do than worry about that. Next.'

I closed my eyes, remembering the flutters of panic when I thought I might not get Pietro to go on stage.

'Much worse ... the absolute worst. Pietro delayed curtain up.'

'Blimey.' Even Felix knew how serious that was. He squeezed my arm with an immediate show of understanding. Felix really did get how important my job was to me.

'It wasn't even my fault but AK immediately assumed it was. She didn't even give me a chance to explain that Pietro got a call and the press ... He's being blackmailed.'

'Ooooo what's he done? Been caught in a compromising position with a rent boy in the box office?'

'Felix! Don't be so horrible.'

'What's he done then? Something worse?' His keen-eyed curiosity had me hesitating for a second, I could almost hear him smacking his lips in anticipation.

I sighed. 'He was so upset. When he was younger, his family didn't have the money to pay for singing lessons. He got a part in a porn film to earn the money.'

'I can't wait to tell Kevin that one.'

'Felix! You can't tell anyone.'

'Just joking. So, what's happened?'

'Pietro's sleaze-ball of an ex-brother-in-law has threatened to contact the press unless Pietro is nice to him. Shorthand for give him a big hand out.'

'Can you imagine it? If the press get wind the film will be all over the internet. At the moment if he can keep a lid on it, it's unlikely anyone will track it down.'

'Blimey. What a boy.'

I shook my head and sighed. Poor Pietro. 'He told me a bit about it, sounded quite racy. Very Lady Chatterley. Apparently, he played the young gardener seduced by the Contessa. Pietro said it was called *Il Gardiniere*.'

'Doing her lady's garden for her,' giggled Felix. 'Classic. Go Pietro. Someone would pay good money for pictures.'

'Felix, you shouldn't say that.' I shook my head. 'It's not funny. I feel so sorry for him. You didn't see how upset he was. He almost couldn't go on.'

'You're too soft. He'll get over it,' dismissed Felix. 'No such thing as bad publicity.'

To: Wig, Hair, and Make-Up Team
From: Director of IT
All members of staff are reminded that under no circumstances should attachments from unauthorised sources be opened or any unapproved material downloaded.

M Walker
Director of IT
London Metropolitan Opera Company

Chapter 3

Dreams of heart-shaped doodlebugs, reducing London to rubble, while AK handed me an Air Warden's helmet, filled my head all night leaving me feeling blurry around the edges by morning. Stuffing my corkscrew curls into a hasty ponytail, I secured it with a silk paisley scarf pinched from the wardrobe department and glared at my anaemic reflection before poking unhappily at the bags under my eyes. All the tricks of the trade weren't going to be able to disguise those babies.

I shot the computer in the workroom a quick look. I was staying clear of that thing today. Vince, who was just arriving, smiled as he caught me.

'Morning our Tilly. Want me to check your emails for you, lovie?'

'Don't. I'm jinxed. I'm not touching it again unless I absolutely have to.'

'That reminds me, you've had a few deliveries.' He nodded towards my work area with a sly smile.

'Ha blinking ha!' I scowled at the pyramid tower of loo rolls which had appeared on my worktable. 'Maybe we should be starting up a comedy club.'

Judging by the number of them, I guessed every last member of staff in the building had received my email yesterday. Blinking marvellous. Alison Kreufeld would just love that.

As I got my materials out to start work, Vince wandered over. 'Can I borrow ... ooh those bags still need some work sweetie.'

'Thanks a ton,' I muttered. 'I've used half a tube of concealer. I didn't get much sleep.' I did a double take, his skin positively glowed. 'Whereas you, you look all bright-eyed and bushy tailed. Have you been at the Beauty Flash Balm again?'

'Me darling? I swear by it, especially when you get home with the larks.'

'Larks? Late night, early morning?'

'All work and no play would make Vince a very dull boy darling. Bit of drinking and dancing, you know how it is.'

Behind him, Jeanie sighed. 'Drinking and dancing? I don't know where you get the energy.'

'High on life, me. High on life,' chirped Vince.

'Oh God,' groaned Jeanie. 'Who is it this time?'

Vince pouted and sniffed. 'Who says there's a man involved?'

Jeanie and I exchanged grins. 'There's *always* a man involved.'

Vince swallowed hard. 'Not this time.' Even trying to sound brave, he managed to be dramatic. 'We're just good friends.'

'Aw Vince,' I reached out and patted his arm. He seemed destined to be unlucky in love and it would be lovely if he could find the perfect partner.

Jeanie rolled her eyes. 'You mean he's straight.' She shook her head. 'Vince. Vince. Vince. What are we going to do with you?'

'He's not straight.' Vince's words spewed out in a brief burst of anger. 'He's in denial.'

'Really?' I reached over and patted his hand. 'Maybe he'll come around.'

He snatched his hand away. 'Easy for you to say.' His mouth flattened into an unhappy line. 'Smugly engaged.'

The sharp words hit like unexpected hailstones and I flinched. It was unlike Vince to be snippy. Jeanie's jawline tensed.

'Sorry Tilly. Sorry.' He gave me a sheepish look. 'I– I sh– I didn't mean to take it out on you.'

She gave him an approving look.

Wary of touching him again, I nodded. 'Don't worry Vince. I understand. If you ever want to talk about it.' I encompassed Jeanie in the look but her face was closed. It struck me that she'd been drawing back more recently.

'Thanks, lovie, but no one can help this time.'

The expression on his face made me want to comfort him but something in his eyes warned me to back off.

'Right, then to work.'

'Come on. My office. We need to get cracking and start thinking about *Romeo and Juliet* for next year's season.' She stopped and her eyes twinkled with sudden enthusiasm. 'And guess what? It's going to have a Regency period setting.'

'Oooh,' I rubbed my hands together. 'Research.'

Vince groaned, '*Research.*' Before adding, 'Tilly will be down to the Portrait Gallery faster than Fagin can pick a pocket or two.'

I beamed, my fingers twitching at the thought of getting started on the hairpieces we would need.

'Well, before you go beetling off on your little jaunt, we can make a start here.' Jeanie pointed to a pile of large coffee-table-sized books on the floor in front of her feet. Despite being no bigger than a broom cupboard, her office housed a huge collection of books.

'Being sexist, let's start having a look at this lot to get some ideas of the period for the ladies and you Vince,' she pushed another set of books with her foot across the floor to him, 'for the gents.'

Vince winked at me. 'Goody, lots of eye candy for me.'

After about an hour, with pages marked with yellow stickies, scribbles in notebooks and the occasional, 'What about this?' Vince got to his feet. 'My knees are killing me darlings. I need caffeine.'

'I doubt it will help your knees but I wouldn't say no.' I held up my empty mug.

As he stepped over me, I shifted onto my bottom and stretched out my legs, taking over what little space he'd just vacated. My back twinged as I sighed in relief.

Jeanie's phone buzzed and she leaned over me to get it. A resigned expression settled on her face.

'I'll send her up now.'

Alison Kreufeld's office was a lot grander than Jeanie's in that there was room to swing a whole cat and possibly a hamster too. With a cursory nod, as I approached the open door she invited me in. I'd only been here a few times before and was fascinated by the patchwork of designs that filled the walls, sets, make-up, wardrobe, lighting rig plans. She had a huge job, like a spider in the centre of the web spinning all the threads to create the final look and feel of a production. I might not be too keen on her but her reputation was fearsome.

'Morning, Matilde. Take a seat.'

She shook her head and sighed. 'Bit of a balls up last night.'

'Yes. Pietro ... He had a bit of a crisis.'

'Do you know what? I don't actually give a ... he's the talent. I can't bollock him. You however, I can. It's your responsibility to make sure he's where he's supposed to be. You, I can sack. And I bloody will if you make a balls-up like that again.'

What did she want me to say?

'I'm sorry but–'

'Like I said. I don't give a toss. And yes, I know it's bloody unfair but that's the way it is and you have to suck it up.'

Alison sighed and turned to the view outside her window. 'You're a good make-up artist. Talented. But there are plenty of good, talented make-up artists. They're standing ten deep in a queue out there.' She actually stabbed her finger at the pane of glass. 'You need to be better than good. Deal with stuff. Like getting Pietro on stage on time no matter what. You're too casual about things. You need to take some responsibility.'

I opened my mouth. I'd got Pietro down to the wings. Calmed him down in the lift. Got him to sing scales. He was two minutes late but it wasn't my fault.

'Your attitude is far too cavalier. Just that bit too laid back. It's not acceptable. You're letting yourself down. The executive board has decided to appoint an assistant head of department to Jeanie in the New Year. It's a management post.' Her eyes bored into mine. 'And it has to be advertised internally and externally. I'd like to see you apply but I need to see you buck your ideas up. I'm going to be keeping a very close eye on you, one more cock-up and you'll be on a disciplinary. Consider yourself on probation between now and Christmas.'

I opened my mouth aghast and for once thought better of it and closed it quickly. The quick calculating glance she shot me suggested she'd seen the brief movement.

'Probation?' What on earth did that mean?

'Yes. For the next few weeks I'll be reviewing your work very closely and at the end of the period, I'll decide whether to recommend you for the job or not. You have a tendency to jump in feet first without thinking about the further consequences,' she continued. 'That is not managerial behaviour. Managers reflect, think and then act.'

'I'd really like to apply. I love it here and–'

'I appreciate that but we want someone who doesn't just get the job done but who also understands the bigger picture. You love it. Great. You're brilliant at it. Wonderful. But you are just one small cog. Make-up ... yes, it's important. But so is the sound, wardrobe, the electricians, the lighting riggers, the props guys. If you're in management, you can't afford to think that your department makes a bigger, better, more special, more authentic, cleverer contribution. I know the detail, the attention, the amount of work that goes in, but,' she paused and gave me a ferocious stare, 'if you don't get the talent on the fucking stage, none of that counts for jack shit and actually shafts all the other buggers who have done their job just as bloody well and don't get the notice. Prima donnas on the stage I can cope with, but not the backstage crew.'

She sat down back at her desk and began to flip through her diary.

'You need to *prove* that you can do more than wield a hairbrush. And not make stupid cock-ups such as sending effing pictures of Dr sodding Who to my opposite number at La Scala when she's expecting shots of our leading lady. Yes, I did hear about that and it makes us all look stupid. Especially when we're in competition with the Royal Opera House only a stone's throw from here.'

'That was ...' One of my ditzier moments.

'Unprofessional.'

'But they ... thought it was funny,' I said in a small voice.

'Funny?' Her voice dripped icicles. 'It undermines the reputation of the London Metropolitan Opera Company, the heart of what we are – a world-renowned institution which employs the very best people, not a bunch of amateurs who can't use modern technology. What does that sort of dumb ass thing say about us? We're a bunch of effing dinosaurs? We're supposed to be at the forefront of artistic endeavour, avant garde, cutting edge, innovative, ground breaking.'

I bit my lip as she continued her diatribe, still hanging on to that brief thread of hope, 'I'd like to see you apply'.

'And then there's the small matter of yesterday's virus. Which brings me to my second point which is going to be a key part of your probation.' She picked up a pen and marked a date in the diary with my initials. Christmas Eve.

My heart contracted slightly.

'Care to explain that?'

I grimaced. 'Yes, I'm sorry I thought it was,' I shrugged, 'harmless.'

'Clearly,' she bit out. 'Do you have any idea how much havoc that little stunt caused?'

'No.' I'd very much hoped that not too many people had realised. 'W-what happened?'

'What happened,' she almost snarled the words, 'was that when you opened that attachment, it attached itself to every email contact you have.'

'Oh.' I wriggled in my chair. That sounded really, really bad.

'Which in turn then attached itself to every contact in all those contacts and so on and so on.'

OK, it just got even worse. My face heated up.

'I'm a layman here but Mr Walker, our new IT Director, did explain that it could have had extremely serious consequences if they hadn't managed to shut things down and get rid of it.' Her eyes bored into mine. 'Great start to his job. Now, thanks to you, he thinks we're all a bunch of incompetent idiots.'

'Oh.' I ducked my head, my face now on fire.

'The IT department spent all night trying to get rid of it. After you'd kindly shared it with every email address in the building.'

I bit my lip and slid my hands under my thighs. 'Sorry about that.' I felt five inches high. 'I'm very sorry.'

'You don't need to apologise to me. You're going to have to apologise to Mr Walker and Fred, the IT assistant, who burnt considerable midnight oil to solve the problem. It's not created the best impression with the new director.'

'Oh dear.' I wilted inside. Our first encounter hadn't exactly gone well.

'Oh, dear indeed. It took considerable persuasion to get him to take the job. Julian Spencer is not best pleased, as you've confirmed any negative perceptions Mr Walker might have had about the ability of the Opera House to move into the twenty-first century.'

I gazed down at her table, trying to imagine how to frame a suitable apology and came up with nothing. I'd rather hoped after that first run in, I'd never have to see Mr drop-dead-gorgeous again.

'Are you listening to me?' She laid her hands on the desk and pinned me with a fierce stare.

I nodded vigorously.

'Good, because I've decided that we are going to convince our new IT Director that all departments are open and amenable to progress. All members of staff are ready to embrace technology and make it serve us.'

What ... afternoon cream teas? I rather relished the thought of the little CD disk drawers popping out on command with a lovely china cup and saucer of tea and a matching plate with a chocolate éclair. Then I realised I'd missed what she was saying.

'... an IT champion, who will provide the link with the IT department and promote the use of new systems within their department.'

She plumped herself down in her grand leather chair as if she were Sir Alan Sugar suddenly discovering that his potential apprentices had a couple of brain cells each.

What? I'd missed something important here.

'As part of your probation, you are now the Hair, Wig and Make-up team's IT contact and you will be working closely with Mr Walker to identify suitable software packages for implementation in the department to streamline and update your processes.'

'*Me?*' She had to be kidding. 'But I'm rub–'

'It's all been agreed. He's expecting to see you today.'

'Who? Mr Walker?' I curled my fingers over the edge of the chair.

She narrowed her eyes, which I took as a yes.

'But ... but ... I've got work to do ... proper work. The designs for Juliet. And Pietro for curtain up tonight.'

She smiled and it wasn't a nice smile. She tapped her diary rather pointedly.

'Mr Walker will be keeping me abreast of your progress.'

I gave her a weak smile. My cup just runneth over.

As I stood to leave, she leaned under her desk.

'A present for you,' she said and pointedly handed me a toilet roll.

'Did she offer you the Assistant Head of Make-up job?'

Vince bobbed up and down, firing the question at me as soon as I returned to Jeanie's cubby hole, half an hour later.

'You are flippin' joking,' I said with feeling. 'She bloody hates me. I'm a "dumb ass", "stupid", "make cock-ups" and I'm an "amateur". I think it's safe to say, I'm not on the short list for that job.'

Jeanie gave me a stern look. 'Is that what she really said?'

I shrugged.

'Or did you just listen to the bad bits and ignore the

positrons?'

'Positives,' I said absently, staring mutinously at the floor. 'She wants me to have a meeting with the Prince of Darkness to discuss the use of IT in our department.'

'What? The new IT Director? Oooh lucky you. Sadly, I don't think he bats for our side.'

Jeanie shot Vince a look.

'Good, that will make life up here a little less precarious when you use that thing.' She nodded at the computer.

'But I don't want ...'

Jeanie sniffed. 'One meeting won't kill you. You are a great make-up artist but these days, it isn't enough.'

My heart sank. As Alison had told me. Presumably she'd had this conversation with Jeanie already, after all she was my boss.

'You need as many strings to your violin as you can get.' She turned back to the stack of books on her desk. 'Now we need to crack on.'

With that clear signal, both Vince and I got our heads down to do some serious research.

At the London Met Opera Company, it's an adventure just travelling in the lift. You might meet members of the orchestra rocking the escaped mafia hitman look in their dinner suits carrying violin cases, a props guy carrying a papier *mâché* lobster, costume ladies buried in yards and yards of chiffon, set designers in paint-splodged clothes and petite dancers of both sexes, who always seemed to be wearing millions of layers and carrying bags double their size. Today, I didn't even take note as my heart plummeted along with the lift.

I wandered as slowly as I could along the corridor to the IT department. Once you passed the sound engineers' offices, it became very different down here in the basement. A million different cables found their way around every surface; coiled and suspended with the sinuous grace of snakes in the jungle, blue wires, black wires, curly cable, straight cable and an infinite amount of silver connecting thingummies at the end of each. Passing a couple of storerooms, I finally came to the IT offices. I'd only been down here a few times but I almost didn't recognise the area today.

'Ah, come to see the damage.' Fred glared at me from where he sat hunched over a screen in a central station in the middle of the room and shook his head. 'What are you like? Here till bloody 3am because of you.'

'Was it really that bad?' I asked, wincing at his outraged face. 'I'm so sorry.' Poor Fred had been my saviour on more than one occasion, the most recent being an unfortunate incident with a can of Coke and a keyboard.

'You will be when his nibs gets hold of you.' Fred sniffed, rolling his eyes and went back to peering at his screen. I took a quick look around the room.

'Blimey, what's happened in here?'

'Marcus.' Fred inclined his head towards the office over on the outside wall.

Ah, so the M stood for Marcus. It suited him, sounded slightly posh.

The entire room appeared to have undergone operation de-clutter. For once, you could see the floor and on the opposite wall, a bank of shiny white glossy cupboards lined it like storm trooper lockers. One open door revealed neatly organised shelves filled with spare mice, keyboards, green circuit board things and various other bits I didn't recognise.

'Very smart. Very Star Wars.'

'Comes of working in the City,' answered Fred, glancing over towards his boss who was clearly visible through the glass door, his back to us, gesticulating with surprisingly graceful hands with a phone tucked under his ear. 'And he cares about this department.'

'Actually, he reminds of Darth Vader, without the breathing problems.'

An animated look came over Fred's face. 'Might be an ordinary bloke doing his job, but he's bloody brilliant at making things happen.'

He'd obviously made quite an impression on Fred. He's usually very laid back, although with his long streaky blonde hair thinning on top and the baggy paunch around his middle he looks more surfer dad than surfer dude.

'Precisely Fred, no one here is ordinary. He doesn't belong. You dress up as Thor, with a Viking helmet and a silver spray painted mallet for Comic Con. You're one of us ... even if you do understand the machines.'

I laughed at his sheepish attempt to study the ceiling.

'Don't deny it. I saw the pictures on Facebook and the props guys told me they made the hammer for you.'

'I had a great time. You should see the outfit Leonie in wardrobe's going to make me this time. A proper one.' His eyes lit up with glee. 'Don't suppose you'd do my make-up for me?'

'Of course, I'd love to ...' I stopped, 'but please don't say you want to be that blue one from X-Men.'

'Mystique? Nah, she's a girl.' Fred pulled a 'yuk' face.

'And you think that dressing as an imaginary alien species is more acceptable than a spot of cross dressing?'

He shrugged.

'So, who are you going as? I'll need to do my research to make sure it's right.'

'The Joker. Leonie's making a purple suit.'

'Batman. Yes. Big red lips. White face? Green hair.' I studied Fred's limp blonde mane dubiously. 'It might not come out for a while.'

'I can live with green hair. It's a Saturday in about three weeks' time.'

'Sure, I'll be working if we've got a matinee or I don't mind coming in. I'll have to see if I have the right coloured hair spray in the cupboard. But seriously if you want green hair–'

'It'll be fine.'

'Can't imagine he'd approve of that,' I nodded towards the office door. 'Surprised he hasn't got you in a suit yet.'

'Give him a break.'

I pulled a face.

Fred nodded enthusiastically. 'Bit of a control freak but OK. Doubt he'll be here long. You lot will drive him mad and besides, I reckon as soon as he's got his shit together he'll go back to the City.'

'Why do you say that?'

Fred checked the room with a furtive dart of his head as if to make sure no one was listening. 'He was at Deutsche bank before here. Bit of a leap. They've got some serious mainframe over there. Why he came here, unless he was fired, made redundant or caught fiddling the books? This is a come down for him.'

I put my hands on my hips. 'This is one of the best places in the world to work.'

Fred laughed. 'I meant in terms of technology, you great muppet. It's not exactly cutting edge and he doesn't have much time for artistic temperament. Knows his stuff, though. Definitely on a mission. Bring this place into the twenty-first century. You have to admit he's got a point. Some of the kit here pre-dates steam engines and you lot in make-up and wardrobe are a blinking nightmare.'

I knew what he was referring to.

I'd once called Fred up because the computer wouldn't switch on. The light on the monitor was on, so as far as I was concerned when he said was it switched on, it was. Not seeing the cleaners had unplugged the hard drive the night before was an easy mistake to make.

'The monitor and the hard drive should switch on together,' I said still feeling indignant even though it had been six months before, 'it's not as if you can use one without the other. It should be automatic.'

'That probably would make good sense in some situations, Miss Hunter.'

I jumped up from the edge of Fred's desk. How had he moved so quietly? My mouth dried.

With his white shirt-sleeves rolled up to reveal strong tanned forearms and the top few buttons unbuttoned, I found myself totally distracted by the skin on display, which wasn't even that much.

'Would you like to step into my office?' He gestured for me to go ahead of him.

'About as much as a fly does into a web,' I muttered under my breath.

His office had the ice-cold minimalism of an executive. See, definitely alien species. A shiny silver laptop sat in the centre of the dark ash wood desk and absolutely nothing else. He did not belong here. Not a single personal item could be seen, no photos, no knick-knacks nor any colour apart from the rich red satin lining of his jacket which hung from the black leather chair at his desk. It contrasted sharply with my little cubby-hole upstairs which embraced a magpie approach, as if one had flown through my life, cherry-picking the best bits to produce a snapshot of memories with pictures of finished make-up designs, photos of me and friends on various nights out, ticket stubs of milestone productions and swatches of fabrics.

He pulled up a chair for me and then took his seat opposite. It felt as cold and chilly as being in a head-master's office.

Any moment now, he'd say 'You know why you're here, have you anything to say for yourself?'

Leaning back in his executive chair, he exuded an air of being relaxed and in control.

'Would you like a coffee?'

Surprised, I nodded. He disappeared and within minutes returned with two pristine white china coffee cups.

'Wow, real coffee. How did you do that?'

'Nespresso machine.'

'How did you wangle one of those? Is that the sort

of perk you have in the City?'

'No, there we have minions who go out and get our double espresso mochaccino lattes for us.'

I nodded, of course they did.

His lips quirked in a brief smile. It took me a second to catch up.

'It's my own machine. I brought it in.'

Oooh, a sense of humour. I hadn't expected that.

I took a sip. Heaven in a cup. 'I'll have to remember this.'

One eyebrow twitched. 'You're always welcome.'

He might have meant, over my dead body, but there was something else in his expression that made my pulse flutter in recognition of something that I thought had long since passed me by. Was he *flirting* with me?

'Thank you for coming to see me.'

Ah maybe he wasn't. There was nothing flirtatious about the grave, business-like expression that had dropped down across his face as if the drawbridge had suddenly been drawn up.

I shrugged. 'Alison insisted,' I blurted out with my usual blunt honesty, instead of slowing down to frame the apology I'd planned. Before I managed to carry on, his face darkened and he stiffened, the brief sense of humour I'd sensed earlier vanishing like smoke.

'It's obvious that for some departments in this building, technology is viewed with the same sort of suspicion as witchcraft in the Dark Ages.' The stilted words sounded a bit rehearsed, the irony of which was not lost on me, given we were in a theatre where people normally played their parts with ease.

He shook his head. 'The place is filled with archetypal Luddites.'

This place! Any thought of an apology dried up.

'I don't think I've ever come across anything quite like it. Alison and I have discussed some changes. My role is to help each department identify where technological applications could help increase efficiency and productivity. I can't believe the lack of computer literacy in some of the departments. It's a bloody nightmare.' He sighed and fiddled with the pen on his desk before looking up and focusing on me. The stern expression in his green eyes made my stomach flip. Lord, talk about masterful.

'And your department takes the prize for being the absolute worst.'

Screw the lovely green eyes, he was horrible.

'That's because we don't really need computers.' My voice rose in indignation. We'd managed perfectly well without his interference or without stupid computers for the last ... well for ever. Could they apply make-up, pin a wig, placate an unhappy singer? No. Unless I'd missed some incredible technological breakthrough which surely would have been broadcast by every paper on the planet. And even *I* couldn't have missed that.

'Of course, you do. Everyone does these days.'

'Rubbish, we're dealing with art.' I shot him a disdainful look. Clearly, he had no soul. 'Not numbers and widgets. There isn't a right way or a wrong way to play Don Giovanni, there isn't a definitive costume for him, or a prescriptive make-up design. It's all open to interpretation. Not that I'd expect someone like *you* to understand that.'

His jaw clenched and I felt a bit guilty. Him and his attitude just reminded me too much of my parents. They didn't approve of my job at all.

'As I said, I've got a job to do here and you people need to understand that technology is here to stay.'

Did he just say *you people*?

'Have you any idea how many of the disparate parts of this building are held together by computer equipment and software?'

I shook my head and shrugged. Like I cared. A computer could not put on a show. We'd managed for hundreds of years without them. Yes, I'm sure for some industries they were essential tools of the trade but we didn't need them.

He leant forward, planting both elbows on the table, steepling his hands together. Again, I noticed they were lovely. Long fingers. Quite artistic looking. Nice nails.

'Miss Hunter? Are you listening to me?'

'Yes,' I lied and focused on the grim set of his jawline. Gosh he was handsome.

I tried hard not to look at the dark hair peeking out of the top of his white shirt.

'Every part of the operation in this building, and I mean every part, is dependent on technology.'

He paused, looking expectantly at me.

'Sorry?'

Oh heck, I could feel myself blushing.

I put on my 'interested' face. Concentrate Tilly. Operation. Building. Technology. Yes, got it.

I nodded at him, with no idea what he was banging on about.

He had one view, I had another. It was all very well giving me this lecture but what did he hope to achieve? Tell me off. Tell me not to pull the plug out or open any more attachments. Blah. Blah. I knew all that, *now*.

I realised he was still talking and I'd tuned out.

'... So, it is vital that everyone can use computers without potentially causing a problem elsewhere.'

I nodded anyway. Again. I'd been doing that a lot since he'd started. Hopefully he'd wind it up soon. Honestly, he could have given *Wagner's Ring Cycle* a run for its money.

Suddenly he threw himself back in his chair, finding something interesting up on the ceiling. I followed his gaze and then realised he'd turned his thunderous expression on me.

'None of this is getting through, is it?' His tone was mild but there was a pulse just under his jawline which tipped forward, just erring on the side of pugnacious.

When he rose to his feet, for a second, I thought he might be about to strangle me. He strode around the desk.

'Come with me.'

With a hand under my elbow he ushered me to my feet. Wow, he smelled good in an understated, subtle aftershave, sort of way. I tried not to sniff too obviously. And since when had I liked that masterful touch? Rather than shake his hand off, I let him lead me out of his office and over the corridor to a large glossy black door.

Bluebeard's den? The IT prison cell?

Inside the room, a steady hum emanated and in the dark lots of green lights flickered and blinked in and out with synced regularity.

'No point in asking if you know what this is,' he said, snapping on the light. His eyes glinted as they roved across the back wall. I turned to look, which wasn't a great move. There wasn't much space and I was conscious of him standing right behind me, his toned thighs almost touching the back of mine.

The room had a bank of cabinets on one side filled with grey and black boxes, all of which had lots of grey wiring leading out of them along the wall and disappearing through the ceiling and away.

'This is the main server. Every computer in this building is linked to it. If that goes down, nothing happens. *La Bohème* doesn't go on stage. Every computer is networked through this. If something goes wrong on one computer in your department, such as it being infected with a virus ...' He paused expectantly. I turned around and gave him a weak grimace.

He responded with a very serious look to underline his very important point, but it just had my heart doing a ridiculous cartwheel. Who knew that stern and serious could be sexy? Except he wasn't sexy and I was spoken for.

'It can impact on the whole network. This server manages a whole host of systems throughout the building. Systems that every production going on stage is totally reliant on. There's the system which manages the ticket sales in the box office. Another one which programmes the lighting desk. No server, no stage lights. Everything in the music library is catalogued on a computer. There are thousands of scores stored here, finding the right one for the woodwind section for *La Bohème* could take months, without that cata-logue. And that's just the tip of the iceberg.'

Now when he stared down at me, I shuffled and swallowed. The blood pounding quite hard in my veins. Fear, obviously at how close I'd come to messing things up. Who knew that a little box with all those wires could have such significance?

'When you happily downloaded your little virus, it slowed the whole network down. Every computer in the building was busy sending out emails to every contact on every email account in the building. To stop it we had to shut down most of the network, in order to ensure that the vital systems could carry on. Luckily for you the real damage only started after the opera had finished for the night. Otherwise the show would not have gone on.'

Shit. That would have been serious. We'd weathered storms, riots outside, transport strikes, but we'd never missed a show.

'But I thought we had virus protection things and isn't that your job to install those things?'

His jaw tensed and I could see his throat working. I got the distinct impression he was holding something in. 'They work just fine, as long as idiots don't open suspect attachments.'

He leaned back against the door with his arms folded. 'Can I ask that you never, ever, ever open another attachment if you don't know where it's come from or who has sent it to you? In fact, don't answer or respond to any email unless you know who has sent it or you ascertain that it has come from a bona fide contact. Do you have any concept of e-safety?'

'Erm, sort of.' My half-hearted smile elicited another narrow-eyed stare.

'It's about keeping yourself safe on-line. Protecting your personal information. Privacy settings on Facebook. Limiting the information you share on-line. In emails. Twitter, etcetera.'

'You can rest easy there. I have a habit of frying my phones, so I don't tend to do much on-line stuff.'

'Frying your phones?' The patient tone radiated scepticism.

'Yes. Phones. Watches. Those Fitbit things. Anything electrical seems to be allergic to me.'

'Really?'

I shrugged. I'd been through enough phones and watches not to care whether people believed me or not.

'When it comes to attachments on emails,' he paused and a brief smile flared at the corners of his mouth. Had he seen Santa Baby in action? 'In future, if in doubt, call myself or Fred.'

'Yes sir,' I said with a sudden smile. He was kind of cute when he was being all earnest and entreating. I decided against accompanying my words with a salute. He was after all a director and only trying to do his job. 'I don't mean to be useless with technology, it just doesn't like me.'

I could see him bite back a smile.

'Tilly, computers don't like anyone. They're not

people. They're machines. They work for us. Do what we tell them. As long as we treat them properly.'

'Are you sure?' I asked doubtfully.

'Yes, I'm sure. Hopefully you'll feel a bit more confident when we've had a few sessions.'

'Sessions?' That wasn't the deal with Alison.

'Yes. As our first champion for the make-up department, we need to spend some time together so that we can identify what processes and systems we can implement to improve the way you do things. While you're here, we'll diarise a few dates to get things moving.'

I opened my mouth. Nothing came out. But I must have signalled my dismay.

He had to be kidding? We were absolutely fine as we were. Hadn't he ever heard the saying, 'If it isn't broke'?

'I think a couple of half days in the next week or two, to get started, and then once we've identified those areas that we can work on, we'll develop appropriate systems, get you trained up and then you can introduce them to the rest of your team.'

'What?' A couple of half days? 'Is it really going to take that long? I'm sure there's not a lot you can help with.'

'Why don't you let *me* be the judge of that?'

I sighed. 'And why me?'

He smiled, not a nice friendly smile, but a shark going in for the kill type.

'I think unplugging a computer to *reboot* it, I think the phrase was, is a perfectly good starter for ten.'

Our eyes met.

I let out a long huff and glared. The room seemed to get smaller as he lifted his head and stared me down. It drew attention to the handsome jaw-line which was smoothly shaven, not like Felix's sexy but occasionally irritating stubble. This man was the total opposite, a corporate robot, looking to improve things, take the soul out of everything with his streamlining and rationalisationing. Well, he needn't think I'd be going over to the dark side. I'd grown up with all that crap and escaped it.

'I thought we'd start with our first meeting a week on Thursday. Have a chat about what you do in more detail and what areas could do with some improvements. I hear you've had a few ...' he was fighting back a smirk, 'issues in the past.' Alison had clearly gone to town telling him how rubbish I was. 'Sent a few emails to the wrong people. Copied in the wrong people. Attached the wrong file?' I could see merriment dancing in his eyes. 'Dr Who, was it?'

'Might have been,' I muttered.

'Tennant, Smith or Capaldi?'

'Tennant,' I muttered, blushing. To be fair, I had been trying to send a picture of the potato headed man, Drax, to illustrate an idea but had got a bit carried away when

I started searching the internet for pictures.

As I turned to leave I noticed one more thing. He had really nice lips.

'You never know you might enjoy it.'

'What?' Was he some kind of mind reader?

He lifted one sardonic brow. 'Learning more about IT?'

Chapter 4

With a quick glance at my watch, I figured there was just enough time to finish the hairpiece I was working on before a mad dash to meet up with my sister. The strand of hair wrapped around a piece of doweling only needed a quick spray with setting solution and the last perfect ringlet would be done. I held up the piece with its bobbing curls and admired it, imagining the way it would look on the dancer playing Juliet.

'Ooh Tilly. You might wanna see this.' Vince let out an alarmed squeal. He bounced up in his seat, where he'd been ensconced in front of the department computer since ten o'clock that morning. Allegedly he was looking for Byronesque style headshots but as far as I could tell he'd done nothing but sigh over pictures of good looking male movie stars who might once have had a brush with a historical film.

Hanging onto the final curl, I gave him a quizzical look.

'I thought you'd decided Mr McAvoy and his appropriate sideburns, in *Becoming Jane*, were what you were looking for. Are you still hunk-spotting?'

'As if I would?' He batted his eyelashes as if he'd never once logged onto Onmygaydar.com. 'No lovie. It's you. You're in trouble, girl. You got email.'

'What sort of trouble?'

'Seriously, doll.' Vince's blue eyes widened, like a small bush baby. 'Looks as if it's your virus.'

It wasn't *my* virus.

I carefully put down the hairpiece, before scurrying over to the computer, to find an email from a complete stranger.

I heartily wished I'd never sent that first email.

To: Matilde@lmoc.co.uk
From: Redsman@hotmail.co.uk
Subject: FW: URGENT – Possible loo roll crisis
Dear Matilda

Do I know you? I've just had an email from you. Don't think you meant to send it to me but

loo rolls? Try Tesco. Although funnily enough, I've literally just finished that book, funny read. Did you know there was a sequel?

With kind regards

A Liverpool Supporter.

P.S. Didn't think Arsenal supporters could read,

not as erudite as us Liverpool supporters.

'Oh pants.' Thankfully, despite his duff allegiance, the Liverpool supporter didn't seem too upset. 'Do you think I'm going to get loads of these?'

Suddenly I realised Jeanie was standing behind us. She rolled her eyes, and squinted at the screen beyond them. 'If they're all as dull as this, you haven't got a problem. A football supporter who sounds very sensible. Probably short, bald and lives with his mum. And likes Liverpool United.' She shook her head, before adding. 'Oh God, a Northerner.'

Southern born and bred, Jeanie was convinced that anyone north of Mill Hill was slightly suspect.

'Come on, some of us have work to do.' She gave both of us a pointed look before turning and heading back to her office.

I shot the screen another look and then my watch. Christelle was incapable of being late, I had no leeway.

'You're not going to email him back, are you?' asked Vince, clutching his throat in dramatic horror, which was a bit rich coming from Mr Online Romance himself. 'What if he's a stalker or one of those people that's looking to groom you for the sex-slave trade?'

With great show, I pointed to my flat chest and raised my eyebrows.

'Seriously, I read about it in the paper.'

'Well it must be true, then.'

'No, honest, girls promised designer clothes and given make-overs and then sold into high-class prostitution.'

In my favourite vintage 1950s skirt, printed with cherries, a matching red ballerina style cross-over cardigan and flat chunky boots, I was hardly sex-kitten material.

Vince inspected my boots. 'Maybe not.'

'Definitely not. Besides, it's not as if we're to become pen-pals.'

'Hmm.'

'I'm not letting him have the last word on my football team.' I shrugged my shoulders.

Vince raised his eyes heavenwards. 'You're a girl, is that normal? You know – the football stuff.'

'You're a boy. You wear yellow. Putrid mustard yellow. That's not normal unless you're a Buddhist monk.'

With another quick check of my watch, I edged him out of the way, pausing only fractionally as I remembered the thing about e-safety his royal ITness had said. But this was different. This bloke had taken the trouble to email me, it was only polite to email him back and thank him. If he was up to no good, he wouldn't be trying to help, would he? Then I stopped, what if he thought I was some sad loser type sending random emails out to try and make friends.

To: Redsman@hotmail.co.uk

From: Matilde@lmoc.co.uk
Subject: Loo Rolls
  I'm so sorry. That email was supposed to be to my fiancé.

There. Not single or desperate.

  I think I might have got a virus.

No shit, Sherlock.

  I opened an attachment I shouldn't have. Thanks for being nice about it.

And for God's sake please don't mention it to anyone.

  I've finished the book now. Don't want to read the sequel straight away but want something as good. I always feel a bit bereft when I finish a book I've enjoyed.

With kind regards

Deciding to keep things formal I put Matilde rather than Tilly which felt like it kept a bit of distance.
  I hate my name. Matilde, written down, looks German and butch rather than French. The 'd' is silent

but very few people get that, so I prefer Tilly. My mother is Parisian – hence the name. Although these days, even she managed to call me Tilly – on the odd occasions we spoke.

'How about that?' I re-read the words on the screen one last time. Mostly harmless.

Vince pulled a mournful face, disappointment filling his big blue eyes.

'It's not that bad, is it?'

He sighed and tossed his head. 'Well, it's hardly *Gone with the Wind*. I mean ...'

'It's not supposed to be.' I read the words again. It was OK. Not like people you heard of, who gave in to the heady temptation of on-line and text flirting, and ended up creating daring alter-egos that bore no resemblance to their real persona.

Although, I rolled my neck feeling the tension. God knows a flirtation would be a welcome ego boost – Felix seemed to find me about as sexy as a moth-eaten camel these days, but I was not going to fall into that trap.

Vince rubbed at his goatee and sighed in theatrical despair. 'Lovie, why don't you compare slippers? At least ask him what he thinks of the book. It's seriously, seriously dull.'

'Thanks a bunch. It's just a response. It's not as if I'm going to get to know him.'

'I should think not.' Vince bristled, folding his arms and speaking with hushed reverence. 'Not when you've got Felix.'

There was only one thing to do with that comment; I ignored his half-pint sized crush on Felix. 'Just keeping it bland makes it obvious I'm not some desperate cyber-stalker on the lookout for a man.'

'Charming. What does that make me? Minced meat.' Vince walked off huffily.

I literally slapped my forehead. God, he was such a drama queen. He'd be offended for the rest of the day now. I hadn't meant anything to do with his predilection for on-line dating.

I gave it one last read through. Vince was right, it did sound slipperish. Ignoring the small matter of already being ten minutes late, I added a quick post-script.

P.S. Liverpool supporters erudite? In which parallel universe would that be?

That wasn't flirty, was it? No. With a resolute stab that nearly pinged the enter button off the keyboard, I pressed send and shut down the email. Oops, even by my shoddy time-keeping standards, I was late.

Of course, she was already there, perched at one of the

high tables in Café Paul and engrossed in her iPhone. I knew exactly what my sister would look like without having to peer through the window. Pristine and pressed to perfection. I could have made easy money betting on the fact that Christelle would be wearing a pure white cotton shirt, peaked tramlines down each sleeve, and a figure hugging black pencil skirt along with a nipped in matching jacket from either Hobbs or Jigsaw. Her glossy brown hair would be scraped mercilessly back into the dullest bun you could imagine and she'd be wearing rubbish make-up. Seriously, she didn't have a clue. Lipstick in a dull nude colour which made her lips vanish into her face and a matt brown eyeshadow over the whole lid that made her eyes recede into her head. With her figure and gorgeous hair, she could have looked like some sixties starlet. It wasn't fair. Stick a button on my nose and I'd look like one of those anime cute cartoon girls, except with way too much curly hair. I would have loved to get hold of her and give her a serious make-over but we weren't that sort of sisters. Oh Lord, no.

'Late again.' Why the hell did she have to look at her watch? I wasn't going to deny it. I was nearly always late to meet her. Maybe it was psychological. It minimised the amount of time we had to spend together.

I shrugged cheerfully. 'Problem with a virus at work.' It sounded almost professional and competent, something she might appreciate.

For once, Christelle appeared vaguely interested. 'Serious? That can be terribly damaging. I heard of one solicitor's company who had to buy a new server because they'd got some malware that corrupted everything. It almost put them out of business. And they're a very smart outfit. They have some very high profile, blue chip clients.'

'Our IT department is very good,' I said smoothly as if it were the sort of thing that I regularly trotted out.

'That's so important,' said Christelle nodding. She stuck her head out, trying to catch the attention of the waiter who acknowledged us with a quick nod before disappearing with an armful of dirty crockery.

We lapsed into silence.

'So,' I said, 'how's work?'

'Good.' She stopped there. I had about as much of an idea about her job as she did about mine. She was a barrister, except she didn't do the exciting criminal stuff, no she did employment law which from the little I understood sounded deadly.

I've no idea why she insisted on these monthly meetings, they were always excruciating. But no, regular as clockwork, she phoned at the beginning of the month to suggest we meet up.

'So, are you busy this weekend?' I asked, praying the waiter would get a move on.

'Yes, it's Alexa's thirtieth birthday and we've hired a gorgeous house. It sleeps twenty-eight, which is perfect.' She whipped out her phone and showed me a couple of pictures of a fantastic view and a rather lovely looking Edwardian mansion perched on the side of a wooded hillside.

You see, that I couldn't fathom. Whatever I thought about my sister, her social life was always busy.

'What about you?'

I smiled. 'I'll be working late on Friday and Saturday.'

'I don't know how you manage to have a relationship. I find it hard enough to get dates with my hours let alone working most nights. Doesn't Felix mind? Do you ever get to spend a weekend together?'

'He doesn't mind.' That was the wonderful thing about Felix. He'd never minded. He understood how important my job was to me. And me working evenings had never been an issue. I paused, trying hard to picture my very uptight sister going on a date. She'd never mentioned any romantic entanglements and I'd always assumed she was too busy pursuing her career to bother with such irrelevancies. For some reason, Marcus popped into my head. He was probably Christelle's perfect date, not that I'd wish her on him.

'Do you do a lot of dating?' I asked, surprising myself.

It took her a minute to answer. In fact, she spent a good thirty seconds rummaging through her handbag, in a most un-Christelle like fashion, before she lifted her head. I could almost see her weighing up how to answer.

The second thirty seconds seemed to hang with unexpected portent between us. Sink or swim. Do or die. Crash and burn. Her foot poised over uncharted territory.

And then she cleared her throat and I felt a pulse of shock at her candid look.

'Not with any success. You're so lucky. You and Felix have got it all sussed. You were friends with him first. I've been on so many dates but I just never seem to click with anyone. On paper, they're absolutely perfect ... and then I meet them.' Her childish expression combined with the most exaggerated eye roll, again so not Christelle, made me break out in a wary smile.

'They're either unmitigated hooray Henry tosspots,' she broke off, 'excuse my language,' she added, giving me a look that dared me to say anything, 'or stuffed shirts who spend the entire date trying to work out whether I'm more successful than they are and whether I've billed more than them in the last forty-eight hours. It's pathetic.'

'It must be hard.' I tried to look sympathetic, but quite frankly they sounded eminently suitable. 'Ah, the waiter,' I said and grabbed the menu. 'What do you fancy? The fruit tarts look gorgeous, but then so do the palmiers and the chocolate croissants here are to die for.'

'Cappuccino for me and a croissant amandes.' Christelle snapped shut her menu and handed it to him, while I had now discovered the enticements of chocolate éclairs, raisin pastries and pear and rhubarb tarts.

I chewed at my lip as Christelle folded her arms. 'Make that two Cappuccinos and I, hmm, I can't make up my mind between the ...' I turned the menu over and then peered beyond the waiter at the glass fronted cabinets. 'Or should I have one of the strawberry tarts. No. I'll have a pain au chocolat ...'

The waiter clearly had my measure, because he whipped away the menu before I could change my mind and go for one of the glistening strawberry tarts.

Christelle put her elbows on the table.

'We need to decide what we're going to get for Mum and Dad for Christmas.'

'It's ages away,' I said. Why couldn't people enjoy the build up to Christmas? Planning this far ahead took away all the fun and spontaneity. Present-buying should be an adventure and a grand expedition to all the beautifully decorated shops, sparkling with glitter and tinsel. It should be full of promise and excitement, like going on a bear hunt, to track down and tease out things that people will like. No, that people will love.

Christelle let out a small huffy sigh. 'You haven't spoken to Mum, have you?'

'No.' Nothing new there. My unsociable working hours didn't fit with her and Dad's nine to seven schedule.

She bit her lip before blurting out with great indignation. 'They're going away for Christmas.' Around her mouth a few tiny lines that I'd never noticed before tightened.

'Really? Where?'

'Apparently,' she stiffened. 'They're going on a cruise.' I shrugged.

'To Scandinavia.'

'Oh.' It was a bit of a surprise but it would save me the scramble to catch the last train from Kings Cross wedged up against over-exuberant drunks in a corridor and then having to make the journey back in two days' time to get back to work. It never seemed fair to book holiday at Christmas when other people in the department had young children and families.

'I don't know why they've suddenly decided to go on a cruise now.' Christelle's voice wobbled.

'Why not? We're not children anymore.'

'But it's a family time. And we always go home.'

'Well maybe this year it's time to do something different.' I shrugged, ignoring the bleak look on her face. 'Break the mould. See it as an opportunity.'

'An opportunity for what?'

'There's loads going on in London, carol concerts, ice skating, shows.'

'Yes, but not on Christmas Day.'

'There is.'

Oh, God, now I had no excuse not to go with Felix to visit his mother on Christmas Day. 'Loads of things still happen, you know.'

Her mouth dipped down in scepticism.

'Jeanie, my boss, often spends Christmas on her own. She's never short of things to do. Last year she went on a walking tour around the city. The year before she volunteered for Crisis and the year before that she went to watch the swimmers in the Peter Pan Cup race on the Serpentine. It's only one day. You could just spend the day watching films.'

A pang of guilt danced in and out of my conscience. Was she worried about being on her own? I hadn't given it that much thought. As I said, Christmas was still ages away.

'Yes, but why don't they want to have Christmas with us? It's not like them. Don't you think it's odd?'

'No.'

She pursed her mouth. 'That's so typical of you Tilly, you ignore the things you don't want to see.'

'No I don't.'

'You do, you've always done it. Making out that Mum

and Dad are so against your career.'

'They are.' I folded my arms, I really didn't want to get into this now. It was old history and nothing was going to change.

'No, they just wanted you to–'

'Whatever. Going home at Christmas is a hassle anyway. The trains are always packed and we're busy at work.'

'What will you do instead?'

'Work.'

'On Christmas Day?'

'No, but we'll probably go to Felix's mum and I'll come back that evening because I'm working on Boxing Day.'

'I guess I could have lunch with some friends, but it won't be the same,' she sighed, 'although Mum has said she'll do lunch with all the trimmings before Christmas. We can go up together. If I drive up, we won't have to worry about carrying all the presents.' She brightened. 'Talking of which, I was thinking about a nice Estée Lauder skin set for Mum, they've got some lovely gift packs this year.'

'I'll be work–' Christelle had never done puppy dog eyes in her life. She worked on pure logic but there was a shadow of sadness about her and a sudden blinking that made me pause and say, 'That's probably a good idea.'

'We could leave late on Friday, miss the traffic and then we'd have the whole of Saturday. I could pick you up straight from work. What time do you finish?'

'Depends on the production but around ten-thirty, eleven.'

She smiled and straightened up, losing the sad uncharacteristic droop. 'I'm glad that's all sorted. Now, I was thinking a nice cashmere sweater for Dad and he's been wittering on about learning coding, so a colleague at work recommended a book for him. Oh...' She looked down at her phone which had begun to ring, 'I need to take this. Will you excuse me?'

'Yeah. It's fine.' Her formality drove me nuts. I was her bloody sister for God's sake, not an effing client. She scooped up her phone and disappeared out of the door, where I watched her pace with considered steps backwards and forwards through the window.

I picked up my Kindle Fire that I never went anywhere without and luckily it seemed to be the one thing that evaded my negative electrical force-field. My idea of hell was not having a book to read. I'm not sure what made me do it, but I logged onto the free Wi-Fi to check my emails and nearly dropped it when I saw I'd got a response to my earlier one.

To: Matilde@lmoc.co.uk
From: Redsman@hotmail.co.uk

Subject: Loo Rolls

Dear Matilde

The sequel is good but if you want something of a similar ilk, how about *High Fidelity* by Nick Hornby. It's about a man who's crap at relationships too.

Regards

R

P.S. - Would that be that same parallel universe in which Arsenal can play?

It made me smile and by the time Christelle reappeared I'd downloaded *High Fidelity*.

'Sorry about that. A client I've been trying to get hold of for a few days.' Any hint of sadness was vanquished as back-in-business Christelle swept back to the fore.

'OK, coding book and sweater for Dad, skin care set for Mum. Do you want me to get them and you can pay me back?'

'I hate to be mean but could we perhaps go lamb's wool rather than cashmere on the sweater for Dad? And set a budget.'

'Don't worry, if you can't afford it now, you pay me back later when you can.'

'I can afford it.'

Just because her income bracket outstripped mine by several thousand a month didn't mean she should contribute more. Pride stopped me saying that things were a bit tight this month because Felix still owed me two months' share of the household bills.

'Well, we can worry about that later.' She gave me a blithe smile and glanced at her mobile phone; it reminded me of a cheeping canary clutched in her hand. It never shut up. She took a long swallow of Cappuccino. 'I've got an appointment with Sir Charles Whitworth's solicitor. I'm going to have to go in a minute.'

'Me too,' I said. 'Pietro D'Angelis waits for no woman.' My rare name drop sent her eyebrows shooting upwards in satisfying startlement.

'What? The Pietro D'Angelis?'

'Yes.'

'You do his make-up? Seriously?'

'Yes.' I sat quite still, contrary to the smug inner squirming, surprised by my petty attempt at one-upmanship. The truly sad thing was that Christelle wasn't name dropping or trying to score points. That was her world in the same way the theatre was mine.

Usually I gave little away about work. As the black sheep of a high achieving professional family, I preferred to keep my triumphs to myself. Obviously putting a bit of slap on a singer wasn't quite in the same realm as saving a company billions of pounds in pay-outs in a wrongful dismissal case.

'Wow. He's really famous. Isn't that a bit, you know,

daunting?'

I laughed. 'Not now, but,' I leaned forward, to whisper conspiratorially, 'the first time, I thought I might poke his eye out, my hand was shaking so much!'

She laughed too and then both of us stopped, stalling in a well-this-is-not-like-us moment of shared confusion. Jumping up to her feet, Christelle gathered her phone, her bag and her gloves, leather ones that matched her bag and shoes, both a bold kingfisher blue, which I hadn't noticed before.

We peeled off in opposite directions with a quick kiss on each cheek, back to our other worlds.

Chapter 5

Everyone caught in the unexpected evening sleet wore a coat of dandruff as they hurried into the tube station, casting worried looks up at the sky. They had nothing to worry about, as this was not proper snow. I'd grown up in Yorkshire on the edge of the Dales and so I knew all about wading to school through drifts up to your thighs.

As the damp bodies started to warm up, the smell of wet dog permeated the packed tube on the Northern Line. I was wedged between a man in a Che Guevara khaki jacket, stained dark with the rain and a girl in a heavyweight rain-coat that rustled with every jolt and bump of the train.

Unable to get enough elbow room to read my book, I twitched like a smoker desperate for a light.

Despite my unknown email correspondent being a Liverpool supporter, he had good taste in books. I'd started *High Fidelity* a couple of days before and was loving it.

Finally, yippee, enough people got off at Charing Cross and I dropped into a seat. By the time the doors closed, chapter two had absorbed me.

By Waterloo, I was deep in 70's suburban life.

Kennington came and went.

Clapham North arrived as I was mid-snigger, and way before I was ready. Stuffing my book away and leaving the summer of '76, I only just got out of the doors in time to join the stream of bowed bodies battling up the escalators into the bitterly cold night where, surprisingly, the tiny pinpricks of barely-there snow had turned into full on flakes, curling and floating down like feathers I still doubted it would settle.

With Felix away for the night, I could carry on reading. Making myself baked beans on toast, I stood stirring the pan of beans with one hand and my kindle in the other and ate my tea, flicking the pages on the touch screen with my fingers.

The washing up was left as I curled up on the sofa, the TV on for background noise, and carried on reading, completely hooked.

Temptation sizzled on the edge of my fingertips.

With half an eye on a very old episode of *Spooks* on the telly, I swapped to the email app on my Kindle.

Ever since I'd finished the last chapter, I'd been mentally composing the message.

I was just being polite. Letting a fellow reader know how much I was enjoying his recommendation.

To: Redsman@hotmail.co.uk
From: Matilde@lmoc.co.uk
Subject: Book
    Thanks for the recommendation. *High Fidelity* is fab. Love it, although I got some strange looks on the tube on the way home. Kept laughing out loud. Just what I needed on a filthy winter night.
    Thanks, again
    Tilly

My finger hovered over the send button. Was this the sort of jump in feet first type of thing that Alison meant? But where was the harm?

The only downside I could think of was that he might think I was stalking him? Would he care what I thought? But then he did recommend the book.

If it were me, I'd be delighted to hear someone liked a book as much as I did.

Then again, he was a bloke.

I groaned out loud. I was giving myself a headache. It was just an email. He'd read it, raise his eyebrows, think it's that dumb girl who sent the virus, delete it and think no more about it ever again.

Then again ... He might just appreciate the feedback.

The argument in my stupid head was getting out of hand. I went with the ref's decision and pressed the send button. Done. No regrets.

Putting down my Kindle, I went back to *Spooks* where things on the screen were tense. MI5 were about to save London for the fifth time that series.

An onscreen flash on my Kindle two minutes later interrupted a terse exchange between the head of division and one of his trigger-happy minions – I'd got mail.

To: Matilde@lmoc.co.uk
From: Redsman@hotmail.co.uk
Subject: High Fidelity
    I'm glad you're enjoying it. One of my favourites. And also a great film.

Phew, he didn't think I was some deranged lunatic stalking him.

Have you seen it? Not often you can say that, when they abandon a perfectly good English setting. Can't understand that? Why didn't they leave the record shop in England? In fact, why do film and TV companies have to fiddle with settings? *The Killing? Life on Mars?* Have we made an English *Friends? Mates? CSI - Southampton?* Thankfully

High Fidelity survived. I'd recommend it if you haven't seen it. One of those rare films that translates well from a book.

R

OK, he had a point with the setting thing, but plenty of other books survived celluloid translation. With tongue firmly pressed in cheek I typed,

To: Redsman@hotmail.co.uk
From: Matilde@lmoc.co.uk
Subject: High Fidelity
Dear M
I think that perhaps being a Liverpool fan might have addled your brain. Loads of good films from books:
What about *Pride and Prejudice, Sense and Sensibility, Bridget Jones' Diary, Atonement?*
M

An email came right back

To: Matilde@lmoc.co.uk
From: Redsman@hotmail.co.uk
Subject: High Fidelity
What no car chases?

I giggled. He was starting to sound a lot less grey cardie and slippers.

To: Redsman@hotmail.co.uk
From: Matilde@lmoc.co.uk
Subject: High Fidelity
    Ok then, what about:
    The Bourne Identity, Casino Royale, Patriot Games!

Yet another new message.

To: Matilde@lmoc.co.uk
From: Redsman@hotmail.co.uk
Subject: High Fidelity
    Depends on the *Casino Royale*. First or second. Bet you're one of those girls who fancies Daniel Craig, although Lazenby is the cult James Bond.

He had no idea.

To: Redsman@hotmail.co.uk
From: Matilde@lmoc.co.uk
Subject: High Fidelity
    Daniel Craig!!!! No thank you. Timothy Dalton, every time!

To: Matilde@lmoc.co.uk
From: Redsman@hotmail.co.uk
Subject: High Fidelity
   Words fail me.

To: Redsman@hotmail.co.uk
From: Matilde@lmoc.co.uk
Subject: High Fidelity
   What's wrong with him?!

To: Matilde@lmoc.co.uk
From: Redsman@hotmail.co.uk
Subject: High Fidelity
   The only positive thing I can say is that he had one of the best Bond girls.

To: Redsman@hotmail.co.uk
From: Matilde@lmoc.co.uk
Subject: High Fidelity
   Which one?

To: Matilde@lmoc.co.uk
From: Redsman@hotmail.co.uk
Subject: High Fidelity
   The blond cello player – they sledged down a mountain in her cello case. I've never read any Ian Fleming? Have you?

To: Redsman@hotmail.co.uk
From: Matilde@lmoc.co.uk
Subject: High Fidelity
    Yes, but not sure I should admit it. I read quite a few Bond books when I was a kid (very precocious reader) – totally (very) unsuitable for a twelve-year-old.

To: Matilde@lmoc.co.uk
From: Redsman@hotmail.co.uk
Subject: High Fidelity
    He did write *Chitty Chitty Bang Bang.*

To: Redsman@hotmail.co.uk
From: Matilde@lmoc.co.uk
Subject: High Fidelity
    And you think that's a suitable title for a kid's book? Although I loved the musical at the Palladium. Bet you're not a musical man.

To: Matilde@lmoc.co.uk
From: Redsman@hotmail.co.uk
Subject: High Fidelity
    I saw Oliver once. Definitely not a suitable title for a kid's book although at that age I was going through my Sci-fi phase. More Isaac Asimov and Ray Bradbury.

To: Redsman@hotmail.co.uk
From: Matilde@lmoc.co.uk
Subject: High Fidelity
 Sci-fi ... Oh dear. Just when I was starting to think ... Although I have read *The Time Traveller's Wife*.

To: Matilde@lmoc.co.uk
From: Redsman@hotmail.co.uk
Re: High Fidelity
 Time Travellers Wife! That's not Sci-fi.

To: Redsman@hotmail.co.uk
From: Matilde@lmoc.co.uk
Subject: High Fidelity
 How come? It's about a man that zips back and forth in time. He might not be Dr Who but how can that not be Sci-fi?

To: Matilde@lmoc.co.uk
From: Redsman@hotmail.co.uk
Subject: High Fidelity
 O.K., I admit it, I've never read it but doesn't sound very SF to me.

To: Redsman@hotmail.co.uk
From: Matilde@lmoc.co.uk

Subject: High Fidelity

HAVEN'T READ *The Time Traveller's Wife*.
Shame on you, a) it's beautiful and b) it's beautiful.

I forgot you're a bloke!

Think you should broaden your horizons and
read TTTW – it's very original. Failing that you
could always try the other Nick Hornby classic –
Fever Pitch.

I grinned at that one. He might take offence at reading
about Arsenal doing the double and winning the league
cup and the FA cup in 1992 and he probably wasn't a
Colin Firth fan either, so wouldn't appreciate the film
version quite the way I had.

This might have gone on all night, except the phone
rang at nine.

'Hey missus, it's me.' Felix had been away for several
days and was staying in some posh hotel in Brighton.
A trip which had been extended by an additional day.

'Hi.'

'You all right?' asked Felix, bouncy as ever.

'Yes. Sorry, long day.' I tried to sound a bit more with
it, and not as guilty as I felt. I'd only been talking to
someone on line, I hadn't done anything wrong, but I
knew I wouldn't mention it to Felix. 'How are you?
When are you coming home? And is it snowing down
there?' Lifting the curtain, I was disappointed to see

that only a few flakes danced across the sky, battling against a brisk wind. There was no sign of the light scattering that had settled earlier.

'Not a speck here. I might stay here for ever. I could get used to this hotel. Five stars is right up my street,' he enthused. 'Might bring you some towels. Lovely, white fluffy ones.'

'Felix! You can't do that.'

'People do it all the time.' His voice took on a wheedling tone.

'No! Don't bring the towels home.' You had to be literal with Felix at times.

'Means we could put something else on the wedding list.'

'At our age, do you think we need one?' Not that we had got anywhere near arranging a wedding list. We occasionally referenced having one but never did anything about it. A bit like the wedding.

'Be a shame though.' He paused. 'I fancied one of those space-age Philippe Starck orange-squeezers.'

'They're too *War of the Worlds*. I wouldn't want one in the kitchen. I'd love one of those teas-made things. We should go for things we'd never buy for ourselves.'

'Or use!' said Felix scathingly. 'You're not one hundred and three.'

We both laughed.

'We don't need a wedding list,' I said. We had pretty

much everything we needed.

'Of course we do. Isn't that the whole point of getting married?' He stopped. 'Maybe we'd better call it off then.'

Silence filled the airwaves.

'So how did–'

'– the presentation went well.'

We interrupted one another.

'Oh good.'

'What have you got lined up on Friday?' Felix paused. 'Would you mind if I stayed down here another night? Save having to battle through the traffic.'

'Aw, Felix. I've got an early finish on Friday, I thought we could do something together for a change.'

'I'll make it up to you.'

'You'd better. I've got to see the IT guy that day. I'll need cheering up after that.'

Felix burst out laughing. 'So will he. I hope they're paying him danger money.'

Chapter 6

I kept chuckling to myself at this morning's email response to my suggestion to *Fever Pitch* as I rounded up my notes and sketches. There'd been email silence for nearly a week and I'd assumed it marked the end of the on-line conversation, but it seemed I was wrong.

Before I could respond, I was sucked into the day's work. Jeanie wanted an update of where we were at with all the hairpieces for the corps de ballet and both of us had to prepare for a make-up design meeting for *Romeo and Juliet* with the Ballet Director and Head of Costume, which meant making sure I had a complete cast list and details of their colouring along with the notes from Costume.

Vince seemed full of beans. One minute he was running to get coffee for everyone, the next offering to redo the rota for the following production in three months' time, then he would settle at the wig he was making and then dart up to wash a few brushes. The whole time he kept his distance from me.

I took time to grab a coffee and took one into Jeanie's office.

'What the hell is the matter with him?' she asked, eyeing Vince over the rim of her coffee mug with deep suspicion.

'Seriously?' I peered over at him, busy texting now. 'He's obviously got a hot date tonight.' Although normally we'd have been subject to all his hopes and fears by now. Vince longed for true love and undying loyalty. A complete romantic.

Jeanie sighed. 'Who is it this time? I worry about that boy.' Her fingers rubbed an invisible stain on the side of the china mug. 'Needs to settle down. He's getting a bit too old for all this promiscuity.' She'd been in the business a long time. Even though it was less prevalent these days, too many of her friends had died of Aids in the late eighties.

'I've no idea. In fact, that's the weird thing, he's not mentioned anyone recently.' I cast my mind back over recent conversations. There'd been no clues. 'Not someone from the orchestra, I know that much.' Vince had a fondness for percussionists and brass instrument players. Whenever a touring orchestra came, he was sure to find a new friend but they only stayed for a brief while before moving on to the next venue.

I squeezed her arm. 'We've given him the safe sex

talk enough times, all we can do is be here to pick up the pieces.' Both of us wished he could find 'the one'.

'Funny he's not said much about it, if it is a date.' Jeanie put down her mug and stared thoughtfully over at him. I could tell by his studied inspection of his mobile phone that he knew he was being talked about.

'Maybe he's growing up?' I suggested.

A beat later, we both burst out laughing and Vince looked up, his curiosity antennae instantly tuned and mouthed 'What?' across the room.

'Yeah and I'm going to buy me a pair of unicorns,' Jeanie responded.

With another fifteen minutes before I had to head downstairs to the IT department, I sneaked over to the computer and quickly logged onto my email. I just wanted to check there hadn't been any other emails resulting from my virus.

Who was I kidding? I wanted to respond to Redsman's email. He clearly hadn't liked my suggestion for a book about Arsenal. Jeanie was still out of sight, so I quickly typed a response.

To: Redsman@hotmail.co.uk
From: Matilde@lmoc.co.uk
Re: Subject: !!!!!

It could be my dead body we're talking about. I'm just off to see his royal ITness, the Prince of

Darkness, the corporate bod who lives down in the lower ground floor. I'm to be given lessons on the correct use of computers. They weren't best pleased about the virus.

I'm still a bit confused how it got to you ... lots of people here received it. You should see my pile of loo rolls. Think they're a bunch of comedians. Oh, how I haven't laughed.

Must go. If you never hear from me again, send in a search party to dig up the basement.

M

P.S. Liverpool will be lucky to win the match this week let alone anything else.

I checked my watch, still a couple of minutes to go. I wandered over to Vince's cubby hole. The make-up team each had one. It was our workspace and consisted of a shelving area, a long work bench and a chair, along with a small chest of drawers.

'Hi Vince,' I said pointedly when he didn't look up.

'Oh, hi,' he said, all smiles and fake bright eyes, as he finally lifted his head, as if he'd had no idea I was there.

I sighed. 'Will you wish me luck?'

Vince's mouth pulled down at either corner. 'Glad it's you and not me.'

'Yeah, he's too bloody good looking for his own good,'

I said dispiritedly.

'Lordy girly, are we talking about the same man. Good looking?'

'Yes, don't you think so?'

'You need to get some new glasses. He's not a patch on Felix.' Vince sounded quite aggrieved.

'I'm not planning to be unfaithful or anything, I just noticed he was,' I shrugged, 'you know, rather easy on the eye.'

'Average, darling. Average.' Vince turned up his nose but kept his eyes down, his fingers nimbly plaiting an intricate hairpiece. 'Unless you like that sort of thing, I guess.' Through his strategically ripped jeans, his knee was jumping up and down with the frantic energy of teeth chattering. 'Shouldn't you be leaving?'

'Are you alright Vince?'

'Fine, why?' he snapped.

'Got anything nice planned this weekend? What are you up to tonight?' I was half hoping that he might be free. With an early finish, I didn't fancy being on my own in the flat again.

'I'm going away.'

'You didn't say anything about that before.'

Vince pouted. 'What? Now you're like the social life police? I don't have to tell you everything. It's called a private life for a reason.'

I took a step back.

Vince shared anything and everything about his vibrant social life.

I put my hands up in defence, said 'Sorry' and got the hell out of Dodge.

Making a strategic retreat, I realised that now I was going to be late.

I skidded to a halt in the doorway to find Marcus ready and waiting, not quite drumming his fingers on his desk. There were, however, two mugs of coffee sitting there.

'Here you go.'

I inhaled the delicious scent as he pushed one towards me.

He'd definitely earned a brownie point or two with his coffee. 'Sorry I'm late.'

'I expected it. I guess I should be grateful you turned up at all.' The rueful shrug accompanying his words robbed them of any malice. A simple statement of fact which irked me even more.

'I do have a job of my own.'

'I know, so I'll try and be quick today. And this will help make that job easier so that you'll have more time. Ready for your first lesson?'

'Not really. But in for a penny in for a pound.'

His green eyes danced with sudden amusement, transforming his face which made my body go into silly mode with my hormones hijacking any common sense and sending my pulse into overdrive. Bloody hormones. What did they know? I didn't even like him that much.

Although I had to admit, it struck me how healthy and wholesome he looked. I might have likened him to the Prince of Darkness but he was clearly a damn sight more used to sunshine than I was. It struck me that I spent too much time with either stick thin dancers or singers with healthy diaphragms and sturdy chests and people whose working hours were principally after dark. The LMOC was my whole world and what a world it was. Most of my friends worked here. Jeanie had worked in theatre for years and had a million and one amazing stories. She'd worked with everyone who was anyone. Vince had come from provincial theatre and had less experience but had lived and breathed theatre life, so had a huge acquaintance of set designers, sound engineers and props people. My friends in the orchestra, Philippe, Guillaume, Karla and Angela had lived all over the world and came from different countries and cultures and Leonie and Sasha from the wardrobe department were slightly alternative and very bohemian. It was easy for us all to stick together because not only did we have the theatre in common, we all worked similar shift patterns.

'Have a seat.' He pointed to the one next to him and I

realised he changed the configuration of his desk so that we could now share his monitor, with me sitting at the end of his desk. 'You never know you might learn something.'

I sank into the chair with all the petulance of a teenager. I didn't like the way he wrong-footed me. It made me feel out of place. This was my world. My place. I hated feeling like this. It made me act even more childishly.

'I do know. I won't learn anything useful because it's not necessary.'

He leaned back and folded his arms and lifted one eyebrow in a superior fashion. I felt about five.

'OK, how about you teach me some things?'

That sounded a bit wanky management approach to me, i.e. he was trying to butter me up. I wasn't completely stupid.

'Like what?'

'How many wigs do you have in the department?'

I shrugged. 'No idea.'

'OK, how many in the current production of *Don Giovanni?*'

'I'm impressed, you know what's on.' My barb struck and I saw a tiny twitch in his eye. It made me feel a bit better and then I felt ashamed that I felt like that. It was mean and uncharitable. He was new in the job. 'There are eight main roles, the men have several wigs each, and the women have hair pieces. And some of the chorus have a wig. For this particular production, I guess we have seventeen for the principals, plus a few spares in case they get a bit untidy and we haven't got time to redo them.'

'What about *Romeo and Juliet*?'

'You have been doing your homework. We have five for Juliet, for the principal ballerina and her understudy, thirty-five hair pieces for the corps de ballet. Wigs for the older male parts and the nurse. I think by the time we finish, we'll have around fifty.'

'And do you keep a record of what you've got? Do you keep them all? Use them again?'

'We used to take Polaroids of everything and then file them. That was the easiest way, although a lot of the time there'll be some one who will remember a production from way back. In that case, we'll go and look through the old Polaroids and then look in the storeroom. Unfortunately, they don't hold their colour too well.'

'Polaroids?' His face said it all. 'You don't have a digital camera?'

'Oh yes,' I said, suddenly relieved that I could reassure him on that front. 'We used it a lot.' Oh shit. 'Weeelll, that was until it got full up and let's say it doesn't work for us.'

'Full up?' Marcus's voice sounded suspiciously choked.

'Yes, you know. It says there's no more space.' I lifted both shoulders. 'When we tried to free up some space, we managed to delete everything, so we decided not to use it anymore. We have a little card index file system, where we write descriptions down.' When we remembered, or got around to it.

Marcus closed his eyes and his lips moved. I think he said, 'Give me strength.' Or it might have been 'For fuck's sake.'

After giving his rather appropriate pound sign cufflinks a thorough visual inspection, he swallowed hard and quickly scribbled down a couple of notes.

'And do you make all of them in house?'

'What?' I was still focusing on the pen and notebook, wondering what he'd written down. I couldn't imagine it was anything very approving.

'The wigs, do you make all of them?'

'No, not all. It depends how many are needed. We have piece workers who will do some.'

'So how do you work all that out? Who's doing what? When it needs to be done by? What's ready?'

'It can be a bit stressful, I guess.' Damn, I'd walked straight into that one. I was not going to elaborate and admit we'd had some major panics in the past. Because it didn't matter. We'd always got things sorted in time.

'Really?' He studied me so quizzically I felt as if he could look straight through and could tell I was avoiding the complete truth.

'Yes, OK,' I hedged, 'it is *very* stressful but it works.'

'But it could work better. Be less stressful.'

'What, you're going to wave a magic wand?'

'No but I could come up with a system to help you. A project management package.'

It sounded a bit too good to be true. 'What's in it for you?'

He laid down his pen and gave me a grave look. 'It's like trying to herd a box of angry kittens with you. Believe it or not, I'm trying to help both of us. What's in it for me, is that, for one thing, you might treat a computer with a bit more damn respect instead of just yanking the plug out when it doesn't do what you want.'

'That was a one off,' I said. 'It was just unfortunate that you walked in when you did. I've never done that before.'

'Unfortunate? Careless I think.'

I narrowed my eyes at him for a second. 'Oscar Wilde?'

'I have been to the theatre occasionally. Despite what you may think, I'm not a complete corporate philistine.'

'I didn't say you were.' Although come to think of it, I might have done. The phrase nagged at me.

'We're straying. Whether it was the first time or not, it demonstrated your complete lack of respect or understanding for a computer.'

Maybe now wasn't the time to volunteer the fact that

I often used the CD drawer to put my coffee on when I was working on a complicated hair piece. If I spilt coffee on any of the expensive human hair we used Jeanie would kill me.

Suddenly he stood up and moved from behind the desk. 'Tell me about your typical day.' Marcus's sudden change of tack threw me for a second until I realised he wasn't asking me about my shower routine in the morning but about my working day.

'We have shifts. We don't need to be at the theatre until a few hours before curtain up. But then there are rehearsals, matinees and evening performances, so our times vary. No one's a clock-watcher.'

We all lived and breathed the job. Most of us probably would have done it for free.

'Tell me, what did you do yesterday?'

'I spent the first half hour cleaning hairbrushes, rinsing out sponges and sharpening pencils.' Nothing that a computer could help with and the look I levelled at him reiterated my thought. A slight smile curved on his lips.

I pulled a face as I remembered that yesterday had been a bit of a fiasco. 'I had to nip out to grab some light pancake because we'd completely run out. Then–'

'Does that happen often?' His face was grave as he asked the question.

I lifted my shoulders. 'Very, very occasionally,' I lied.

'Only because we don't tend to use that one very often. After that we had a big delivery from the wholesalers, which I had to unpack with Vince.' Which we'd forgotten was arriving and had chucked a spanner in the works as the boxes took up most of our working space until we'd got everything put away.

'What sort of delivery?'

'Hair stuff. You know Kirby grips, hair nets, hairspray, mousse. We get through buckets of the stuff.'

'And how do you order all that?'

'The wholesale people are quite good at giving us a call every so often and we just place an order. What?'

He didn't exactly pull a face but I could see precisely what was going on in his head.

'You can never have too many hair pins,' I retorted.

'It just doesn't sound very,' he clicked his pen off and on again, 'organised.'

If I'd been a cat, my back would have been arched and I'd have hissed at him.

'Are you trying to say we're not very professional?' I could feel my mouth creasing into mulish lines. What was it about this man that made me revert to being so juvenile?

'No, not at all.' Exasperation was written across his face. 'But I can already see ways in which I could help you. The computer is not your enemy but it's only your friend if it does what you need it to do. Using it could help enormously. Help you create orders of things you need and stop you running out of them. For example, remind you when you're low on pancake ... what is that by the way?' He gave a self-deprecating smile, which made the green eyes twinkle. 'I'm assuming you're not talking the maple syrup variety.'

I bristled for a second and then realised he didn't have a clue what I was talking about. Maybe it was time I cut the guy a little slack.

'Base. Make-up base. Not pancake anymore but we still call it that. I think some of our prima donnas would get very irate if you tried to smear their faces with anything that went with maple syrup.'

'I thought as much.'

OK. Brownie points to him. I could see he was trying to help but really, we were fine as we were.

'We're actually quite good at that,' I started, 'although I guess it could be helpful to keep some sort of list of what we have.'

'Ever used a spreadsheet?' he asked with a grin.

'Now you're just trying to blind me with science. I hate the damn things.'

I stared at the very posh leather-bound notebook as he quickly wrote something with a silver Cross pen.

It reminded me of my mother. She always used Cross pens and Smythson notebooks. She would approve of Marcus.

'You're looking pissed off again,' he commented.

'Sorry, I was thinking about my mother, it does that to me.'

He looked startled. 'Right. OK. I've got a few ideas about some software and asset management programmes to help you manage your inventory that would be easy to implement and would, I promise you, be of practical help. Once they're installed and you know how to use them, you won't believe how you ever managed without them.' He gave me a wry grin. 'We can explore some off-the-peg solutions which will be straight forward to install.' His face sobered. 'The hard bit will be down to you and you're going to need to commit to it. The final success will be totally reliant on you. There'll be a lot of set up work, inputting data and information. Stock-taking.'

I sat up straighter and shook my head.

'I haven't got time. And like I said, we're very good at managing our supplies.' And the thought of it all being down to me scared the pants off me. I didn't want the job. 'This is a very busy time of year for us. *The Nutcracker* starts in three weeks, we're full on. I just won't have time.'

His eyes narrowed.

'Are you going to tell Alison Kreufeld that?'

Chapter 7

My day didn't get any better after I'd begrudgingly agreed to another *information sharing session* the following week with Marcus. When I returned to the make-up department Vince barely spoke to me and when Pietro rocked up for his call, he wasn't himself at all.

'Is everything alright?' I asked. Stupid question because anyone within two feet could feel the waves of anger radiating from him.

He threw himself into the cream leather seat in front of the well-lit mirrors, a scowl creasing deep lines across his forehead. Leonie hurried into make-up after him, still trying to lace up the ornate brocade jacket he wore. She threw me an anxious look as with ill-grace he submitted to her, tying the laces and adjusting the elaborate trimming at his neck and cuffs. She worked with jerky movements, tight-lipped and frozen jawed. Pietro stared stonily at himself in the mirror.

Oh God, I had to get him on stage on time tonight.

I felt slightly sick as I dabbed my sponge in the pan stick. It was like having to go head to head with a dragon who might roar at any moment and singe my eyebrows into oblivion. If that was all he did, I'd count myself lucky. An hour to curtain call and he was still a long way from the zone. No amount of scales in the lifts would help if he didn't start making that mental shift into character. Actors, singers and dancers all prepare themselves before they go on stage. They use a variety of methods to put themselves in the zone. For some it's very casual and only a five-minute job. For others, from the minute they enter the theatre, they start thinking about their character. Dancers begin warming up and stretching their muscles. Singers start to tune up their voices, practising their breathing, running through scales and vocal exercises with their mouths and cheeks to get all the musical juices flowing.

Pietro normally prepared with painstaking thoroughness. Last time the phone call had interrupted but he'd already been in character. This zombie-like stillness and sense of brooding made me very nervous.

I approached with extreme caution, taking my lead from him. He clearly didn't want to talk.

Without making eye contact, I busied myself with my kit and then got straight down to work without any further preamble, brushing his face with quick, nimble strokes, blending the foundation to create my blank canvas, working my way right into the roots of his hair. Next I brushed his hair, applying a light coat of wax before pinning it away from his face in readiness for the long wig.

He grunted as I tugged it into place and then firmly pushed hairpins through the mesh to ensure that it didn't slip.

He closed his eyes and kept them closed as I started work, shading the lids and outlining them with eyeliner.

When he opened them, my heart contracted in pity. Despair shadowed them.

'Oh Pietro, are you OK?' I asked unable to stop myself. I'd never seen him look so down.

'No, my bastardo brother-in-law just asked for more money,' he whispered. 'And my agent says that he can't get an injunction. I'm going to have to pay the little shit again.'

Once Pietro strode onto stage, I joined Jeanie and Vince in the wings and let out a huge sigh, feeling the tension in my shoulders release. I'd got him there, although I wasn't convinced I'd done him any favours. As the curtain rose, I caught Alison's eye and she gave me an approving nod. It didn't make me feel any better.

I watched anxiously as Pietro took centre stage and began to sing.

'God, that was awful,' I muttered in Jeanie's ear.

'What was wrong with him?' Her low voice was barely audible. 'I don't think I've ever seen him quite like that before.'

I just shook my head, unable to take my eyes from him. We watched as he moved about the stage. The voice was off, and his movements stiff. He missed a couple of cues that the audience would probably never know but a frisson of alarm ran around the wings.

After ten minutes, Pietro's consummate professionalism and innate talent rescued him.

When we left the backstage area at the end of the performance to go to the canteen for a cup of tea, I was able to heave a sigh of relief.

'Shit.' Jeanie turned to me. 'That was a bit hairy.'

'He's had some bad news,' I hedged. 'You know I told you about the porn film.'

I filled her in on his latest fears.

'Bastard. His own family,' said Jeanie as we queued up. 'But better to keep it out of the papers. Something like that would spread faster than wildfire on the internet.'

'That's what he's worried about. Never getting the genie back in the bottle.'

'You got him on.' Jeanie clapped me on the back. 'That's the most important thing. All part of our job.

You handled him well. Didn't press him. I think if anyone else had, he would have detonated.'

'Think you can tell Alison Kreufeld that?'

'She saw it for herself.'

'Yeah and she probably saw how crap he was for the first ten minutes and I'll get the blame for that too.'

'She's not so bad you know. She rates you.'

'Yeah right. So maybe you could have a word with her?'

She didn't even turn and look at me.

'You don't even know what I was going to ask?' I wailed.

'Tilly, you are doing the computer stuff and that's the end of it.' Darn it, I could have been asking anything. How the hell did she know that was what I was trying to wiggle out of?'

'But it's not my thing and it's going to take ages and it's going to be dead boring ... I don't want to do it.'

She gave me the look. I winced. 'The virus was a one off. I won't do it again.'

'No, you won't because you're getting some training and support from the IT lot.'

'Why can't Vince do it?' I turned to him. 'You'd quite enjoy it, wouldn't you?'

'Not really, I get by just fine as I do.' Tight-lipped, he concentrated on the floor.

'Hmph.' I crossed my arms.

'Come on the pair of you. We've got some tidying up to do.'

'But it's our early night,' protested Vince. 'Well ... it's ...' his voice dried up, withered no doubt by Jeanie's arctic gaze. 'I've ... it's ...'

Turning on her heel with a distinct majestic toss of the head, Jeanie marched off down the corridor ahead of us, her feet clipping the floor with military purpose.

'Now you've done it,' I whispered to Vince. Jeanie affronted was not conducive to a quick getaway.

'Just because she hasn't seen any action in fifty million years, doesn't mean she should begrudge me some fun.'

'Oooh, where are you off to?'

He paused, suddenly shifty.

'You've got a date,' I accused him.

'No, I haven't.' His lips pursed into the giveaway pout that always told me he was lying.

'Yes, you have. I can tell.'

'No. I. Have. Not.' He folded his arms and glared at me before adding with a snarl, 'I'm just meeting a friend. Sometimes Tilly, you just don't know when to stop.' He paused and I saw the flash of pain in his eyes. 'I'm seeing a friend. OK. That's all it is.'

I stepped back as if he'd hit me. 'I'm ... I'm sorry.'

'Yes, well you should be,' he spat. 'It's easy for you. You don't know how bloody lucky you are. You've got it all.'

I waited a moment as he marched off down the corridor following Jeanie to the lift, almost tempted to give in and burst into tears.

To: Matilde@lmoc.co.uk
From: Redsman@hotmail.co.uk
Subject: Defeat
   Hi Tilly
   Oh dear, you might be wishing you were buried in the basement.
   Disastrous result for your boys yesterday.
   Was it miserable down your street in Camden?

Chapter 8

I stretched, the longing for a cup of tea outweighing the urge to go back to sleep. It would have been so nice to have one of those teas-made thingies.

I nudged Felix who was pretending to be asleep.

'It's not even seven o'clock, missus,' he groaned and burrowed back under the duvet.

I nudged him again. It wasn't my fault he'd come home sometime in the wee small hours of the morning.

'You know what day it is, don't you?' Every once in a while, on a Sunday, we blitzed the flat usually when Felix's mother, Judith, was due but occasionally for the good of our health and today was for the latter.

'Yes, it means you go all mental on me and get an obsession with rubber gloves,' he gave a sleepy laugh, 'that sounds more exciting than it is.'

'Seriously Felix, we have to tidy up. The cobwebs in here pre-date last Christmas.'

The whole flat was starting to look a little tired and

in need of some serious DIY. The tap in the kitchen was leaking, one ring on the oven had stopped working and the window in the lounge had a large crack down one pane.

'Chuck a bit of glitter in them and they can be our decorations.'

I brightened. 'I love that idea but it's a bit early.' Christmas was a month away, which seemed like ages but it would soon race by.

'Then we can stay in bed and not worry.' He made a move to turn over and wriggle back under the duvet.

'Felix, there are dust bunnies in the lounge the size of small elephants, the kitchen sink has defied the concept of stainless steel and the hall floor is so sticky that the people from superglue will be round to find out the secret of our formula.'

He pulled the duvet tighter over his head.

'If we're not careful we'll get nominated for one of those awful, *How Clean is Your House?* TV programmes.'

'Alright. Alright. You've made your point. I'm getting up.'

'I'll make a start on the hoovering, you do the kitchen and ...' I took a quick peek at the time on my phone on the bedside table, 'I'll do the lounge while you clean the shower. It's your turn.'

He raised an eyebrow. 'What with *Match of the Day* to accompany you?'

I tried to look innocent and scooted out of bed quickly. Busted. The repeats were calling.

'Multi-tasking,' I shrugged, pulling on a ratty T-shirt and leggings. 'I set the thingy to record it so I can catch the highlights as I round up the marauding elephants.'

'I thought Arsenal lost.'

'They did but ...' I was one of those sad people that needed to see the train wreck.

By the time, I got to the lounge, feeling slightly sweaty and grimy, I felt I deserved the treat of football.

I switched on the telly as I set up the hoover with all the right attachments ready to attack the huge cobweb draped across the corner of the room, hugging the picture-rail.

The football depressed me further, although Redsman's crowing email did make me smile. Liverpool had won their match yesterday. Three nil at home, as opposed to Arsenal who'd managed to snatch defeat from the jaws of victory in the eighty-ninth minute.

To: Redsman@hotmail.co.uk
From: Matilde@lmoc.co.uk
Subject: Re: Defeat

Watching MOTD by any chance?

You know what they say, you only sing when you're winning.

Camden? I live in Clapham, not quite so hipsterish.

Tilly

To: Matilde@lmoc.co.uk
From: Redsman@hotmail.co.uk
Subject: Re: Re: Defeat

Would love to be watching MOTD but have hot date with Harry Potter DVD and niece and nephew who have been up since 6.30am.

Clapham? Posh bird then.

To: Redsman@hotmail.co.uk
From: Matilde@lmoc.co.uk
Subject: Re: Re: Re: Defeat

Love a bit of Harry Potter, I've read all the books ... and can't even claim to have nephews and nieces as an excuse.

Clapham North, the less posh bit. Trewgowan Road, decidedly unposh.

Tilly

To: Matilde@lmoc.co.uk
From: Redsman@hotmail.co.uk
Subject: Harry Potter

Confession time. I was one of the army of disapprovers, rolling my eyes on the tube at grown-ups, until I had to read a chapter of *Harry Potter and the Prisoner of Azkaban* to said nephew. Course I had no idea what was going on but was so hooked on the whole Hogwarts thing that I had to go out and buy the first two books in the series. The rest of that weekend got lost (good job I live on my own – I didn't move off the sofa for two days). Ever since then, I have been a fan (even queued at Waterstones the night *Deathly Hallows* came out – although that might have had something to do with the fact that I also happened to be staggering out of the pub at that time).

I'd giggled as I read. Just as Jeanie had surmised, he lived alone. But he didn't sound quite so dull any more, not that he had to me. I read on, ignoring the call of housework. This was more fun.

Have a good weekend – got to be better than mine. Earlier mentioned nephew and excessively precocious four-year-old niece aren't being collected until this afternoon. By six pm I will be a mere shadow of my former self. Last time Meg (niece) came, she used my entire stock of reject Christmas present aftershave to create her own unique blend (potential to market it as Gigolo's Boudoir) which she then doused my bedroom in because, 'Mummy said it smelt of old socks and knickers.' (It doesn't by the way)

How funny I've got a friend who lives on that street. Number 16, what number are you?

The kitchen could wait a while longer. I pulled up the chair and sent him one back.

To: Redsman@hotmail.co.uk
From: Matilde@lmoc.co.uk
Subject: Harry Potter

Just about to do my housework, hazmat suits may be required. No old socks or knickers lurking, just a year's worth of blood and sweat from an army of spiders. Would far rather be reading. Hope the day with the small relatives goes well.

What a small world, I live the other side of the street, 21, who knows I might pass your friend every day on my way to work.

Mx

I stopped. Without thinking I'd added the x. To x or not to x?

I deleted it. And then typed it back in again. Then deleted it again.

For God's sake, it's an email to a friend. Nothing wrong with a friendly x. I stuck it back in and pressed send before I could change my mind.

I wandered into the kitchen to find Felix texting on his phone. He quickly stuffed it in his back pocket, trying to look innocent. I could hardly say anything, I'd been slacking too.

I grinned at him. 'How you doing?' I nudged one of the crumbs dusting the kitchen table. 'I'm bored now.'

He gave me an impish smile. 'What happened to, Missus we've-got-to-clean-for-the-Olympics?'

'I qualified for bronze, that's good enough. Come on, I'll give you a hand.'

Twenty minutes later, when the kitchen had been tidied, I straightened up and rubbed my aching back. The floor was clean. The sink cleared and the counter tops wiped.

'Can we go to the pub now?' Felix wheedled pulling a silly face. 'Pretty pretty please, boss lady.' He put his arms around me and spun me around the kitchen. 'Let's go get a pint in at The Windmill. Have some fun.' He buried his head in my curls.

I slipped my arms around his neck. 'We could always go back to bed.' I nuzzled his neck.

He pushed me away, shaking his head. 'Down girl. I've just got out the shower. Come on leave that, let's go out.'

'But Felix there's still the hall ...'

'But Tilly ...' he teased, 'you know you want to...' His dark eyes twinkled as he said it, his whole face alight with laughter. 'Clean house and no fun makes Tilly just like her parents.'

I thought of the pristine home I'd grown up in. 'Give me ten minutes to get showered.'

With his usual bouncy exuberance, Felix pulled me along to the pub, not allowing me to dawdle and giving me affectionate hugs every time I slowed down as we passed the row of shops around the corner from the flat.

Luckily in pub terms it was still early and we managed to grab a table. Felix had texted a few friends who joined us, the usual crew of his best friend Kevin and girlfriend, Sarah, and their nearest neighbours Jason and Kelly. Jason had brought a couple of Sunday papers which he dumped onto the slightly sticky round table, a serious broadsheet and a tabloid.

Felix seized them and placed them on the chair nearest him. 'We're here to drink beer and socialise, not read the papers.'

'Mate, I want to read the match report,' said Kevin, grabbing them back.

'So do I,' I added.

Felix folded his arms and pouted. 'Sport only,' which resulted in Kevin and me having a quick tussle to grab the sports pages. He was a West Ham supporter and we routinely abused each other.

'Rubbish result, yesterday,' he grinned, snagging the tabloid.

I pulled a face and picked up the broadsheet. 'Woeful,' I agreed and started leafing through the back pages to find a match report.

Kelly, a very natural redhead, tossed her page boy bob and head, screwed up her petite freckled face. 'Isn't it a bit weird that you're into opera and football? And that Felix can't bear football and he's a bloke.'

'He's gay,' Kevin chipped in, peering over the top of his paper.

Felix grinned and swiped at the paper making the pages crumple. Kevin folded it and whacked him over the head.

I ignored the two of them and turned to Kelly as Kevin began flicking through the paper. A text pinged on Felix's phone which immediately diverted his interest.

'My dad didn't have any sons,' I explained. 'He used to say the only person in the house on his side was the cat, George. He took me to a couple of Leeds United matches when I was a kid. I got into it.'

'So how come Arsenal?' asked Kevin.

I pulled a wry face. 'Leeds kept losing. Dropped out of the premiership. Arsenal kept winning. Became a habit and then when I moved to London I lived in Highbury for a little while.' I shrugged.

'I still don't get how you like opera as well ... I mean it's like well pretentious.' Kelly sneered. 'For stuck up rich people.'

I smiled. I'd heard that sort of comment so many times. 'You just get to know the music and the stories, and they're not that different from a soap opera; just set several centuries ago.'

Kelly wrinkled her nose in confusion. 'What like EastEnders in Italian?'

'Not exactly ...' I laughed. 'But they share universal themes. Love, jealousy, betrayal.'

'Hey, Tilly. Look. Is this one of your lot?'

Kevin held up one of the pages. 'The Snow Queen.'

'Oh my God, it's Katerina. What does it say?'

I scooted round the table to sit next to him.

Kevin read out, 'It says, "Prima Ballerina, Katerina Petrova, 26 ..." Why do they always give people's ages? "denies cocaine addiction, but it looks like the *Swan Lake* star might be partial to a little pick me up between scenes."'

'Oooh that's not good. She's in full costume and ... oh God that's backstage. Oh shit ...' The picture was more than familiar. One of the backstage crew had taken it and shared it on WhatsApp. Jeanie had been furious when she'd heard that Vince had shown it to me and Felix on his phone one night when we were all out together. I tried to catch Felix's eye but he was absorbed in his phone.

'Do you know her then?' asked Kelly.

'Yes … well, I mean I work with her.' I did her hair and make-up, knew her to say hello to in the corridor but not much more than that. 'I don't know her socially.'

'Does she take coke a lot?'

'Yeah. Does she?' Jason piped up.

'Bet she does, all those dancers do. They live on fresh air, stands to reason,' said Kevin knowingly. 'Jonno will be here in a while, he can give us the low down. He works at the Mercury. He says coke is the same as a glass of wine to everyone in the media and show biz.'

'Well they're all anorexic, aren't they,' added Sarah. 'No calories in drugs.'

For a moment, I paused, the four of them focused on me, making my skin prickle at the avaricious interest shining in their eyes. Only Felix seemed totally disinterested. I sighed. There had been rumours, among the backstage crew, that Katerina liked a sniff now and then but this avid interest in someone they didn't even know felt wrong, along with the blithe dismissal of 'all those dancers' as if they were somehow a different species of human and therefore didn't qualify for any sympathy.

Knowing how upset Pietro had been the other day, and seeing first-hand the impact just worrying about a story appearing had on him, made me pause before I made any comment.

Poor Katerina. How must she be feeling this morning? Dancers like her worked all their lives to make it into a ballet company, making enormous sacrifices. I wanted to cry for her.

'It's awful,' I said. 'She's going to be in bits about this.'

How had the paper got hold of that picture? I glanced at Felix trying to catch his eye. It had done the rounds on WhatsApp. Anyone could have texted, emailed, tweeted, instagrammed it. Suddenly it was clear how easy it was for something to go viral. Anyone of hundreds of people could have sent that picture to the paper.

Felix shrugged, still not meeting my eye. 'I don't see what the problem is. Celebs love getting their face in the papers. It'll up her profile. She'll love it.'

'But what about her family? Her friends? Her fans?' Surely Felix could see how that might affect her. 'What about her job? It's not good for her profile with management.'

'Rubbish,' scoffed Felix. 'I wouldn't be surprised if it was leaked deliberately. Great publicity for the theatre. Just think of all the extra tickets you'll sell.'

Had Felix lost his marbles? 'Tickets are harder to get than gold dust ... our shows sell out, sometimes a year in advance.' I still couldn't believe he was thinking like this.

'No one leaked this picture. Some mercenary bastard sold it for a quick buck I bet.' I tossed the paper aside in disgust. Felix looked up briefly and then his eyes slid away to a spot below my feet. My stomach flipped with a roll of nausea.

'Hello, hello, hello,' a nasally voice with a decided tinge of Essex rang out as a wirier version of Kev with the same shade of gingery blonde hair appeared.

I took advantage of his arrival to slip away to the toilet, where I pressed my hot face against the cold mirror.

'You the make-up lady, then?'

I jumped and turned. Kevin's brother swaggered into the toilets clutching a pint of lager, all tight jeans and slip-on shoes. The thin, gingery moustache on his upper-lip combined with his round-shouldered slouch brought to mind a small weasel.

'This is the ladies. Do you mind?'

He shrugged and took an insolent sip of his drink, his eyes boring into mine over the top of his glass.

'So, make-up lady.' He leaned a hip against one of the basins crossing his legs so that I'd have to step over them to pass.

'Tilly,' I snapped. 'And you are ...?' I asked, determined not to give him the satisfaction of acknowledging that I knew who he was.

'Jonno'

When I didn't say anything, he added, 'Kev's brother', with an are-you-stupid roll of his eyes.

I stepped back from him, his closeness discomforting and pulled at the soap dispenser hoping the trickle of pink liquid would help make me feel clean again, but he leaned towards me, his breath hot on my neck.

'I hear you have the inside track on a few of our top operatic and balletic celebs.'

Flustered, I tried to move back and smeared the pink soap all down my sleeve. 'I don't know what you mean,' I said, my heart starting to beat uncomfortably.

'Come on. Nice story about the Snow Queen. I got a by-line out of that one.'

'You're a journalist!' My heartbeat rocketed to warp speed and the bottom of my stomach fell away.

'Yup. Celebrity stringer. News reporter. Always on the lookout for a good tip.'

Images of Pietro's strained face, singing in the final scene of *Don Giovanni*, popped into my head.

'Reporter?' I clenched my fists at my sides, resisting the overwhelming urge to punch his nasty, smug little face. 'That's not news. Gossip rag, more like.'

A tide of red rose up his neck, spilling along his cheeks. 'We're performing a public service,' he snapped. 'People do crappy things – we report it.' His narrow lips, too red in colour, firmed into a crumpled line.

'Public service?' I echoed and copied his tone. 'Scurrilous gossip sells – you get paid.'

He narrowed his eyes and glared at me. Jutting out his chin, he said in a growl, 'We uncover the truth. You might not approve Missy but that's what we do.'

'No.' A hot flush ran through me. How could he be so ... so indifferent to people's feelings? 'You harass decent people. Take photos of them when they're going about their daily business and deliberately smear their names unnecessarily. You wouldn't know the truth if it ...' I ran out of steam, too worked up to finish.

'What like Katerina Petrova? Hardly whiter than white?' He sniggered.

'She's human. No one is perfect. Printing that picture was just mean.'

'Mean,' he teased in a high voice with the maliciousness of a nasty playground bully. 'Public has a right to know if celebs are up to no good.'

'Not if it's a private picture.' As soon as I said it, I knew I'd stepped out on treacherous ground.

He lifted an eyebrow, smirking. 'Not that private. I heard it was shared around.'

I felt a deep sense of shame. Like so many others backstage in the cast, we'd all seen the picture. Been complicit in sharing it. Were we any better?

His face turned sly. 'I hear one of your boys has been a bit naughty.'

I went cold. 'I don't know what you mean,' I said, turning my back on him scared I might give something away.

He grabbed my arm and turned me round, bringing his face close to mine. I so wanted to wipe the smirk from his weasely face.

Rancid lager breath fumes hissed out of his mouth as he said, 'Oh I think you do. I heard a rumour.'

I swallowed and like a rabbit I froze, unable to escape his intent stare. What did he know? Was he just fishing? My heart thudded so hard it hurt. My face burnt with florid heat.

'I don't know what you're talking about.' I lifted my chin in the air, praying that the pulse thundering in my neck wouldn't give me away.

'Oh, I think you do.' Jonno's eyes narrowed to slits and his lips virtually disappeared in an unpleasant smile.

'No comment,' I said. It was the first thing that came into my mind.

He smirked. 'I could sweeten the deal.' He raised his eyebrows with Groucho Marx emphasis.

'You think I'd tell you things ... for money? Is that how you got that picture? The one of Katerina? Well you can get lost, I wouldn't tell you a thing. I wouldn't want your money.'

He gave a nasty smile. 'Doesn't matter, there's always

folks that do. It only takes a little whisper and we can do the rest. A bit of digging. It's amazing what you can turn up.' He winked.

I closed my eyes. Pietro's drawn face popped into my head and then Felix's, his expression bright and inquisitive as he'd said, 'No such thing as bad publicity.'

Jonno's eyes shifted to the doorway back towards the pub and he laughed.

'Paid a fair price for the tip off about Katerina – twenty pieces of silver.'

Chapter 9

'No offence, Tilly, but you look like shit this morning,' said Jeanie, standing in front of me, tilting my chin towards the light.

'So would you if you had a night like mine,' I growled. I didn't need her to tell me how crap I looked. It was nothing compared to how I felt.

'Want me to sort those bags under your eyes out?'

I shook my head, loathe to reject the rare inner mother hen of Jeanie wanting to help. I was worried I'd end up blabbing the whole truth to her and that would have been disastrous.

'To be honest Jeanie, I've had a massive row with Felix and I'm still steaming.'

She took a step back, holding her hands up as if to ward me off.

''Kay. You just hold right on to that anger.'

I'd been doing that for the last two hours, although the middle-aged man who'd bagged the last seat on the tube right from under me might disagree. He probably had a broken toe. Served him right. That's what you got for messing with an irate female in kitten heels.

'You could sort out the cupboard?' Jeanie tilted her head to one side in hopeful anticipation. 'Coffee at eleven.'

'Fine.' It was unlikely she was even half-way fooled by my weak attempt at a smile. God I wanted to kill him. 'I'll just check my emails first.'

I'd been hoping to hear from Redsman and my heart plummeted in further disappointment at my empty inbox. Oh God, it was the kiss. I shouldn't have sent that email with the kiss. Should I send another and explain it was habit, a mistake ... or would that compound things. Maybe I should send him another email, this time without the kiss. I could ask him about a book. Go back to our roots, as it were.

From: Matilde@lmoc.co.uk
Subject: Harry Potter
Hope the weekend with the small people went well.
Looking for another book recommendation, any suggestions?
Tilly

There, no kiss. I pressed the send button. And immediately regretted it. Was that what things had come to? Relying on the next best thing to an imaginary friend to lift my mood.

Casting the computer a sour look, I stomped off towards the chaotic, tiny room with its jumble of hair dyes, perming solutions and other noxious chemicals. It was easily the worst job on the watch but that morning, it suited me perfectly. As I scoured the stained sink with an ancient bristled brush, I imagined using it on Felix's pearly white teeth. That would teach him, wash his mouth out and make sure he never spilled another secret again.

Oh yes, the apologies had been profuse, between mouthfuls of cereal, as soon as he knew Jonno had spilled the beans. I'd slept in the spare room, mainly to ensure I didn't give into the temptation to strangle him at some point before dawn. But it didn't stop me thinking that I only had myself to blame.

'Look Tilly, I'm really, really sorry that Jonno ...' Felix had peered up at me from a hunched position at the kitchen table, reminding me of a tentative turtle testing the water, wondering whether he dare pop his head out of the shell.

'What?' I snapped, my hands gripping the back of the wooden chair, ignoring his submissive, apologetic stance. 'Told me?' My voice went up several decibels. 'Or that you sold ... sold that picture to him? I can't believe you did that. You do know I could lose my job?'

And it would be my own fault, not his. It didn't matter what he'd done. I shouldn't have told Felix any of the things that went on at work. That was the plain fact of the matter. I had broken the code. I should have known better, although I wasn't going to let him off the hook that easily.

Felix opened his mouth to say something.

'Work stuff I tell you is in confidence. We're not supposed to tell anyone. You knew that...'

'I know ... but ...it just sort of came out, you know ... I told him about the picture of the dancer and ...' He shrugged helplessly as if it had all been out of his control.

I clenched my fingers so tight my ring pinched at the next finger. 'Really? And what about the money side of things? I'm not stupid, you know.'

I'd had plenty of time during a sleepless night to join all the dots.

'I didn't mean to...' Felix's eyes widened, beseeching me to believe him. 'It just ... came up in conversation. You *have* to believe me.' He finished his words with another appealing sorrowful look but by that stage the puppy dog thing was wasted on me.

'Bollocks,' I spat. I'm not sure who was more surprised by my vehemence. It was so rare that we rowed. Was it because when it came to it, there was little for either of us to get that worked up about?

'Look. I'm sorry. It just slipped out in front of Jonno ...'

'What and a few hundred quid just slipped into your back pocket, did they?'

The blush that stained his cheek said it all. I'd hoped it had come out by accident. Bragging that he knew something. But the minute I said that I realised, the intent had been there all along.

I stared at him, feeling disorientated. The axis of my world had tipped over. I didn't know where I was any more.

Felix concentrated on the contents of his breakfast bowl, his spoon rescuing the last bits of cereal from the chocolate coloured milk. I scowled at the top of his head. Him and his bloody Coco Pops. He was a grown man for God's sake.

There was silence as Felix swallowed and then looked back up. 'No one's going to find out. Jonno won't reveal his source.'

I stared at him, numb, trying to find something to say. How could he believe that made it OK?

'Tilly. You're over-reacting.' Felix was all wide eyed and optimistic. 'No one knows it came from you.' He shrugged. 'You're off the hook.'

'Off the hook!' I echoed, sitting down on the chair

and putting my head in my hands. 'You don't get it, do you? It's about trust.' My voice was dull. No, it was also about personal responsibility and I had let myself down badly. 'It's about *us*. Where does this leave us? How can I trust you again?'

Felix's shocked expression suggested none of that had occurred to him before.

I took in a deep breath. 'Please, please tell me you didn't tell him about Pietro. Jonno alluded to rumours about someone.'

Felix's eyes met mine full on, wide and bright. Too bright, too wide, too keen to please all of a sudden. 'No, I haven't.'

A tiny bit of me inside relaxed but his next sentence cancelled it out.

'But you said Pietro's brother-in-law was threatening to go to the papers. Say, hypothetically, that I did, it wouldn't have mattered. That story's going to come out. Someone will tell all, there's big money in it.'

His smile widened as if trying to coax me into seeing the positives. 'Let's face it, the money would be handy. For the wedding and ...'

'Money? Is that all you think about? I don't want a fancy wedding.' I twisted my engagement ring, ready to hurl the damn thing at him.

'It wasn't just for the wedding, there were other things.'

'Other things! Like what?'

Felix scowled and I hated myself. I'd never wanted to be the penny-pincher but I'd been forced to be the responsible one. Even boiling mad, I had to ask. 'What other things?'

He sighed. 'I lost a bit too much at poker.'

'How much?' I had to ask even though I wasn't sure I wanted to know the answer.

He shrugged.

'Why didn't you tell me?' I asked, unable to believe that he'd kept all this from me.

'I'd already ... you know.'

I did, he was always short of cash. I stared searchingly at him, watching as his hand worried at the big knot in his silk tie, tugged it one way and then another.

Studying his face, I saw someone I didn't know. What other secrets did he have? The freshly shaven jaw-line suddenly embodied weakness and although his eyes met mine, there was no sense of shame or humility in them.

I sighed and rubbed my forehead with the heel of my hand. I looked at him again.

'You've done this before.'

As his gaze slid away from mine, I remembered.

The unexpected bonus six months ago, around the same time as the papers got wind of Elvira Bennetini's top secret pregnancy. At the time, it hadn't been so bad. She hadn't been too upset because it had only been a matter of time. I'd happily ignored that tiny niggle that the leak was no accident.

I closed my eyes, numbed by the sense of disappointment at my own blithe ability not to probe too deeply.

No wonder he'd shown so much interest in my life at the theatre.

My heart twisted in my chest and I swallowed. There was nothing more I could say, even if I could have got the words past the blockage in my throat. I couldn't bear another second with him or to be truthful, myself. Grabbing my coat, I fled down the stairs.

I'd slammed the front door so hard, it had bounced open again and I left it as I flounced down the street, my wide fifties skirt bouncing and the heels of my sling backs clicking furiously.

I looked down at my skirt now, it would be ruined if I spilled any of the bleach I was using to scrub the sink over it. Some part of me wanted to ruin it as a punishment. All the cleaning had made me feel better. Although, that was relative. This morning's burning anger had gone. Now I felt numb, anaesthetised by a sense of loss. Not just Felix's perfidy but my own spineless complicity. I desperately wanted to talk to someone.

But who? Jeanie would go ballistic. As it was I could barely bring myself to look her in the eye. Vince would be horrified. He adored Felix – his heart would be smashed to smithereens. Felix had broken the absolute number one commandment in the make-up world. And I was already in enough trouble. If management found out about this ... Oh shit. Tears of self-pity welled up. God I'd really messed up.

I took a solitary lunch wandering aimlessly around Covent Garden, indifferent to the scent of winter in the air and the cherry pickers putting up Christmas lights and huge swathes of fake giant mistletoe and huge silver baubles the size of demolition balls.

On my return to the opera house, the moment I stepped over the threshold of the stage door a sense of tension in the air hit hard. Cheerful Charlie, the doorman, had lost his characteristic manner, instead he seemed particularly grim as I flashed my staff badge and as I passed various members of backstage crew I noticed everyone kept their heads down.

In her office, Jeanie held the phone to her ear, her face set in stern lines, her mouth dipped at either end. She nodded several times, barked a couple of staccato questions and rubbed at a spot on the back of her neck. With depressed lethargy, she replaced the handset. I wanted to look away so she couldn't see anything in my eyes.

She straightened and I could virtually see her donning her management cape, pulling the strings of serious and grave about her.

'There's an emergency meeting downstairs on stage. At two-thirty. Memo on your desk.'

'Yesterday's papers?' I asked, my voice faint. After a very sleepless night, every tendon in my body felt tight.

'You'll have to wait until the meeting. The department heads have only been told a brief outline. And where the hell has Vince got to? He was supposed to start work at twelve today.' She tapped pointedly at her watch.

I presumed she wasn't expecting me to answer as a) I wasn't his official time-keeper and b) given the hugely varied hours productions finished, clock watching had never been a feature of our employment.

'I'm sure he'll be here soon.' My placating attempt fell on deaf ears as she wheeled to watch him drift in through the door. Drift being the operative word. He had a sad and lost air about him.

'Are you OK?' I asked. Another disastrous date? Normally Jeanie and I would patch him up with hot sweet tea and within half an hour, he'd let it all out in his usual camp comic fashion and be laughing as hard as us at the memory of the night before.

With a curl of his lip, he glared. 'No. Just a ... bad weekend.' His bush baby eyes filled with tears. 'Sorry, just feeling a bit sorry for myself.'

'Well, what's the problem then?' asked Jeanie, not being at all nice as her mouth pursed with impatience.

She had no time for Vince's dating dramas which, to be fair, were frequent and each one seemed to be a bigger production than the last.

'Urnggg,' wailed Vince and burst into tears, pushing past both of us and fleeing down the corridor.

'Oh, for Pete's sake. Today of all days. Spare me the histories.' Jeanie rolled her eyes. 'That boy will be the death of me.' She hissed out a breath and rounded on me. 'And you shouldn't be encouraging him.'

'Me! What did I do?' Now wasn't the time to correct her.

'If we've got this meeting, we need to get some work done.'

It was official; I was working in a mad house. Both her and Vince were obviously mentally imbalanced at the moment. It was the only explanation I could find. That or they were both in love, with Vince that was always a possibility, with Jeanie an absolute impossibility.

The Head of PR, Elizabeth Tansley, had a distinctive style of her own, consisting of floaty tea dresses and 1940's shoes, and was about as un-public relations-like as humanly possible. She reminded me of a rather chic forgetful clairvoyant with her deep, sincere voice which probably hypnotised journalists into giving the LMOC acres of positive publicity. When any negative stuff was printed, she took it very personally. Today her face kept crumpling into unhappy lines and I knew it wasn't going to be a good meeting especially when I realised who flanked her on either side; the Chief Executive, the head of HR and to my surprise Marcus Walker.

He had the full pin-striped Monty on today and an impassive expression on his face as he stared out across the assembled audience.

'Thank you all for coming. I will be having several of these meetings with various departments.' Her voice shook. 'I'm sure you have all seen the unfortunate story in this weekend's paper which has obviously caused terrible anguish to poor, poor Katerina.' Her voice hitched and she peered over her glasses at the assembled audience. 'I hate to think that this story originated from the LMOC,' she peered over her glasses at the assembled group, her lower lip trembling, 'but ...' I worried that at any moment she might burst into tears, 'there is a v-very s-strong poss ...'

Her mouth worked furiously and everyone shuffled awkwardly at her distress. 'Personally I ... I can't believe that any one of you could ... would even c-consider b-but there is,' she shot Marcus a poisonous glance, 'some thinking that it might have come from someone here.'

I swallowed hard and tried to keep an impassive expression on my face.

'An investigation is underway but I'm sure it won't

happen again. I've been asked to remind you all of the consequences should it transpire that someone has deliberately fed information to the press. Any such transgression will lead to disciplinary actions and possibly prosecution.'

Both Marcus and the Chief Exec straightened like a pair of soldiers on sentry duty. It enhanced the message and then she stepped down and walked away. Chatter immediately erupted, a buzz of angry wasps in horrified condemnation, appalled at the potential accusation.

Then the Head of HR stepped forward. Unlike Elizabeth, Marsha Munro was every inch the exec in her tailored dress and jacket. 'I would like to remind you all that there is an official code of conduct.' Irritation and anger rolled off her in waves of pissed offness, her mouth working as if there was a very nasty taste inside. 'You should have received one with your contract when you first commenced working here. However, in case it has been misplaced, I would urge everyone to take a copy away with them today. We will also be issuing a confidentiality clause to all contracts.'

'She's hacked off because she's been caught out,' muttered Leonie from wardrobe in my ear.

'What do you mean?'

'There's no confidentiality clause in any of our contracts ... now this has happened it doesn't look good for her. Did you ever get a code of conduct?'

'Not that I remember. Just a letter ...'

'Yeah, I bet no one got one. She's shitting herself ...'

Jeanie remained tight-lipped as we made our way back up to the studio while Vince, who had bounced back with the verve of Zebedee on acid, hit Agatha Christie mode, with a rapid run through of potential suspects.

'Could be someone in the box office ... or front of house. One of the cleaners, could be an undercover reporter.' Vince screwed up his face in thought.

Or it could be the partner of someone who worked here, who thought he'd make a fast buck. Acid swirled in my stomach.

'Or what about hidden spy cameras. Rigged up in the middle of the night.' Vince threw his head back and posed towards the ceiling. 'Hello darlings.'

Jeanie stopped dead in the corridor and turned around with a ferocious glare.

'Not another word,' she snapped, her eyes glinting with fury.

'What did I say? Wh–'

I gave him a sharp kick from behind and he shot me an aggrieved look as I shook my head at him.

He tossed his head in the air and thankfully shut up.

When we got back to the studio, Jeanie shut herself in her office. All I could do was sit and sort out hair pins, my hands shaking slightly, the least demanding job I could manage.

Chapter 10

Grim lines etched by years of smoking wreathed Jeanie's mouth, as she pushed a cinnamon Danish towards me. 'This business is hateful. I've worked here for twenty years and nothing like this has ever happened before. That meeting on Monday ... I've never known anything like it before.' She cast a quick look around the crowded canteen. 'I hate the amplification that it has to be one of us.'

Leonie put down her cup with a bang in the saucer. 'Who says it is? Anyone could go to the papers. That picture was doing the rounds for months.'

'No, the paper is insisting the source came directly from someone here.'

'Really?' I asked, my voice shaking, hoping it sounded horrified rather than scared.

Thankfully Felix had gone away again, as I couldn't bring myself to speak to him. I'd relished the peace and quiet at home for the last three days.

Jeanie gave a heavy sigh and turned sharp eyes my way. 'They've launched a full-scale investigation.'

'You mean there's a mole!' squeaked Vince with inappropriate animation. He furtively peered around the room as if it would suddenly become apparent and a big neon arrow might suddenly start flashing.

'I can't believe we've only got a few more performances of *Don Giovanni*,' I said, unsubtly changing the subject, which was clearly a relief to everyone, as they all started dipping their heads in agreement. 'It's gone so quickly, although I'm looking forward to doing *The Nutcracker*.' The popular ballet production was due to open for its usual Christmas run and would be an easy gig.

'Yes,' Leonie nodded, her burnished copper curls bouncing, 'and I'll be relieved that we've got those hairy high-speed costume changes done. Honest to God, my heart rate doesn't return to normal until the end of the show.'

'Good job they decided not to do that scene in the Christmas Gala Performance,' I said, teasing her.

'Oh, that's a breeze. All excerpts from different operas, so we can just reuse existing costumes.'

I wasn't sure I'd agree that the annual Christmas performance was a breeze. The special charity night with invited VIPs, sponsors and friends of the theatre was a bit of a showcase that senior management set great store by.

'Lucky you, darling,' piped up Vince. 'It's a nightmare for us. All those principals, all jostling to be first.' He shuddered. 'It'll be a right cat fight in the make-up room. We're having to have a couple of freelancers on board those nights. It'll give *her* an opportunity to dig in,' he jerked his head indicating someone behind us.

I turned around trying to be subtle. The canteen was just starting to fill up with the lunchtime crowd and was extra busy today as most of the orchestra were in for the first rehearsal for *The Nutcracker*. A few tables back sat Arabella Barnes, my least favourite person in the known universe. Annoyingly perky and upbeat about everything, she also had a particular speciality in pointing out the tiniest fault with saccharine, apologetic sweetness as if she were doing you a favour and not being a superior, know-it-all super-bitch. A regular freelancer, she was desperate for a permanent position and never missed an opportunity to make herself helpful.

What the hell was she doing sitting with Marcus?

They were holding a very animated conversation, although her long swathe of blonde silky hair seemed to be doing an awful lot of the talking as she tossed it over her shoulders with a tinkly laugh every couple of seconds.

'What's she doing here? And with him, I wonder?'

'Sniffing around after your job, no doubt,' said Vince. 'You know it went up on the noticeboard yesterday.'

I did and I'd been trying not to think about it too much. Every job had to be advertised externally and internally.

'She hasn't wasted any time then,' I sighed. 'Please don't tempt providence.' I touched the table and his head, 'It's not *my* job. She has just as good a chance. Alison really likes her.'

'Alison might,' said Leonie with a kind smile, 'but the talent doesn't. She doesn't have the bedside manner with them.'

'Looks as if she's got one with him,' observed Vince, watching them through half-closed lids. 'There's some serious flirting going on over there.'

'They're perfectly suited. Very professional. Ambitious.' I might not like her but I had to admit Arabella was good. Organised. Efficient. She even dressed with the smartness of a manager. I sneaked another look at her. Black shift dress. Smart leather handbag and matching shoes. She reminded me of Christelle. I could never emulate that sort of unconscious elegance or style in a million years.

'Yeah but Tilly, she doesn't have your experience. You can make a mean wig, and,' Vince's elfin face creased into a wicked smile, 'you are going to be an IT expert.'

I shot him a sour look as Leonie laughed. 'How are

the lessons going?'

'They're not. In fact,' I slunk down in my seat, 'I've successfully managed to cancel the last two.'

Almost as if he'd read my mind, Marcus glanced over just as he and Arabella stood up.

'Pants, he's seen me.'

The two of them laughed as I hauled myself back up, trying to pretend I hadn't been hiding at all.

They came straight over to us, like a pair of Exocet missiles homing in on the target.

'Tilly. Glad I caught up with you.' Marcus looked anything but glad. Irritated more like, but he put on a good show with a stiff little smile. 'You stood me up.'

I shifted in my seat, but before I could say anything Arabella butted in. 'And I'm just leaving, so hi and goodbye, guys.' She gave a casual, half all-encompassing wave with her handbag looped over her arm. 'See you all soon.' She pitched up on her tip-toes to give Marcus a quick peck on the cheek. 'Bye sweetie and thank you so much for sparing the time to have a chat. It's been a great help. I've got lots of ideas about how I can introduce improvements.' She flashed a sunny smile my way.

I waited until she'd gone and rolled my eyes only to find Marcus glowering down at me. I screwed up my face. 'Bu ... b-bother, I'd forgotten about you, I mean, sorry I er, forgot the time the other day.'

He raised an eyebrow and made me feel even smaller. I really had forgotten, but it was obvious that he thought I was avoiding him.

'I didn't write it in my diary.' I pulled out my well-thumbed diary and showed him the blank page.

'You still use a diary?' He sounded pained but he had that look on his face that questioned why he should be surprised.

'Yes.' I smiled up at him and then stood up to whisper conspiratorially in his ear, 'and the clever thing about them ...' Damn, I'd forgotten how much I liked the way he smelled. I ignored the missed beat sensation that hit my chest and stepped back to give him a nonchalant wink as I added, 'they don't need batteries or charging.' I didn't feel the least bit nonchalant. Inside, everything felt mixed up and antsy. What the hell was wrong with me? I didn't even like Marcus.

His lips curved with a reluctant smile and he reached out, taking the diary from me, his fingers brushing mine which turned my internal temperature gauge up to maximum. 'And there's nothing else in said diary for the next hour, so we can safely assume that you're free to meet as planned.'

He had me there. Jeannie and Vince watched with avid interest as if we'd laid on a show especially for them. And then realising that I was glaring at them, both rose and made their goodbyes, leaving Marcus and

I facing each other with the animosity of a pair of boxers who'd just been separated by the referee.

'Well, now you've tracked me down ...'

Marcus sighed, not out loud but I could see the way the collar on his shirt rose and his shoulders lifted. It didn't give me any satisfaction.

'OK, I'm sorry I forgot about the meeting.' It was the truth, I wasn't the best diary manager in the world, but I could see that he wasn't sure whether to believe me or not. 'What would you like me to tell you?'

He looked around at the busy canteen and let out a self-deprecating half-laugh which left his mouth turned down. 'How about everything?' If I hadn't known how super confident he was, I might have thought he seemed a touch vulnerable. I could have ignored it but I made the mistake of looking down towards his feet.

The sight of his highly polished black brogues, their glossy leather shining with the reflection of an overhead light, next to the battered leather Chelsea boots of one of the musicians sitting to his right hit me, the stark contrast socking me right in the chest with a punch of sympathy.

Dressed in a smart grey wool suit, which had that cost-a-fortune sheen to it, a crisp white shirt shouting Savile Row and a sedate silk tie, he stood out like a brand-new Ferrari in a second-hand car showroom.

Worse still, he suddenly appeared uncomfortably

aware of it.

'I tell you what,' I rose to my feet, 'why don't I give you the grand tour?' He opened his mouth and I held up a hand. 'Yes, I know. You've already had the official tour, with its shiny-look-how-professional-and-amazing-we-are agenda. And yes we are, but I'll give you the one that explains how we all work together and what really goes on. The highs and the lows, which I'm sure management wouldn't have shared when they were selling this place to you.'

His eyes sharpened, a few lines appearing on his forehead. I could tell he was intrigued and the quick, sudden flash of respect that crossed his face made me feel just that little bit taller.

I gave him a grin. 'What have you got to lose?'

'Put like that, not a lot. Just be gentle with me.' The tentative, pleading smile he sent my way melted any last residual doubts about consorting with the enemy.

Without stopping to think, I tucked a hand into the crook of his arm and steered him towards the exit. 'If it's gentle you want, you're never going to survive here.' Not that I'd worry on that score. On Monday on the stage with the senior bosses, he'd looked plenty tough enough. Ignoring a quick shiver of unease, I smiled at him in a business-like way. I wasn't going to think about any of that.

We started with the foyer, which in keeping with most theatres was a relatively small area when you considered the numbers of people that came through the doors. I always thought of the building as rather like an iceberg. What you saw on the surface by no means reflected the vast spaces backstage and underground.

There were plenty of people about, a few tourists who popped in to take a quick peek, probably unable to get tickets for anything, a couple of discreet cleaning staff polishing the Georgian panes of glass in the doors and a team of props guys who were decorating a huge fir tree which had been placed in the well next to the staircase.

'Oooh, what's the theme this year?' I asked Dean, the senior props builder who was unravelling a long paper chain.

'Hey, Tilly. Music. And I have to say the library has done a brilliant job.' He held up a sparkly gold treble clef and a string of lights which was a replica of the five-lined staff you see on sheet music.

'Clever,' I said as one of his colleagues held up a handful of golden sharps, flats and notes.

I turned to Marcus who was staring up towards the top of the tree which reached the upper balcony of the stair case. 'Each year a different department is elected to design the decorations for the tree.'

'I can't imagine that happening in the bank,' he

responded, looking back at the collection of decorations heaped on the floor.

'It's very competitive. We did sugar plum fairies and nutcracker soldiers last year,' I said before adding, 'I wonder what the IT's contribution would be.'

He gave me a lazy smile. 'Something hi-tech, flashing lights in binary sequence perhaps.'

I rolled my eyes. 'I'm not even going to pretend I know what that means. Come on,' I inclined my head and led him over to the opposite wall. 'The theatre was built in 1822 but didn't become home to the London Metropolitan Opera Company until 1956.' I pointed to a marble plaque on the wall celebrating the creation of the company. 'We're not as old or as famous as the Royal Opera House but we have established a reputation for staging innovative and avant-garde versions of established works.' I gave him a cheesy curtsey. 'That's the official line. And now for the low-down.' I tried to gauge his response, to see whether he'd stick with being corporate stiff or go with the flow, watching his lips which I think twitched ever so slightly. 'In the industry, we're known as a little bit maverick and willing to take a risk.'

I led him over to one of the posters on the walls and pointed to it.

'Sometimes, it can be successful, but very occasionally it backfires spectacularly and we have a right turkey on our hands. Ever heard of the *Sailors of Pompeii*?'

'Is that title for real?' The purse of his lips suggested he thought I was having him on but he studied the poster carefully, giving me a chance to take a good look at his rather perfect and manly profile. He might as well have been some carbon copy of a Greek statue with the strong chin, nothing double about it and a fine forehead and brow.

'Oh yes. An unmitigated disaster. You don't want to go there. The critics hated it. There wasn't a single redeeming comment. They gave us such a mauling and ironically,' I leaned in, standing on tip-toe to whisper conspiratorially, 'we didn't lose money because the tickets sold out with audiences coming to see if it was as bad as they'd said. Bet management didn't tell you that.'

Spatial awareness is not my strong point and I'd clearly misjudged the distance and got a little too close because he whipped his head around as my hot breath hit his ear. The surprise move had me wobbling on my toes and him grasping my forearms to keep me steady, leaving his lips level with mine. A bizarre thought flashed through my head. What would he say if I leaned forward and kissed him? I think I might even have started to lean forward. Luckily, he was pre-occupied with pushing me back upright and I don't think he noticed or if he did he was far too gentlemanly or horrified to acknowledge it. Avoiding his gaze, I busied myself by smoothing down my skirt.

'No, they didn't mention any of that. I think my guide read from the *this foyer cost several million to refurbish and the pure white marble came from the Apuan Alps in north-central Italy* tour script, which included detailed financials on how the renovation costs were part-funded by the Arts Council and a generous legacy.'

'Thought as much,' I said in a business-like tone, relieved that he hadn't noticed my brief moment of lunacy, and led him back through the doors and down a long corridor.

The lift pinged, announcing that we'd arrived on the second floor. 'The wardrobe department,' I said as we walked out into the corridor, which was a tight squeeze thanks to the clothes rails lining the walls.

'What's all this?' He indicated to the line of at least five clothes rails crowding the way.

'This?' I waved a don't-worry-yourself hand and picked up my pace to move on but he'd stopped and was flicking through the hangers.

'Yes, this.' Was there a touch of amusement in his eyes?

'This,' I flashed him a bright smile, 'is probably on its way to our storage facility.' The bright red plumage of feathers we'd brushed alongside were unmistakably from a recent production of *The Firebird*.

'And what happens to it then? I'm assuming they don't all sit here like the patients in A&E until a home can be found for them?' He cocked his head to one side.

'They're amazing, aren't they?' I sought out the principal dancer's costume and pulled the froth of feathers, net and sequins from the rack, pushing it towards him.

For a minute, I thought he might ignore it and all I could think was how strongly the brilliant red contrasted against the dark charcoal of his suit.

'You ought to get a tie that colour, it would look great with that suit,' I blurted out.

Yup, definitely amusement this time, I saw the quirk of his lips even as he ducked his head to hide it.

'Wouldn't it?' I pushed the tutu towards him again.

He reached out to stroke one of a series of large red and black feathers standing tall and proud from the bodice. 'This is ...' I waited as his face changed, 'it's amazing. And it was made just for one play?' He bent over to study the tiny stitches on the many frilled layers in shades of orange, red and yellow of the tutu skirt. 'Don't tell me, this is all done by hand.' He stepped back as if it might bite.

I shook my head, he had so much to learn. 'Yup and not a computer in sight.' I looked him straight in the eye. I deliberately omitted to mention that the wardrobe department also owned quite a few very hi-spec sewing machines, probably with computer chips in them, which did all sorts of clever things including over-locking, embroidery and button-holing.

Most people might have turned away but he took it head on and looked right back at me, and gave a considered nod. 'Must be very time consuming.'

What was he thinking now?

'Is it worth it?' he asked, fingering the feathers again. 'These look expensive. Can anyone really see them at the back of the auditorium?'

He had no idea but it was rather endearing to watch him as he evaluated everything so carefully.

I guess a lot of people would have thought that sourcing the feathers and dying them an exact shade of red was a lot of faff. I was used to it, and to be honest, had never had to justify it before now but I assessed the costume from a fresh perspective.

'From a financial point, possibly not ... but,' the thought struck me, 'we're asking audiences to come to productions featuring the world's greatest talent. If you're an actor and you're trying to immerse yourself in the character and you get a nasty cheap nylon costume to wear, it undermines the integrity of what you're trying to do.'

Cynicism danced on his face, indicated by a subtly raised eyebrow.

'And afterwards, what happens to ... all this work?'

Keen to impress him, I went and let my enthusiasm get the better of me, letting my guard down.

'Most of this goes into storage, although it can vary. Sometimes our productions go on tour, so the costumes are used again. Some are hired out to other companies.'

I could see him taking all the information in a moment too late.

'I can almost hear the cogs turning and tumblers clicking into place,' I heaved a resigned sigh. 'And no, I've no idea how they keep track of everything.'

'Would be interesting to know.' He raised his eyebrows.

'I'm sure it would.' And then because he'd been rather accommodating listening to me ramble on, I added with a teasing grin, 'They might need a system or two.'

'I'm sure they do. And I'll get to them after I've sorted you lot out.'

'Maybe you should start with them,' I said with cheeky perkiness as if the brilliant brainwave had literally only just struck me. 'With all these costumes being picked up any day now.'

'No.' His implacable tone made me jump. 'I think your need is just as great.' He turned and pushed the feathered tutu back into place, making it clear I was on a hiding to nothing but I caught the quick twitch of his lips.

'As you said earlier Tilly, this place has a reputation

for the avant-garde and leading the way with innovation. It would be a shame for your department to miss out.' The green eyes twinkled and the unexpected smile sent my pulse haywire as it broke out into a merry trot.

This man was dangerous. The absolute last thing I needed at the moment was wilful hormones leaping about with ill-disciplined intent, complicating things.

As we were making our way back to the lift we bumped into Alison Kreufeld and she was clearly delighted to see us together.

'Ah, Tilly ... and Marcus you've saved me a call. How's the IT project going?'

'Good,' I said nodding my head, crossing my fingers in my pocket.

She beamed. 'Excellent, I'm looking forward to an update at the end of the week. Marcus told me you've identified a potential project and how confident he is that you can handle the implementation for the make-up department.'

He had?

'Yes, we've just been discussing how best to move forward, haven't we Tilly?' Thankfully he sounded suitably vague. 'We're meeting next week, Thursday isn't it?'

'Yes,' I said still nodding, praying she wouldn't ask for any more information, keeping my foot pinned to the floor instead of delivering a sharp kick to Marcus's shins.

'I'm very pleased to hear it. I can't wait to hear more details.' Her smile was positively warm. 'Great to see you taking this on board. Well done Tilly.'

She turned on her heel and walked off.

'Thanks,' I muttered to Marcus.

'For what?'

'Not dumping me in it.'

'Does that mean you owe me? I'll see you on Thursday. Eleven o'clock, suit?' He flashed a wicked grin and I knew that payback would be coming big time.

Chapter 11

'Missus, you're home.' Felix flashed me a sheepish smile, as he bounced into the kitchen like an enthusiastic Labrador, a smart bag with silky ribbon handles dangling from his hand.

'I bought you a present and,' he held up a hand as to halt any objection, 'before you say anything. I'm really sorry. I messed up, big time.' His face sobered and he came over to me, put a hand under my chin, staring intently at me. 'I shouldn't have listened to Jonno. I swear I'll never do it again. I'm a pillock, I know. And you're far too good for me.'

He said these last words with such a sad, sweet smile and my heart turned over with regret.

He took my face in his hands and looked down with such intensity, I wanted to cry. 'Tilly, you are the best thing that ever happened to me. I don't deserve you. I promise I won't ever tell another soul about anything you tell me. Please, please darling Tilly, forgive me. I love you so much. You're my bestest friend in the whole entire wide, wide world.'

My heart hitched.

He dangled the bag at me, his big brown eyes beseeching, worry and contrition written all over his face.

'Open it.' He pushed the bag into my hands. 'You'll love it.'

Peeling back a layer of tissue paper, I pulled out an exquisite hand-stitched bag made of rich purple velvet and lined with fuchsia-pink marbled silk. The fabric slithered through my fingers, soft and sensuous. It was utterly gorgeous – and *so* me. I stared up at Felix, and bit my lip. The extravagant gift immediately evoked the plaintive notes of the song from *Chess*, *I Know Him So Well*. I'd always thought it a particularly poignant line.

'It's beautiful,' I whispered. I couldn't resist stroking the rich material.

Felix didn't just know me, he got me. Understood what made me tick. As soon as Granny had left me the money for the flat, when I was working at the ad agency, desperately unhappy, he'd told me he would sack me if I didn't get off my arse and go and sign up for a theatrical make-up course. And when my parents had been disapproving, he had been there for me. It was just the two of us. He didn't think I was flaky.

I had to share the blame in this, it was my own fault. Telling him things I shouldn't have because it made me feel big and important. With a sense of shame, I realised I'd done that out of my own petty insecurity. To make me feel better, score a few points against my parents' poor opinion of my achievements.

Did I owe him another chance? He'd made the mistake but I'd made the far bigger one in the first place.

I leaned up and pasting a smile on my face, kissed his stubbled cheek. He'd been my best friend for so long, I didn't want to lose that. 'Thank you, it's absolutely gorgeous.' I hitched the bag over my shoulder, the velvet whispering against my neck.

'My pleasure, missus.' He grinned, his teeth white against his olive skin. 'Now what do you fancy for dinner? There's bugger all in the fridge. Shall we go out?'

There was enough to rustle up an everyday sauce and dried pasta in the cupboard but I knew from experience, he didn't fancy everyday.

Determined to keep the mood light, I quipped, 'How about a trip to Sainsbury's then?'

I pushed back the slight feeling of annoyance that he could move on quite so quickly, but then that was part of his charm. Nothing quelled his perpetual upbeat outlook.

'Do we have to? Can't we get a take-away?'

'No. It's only quarter past eight. This will be cheaper.' Especially when I knew the bag of pure silk and velvet in its fancy boutique-branded tissue paper wrapping must have set him back at least £100. He would have been better paying a glazier to repair the window in the lounge or getting a plumber to stop the dripping tap in the sink.

'We can be done and dusted in half an hour.' I rubbed at the stubble on his face, feeling him pull away. 'Cheer up, I'll knock up that green Thai curry you love.'

He'd pulled right away now and for a moment I wanted to pull him back and see if I could feel the sense of closeness we'd once had but then he perked up immediately. 'What, with jasmine rice and poppadum. And chutney. Oh and those spring rolly things?'

I laughed at him jumping up and down with gluttonous excitement and that joie de vivre that was Felix all over. 'Yeees. Come on, let's go before I change my mind.'

This was more like it. Back to normal. But a little voice in the back of my head insisted in asking if normal was necessarily right?

'Give me five minutes, I need to make a work call.'

'OK, but if it's more than five, you can have baked beans on toast.'

While I was waiting for him, I pulled out my Kindle and burst out laughing. Clearly, my wayward digital kiss in my last email hadn't done any damage.

To: Matilde@lmoc.co.uk
From: Redsman@hotmail.co.uk

Re: Book Recommendations
  The Anatomy of Liverpool – A History in Ten Matches by Jonathan Wilson
  Red Machine – Liverpool FC in the 1980s by Simon Hughes
  Ex-Reds Remembered by Steven Speed
  Red or Dead by David Peace.

I couldn't not respond to that!

To: Redsman@hotmail.co.uk
From: Matilde@lmoc.co.uk
Re: Re: Book Recommendations
  Lol! If I wanted to read horror stories, I'd read Stephen King.
  You are to comedy what Liverpool is to goal scoring. Pitiful result last night.
  Tilly

'Come on missus, stop reading. There's food to buy.' Felix bounced in, wrested my Kindle from me and bundled me out of the flat.

After Thai chicken curry with all the trimmings, I curled up on the sofa leaving Felix, who was still in grovelling mode, doing the washing up.

'Fancy going to the pub?' he asked, appearing at the

door with his mobile in hand. 'The lads are down the Windmill.'

I should have known there was a plan hatching from the prurient gleam in his eyes during dinner when his phone kept chirruping.

'Not really,' I sighed. 'I'm all warm and cosy. It's freezing out there.' The weather had turned this week and a vicious icy wind from Siberia had swept and swirled around the buildings of London, catching you unawares and robbing you of your breath as you turned a corner and left the leeward shelter of a building.

'You don't mind if I go?'

Funnily enough I didn't. After a frenetic trip to Sainsbury's I felt exhausted. Felix had entertained the check-out lady with a running commentary on our shopping starting with, 'Have you tried these?' as he held up a pack of new finger-shaped chocolate and oat biscuits. 'Dunked in tea.' He'd winked at her. 'Lovely.'

'Tastes like cardboard, you know,' he followed up with a minute later, rattling a box of Shreddies and nodding his head towards me before wrinkling his nose and lowering his voice, leaning towards her. 'But better for me apparently than Coco Pops, if you know what I mean.' He raised his eyebrows Groucho Marx style.

By the time everything had been scanned, the cashier, squeezed into her nylon uniform laughing along with him, her chins wobbling in enjoyment, I'd ended up feeling like some kind of mean old kill-joy.

'No, you go. I've got a good book on the go.' I raised a smile. 'I'm knackered.'

'Lightweight.'

'I must be growing up.'

'Never,' declared Felix, shaking his head vigorously, a few strands of hair coming loose from the trendy quiff which he quickly slicked back in a familiar gesture, which gave me a slight pang. Maybe I wasn't making enough effort.

I swung my legs off the sofa. 'Am I being a boring old bat? Do you want me to come with you?'

'No,' he waved his hands as if wanting to push me back into place, 'you're fine lovie. It could be a late one. Might go up to town.'

I flopped back into the sofa.

'Really? I thought you said you were going to the pub.'

'Yeah, well the lads might have plans.'

I'd have thought Kev and Jason, who both worked in the building trade and needed to be up at an ungodly hour, would have been preparing to turn in, not go out on the lash.

'Yeah, not sure I can keep up with that. Don't wake me when you come in.'

'Will do ... I mean, I won't.' He bounded over, shrugging into his coat, which had already been in his hand and plonked a quick kiss on the top of my head. 'You're the best Tilly.'

After he left, unable to help myself I checked my email.

To: Matilde@lmoc.co.uk
From: Redsman@hotmail.co.uk

You should be used to a good laugh. Your team are a right bunch of comedians. Reckon you're doomed to disappointment tomorrow night. Two of your strikers on the bench ... not a chance in hell you'll beat Chelsea.

Stephen King, best book *Misery*. Have you read it?

Unfortunately, I was inclined to agree with him, not that I'd let him know that.

To: Redsman@hotmail.co.uk
From: Matilde@lmoc.co.uk

Just a mid-season slump, we'll soon bounce back. And let's see your result before you start singing.

Not read any Stephen King, although I saw *Misery* (liked it) and *The Shining* (did not like it – scared the pants off me).

Tilly

Chapter 12

'Ooof.' I bounced off Marcus's chest as I dashed around the corner. He was wearing another of his fine wool suits, which I could bet probably cost as much as I earned in a month, and once again he made me think of an elegant swan among a brace of unruly ducklings. Today, I was rocking the Audrey Hepburn does Paris look with a white shirt, a black pencil skirt, but not the pure wool, neatly tailored sort my sister would wear, and a striped neck scarf.

'In a hurry?' His lips narrowed into a firm line of disdain.

'Yes,' I gasped.

'Tilly, this isn't good enough.'

'What?' I frowned and then I remembered. 'Oh bollocks ... I mean. I'm sorry. I forgot again. Honest.' My foot tapped as my stress level suddenly spiked, remembering Alison's comments the day before. 'We could do tomorrow. I promise I won't forget.'

'Where are you off to?'

'Er ...' I examined the corridor walls. Inspiration was in short supply, so I fessed up. 'I've got to nip to Fox's to get some supplies. Well, one supply actually. It's this special hypo-allergenic adhesive we use for facial hair. George Fordingbridge is popping in for a publicity shot and he's got very sensitive skin, so we need the non-allergic stuff.'

'What? *The* George Fordingbridge. The actor?' His voice held a touch of fan-boy excitement.

I just about refrained from rolling my eyes.

'It's a theatre. We get quite a few of those actor types through the door.'

My dry tone made him straighten and rub at the collar of his shirt and immediately I said, 'Sorry. I guess he is quite a big name and I'm used to it.'

'Yeah.' His rueful expression made me glad I'd jumped in with the apology. 'Yeah. A visit from the under-secretary of the Department for Business, Energy & Industrial Strategy doesn't quite cut it on the name-dropping front. That was the highlight in my last job. Because clearly, here, it's not name dropping. Takes a bit of adjustment. You're all so blasé about it.'

'Soon you'll be name dropping with the best of us.' I squeezed his arm and as he flinched I realised what I'd done. He probably wasn't used to us touchy, feely types either.

'I tell you what …' Oh God, I was probably going to regret it. 'Why don't you come with me?'

'As it's the only way I'm going to pin you down today.' He gave a sudden grin, like a cat that had swallowed a canary and the golden goose in one neat swallow. 'Yes. I could do with some fresh air. And perhaps we can talk about developing a system that stops you running out of things. And we can further refine the discussion with a proper meeting tomorrow.'

Damn. I'd walked right into that one.

From the end of November onwards, stepping out into Covent Garden is magical and as soon as December first hits, it's positively enchanting. There's a pervasive atmosphere of Christmas that seems to seep into every nook and cranny of the historic buildings and pavements. There's nowhere else quite like it in London with its cobbled piazza, the columns and porticos, the old houses – all of which lend themselves perfectly to the traditional trappings of Christmas. Everywhere you look it's as if a festive wand has been waved, leaving a drape of evergreen here, a touch of holly berry red there and a dust of shimmering gold just about everywhere. This year's crowning piece dominating the north side of the piazza was a huge topiary stag, head turned to look out over the shoppers and tourists like the king of some faraway forest transplanted to reign over the urban domain for a few weeks. Diamond studded with twinkling brilliant fairy lights, the stag made me think that at any second he could make a mighty leap and bound away back from whence he came.

Christmas brings out the fanciful in me. I can't help myself. I loved this time of year and the infectious attitude in the streets.

'Come on,' I said, darting around the tourists who were busy taking selfies of themselves and the street artists, to take a roundabout route designed to take in the new Lego display which I was hoping had now been unveiled.

'Where are we going?'

'Officially to Charles Fox. Unofficially,' I beamed at him, 'the long way around.'

I'd been watching the twitching tarpaulins for a couple of days now waiting for the display to be completed.

I led him through the quieter streets to avoid the tourists who were out in full force and then cut across the corner of the piazza, my heels slipping on the cobbled stones in my haste. I did need to be quick but there was always time for this.

I stopped and turned to Marcus with a big smile, grabbing his arm. 'It's finished.'

He looked a little startled and I dropped his arm to get closer to the barrier to peer at the amazing scene of brilliantly coloured bricks. There were elves, with curly-toed slippers, gift boxes complete with bows, Santa with a rounded belly, a flowing beard and his scarlet suit finished off with ermine trim. It never ceased to amaze me how little squared off bricks could be transformed into these varied shapes.

Even Marcus, Chief Philistine, leaned closer to take a second look at the incredible detail.

'I must bring my neph ... my family to see this,' he said.

I stopped suddenly as we moved off, putting my hand onto his sleeve and looking up.

'Oh!'

'What?'

Disappointed, I shook my head. 'I thought I felt a snowflake. The weather forecast man said that there was chance of snow today.'

'In the Scottish Highlands possibly, but not down here.'

Giving the sky a last hopeful look, I led him through the old apple market, giving the stalls a quick inspection, ticking them off in my head, reassured that all were present and correct. Leather clutches in pale pastels on the corner, Devore scarfs third stall in, the new girl on the end with the rather fabulous felt flower brooches, the usual bloke in his cloth cap with the silver jewellery made from old cutlery, the weird and wonderful clocks in the middle of the row.

I stopped quickly while Marcus overshot me, carrying

on before he realised I'd ditched him. My eye had been caught by a new stall with the most fabulous silk scarves and more importantly the perfect present. I reached up to touch one of the lengths of silk, coloured with swirls of teal, pink and black and embellished with little dark grey bugle beads that gave it additional weight and movement. It could have been made for my sister. The colours would suit her perfectly and, even better, would jazz up one of her little black suits no end as well as co-ordinate with her fancy shoes and handbag.

'Er, Tilly?'

'Sorry, I just spotted this. Isn't it gorgeous?'

'Seriously.' His eyebrows rose in horrified surprise, clearly taken aback at me even soliciting his opinion, let alone having one. I was too used to shopping with Felix. 'It's not my thing, but ...' he shrugged his shoulders.

I eyed his usual white shirt. 'No, I can see you don't do colour. Do you mind?' I pulled out my purse and thrust my bag at him.

Before he could complain, I'd haggled the price down from thirty-five pounds to twenty-seven and eyed up another scarf for me come payday.

I almost skipped the rest of the way down through the other market stalls, swinging the white paper carrier bag with its twisted cord handles to and fro.

'You're really pleased with yourself, aren't you?' observed Marcus.

'Yup. It's the perfect present. I love it when that happens. You just see something and it's exactly right. The best presents are things you didn't know you wanted but you love them.'

'No, the best presents are useful things.'

'Well you would say that, wouldn't you? I bet you love getting things like socks, slippers and pants.'

'Pants?' he raised an eyebrow. 'Slippers? You do have a dim view of me.'

'Well, what's your best present ever?'

'Er ... What, ever?'

'OK, last Christmas. What was the best thing you received?'

His face fell. 'Quite a cool tie.'

'Cool? I've seen your taste in ties.' Bland in the extreme in varying shades of grey.

'I don't wear this one any more.' His clipped tone suggested he'd said too much and immediately regretted it.

And I couldn't leave well alone. 'Oh dear. Present from an ex?'

'Yes.'

'OK.' His clipped tone recommended that I didn't pursue that line of conversation any further. 'What's the worst present you've ever been given? Apart from the pants and slippers. You must have a dodgy aunt or someone who always buys naff presents.' I paused by my favourite jewellery stall but decided not to risk his patience any further. 'My Aunt Jane, Dad's side of the family, bought me one of those tartan travel rugs. I don't even have a car. Mind you, she bought one for Christelle too and Christelle loved hers. It was a nicer colour than mine.'

'Ah, now I can top that. My Mum's sister bought me a slanket.'

'A slanket?' I slowed my steps and shot him an incredulous look. He so was not a slanket type of guy.

'Blanket with sleeves. Purple.'

I pinched my lips but couldn't hold back the unladylike snigger. 'I know what it is … but … you.' I started to laugh while with a nudge he urged me to keep walking.

Trying to keep a straight face now that I'd got my giggles under control, I said, 'You'll never be short of a fancy-dress costume. You can go as Barney the Dinosaur.'

'I'll bear it in mind,' he said in a grave, dry voice that had my insides curling with interest. He really wasn't my type but there was something rather appealing about him.

'Doesn't she like you?'

'Hmm I always assumed she did … maybe you're onto something. Or she just worries that I can't afford the heating bills since I moved out of home into a place of my own.'

'How long ago did you leave home?'

That smile burst out. 'Over ten years ago.'

I was dying to ask if the place of his own was shared with anyone but it would sound as if I was interested in him and I wasn't. He was a work colleague. And once this pesky project was over, I wouldn't have to have anything more to do with him. The thought didn't give me as much pleasure as I thought it would.

'Look, it really is snowing,' I said, as we emerged from the Piazza. White flakes twirled and danced through the sky and I stopped dead lifting my face up and closing my eyes.

'What are you doing?' I could hear the bemusement in his voice.

I waited a bit longer, until I felt a snowflake settle on my eyelashes. I fluttered them. 'Angel's kiss. When a snowflake lands on your eyes, it's like a kiss from an angel. As soon as it snows, you have to wait for the first kiss before you can move. Me and my sister always used to do it.'

'I've never heard of that before.' He had that superior I'm-humouring-you-but-you're-barking-mad look on his face.

'Of course you haven't, it's a family thing. But I love the snow. It's magical, isn't it?'

'No, it's cold, wet and everything grinds to a standstill at the first sign of it settling.'

I gave him a pitying look; the man really did have no soul.

The shop had had its Christmas make-over and the window featured a Cinderella panto theme, with Cinders' skin sparkling with crystals, the ugly sisters with animal print hair extensions and mice wearing the most amazing feathery rainbow false eyelashes. With the familiar buzz of anticipation, I pushed open the door, shaking the snowflakes from my hair.

'Is this a regular occurrence? Running out of things?' asked Marcus as I stopped to pick up a palette of pastel eye shadow, a sneak preview of the new spring collection apparently.

'No,' I said airily, putting down the palette quickly. 'Only occasionally. Just specialist items.'

'Tilly! Brilliant timing. Look, what's just come in.' Ava, the girl who'd worked there for the last eighteen months, darted over and grabbed my wrist, dabbing at my skin with a loaded sponge to leave a smear of iridescent blue, the liquid colour shimmering with radiance.

'That's gorgeous.' I held my arm to the light.

'And it comes in eight colours including pearl and copper. Isn't it to die for?'

'It is,' I looked with naked longing at the display of little pots lined up in front of a poster of a woman with the same blue painted on her face in a snakeskin design and then remembered Marcus standing beadily watching me. 'I've just popped in to get some spirit gum, the non-allergen one.'

She pulled the bottle from the shelf. 'On account?'

'Yes please.' I could see her giving Marcus an appraising look and clearly liking what she saw.

'Nothing else?' The smile she shot his way had ramped up to downright flirtatious.

'No. Not today,' I said, trying to sound professional, fighting an odd urge to stand in front of him and protect him from her downright frank interest.

'You always say that ... and then you remember loads of things when you're in here.' She turned to Marcus. 'The LMOC's one of our best customers.'

I gave her one of those please-stop-talking half grimace half smile and very subtly nodded my head Marcus's way. 'This is my colleague Marcus. He's just started working at the LMOC, in IT.'

'IT eh? Shame, we won't be seeing you as often as we see Tilly in here.' She gave him a very obvious wink. 'They're always running out of things.'

It was one of those bang your head on the desk, 'doh' moments.

We'd only taken three steps down the street, the snow having stopped as suddenly as it had begun, before Marcus said, 'Shall we talk stock control systems?'

Chapter 13

Bliss. The hot water lapped around my body, loosening the knots in my neck. Once, I might have tried to persuade Felix to join me in the bath and work his way up. Looked like it was just me and a good e-book. Recently my libido had been feeling very neglected. The fortune I spent last – no, it wasn't last month – it was way back in September when I had spent a ridiculous amount on a new lacy push-up ultra-bra which had delivered the promised balcony but, sadly, my Romeo didn't appear to be the least interested in scaling it.

'Drink, modom.' Felix appeared with a gin and tonic, the cold glass condensing immediately in the steamy atmosphere. 'Candles?'

'Why not?' I raised myself out of the bubbles, trying to look more come hither than I felt. 'Coming in?'

'Just check my ...'

Before I could say another word, he'd vanished and

I nearly choked, the tonic in my drink had gone walk-about.

A small part of me wilted. OK, so I was being contrary but did my bum look big in the bath or something? A girl could get a complex. Clearly, he'd rather play with his computer than me. At least I was trying to make an effort. Maybe he realised my heart wasn't really in it. It had its own ideas at the moment, sending my system into a tizzy whenever Marcus appeared in my vicinity. How did that happen when I wasn't sure I even liked him that much, let alone fancied him?

I brooded a while and then picked up my Kindle to lose myself in an old Sophie Kinsella book I'd read before. I loved re-reading books. Did Redsman? At the end of the chapter, with a suddenly empty glass, I switched to the email app.

To: Matilde@lmoc.co.uk
From: Redsman@hotmail.co.uk
     Wouldn't want you to go without your pants. ;-)
     R

What! I sat up quickly, water sloshing over the edge of the bath. This was new territory and even when I scrolled back to my previous email and the reference to seeing *The Shining*, I wasn't sure. Was this flirty?

I typed a one word response

To: Redsman@hotmail.co.uk
From: Matilde@lmoc.co.uk
    Cheeky

My fingers hovered over the touchscreen. Was this straying over a line? I let the gin do the talking and pressed send.

He immediately back came with:

To: Matilde@lmoc.co.uk
From: Redsman@hotmail.co.uk
    It would be if you made a habit of it.
    R

To: Redsman@hotmail.co.uk
From: Matilde@lmoc.co.uk
    I'll have you know I'm a very respectable young lady, with a fine selection of pants, thank you very much.

To: Matilde@lmoc.co.uk
From: Redsman@hotmail.co.uk
    I'm intrigued as to what constitutes a fine selection of pants.
    R

This constituted flirty and with it came a little buzz. I

couldn't resist typing back.

To: Redsman@hotmail.co.uk
From: Matilde@lmoc.co.uk
    And that my friend, is where we'll leave it for this evening.
    Tx

Oh shit I'd done it again, another kiss. And along with it the intimation that I was happy to leave him pondering my underwear.

Felix was engrossed, his fingers tapping away at his iPad.

Guilt gnawed at me. They were just emails, it wasn't as if I was doing any harm to anyone and Felix wouldn't mind, he'd probably find them funny.

'Thought you were going to join me in the bath,' I said, adding a teasing smile to keep things light.

'Oh, sorry. I ... um, forgot.'

'Charming. Going off me?' Even as I said the words, they felt wrong. Since he'd given me the scarf, I'd been trying to make a real effort, even though that night he'd got so drunk with the lads he'd ended up crashing at Kevin's which should have made me cross. Instead I'd felt relief.

'Never Tilly. My gorgeous darling. Come here and

have a cuddle.' He sniffed deeply. 'Mmm, you smell nice. What's that?' he asked as he pulled me towards the sofa.

'The posh rose bubbles that Jeanie bought me for my birthday.'

'How is the poison dwarf?' he asked grinning. He and Jeanie had a bit of a love-hate relationship, tolerating each other for my sake.

'Don't be mean.'

'Sorry. Just wondered if you two had had a falling out or something.'

'No, why?'

'You haven't been over there for a while, that's all.'

And I didn't need him to remind me. At least once every couple of weeks, I'd go to Jeanie's tiny cottage in Hammersmith for the night, usually to avoid poker night, but I hadn't been invited recently.

'She's very busy,' I said, concentrating on tracing the base of my glass. But busy doing what?

Felix grinned, his left eyebrow lifting with a devilish twist. 'Don't tell me ... she's got a boyfriend?'

'You think?' I said trying to laugh. 'She's been off men for the last fifteen years. I don't think she's going to change now.'

'Bit like Mum,' said Felix shaking his head.

His mum had been on her own since Felix's dad left her for a dancer down the working men's club, putting her off all men except for Felix, who she doted on, almost unhealthily so.

She might be resolutely single but ever since we'd got engaged she'd been determined to get in on the act, even taking us to visit the Gideon Hotel three miles down the road from her house. Talk about ordeal – death by afternoon tea; china cups balanced on paper thin saucers that held three sips of watery tea, supercilious staff who looked with suspicion at my vintage dress, all but sniffing out loud, and bridge types rustling their *Telegraphs* ostentatiously every time someone new walked through the lounge.

It had represented everything I hated. Too much formality and stilted manners. My parents would have absolutely loved it.

'And talking of Mum, have you decided about Christmas yet? She asked again last night.'

Oh God, she'd be dropping more hints about the wedding. I could see Felix caving in and forgetting about the raspberry mojitos, paso doble and no extended family wedding we'd talked about rather loosely when we first got engaged.

I had no excuse this year. My sense of depression deepened. Christmas Day with Felix's mother. I couldn't think of anything less I'd rather do.

Chapter 14

Today's meeting with Marcus was taking place in our department and in his honour, I'd tidied the space around the computer or rather hidden the evidence of its misuse by removing the empty Costa coffee cup and closing the CD rom drawer. I tidied the skeins of hair that I'd left hanging over the monitor and given the desk a hasty swipe with a damp cloth to get rid of all the coffee rings. It wouldn't do to get coffee stains, old or otherwise, on his pristine shirt cuffs. I'd been wondering if he owned anything other than white shirts. Today's evidence suggested not. Brilliant white again. Did he have stocks and shares in a washing powder company?

'Hello there.' Jeannie gave him a welcoming smile. How come he warranted one? She had the same view of computers as me but then again, she hadn't been co-opted.

Vince exchanged an eye-roll with me. 'Come to sort

our Tilly out.'

'Well, I'm going to attempt it.' To be fair he included me in his warm smile and then went and spoilt it. 'Although miracles are beyond my job spec.'

'I'm sure you'll do your best.' Jeanie shot me a wicked grin.

I tapped an impatient foot on the floor.

'Shall we get started then? Time is money,' I snapped at Marcus, every inch the corporate banker today. My libido threatened to have another moment. What was it about this man? He absolutely was not my type.

With the sudden adrenaline slushing around my system, I could feel my knees going a bit wobbly, so I straightened and indicated the corner desk that housed the solitary computer.

'You're keen.'

'No, keen to finish. I've got proper work to do today.' I cast a longing look over at a half-finished wig on my work table.

'I've found a piece of inventory management software which is very intuitive, so will be easy to use. I'm quite pleased with it. I've installed it on my laptop as I think that antiquated dinosaur would only contribute to the frustration factor.'

'There's an easy way to avoid it.' I gave him a hopeful grin.

'Do you want ... to take notes?'

'No, I'm sure I can remember. Didn't you say it was intuitive?'

He shot me a sharp look as I parroted his earlier phrase back at him.

Without pausing to pay any attention, he opened his laptop and for the next half hour proceeded to show me a stock management system he'd set up, bandying around words like response thresholds, expected accuracy and inventory optimisation metrics.

To give him credit, Marcus was incredibly patient and after half an hour it was actually me that was starting to lose the will to live.

'I've only typed in half the stuff we use.' Roughly translated as precisely four items. 'It's going to take forever.'

'You'll get quicker.'

'I wouldn't bet on it,' I muttered. 'Do I really have to put in every single product? Can't I just put in the things we use a lot?'

'No, because it defeats the object. Once it's done, it's done and it will save you hours in the future. Would you like me to go and get us coffee? As you've been ... quite a good student.'

When he came back I was close to throwing the computer out of the window.

'What's the matter?'

'I've lost it all. Stupid laptop's eaten everything.'

'It's a computer, Tilly. It doesn't eat things. That's the great thing about them. They only do what you tell them to do.'

'Not this one, it has an aversion to me.'

'No, you have an aversion to it. You're in charge. If you've put the information in there, it should still be there. I showed you how to save each product. Did you do that?'

'Yes, I'm not a complete numpty.'

With an impatient sigh, he took the mouse from me and wielding it with the ease of a sleight of hand card player, a couple of clicks later he opened various things up to be faced with a completely blank screen.

His face creased with a puzzled frown. 'They should all be there, what have you done?'

'See I told you. It eats them.' I cast the computer a baleful glare.

'That's not possible. They must be there, somewhere. The system has several fail-safes and if you press save, it's saved somewhere.'

I pursed my lips in a pout.

'Show me what you did?'

I showed him.

'Now I see what you're doing.' Quickly and calmly he showed me again. He was a very good and incredibly patient teacher. Whenever Felix tried to show me anything vaguely technical, he usually ended up

186

laughing uproariously at my utter incompetence and not helping at all and then finally walking off in a strop because he'd run out of patience.

'Oh God, I'm sorry. I'm an idiot. Thank you. I'll get a notebook and write this down.'

To his credit, keeping an amazingly bland expression on his face, he nodded and said, 'That's probably a good idea.'

I nudged him in the ribs. 'Which is what I should have done at the beginning.'

He pinched his lips together. 'It wouldn't be very gentlemanly to say I told you so.'

'No but honest.'

'So, Marcus.' I knew what I was doing now and the prospect of having to type in a gazillion items was mind numbing. 'Do you actually know of any operas?'

'Yes.' He pointed to the screen. 'See you can create order profiles for the future based on previous records. Create folders for each production you're working on.'

'Seriously, how many operas have you seen?' I looked around the room. Most of the walls were decorated with pictures of previous productions, principals in their costumes and publicity shots.

I watched his jaw tighten.

'What do you think? Would it make sense to do it by production, for example? If you were doing *La*

Bohème – for example, you could create a list of products you know you want to use.'

'You like *La Bohème* don't you?'

'What?' He had a pretend puzzled look on his face. 'Tilly, are you paying attention?' Although he was trying to be stern, all uptight and professional, amusement definitely lurked in his eyes.

'Do you know how many times you've mentioned it?'

He went very still. 'No, but it's a famous opera.'

'So are *Carmen*, *The Magic Flute*, *The Barber of Seville*, *La Traviata*, *Tosca*, but funnily enough *La Bohème* is the only one you've ever mentioned. Have you seen it? Do you even know the story?'

Body language tells you a lot and his suddenly read shifty.

'Have you ever seen an opera at all?'

Like an older brother targeting the most ticklish part of a sibling, I kept going.

'You haven't, have you?'

'Not recently.' He shifted in his seat. 'Now.' He pointed to the computer screen. 'See. We've created a list ...'

'Not recently? When do you think the last opera you saw was?'

'See if you do it like this, you can save yourself a lot of time, because you can duplicate ...'

'Opera? What was the last one you saw?'

He seemed to find a spot on the ceiling of intense interest suddenly.

'What about ballet?'

Letting out a huffy sigh, he muttered, 'I'm not a ballet person.'

'Marcus, you're not even an opera person, are you?' I started laughing at his schoolboy squirming even as I found it rather cute. 'Have you even been in a theatre?'

'Course I have ... I just.'

'What was the last thing you went to see?'

'I took my mum to see *Oliver* about five years ago.'

'Under sufferance?'

I watched him fidget with the keyboard, his index finger stroking the keys in a circular motion that suddenly made me feel rather hot.

'I'm not really a theatre person.' He shot me a slightly shy smile that raised my temperature another thousand degrees.

I folded my arms firmly over my chest, which had been having an errant and totally inappropriate response to his hand movements. 'And I'm not really a computer person.'

Touché Mr IT.

He grinned, his face lighting up. Oh boy, those twinkling green eyes socked a powerful punch when he became a human being. I crossed my legs, squeezing my thighs together. 'Tough! It's not my job to know about the opera, just to make sure the computers in this place run smoothly to ensure that the show goes on.'

'That's not fair,' I said, unable to stop looking at him.

He just smiled again. My heart bounced oddly in my chest.

'Shall we set up these sub folders and lists? Here, you do it. And talk me through it.'

I'd have been absolutely fine and back in control of my wayward chemical imbalance if he hadn't chosen that moment to lay his hand on mine resting on the mouse. I might as well have stuck my finger in the socket. 5,000 volts of pure lust zinged through my system.

'You click on this icon.' I tried not to stutter. 'And then save as?'

'Show me.'

I gripped the mouse tighter and again he moved my hand. I watched his jawline as he stared intently at the screen. I could smell his aftershave.

'What?'

'Save the list but create a new master list to put it in.'

'Right. Save the list.' I couldn't bring myself to move the mouse. It would bring his arm closer to me and any minute now I might melt all over him.

My whole body hummed. Surely, he could feel it.

I forced myself to keep still, trying to focus on the computer screen, ignoring the slight weight of his arm against mine, but I couldn't help sneaking a quick look at him. For a few very long seconds we stared at each other, his green eyes darkening with sudden smoky awareness.

I swallowed and he moved his hand from the mouse, straightening up and pushing his chair away to put some distance between us. I let out a tiny sigh.

'I think we're just about done here for the day.' He stood up and tugged at his tie.

'Great,' I said with false bright enthusiasm, jumping up from my seat, brushing invisible lint from my skirt.

He collected up a sheaf of papers from the table. 'Come on, it wasn't that bad.' He smiled. 'Once you started listening properly instead of trying to distract me.'

If only he knew. Who knew that a man's neck and throat could be so distracting?

I shrugged and he nodded, terribly professionally and formally. It was as if I'd imagined that brief moment.

'So why don't you give me a bit of a tour up here, so that I can get a feel for some ways you can use the computer to help a bit more.'

Nooo. I wanted him to go. I didn't want this confusing rush of lust, fascination, whatever it was. It made me feel a bit panicky.

'I think it's going to take a few more lessons before I dare attempt to unleash you on a spreadsheet. Let's just shut this down.'

'Hi Marcus, so how did you get on with our resident computer numpty?'

I opened my mouth and glared at her in outrage. Jeanie tossed her head with an insouciant shrug.

'Not bad. Although Tilly needs to carry on inputting data. There's a lot of work involved I'm afraid.' He turned to me. 'Plenty of homework.'

I pulled a face. 'But what if I delete something?'

'It's all retrievable.'

Good job he felt so confident. I wasn't convinced that without him as wingman I wouldn't make a complete muck up of things.

'I'm sure there'll be more efficiencies I can help your department with.'

Jeanie nodded her head briskly. 'Excellent. It's about time we embraced the modern world. Perhaps Tilly can give you a tour, so you have a better idea of what we do. I'm sure you can come up with some ideas about how we can do things differently.'

Had an alien taken her over? Normally she was as change averse as I was. In fact, she, Vince and I had all previously agreed that there was no place for technology up here. What had changed her tune?

'I must dash, I've got a meeting.' With that she darted out the door with an amused smirk on her face. Wait till I get hold of her later.

My guided tour started with Jeanie's office. Over the years, she'd made the space her own with an eclectic mix of furniture and bits rescued from the props department which included a brass hurricane lamp, an old-school blackboard tucked in the corner covered in pictures and fabric swatches and a collection of walking sticks and umbrellas, slotted like giant jack straws into a faux elephant foot.

I was used to the papers and piles of books covering every available flat space but I did wonder what Marcus was going to think. More so of the vibrant purple velvet chaise which took up the whole of one wall. Vince and I were rather fond of it, maybe because we'd been commandeered by Jeanie to rescue it from a skip two streets away. We felt that gave us joint ownership and entitled either of us to full reclining rights as and when required and only when Jeanie wasn't in.

As I showed him in through the door, I watched his expression feign polite observation as he desperately tried to hide the bolt of horror that flitted across.

'It's not that bad.' Although compared to his desk, mine could be likened to the aftermath of a hurricane in a rubbish tip.

He simply looked at me.

Maybe he had a point. Some of the papers were yellowing with age and apart from the books which we did frequently refer to, I couldn't remember the last time Jeanie had so much as touched any of the piles of paper. Whenever they got too big, we just moved them and added them to the dust-coated collection under the chaise.

'Tell me you don't have meetings in here?'

Just looking at the crowded, cluttered space made my back twinge.

'Sometimes.'

He just shook his head and moved past me, back out of the office. I stood there for a moment looking with fresh eyes. If we tidied up in here, got rid of the chaise and put up some proper book shelves, there'd be plenty of room to sit at a desk with the books spread out, without having to crouch on the floor.

I glared at Marcus's broad back. I was not going over to the dark side. My hormones had a lot to answer for. Now they were messing with my brain.

Suddenly anxious to get rid of him, I speeded up and waved my hand vaguely in the direction of the four corners of the department. 'Make-up store over there. Vince, Jane, Sasha, Jason over there. Dyeing area over there.' I pointed to an industrial sink and drying racks.

'Dyeing?'

'Hair dye.' I didn't bother elaborating.

'My work space over there.' I wafted my hand once more, my pace picking up. We were on the home stretch, two seconds more and I could usher him out of the door.

And bugger me if he didn't take a detour that way.

'Looks like something out of a horror film, Stephen King would be proud,' he said, poking one of the pins stuck into the wooden head block on my work bench and giving me a rather penetrating look. 'Is this a wig?'

Damn, but didn't he have nice hands.

'Yes,' I said, impatience tinging my voice. What did he think we did up here? Play tiddlywinks?

'You make them from scratch?' Damn, he sounded impressed.

'Yup.' I was immune to flattery even in a low-pitched chocolate voice.

He fingered the length of hair. 'Is that real hair?' he pulled back.

'Yes, we harvest it from fresh corpses over at the hospital.' I didn't need to say that, I didn't.

Of course, he laughed, as he was supposed to, and of course he looked even more attractive. His eyes all crinkled and smiley, his teeth perfectly dazzily. Sole attention on me, a brilliant sunbeam directed full on. And bugger I lapped it up, like a daisy lifting its face up for pure photosynthesis bliss, I reacted and all the barriers I'd been trying to keep up just toppled over.

Laughing again, he said, 'Somehow I don't believe you.'

'Damn.' I smiled back at him. 'I kept that one going for months with one person.' I smoothed the hair where his fingers had just touched it. 'It is real hair but we buy it in.'

'Isn't that very expensive? Why don't you use synthetic?' His interest sounded genuine.

'It is but real hair performs better.'

'Really?' He quirked one eyebrow and leaned a hip against the table. 'Performs? What – it joins in the singing and dancing?'

'No.' I laughed and gave him an involuntary poke, surprising myself. 'Not that sort of performs. It lasts longer and it moves better – which for a dancer is quite important. You don't want a beautiful fluid and lyrical dance with static hair that doesn't move and flow with it. It would spoil the overall look. And I promise you, audiences notice that sort of thing.'

'I hadn't thought of that.' He thoughtfully reached out to take a hank of hair, swishing it from side to side, watching the movement with intrigued intensity.

'See.' I pulled a long nylon hairpiece out of one of the drawers and offered it to him.

'And it's not just about aesthetics. Real hair doesn't get frizzy or damaged as easily as synthetics. We do use a lot of yak hair, as an alternative to human hair.'

'Yak hair, as in Himalayan cows?' Marcus shook his head. 'No, you're taking the piss now.'

'I'm not. Honest.' Rising to my feet, I went over to another set of drawers to find a sample. 'Here, feel this. See how soft it is. We use it a lot. Most of the high-quality Father Christmas costumes will use yak hair for the beard and hair. Also, it takes colour well.'

Marcus fingered the soft strands, looking slightly bemused. 'I had no idea ... you do all this.'

'What? You thought I pinned on a wig, slapped on a bit of make-up and hey presto. Off they go.'

'Something like that.'

I liked the way he came straight out and admitted it. No trying to bluff or bullshit.

'Attention to detail. That's what we do here. No detail is too small to overlook.'

'But it's, don't get me wrong ... but why? I mean it is just ...'

'Just a performance?' I asked.

'I hadn't appreciated how much work goes on behind the scenes. Is it all worth it?'

'Have you been to many other departments yet?'

'No.' He gave me a candid stare. 'I guessed that this was the worst, so decided to start here.'

I tossed my head with a mock sniff. 'They're just as bad in wardrobe.'

'I don't doubt it.' There was that quick smile again. 'Do I detect a bit of rivalry between you and wardrobe?'

With a demure grin, I widened my eyes. 'We're all one big happy family. Well, there may be a bit of professional rivalry and we might have the odd little digs at each other but for the most part they're tongue in cheek and we get on. We have to. We work together quite a bit, especially backstage. If there's a quick change, it has to be precision timed. Just like a pit stop in Formula One. There was one production where we had exactly thirty seconds to transform the actor playing the lead into someone who'd been beaten and had her hands cut off ...'

He blinked. 'Sounds a bit gruesome.'

'Yes, well it's supposed to be and it looked it. But that's vital. It's all part of the willing suspension of disbelief. It's going to ruin it for the audience if she comes out with a couple of spots of tomato ketchup. They've got to believe. If we get it wrong its neither fair on the audience nor the cast because we're taking them out of their performance. It *has* to be right.'

From the serious expression on his face, I could tell this was all new to him.

'I've never considered it that way.'

'If you were watching a film, you wouldn't want one of the characters suddenly turning around the camera and saying, "By the way, I'm just standing in front of a green screen, these buildings behind me are all computer generated." You probably know they are but you buy into it.'

'You're so passionate about this, aren't you?' The words, tinged with admiration, lit a small glow.

'I am. I love what I do but I'm just a small cog in the whole thing. People pay an awful lot of money to come and watch a production here. Some seats cost hundreds of pounds. Singers, dancers, performers – they all train for years. The competition for parts is intense. Every member of the orchestra is at the top of their game. World renowned musicians. The conductors are the best in the world. To support that we must make sure that what we do supports every last bit of all that.'

'What are you working on here?'

'It's going to be a wig for Juliet Capulet. They've chosen the Regency period as the setting, which requires quite elaborate hairstyles. It's easier to use a wig than style the dancer's hair each night and for some scenes, for example, in her death scene, the director wants her hair to be loose and long. To change the style between scenes isn't that feasible, so we'll have a series of different wigs for her to wear.'

'Isn't there a danger it might fall off with all that dancing.'

I half-snorted and covered the vicinity of ears on the wig block with protective hands. 'Whatever you do, don't say that in front of Jeanie. You will get "the lecture".'

Mimicking her clipped tones, I said, 'I don't care if you draw blood as long as the wig stays put.'

'Ouch.'

'I promise you, there'll be enough grips and pins in there to anchor a liner to dock. Any slippage with a wig is a hanging offence around here.'

He touched the silk foundation mesh. 'So how do you do it?'

'Do you really want to know?' Felix had been in to work with me a couple of times but had never shown this much interest. He'd have got bored by now and darted off to chat to Vince.

'Yes, I do. It looks fascinating.'

I picked up a skein of hair and the hook I used to pull the hair through into a knot. Beckoning him closer, I carefully separated enough strands and then with the hook, I showed him how I looped it through the tightly pinned mesh, using the hook and then back again before tying the hair into a secure knot.

The earlier sizzle between us had subsided but I found I was enjoying this shared, measured, professional exchange. The quiet respect he showed made me stand a little taller.

'Wow, that looks painstaking. How long does it take you to make one?'

'At least a week, depends on the complexity and the size and whether I'm working backstage during that time. *Don Giovanni* finishes this week and then *The Nutcracker* starts. I'm not as involved in that, I won't be looking after any principals so most of my work will be up here on wigs and working with the design team to make sure that the overall feel of the next production all matches.'

'Matches?'

'Yes. For example, the treatment of *Don Giovanni* is very traditional. It's set in the original period, so the hairstyles and costumes are dictated by the setting. However, as I said, *Romeo and Juliet* is going to be set during the Regency, and we've decided on her hair and what it will look like but we need to make sure that corps de ballet have appropriate styles that fit the period, although they won't be quite so elaborate. Part of our job is to research the right hairstyles and then submit our ideas and suggestions to the production team, the director, the artistic director along with the ideas from the costume team, the set designers, so that it all fits together.'

'I never realised there was so much involved.' With a thoughtful gaze, he examined the room as if seeing it properly for the first time.

'You ought to come backstage during a performance.' I had no idea what made me blurt that out. Was I trying to impress him? 'Or ... I've promised Fred I'd do his hair and make-up for Comic Con this Saturday.'

'You are?' His eyes lit up and I felt like I was missing something.

'Yes.'

'Fred didn't mention it. I'm going with him.'

'What? Going to Comic Con?'

He gave me a sheepish smile that transformed his whole face and made him look totally disarming.

'You're dressing up?' I asked doubtfully.

He coloured. 'Not normally ... Fred and Leonie talked me into it.' The sudden stiffness in his body language suggested that he wasn't that comfortable with it but was trying to be.

I stared at him, trying to ignore the wobble of my heart. Human, self-deprecating Marcus suddenly seemed a whole new man. 'What are you going as?'

He swallowed hard, white teeth gnawing his lower lip. 'Wolverine.'

Oh yes, I could see that.

'The costume was the easiest.' He ran a hand through his dark hair. 'Do you think you could do something? If ... if you're doing Fred anyway.'

'Oh yeah. Wolverine's pretty easy.' I stopped and swallowed. I stare at people's faces professionally all the time but suddenly it seemed really hard to look at his chin.

'Do you ... er ... um,' I nodded at his face. 'Shave?'

Puzzlement creased his face and he looked horrified for a moment. 'Where?'

'On your chin?' Oh God, now it was my turn to blush, just what did he think I was suggesting?

His face cleared but he was still doubtful when he answered, 'Yeees.'

'I meant how ... how often. I mean, will you, er, be able to, urm, you know, grow the sideburns and er a beard. Does it? You know. Grow quickly?'

Gosh, it felt so intimate asking probing questions about his shaving routine, in a way that never had with anyone else. What the hell was wrong with me? Although I guess, beards and facial hair are all to do with manhood and testosterone.

Stroking his chin, he shook his head. 'I'd rather not ... not shave when I'm at work the week before.'

'No problem.' Phew the relief at being able to move on. 'I can create sideburns and the shape of Wolverine's beard easily. And your hair's probably just about long enough.' I gave it a quick assessment. Would be tricky. 'It's a wee bit short, but we'll manage. How about the blades?' I waggled my hands. 'A set of butter knives?'

He laughed a little bit too loudly. 'Have you got a better idea?'

'I'll have a think, but if we start doing prosthetics we'll be here for hours.'

With a grave nod he agreed but from the steady look he gave me I suspected he had no idea what I was talking about. I realised this was his default when he didn't understand. Not because he was trying to hide any ignorance but rather like a touch of respect as if he felt he should have known.

'Prosthetics like prosthetic legs and arms. Any kind of false parts we can apply, usually latex or similar compounds which we then blend in so they look totally realistic. False noses, really bad scars.'

The smile returned and I saw him relax. 'Of course. Yes. That sounds far too much work. I think the butter knives will do just fine. And going backstage sounds a good idea. It would be good to see all aspects of the whole operation.'

I rolled my eyes. I'd suggested it so that he might get a flavour of what we did, not so that he could view it in terms of operational controls.

'You'll need to check with Jeanie ...' I nodded towards his habitual pure white shirt. 'And wear black.'

'Black? Are you having me on again?'

'No, it's the same in every theatre. You don't want to be able to see anyone in the wings.'

'The side bits.'

'Well done, yes the side bits. See how much you're learning and I thought you were supposed to be teaching me!'

'Hmm.' He glanced at his watch. 'Hell, I've been up here for hours. I need to get back.'

He straightened, pushed his watch back under his cuff and turned back into Mr IT.

'Thanks for the tour. Very enlightening.' He paused, his brow furrowing. 'Yes. I'll be in touch about your next lesson and doing the backstage thing.'

'And your make-up?'

'Right.'

We stood facing each other. Did I shake his hand? Say goodbye.

Abruptly he wheeled around and strode away without a backward glance.

Chapter 15

Was it relief or disappointment I felt when I logged onto my emails at lunchtime?

To: Redsman@hotmail.co.uk
From: Matilde@lmoc.co.uk
After your last rejection of my excellent recommendations, I wonder where you stand on forensic crime. Just picked up a Kathy Reichs and really enjoying it. Have you read any?
R

No sign of the previous playful tone. I was toying with my response when Vince came back from lunch sporting a lime green spotted cravat, a pin striped waist coat and matching trousers. He'd clearly had a payday splurge.

'Very nice. You've been shopping?' He had so much in common with Felix who was another one who could never resist trying everything on the minute he'd bought it. 'Are you going out?' The odd ensemble almost worked. I think if the cravat had been slightly less lurid, the outfit might have suggested genteel eccentricity instead of lunatic show off.

'Might be.' Gosh he was very cagey these days.

'You look very smart. Loving the cravat.'

'Eyes down darling.' He pointed with both hands to his feet and did a quick twirl. 'Get a load of these. Aren't they simply gorge?'

I stared at the yellow crocodile-skin leather brogues. 'No.'

'No?' Vince's voice shot up several octaves. 'They're all the rage.'

'I'd be raging if I were the crocodile that had been dyed that colour.'

'Tilly, you're just being mean.'

'No, Vince, I really am not. They are truly, truly hideous.'

He pouted like a five-year-old. 'Not truly scrumptious?' he asked with a discernible wobble to his lip.

'Sorry, Vince, no, not even *Cherry Peach Bombay*.' Our favourite song in *Chitty Chitty Bang Bang*, which we'd seen together five times before it finished its run in the West End.

'But they're sooooo delicious.'

'Vince.' I put my hands on my hips. 'Did the man in the shop tell you that?'

He nodded.

'You know he tells you anything. Have you worn them outside yet?'

He shook his head. I might as well have been trying to make conversation with a puppet, even his eyes had glazed over.

'Take the shoes off.'

With a sulky slump, he fell into the nearest chair and busied himself untying the cream laces. Seriously, they were the stuff of fashion nightmares.

'Are you going to take them back?'

The lower lip extended in a full pout.

'Don't look at me like that Vince. We had a deal, remember?'

With a very sad nod, he agreed. 'I remember. You're the mean old, fashion police who confiscates the good stuff and spoils all my fun.'

'No Vince, I'm the lovely friend who stops you making a complete prat of yourself and gets your money back from the unscrupulous charlatan parading as a shoe salesman around the corner.'

'Bernie's alright.'

'Yeah.' I rubbed my hands together in a good imitation of Fagin. 'He's gotta make a crust or two. What have Jeanie and I told you about going shopping on your own?'

'FaceTime her and text you before I buy anything?'

He trotted it out like a good little lamb. If only he were.

'And what happened? Lose your phone? Forget?'

With all the graciousness of a dowager duchess and the sniff to match, Vince held out the horrific shoes for closer inspection. They were the bubonic plague personified in leather. 'Look, are you sure you don't like them? Genuine Italian leather.'

'Receipt.' I held out my hand.

The reluctance alone to hand over the slip of white paper told me all I needed to know.

'Three hundred pounds!' I screeched, one hand clutched to my chest.

'I really love them,' pleaded Vince.

'You really loved the blue patent Gladstone bag, which you used once and cost £500. You really loved the Driza-Bone authentic Australian cattleman's coat and it was nicked the first time you wore it. And you really, really liked the vintage spats which you wouldn't tell me how much they cost and then you got beaten up by some idiot who took objection to them. And while I don't condone violence, I'm not sure a jury wouldn't have sided with him.'

'You're mean.' He looked as if I'd nicked his brand-new puppy.

'Not as mean as Jeanie would be. She'd make you go with her to take them back.'

'Still mean,' muttered Vince as he put them back in the box.

I closed my eyes and counted to ten. Mean or sensible? I touched my third finger. It's all very well having a princess-cut diamond Tiffany engagement ring but the grand gesture loses its lustre when it's you paying off the loan instalments each month.

'Tilly! Vince!' With a machine gun rattle, Jeanie spat the words out. Neither of us had noticed her walk into the studio.

She snatched up the box, looked inside and recoiled immediately.

'Oh, my good lord, heaven's preserve us. What were you thinking? They are ...'

'See!' I pointed at Vince.

For a moment, she shuddered before closing the shoe box again. 'I most fervently hope that they are on their return journey.'

'Yes,' said Vince, over brightly. 'Just on my way now.'

'Honestly the pair of you. I let you out of my sight for one minute.' She stopped, looking suspicious. 'Hang on a minute. These are shag-me shoes, aren't they?'

See Jeanie's so much more on the ball than me. Of course, they were.

He froze, reminding me of a cartoon character teetering on the precipice of danger, looking extremely sheepish. 'I don't know what you mean.'

'Hot date,' said Jeanie and I in perfect unison, we exchanged grins and then my face fell as Vince coloured and wriggled on the spot.

'I'm just meeting a friend,' he squirmed, crossing his feet and looking like an incontinent penguin.

'What friend? We're your friends. We don't know other friends,' said Jeanie.

'No one you know,' Vince said with an airy smile belied by the rigid set of his chin.

Jeanie and I watched him go. 'He's up to no good,' surmised Jeanie narrowing her lips.

'Leave him be,' I said. 'He obviously doesn't want us to know. All we can do is pick up the pieces when it turns out to be a disaster.'

Chapter 16

London at this time on a weekend was always a pleasure. No tourists, no commuters, uncluttered pavements and empty roads. Even the taxi drivers seem to slow down. Getting a coffee in Costa took seconds as there was no queue and I turned up outside the stage door five minutes before Fred.

Cautiously sipping my coffee, I watched deliveries being unloaded, a set of flats being manoeuvred through the huge stage doors and listened to the crash and bang of van doors, as new scenery and props were carried into the building.

'Morning.'

I whipped my head around in the direction of the smooth voice.

'M-morning.' Oh lord, he looked good.

He had a coffee in his hand which he toasted me with and then stood there taking the occasional sip and watching the scenery guys with interest. He'd got the

Wolverine, tough guy leather jacket and jeans look to a T. On a purely objective basis, even I could see that he rocked it as confirmed by a couple of girls passing by who wheeled around to take a second look.

'Have you any idea what they're doing?' he asked after a few minutes of studying the scenery shifters.

'They're taking the set down and putting it into storage.'

'Right,' he said, followed by the grave stare I was becoming used to.

'So many of the sets can be reused or are used if the company tours with the production but there isn't room to keep them all here. We have a huge storage place out in Elstree.'

He nodded and we lapsed into an uncomfortable silence.

'Are you looking forward ...' I asked.

Marcus was supposed to ease my social discomfort by filling in the appropriate gap. He didn't, instead he just nodded politely as if waiting for my next words.

An unearthly cackle right in my ear broke the awkward silence.

'Getting into character?' I asked, glaring at Fred who'd made me jump.

'Sorry darlin'.' He embodied the part already in his purple suit, orange shirt and green waistcoat. 'Hiya boss.'

'Nice costume Fred.' Marcus leaned over and felt the fabric. 'Where the hell did you get that?'

'Leonie made it for me, bless her.'

'Yeah, but this is pure wool. It's a proper suit.'

'She is brilliant,' I piped up. 'Made a skirt for me in October. Copied a vintage one I already had.'

'Leonie made this?' asked Marcus, still eyeing the purple suit. His expression suggested he couldn't make up his mind whether he was appalled or impressed. 'The one in costume.'

Where else? What did he think we all did?

'But it looks as if it were made by a proper tailor. Savile Row or Armani or something.'

'She is a proper tailor,' I said with a touch of snark. 'Where do you think we get the costumes? On eBay?'

He glared at me.

'Come on then, let's get this show on the road,' Fred piped up. 'We need to get to ExCeL by 10.30. Promised my mate I'd meet him. Tourists are gonna love this on the tube.'

'They'll think you're a nutter,' observed Marcus.

'They won't be wrong,' I muttered.

'And why do we have to be here so early?' Marcus scowled and took another sip of coffee. I surreptitiously took stock. In casual clothes, he packed an even more powerful punch, all man. It bloody irritated me. I didn't like this stupid out of control feeling. You should be able to decide who you fancied or not. It made me glare at him even more which he managed to ignore or at least seem completely oblivious to.

He checked his watch. 'You're dressed. Surely putting a bit of face paint and lipstick on isn't going to take that long. Or sticking on a couple of sideburns.'

Fred turned his back on Marcus, with an exaggerated wince and winked at me.

'Sorry he doesn't know what he–'

'Putting a bit of face paint and lipstick won't,' I said with bite and an insincere smile. 'Doing a decent job will take a tad longer. Sideburns. We'll just have to see.' If he wasn't careful he might end up looking more werewolf than super-hero.

'Ooh I like this.' Fred settled himself into one of the throne-like cream leather chairs and turned himself round. 'Feel like a proper star.'

I pulled out a selection of pictures and sketches I'd made and laid them on the bench in front of him. 'Don't get too comfortable yet. I need to know what you want.'

In the mirror, I caught Marcus frowning but I ignored him. This was my domain, he could frown all he liked.

'I did some research. Obviously, there's the Heath Ledger Joker. Seriously scary and you might frighten small children on the tube. Or there's the proper DC Joker from the original series which is more the look they used for Jack Nicholson from the earlier *Batman* film.'

Fred peered at the pictures, taking his time. 'I think Jack Nicholson, more classic Joker. What do you reckon?'

Marcus's attention had been captured by the framed pictures and photos on the walls.

'Whatever gets us moving,' he said with an ostentatious pull back of the leather jacket sleeve to indicate his watch.

Fred grinned. 'Mr Efficiency. He's into all that time and motion stuff.'

'Hmm,' I muttered under my breath.

Whatever Fred chose, I would need white base, red lipstick, pencils, brushes and some smoky eye shadow as well as the green hairspray. In my usual anal fashion, I laid them out in neat lines, the brushes and pencils at precise right angles to the palettes of shadow, everything spaced at even intervals.

Eventually after a bit of dithering, Fred settled on the Jack Nicholson version of the Joker, which was more structured and would take more effort. As I got started, Marcus perched his bum against the bench at my left elbow to watch.

Draping a cover around Fred's fancy suit, I brushed back his hair and gathered the long wispy bits into a tight ponytail which I then pinned up and under.

Luckily his receding hairline worked perfectly and I had virtually no work to do to create the Dracula shaped V at his forehead. With a good steady application of the hair spray, I turned his dirty blonde hair into a luxuriant green. The hairs on the back of my neck prickled slightly as I stepped back to review my progress. Marcus had settled into a relaxed pose, legs crossed at the ankle, arms folded and leaning back against the bench.

Determined not to let him put me off, I did my best to ignore him but every time I reached out to pick up anything I was conscious of his thoughtful observation.

Thankfully Fred, as instructed with no awkwardness, had close-shaved, so the sponge didn't drag and the white base went on quickly and easily. I smoothed it over his face with regular, even strokes making sure he had no tidelines and I didn't spoil the green hairline.

Fred's face had been rendered utterly featureless and this was where the real work began and my favourite part. I took a quick look at one of the pictures to remind myself of the shape of the brows. Slightly maniacal.

Fred stared at himself in the mirror as I worked, keeping perfectly still as if too scared to move. It made my job easier although once I'd finished his eyebrows, painted in with a dark black glossy finish, he waggled them with villainous intent.

'Cool Tilly.'

'They do look good.' Marcus picked up the picture of Jack Nicholson. 'What next? Lips and then you're done.'

I held the picture next to Fred's white face which was now totally featureless. 'Notice a difference.'

Facing Fred, I stepped between his legs. Although I needed to concentrate, it's highly personal working on someone's face, touching them, stroking them and when you are up so close they often have nowhere else to look, so it's important to put them at their ease. I could feel that Fred had stiffened up and was staring with a fixed gaze at himself in the mirror.

'So, going anywhere nice on your holidays, Mr Joker? I hear Gotham City's nice this time of year.' I shaded the side of his nose to give greater contour and shape to his face and made sure I stepped right back each time to give him a bit of space.

'I'm saving. To go to Comic Con. San Diego. That's the big one.' His shoulders moved marginally, so they weren't quite up by his ears.

'So what do you do at these things?' I faffed about cleaning my brush on my hand.

'Just get together with other comic fans.'

I lifted his chin, all business. 'Look to the right for me.' His nose was starting to look sharper.

'What about you?' I tossed over my shoulder and

then added a bit more shade to Fred's nose. Getting Marcus to join in the conversation would also help Fred.

'I've never been before. Enjoyed Marvel when I was a kid, so I thought I'd tag along.'

'You just want to catch an eyeful of Wonder Woman,' said Fred, drawing his eyebrows together in an alarming slash and waggling them.

With hesitant strokes, I started shading Fred's cheeks. I wouldn't have said it to him but he had quite a pudgy face, so getting the Joker's angular look was going to take quite a bit of work on the cheekbones. When I'm working on a production, I've already studied a person's facial structure, the contours of their face and the texture of their skin and I have a pretty good idea of what I need to do.

'Not too much longer,' I said cheerily. And then, oh hell, I'd have to start on Marcus. Fred had relaxed a lot but he still sat quite stiffly. Now, on the home straight, I became aware of Marcus, just on the periphery of my vision, watching with the intensity of a hawk, tracking every stroke of my brush, each dab and glide of my fingers.

I felt unaccountably nervous as I drew around Fred's lips with a lip pencil. The shape needed careful attention; it was the trademark of the Joker. There was absolute silence in the room as I unwound the bright red lipstick from its tube. Inking in the thin lips with the matt finish took forever but I couldn't afford to let one tiny bit bleed into the white base, it would ruin the whole look. The lips need to be a perfect, cruel slash in the face to complete the look.

When at last I finished, I wound the lipstick back with a sharp twist, and moved to the side so that Fred could see the full effect in the mirror. I caught Marcus's eye. The look between us held, his eyes darkening.

I blushed but couldn't look away. His glance dropped to my lips and I froze, not knowing what to do with them.

'Wow Tilly, that's amazing.' Fred had leant forward to look in the mirror and grinned a horrible wide grimace which gave the full grisly Joker effect. He sprang to his feet and posed in the mirror in sheer delight.

'Here, Marcus.' He thrust his phone out. 'Take a few pics. I've got to get these on Twitter, man.'

'Tilly, you are a bluddy genius. Genius, mate. Don't you think?'

Marcus nodded. I felt rather smug at the slightly shell-shocked look on his face. See Mr IT, I do know what I'm doing. As with so many people, where make-up created a mask of invincibility, Fred slipped straight into character, laughing and hopping about with a manic energy that frankly made me feel exhausted and fervently glad I wasn't going with them.

'Right,' I said briskly and offered the chair to Marcus. 'Your turn.'

'The Wi-Fi signal up here's shit,' announced Fred. 'I'll be back in a bit. Want to get online.'

Completely in character he danced out of the room.

Marcus hung back, eying the white leather chair with something akin to terror.

'I won't bite,' I snapped. Inside I felt equally terrified. I hadn't actually thought about touching him before. Now I wasn't sure I could.

Marcus sat down and looked down at the bench and then up at me. 'Where ... I thought you'd have some ... things to stick on.'

'That's what joke shops are for. We do things properly up here,' I said severely. Why were my legs so wobbly all of a sudden? This had never happened before, not even when I'd first done stars such as Bryn Terfel, Jonas Kauffman and Placido Domingo and managed it without batting an eyelid.

Stalling for a moment before I had to make the first move, I took a quick look at the picture of Hugh Jackman dressed as Wolverine. Tensing, I gave Marcus's face an assessing look, focusing on his jawline and making sure I avoided looking into his eyes. Recreating the shape of the facial hair would be dead easy but would look impressive.

Focus on the job in hand, I told myself, gripping the

brush tightly, as I dipped it into the small bottle of adhesive gum and began to carefully paint a small patch of his face, taking care to avoid any skin contact. The brush skated over a tiny mole just below his cheekbone, a shallow chicken pox scar and the shadow of a dimple. I focused on each of these landmarks on his face with each stroke of the brush, ignoring the tightness in my chest as I tried to keep my breathing steady. Inside, I had a Mexican jumping bean bouncing around in my diaphragm.

Now, I had to apply the small strands of wiry wool while it was still sticky, a fiddly job. Touch his face. Press the fibres down. There was no avoiding it, I was going to have to take hold of his face to gain purchase.

'Erm ... do you mind if I ... er ... just ...' Taking a discreet breath, I lifted my hand to cup his chin, it shook slightly.

'No ... that's ... it's OK.'

A tang of soap and shampoo teased the air. Clean, smooth shaven skin beckoned and as I lay my fingers along the contour of his jaw, I fixed my gaze on his lower face. The intimate touch weighed heavy in my hand and for a moment my mind wandered, my fingers twitched as if they followed the path of my wayward thoughts. Tracing under his jaw, around his neck into the thick dark hair at the nape and drawing him forward. I flicked a quick glance to his lips, slightly open and felt my stomach flip as he caught my eye.

'So ... what I'm doing ... this is gum,' my voice sounded overly loud in the room highlighting that it was just the two of us, 'and then I'm going to attach lots of tiny fibres ... see ...'

Almost tipping the packet of wiry wool on the floor, I grabbed at a tiny handful and held them up.

'Oh, right.' Marcus nodded, his face determinedly expressionless, gazing at himself in the mirror.

I took a breath. 'Keep still ... please.' Still holding his face in one hand, with the other I applied the first of the coarse strands to him. I leaned in. So close, his lips only inches from mine.

Under my fingers, I could feel the pulse in his neck, strong and steady. Like him.

Focusing on making sure the tiny fibres adhered, stroking them down and combing them into place with my fingernails, I did my best to ignore the tiny prickles threatening to break his skin and his warm breath whispering over my skin. Although he stayed perfectly still, I could tell by the rigid hold of the tendons in his neck that he was acutely uncomfortable. He kept up a stoic stare straight ahead into the mirror. Part of me regretted my pride. I could have made things a lot easier for myself. Stick on sideburns would have been so much easier. I frowned. Served me right for trying to make a point.

'You look fierce. I dread to think what thoughts are going through your head.'

'I might be thinking about stock control systems,' I said. What would he think if he had any inkling? 'You can't smile. Keep your face still.' He wasn't supposed to smile like that. I didn't want to like him, not when I was so obviously not his type. We were work colleagues; that was all.

The chat slowed as I needed him to be still. I slowly built up the heavy sideburns before moving down to his chin. The silence hung heavily as I worked down his face, thankfully the weird beard shape dipped below the mouth and I didn't have to touch around his lips. Only a brief foray just below his lower lip which gave my pulse a run for its money so I touched it as quickly and impersonally as possible.

'Right.' I took a step back. 'Almost done. Just your hair, although to be honest, it's a little bit short for me to be able to do that much.' For some bizarre reason, I managed to make 'little bit short' sound disapproving and was pleased when he frowned.

Short, however, meant that I had to run my hands through it, sliding over his scalp.

I felt him tense.

'Sorry, did I pull?'

'No ... it's just ...' He squirmed.

With brusque quick moves, I back-combed hoping

that the quick, sharp moves would be less intimate. Why the hell had I signed up for this? Was I some sort of masochist? But in all my time doing hair and make-up, I'd never felt like this, every touch charged with sexual tension.

'What do you think?' I held his gaze in the mirror.

He stroked his cheeks and his face broke out into a delighted beam which sent a zing through me.

'Brilliant ... really ... really brilliant. I had no idea ... it's so effective.'

He stood up and peered in the mirror. 'It's great.' A worried look crossed his face. 'How do I get it off? I'm going out tonight.'

'Don't worry, your City mates need never know.' I didn't like the way I sounded. Sharp and bitchy. 'Or your girlfriend?'

Realising it sounded as if I were fishing, I added quickly, 'It will come off with soap and water ... hot water. Make sure you rub it in thoroughly. Any stubborn bits just put a bit of olive oil on cotton wool and rub with that.'

'Right. That's useful to know.' He eyed the shaggy growth.

Fred reappeared through the door.

'Whoa man ... bearded wonder. That's cool.'

Marcus stroked his chin again. 'I'm not sure what Mum would say if I rocked up tonight all made-up.'

He laughed. 'I'd never hear the end of it if my Dad caught sight of it. I'm going home tonight to watch the football with him down the pub.'

I ducked my head, flushing at his words. It didn't answer the girlfriend question completely but it was an answer to my question.

'Do you want me to take some pictures?' suggested Fred grinning evilly, he was getting into his part.

'No!' Marcus said. 'Definitely not. If they end up on Facebook, I'll kill you. I can't believe you talked me into this. I'm beginning to have second thoughts.' His body stiffened again, his shoulders hunching slightly upwards.

That slight air of vulnerability pricked at me. 'Not after all that work, you're not,' I said, pushing him towards the door.

'Thanks Tilly. I'm only having second thoughts because it looks ... well, so authentic. Serious. Having a couple of stick on sideburns sounded like a laugh. This is a bit too nerdy.' He gave a mock glare at Fred. 'You're a bad influence.'

'Loosen up bro. You'll have a great time when we get there ...'

'That's the bit I'm worrying about. Everyone on the tube staring.'

Fred scrunched up his face in denial and shook his green hair. 'You wait till you see everyone else. This is tame.'

I laid a hand on Marcus's sleeve, wanting to chase away the uncertainty suddenly shadowing his eyes. It didn't look right seeing Mr Big Bad and Confident look unsure. 'Look at Fred. You don't need to worry. He'll be causing enough of a stir. You'll blend into the background. You'll just look like an over-enthusiastic hipster.'

Gratitude flashed in his eyes and the shoulders dropped. 'Hipster? Christ ... that's even worse.'

Chapter 17

The last sight of him walking out of the building adopting a suitably Jackman swagger had just about finished me off and it was a relief to walk in the opposite direction, making a lot of looking down at my phone.

With a whole day to myself, I decided to head to Foyles and pick up a few books. Although I liked the convenience of my Kindle, I still enjoyed the feel of a book in my hand.

I'd just paid for a copy of *Déjà Dead* by Kathy Reichs, prompted by Redsman's last email, when I saw I had a text from Christelle.

Are you working today? Can you get out for a coffee? Going shopping for Mum and Dad's presents. I'd appreciate your opinion. Cx

Rather than faff about trying to text her back, as I walked along the busy street, I called her.

'What do you want my opinion on?'

What would her opinion be of Marcus? She'd never said anything but I got the impression she wasn't overly impressed with Felix and he certainly didn't like her. Guilt tugged at me. In fairness, most of what he knew about her had come from me.

'Well, I was going to get Mum an Estee Lauder gift set, then I remembered I got her one for her birthday. You're good at presents. Any ideas?'

'Where are you?' I asked.

'I'm just walking up St Martins. Are you free later?'

'I'm free now. I'm not working today, I just had to pop into the theatre. I'm in Henrietta Street.'

There was a pause. 'Can you meet me?'

Her uncertainty ratcheted up my guiltometer. Was my usual reticence so obvious? Suddenly I felt sad that we'd grown apart. We used to love going shopping together on Saturdays in Harrogate.

'Yeah, of course.'

We arranged to meet in front of the piazza at Covent Garden in half an hour.

Heading that way, I brightened as I spotted crash barriers in front of St Paul's Church and heard Slade's *I wish it could be Christmas* blaring out. I'd forgotten it was the Annual Christmas Pudding race today.

A team of marshals was busy fighting with an inflatable slide and laughing as the billowing plastic fought

229

back. Behind them, two men were unloading crates of Christmas puds and as I drew closer I could spot the teams of competitors in fancy dress. It was very amusing to watch tourists' reactions to men in blow-up Santa suits, the set of furry penguins and the scantily clad group of girls who'd called themselves The Christmas Crackers.

Things were still being set up but I decided I'd bring Christelle back later to watch the crazy race.

Everyone was wrapped up warmly in down coats, hats and scarves, their gloved hands clutching bulging shopping bags and as I walked quickly, weaving in and out of the groups, I stopped to admire the Christmas tree. It reminded me that I needed to sort one out for the flat even though getting a real one was a major hassle. Unfortunately, even a smallish one wasn't the sort of thing you could carry home on the bus but I refused to have an artificial tree. I'd have to persuade Felix to come with me to help carry it home.

I spotted Christelle and her scarlet red bobble hat, which contrasted gloriously with her Snow White complexion and glossy brunette hair, before she spotted me. Casual for once, she looked gorgeous, her skin glowing from the brisk walk, although I homed in on the sad nude lipstick.

'Hi.'

'Hi,' I replied, narrowing my eyes at her lips.

'What's the matter?'

I grabbed her arm. 'First up, we're going shopping.'

'Well, yeah. That was the plan.'

'No, I mean for you. Come on.'

'But ...'

'No buts.'

I linked my arm firmly through hers and marched northwards up James Street.

'Where are we going?'

'Mac,' I said. 'To get you a new lipstick.'

'OK.'

I stopped. 'What? No argument?'

'Tilly. Do I look as if I have a clue about make-up?'

'No.'

'Well, thanks for the vote of confidence.'

'You asked.'

'Well you didn't need to be so blunt.'

'Sorry, it's just that colour ... in fact calling it a colour should be illegal, it's hideous and it doesn't do you any favours.'

'Legal is my department, make-up is yours,' she said sulkily. 'We can't all be brilliant at it, like you. I know I'm rubbish but ...' She shrugged, looking a little embarrassed. 'I never liked to ask.'

'Why ever not?'

Her eyes slid away before she looked at me. 'You

231

would have laughed.'

Her words left me speechless. My ultra-confident, super-successful sister thought I'd laugh at her. I bit my lip, studying my leather gloves, unable to meet her waiting gaze. Yeah, I probably would which wasn't very nice at all.

'Lipstick is never a laughing matter,' I quipped. 'Come on.'

The Mac shop was busy and noisy and I joined in with the chorus of *Rocking Around the Christmas Tree* coming from the speakers. As soon as Antonio, the manager, spotted me he waved and somehow managed to disentangle himself from an intent customer.

'Tilly.' He kissed me on both cheeks. 'How are you?'

'Good thanks.' Christelle had managed to hide behind me. I pulled her forward. 'This is my sister. We're looking for a lipstick. I'm thinking Ruby Woo or Cherry Glaze.'

'Excellent choices.' He beamed at me and before she knew it, Christelle was on a stool and Antonio was wiping her lips clean with ruthless efficiency.

When he'd finished, making a great show as he outlined her lips, before carefully painting them with a deep red colour, she stared at herself in the mirror.

'See, that lights up your whole face.'

'She's good,' interjected Antonio nodding my way. The colour drew attention to her perfect cupid bow lips making her look even more like Snow White, but perhaps the older sassier sister. 'But we'll try the other one.'

'Sorry, *cherie*,' he said, handing me the lipstick and brush. 'I'll leave you to it. I see customers with fat purses.' He winked and glided over to a pair of women in fur trimmed designer coats and matching Chanel handbags.

As Christelle was seated at my mercy, I decided to make the most of it. She waited patiently as I perused the colours, every now and then looking back at her face. To be honest I'd been dying to get hold of her like this.

'We're supposed to be shopping for Mum,' she said but she didn't sound particularly convincing.

'Are you in a hurry? Need to be anywhere?'

'No,' she scrunched up her face. 'I did have a date tonight.' A resigned expression set in. 'But he cancelled.'

'Excellent. Sorry, not excellent that he cancelled. Idiot. But it means we've got all the time in the world.' I tapped at my watch. And we could watch the race.

'I'm not sure that's such a good thing,' she said with a sudden smile looking at the pile of goodies I'd amassed.

'Sit back and enjoy. You won't feel a thing.'

'Promise?'

I grinned at her and set to work.

There's something satisfying about giving someone a make-over, especially when you see the spring in their step afterwards. Christelle looked positively frisky when we stepped out of Mac.

'I think we deserve a drink,' she said, this time linking her arm through mine.

'I thought you wanted to shop.'

'Have you got plans?'

I shook my head. 'Nothing specific.'

'Well this is your stamping ground. Where can we get a glass of Prosecco round here?'

'Great idea. But first ...'

Christelle and I were almost breathless with laughter.

'That is mad,' she said, wiping away tears as the last hapless competitor stumbled past us, clutching her tray in one hand with its battered looking pud, decorated Mr Potato Head style, sliding precariously to and fro and an outsize Christmas star decoration in the other. Dressed in a fluorescent pink tutu and matching leg-warmers, the poor girl was covered in fake snow, had a streak of something across her face and a massive hole in her tights but she was giggling so hard she could hardly run straight and was in danger of missing the finishing line completely.

We spent a good hour watching the warm up for the

next heat of the race, joining in the silly singing and moving to a different section of the course to watch a reindeer, Alice in Wonderland and Superman bounce and tumble down the inflatable slide desperately trying to hang onto their precious cargo before the cold began to bite.

We were still laughing when we stumbled out of Mabel's two bottles of Prosecco later.

'I can't believe that guy.'

'Why not?'

'He kept staring at me.'

'Yes, because you look gorgeous.'

'Only because of the make-up.'

'Not true, it just enhances what's already there.'

She made a psht noise but didn't say anything more as we wandered along Maiden Lane back towards the piazza. The race was over now and the clean-up was almost complete, the only sign of the earlier craziness was the bunches of balloons tied to stacks of crash barriers.

'We still haven't done any proper shopping.'

'And we've still got the rest of the afternoon. Let's go to the market. We might see something for Mum there.'

'Like what?'

'We won't know until we see it,' I replied firmly, expecting her to come back with some argument but instead she complied with unexpected docility.

We browsed the stalls in the Jubilee market before returning to the piazza. We stopped at one of my favourite jewellery stalls.

'Oh, that's lovely,' said Christelle, pouncing on a pretty bracelet. 'I'd never thought of coming here. That will be perfect for Alexa. And Sarah at work.' She bought two while I bought Jeanie a pair of earrings that I knew she'd love. We were about to move on, when Christelle also decided to buy a pair of Batman cufflinks for her boss. 'They'll be a bit different from his usual ones but, do you know what, I think he'll like them,' she giggled. I picked them up. They'd be a good present for Marcus too. And where had that thought come from? Quickly I put them back. Marcus and I certainly weren't on present buying terms. How was he getting on at Comic Con? An image of him flashed into my head, green eyes assessing mine as I'd done his make-up this morning. Turning and picking up a silver bangle, I pushed the disturbing memory away.

'I know. Let's head towards Seven Dials, the decorations up there are really quirky this year and they have some cool shops,' I said, wanting to get away from the market stalls as thoughts of my previous visit the week before and our conversation about gifts wormed their way into my head. Did he have a girlfriend? He'd mentioned an ex but nothing current. The thought didn't sit well.

'Ok,' said Christelle. I wasn't used to this compliant, unsuspicious version of my sister. We were going to have to do the Prosecco thing more often.

The streets were swollen with people, and progress was slow, although no one seemed to mind. An atmosphere of general happiness thrummed in the air as if everyone brimmed with bonhomie.

'I love Covent Garden at Christmas,' I said looking around. 'It just feels different.'

'That's because they roast chestnuts here,' said Christelle, pointing to a man on the corner. 'I don't know what all the fuss is about. All that roasting chestnuts over the fire malarkey.'

Despite being surprised at her use of the word malarkey – it didn't sound very her – I nodded, imagining their horrible floury texture on my tongue. 'They smell good but taste disgusting.'

'And Mum always sends Dad out to get them for the stuffing.' Christelle mimed walking fingers recalling memories of Dad, in his red jumper, being despatched to Waitrose on an almost daily basis in the final run up to Christmas.

'And we always picked them out.' We both burst out laughing. Every year without fail there had been a line of chestnuts ringing our empty plates on a table strewn with the remnants of crackers, jugs of gravy and bread sauce and Mum's special Christmas napkins with their matching Santa and snowmen napkin rings. Christmas back then, when we were young had been fun, when lunch was a long-laid back affair, in which Mum insisted we all wore our cracker crowns and Christelle, Dad and I contested as to who could be the first to slip them off before Mum noticed and in between turkey and pudding we had the one pound challenge, where we competed to buy the nastiest, tackiest gift for a pound.

'I wish they weren't going away.' I just heard Christelle's wistful words. I wasn't sure she had meant me to. I stuffed the memories away and steered her down the next street.

A couple of hours later, having done a full circuit and walked non-stop, we emerged from Jo Malone's with a huge cream and black carrier bag brimming with Lime, Basil and Mandarin scented tissue paper.

Early evening darkness lit up by brilliant white fairy lights threaded through the decorations overhead, making the street look like some enchanted grotto. We both stopped to crane our necks at an ornate garland of dancing cherubs and little berry red lights that festooned one of the shops.

'Cute,' observed Christelle, nudging me with her elbow. 'Mum is going to be thrilled with this.' She held up the bag. 'I'd forgotten what a brilliant shopper you are.' She lifted her wrist and sniffed. 'And I love this Bay and Blackberry.'

'You tried enough; I thought I was never going to get you out of there.'

'Yes, but look at the free samples.'

'Free? Not if you think about the amount you spent in there.'

'Yes, but I've almost finished my Christmas shopping.' She swung the bag to and fro with the easy joy of a small child. 'Do you think Dad might get a kick out of some Captain America cufflinks?'

'I think all that scent has gone to your head.'

'Or the lipstick.' She flashed me a happy smile, her teeth white against the Cherry Glaze and linked her arm through mine. 'So how about dinner? My treat.'

Chapter 18

Dressed head to foot in black, I waited in the wings and caught sight of Marcus on the other side of the stage. What the hell was he doing over there?

My poor system was going to have sensory overload. I'd only just recovered from Saturday's run in with him and now three days later here he was again.

Following his visit to the department last week, he'd wasted no time in speaking to Jeanie. For some reason, she seemed to think he was the bee's knees and thought it was a wonderful idea and even more wonderful if I chaperoned him backstage.

He vanished and a few minutes later materialised at my side.

'Anyone would think you're avoiding me. You said to meet stage right?'

His whispered words right in my ear startled me and, irritatingly, the warm breath on my neck did other things.

'This is stage right.' I wasn't going to point out to him that stage right was the actor's right when they were facing the audience, so in effect the opposite way around.

As he opened his mouth to say more, I put my finger to my lips and pointed to a large notice behind his head.

Silence in the Wings

A sceptical expression crossed his face and he nodded towards the pit where the orchestra were tuning up.

'It's a good habit to get into,' I muttered and busied myself checking that I had everything, ignoring the sudden lift I felt at being so close to him.

In this particular opera, one of the team stayed for the first scene which involved a very quick change with a lot of fake blood and as speed was of the essence, I needed to be on hand to supervise the effect of the Commendatore bleeding to death. Even without a lightning change, one of us always stayed throughout a performance in case a wig became skew whiff, started to fall apart or to do any touching up or repairing if anything went awry. There's nothing more distracting during a performance than a wardrobe or make-up malfunction.

The minute the curtain went up, my awareness of Marcus switched to a low-level hum as the orchestra merged seamlessly into flow of music that rose and billowed, the notes taking to air like birds on the wing. The overture was in effect our starter gun. Backstage we became shadows cocooned in a world between reality and fantasy. I loved these moments, tucked out of sight but so close to the action unfolding on stage. They held a special indefinable magic that I always wanted to hug close to me, a time when nothing else from the world intruded.

As the familiar section of music began to play, I spotted a figure on the other side of the wings. Carlsten Kunde-Neimoth? What was he doing here? Maybe he'd been practising here today. We had several rehearsal studios on site.

A phrase of music I'd been listening out for was played. I ducked down into my make-up kit, to grab the capsules of blood. Next to me, Marcus watched avidly. Damn, he was in completely the wrong place. With only a few beats of the bar left, I gave him a sharp jab in the ribs and motioned him to move quickly.

He bristled, clearly affronted but I didn't have time to worry about it. A few more notes and scant seconds later, the Commendendatore staggered off stage, ostensibly just having been thrust through with a sword. Like iron filings drawn to a magnet, the team drew around the actor. Ed, the assistant stage manager started his stop watch, counting the seconds off in whispered numbers.

'Ten.'

Leonie from wardrobe whipped off his shirt.

'Nine.'

Hetty, another member of the wardrobe team, already waiting with the material bunched together in her hands, dropped a blood-soaked replica shirt over his head.

'Seven.'

She pulled it down and tucked it into his breeches.

'Five.'

I pulled several Kirby grips from his wig to release a few strategic locks, dropped the grips on the floor and tousled the hair.

'Three.'

Popping the blood capsules in my fingers, I grabbed his hands and smeared them with the sticky liquid.

'Two ... good to go ... one.'

With a flash of teeth in the dark, the actor playing the Commendatore nodded and dropped back into character and staggered back onto stage clutching his side; scarlet blood oozing through his fingers, high-lighted by the single spot trained upon him.

Ed gave us all a thumbs-up and through his head-phones spoke to the stage manager in the regulatory dulled down volume and moved back to his usual posi-tion. The rest of us heaved a collective sigh of relief. Ed pocketed his stop watch and to a man we all relaxed.

No matter how many times we did that change, it always felt hairy.

Marcus had a rather stunned expression on his face. Smiling to myself, I dropped to my haunches to pick up the grips which I'd abandoned. With a quick change at that speed there was no time for tidiness.

He stayed put for the rest of the first act and until the interval. I couldn't help but keep watching him and every now and then I'd catch his eye. I got the impression he took it all with the hunger of a scholar desperate to learn every last detail in one go.

When the curtain went down and the performers came off, immediately reverting to laughing, joking and teasing, his face was a picture, as if the illusion had totally shattered. Which I guess it had.

'Where are they all going?' he asked still whispering.

'Cup of tea in the canteen. Want one?' I was gasping for one. The dry air backstage could make you very thirsty.

Uncertainty crossed his face.

'Come on.' I led the way down to the canteen following in the wake of the two actresses playing Donna Anna and Donna Elvira, the lead female roles, who were debating the merits of brownie recipes. Jane, the elder of the two, was swearing by a Nigella recipe, Constance the younger, vowed Mary Berry's was better.

The canteen buzzed as usual with an orderly queue

lined up, musicians in black tie, actors in eighteenth century dress and various members of backstage crew in their ubiquitous black.

Marcus didn't say a word apart from ordering his coffee. Around the room, with its plastic chairs, round tables and leatherette banquettes around the edges, there were probably close on to one hundred people enjoying a tea, coffee, water or cake.

We sat down at one of the tables along with a couple of the chorus.

'Alright Tilly, how's it going?'

'Good thanks. How's your wife doing?'

'Got a job teaching at Guildford. Regular income which is nice.'

'That'll pay the bills for a while,' said Jill, the other chorus member. 'It's such a relief now my husband has a permanent contract.'

'I wish,' I said.

'What? Are you freelance?' asked Marcus with a genuine look of surprise on his face.

'Fixed term contract. Which has been extended twice.' I pulled a face. 'But I'm currently on probation after my little virus fiasco.' I shot him a mocking smile, although hopefully now that I'd been doing my computer lessons like a good girl, getting Pietro on stage on time for every performance and had Jeanie's backing, I stood a good chance of passing it.

'Is that the same for everyone?' Marcus scanned the room.

'Depends. Some of the orchestra are permanent and the very techy backstage bods. The stage manager and his team. Just depends when you join, what you do.'

'I had no idea.'

I sighed. 'There's a permanent job coming up.'

'You'll be fine Tilly.' Jill offered me a reassuring smile. 'Pietro loves you. And so do the rest of the cast. I can't see why they wouldn't keep you on.'

'Fingers, toes and everything else crossed.'

The four of us chatted, with Marcus asking lots of questions, as we finished our tea.

Jill looked at her watch. 'Does anyone know if it's still snowing? It had just started when I got to the theatre at four. It'll be a devil to get home, if it is.'

'It's bound to have stopped by now,' said Marcus.

'Yes,' I said gloomily. 'It never snows properly down here. There's a weather warning for East Anglia, they're predicting ten inches of snow fall.'

'And that's why I'm so glad I live in London,' said Jill. 'The tubes should be fine.'

The interval bell rang and like lemmings, everyone abandoned their drinks and filtered calmly back along the corridor backstage.

By the time the curtain came down, it was gone eleven

and the performance had met with an enthusiastic response, with standing ovations and stamping feet that rivalled anything you'd see at the Last Night of the Proms.

Backstage, we were all on a massive high. This was the last show of this season and the festival atmosphere, reminiscent of school breaking up for the very last time, was contagious.

'Drinkies, Tilly?' asked Philippe, second violinist in the orchestra, as he passed in the corridor as I made my way back upstairs, Marcus still in tow. Funnily enough, he felt like one of us at that moment.

'Definitely.' Sod my aching legs. 'I'll ask Jeanie.'

'OK, darling. Be at the stage door in twenty.'

I turned to look at Marcus. 'Want to come?' It only seemed right to invite him and to be perfectly honest, I preferred this slightly shell-shocked and impressed version of himself. For once I felt in control, the consummate professional who knew what she was doing, instead of the daft floozy who lurched from computer disaster to computer disaster.

'Yeah, OK.' He nodded.

'You'd better give me half an hour,' I said to Philippe.

I found Jeanie in the department, a wig block under each arm. Her eyes might have been ever so slightly damp.

'You OK?'

'Fine,' she said curtly.

'Did I see Carlsten backstage?'

Jeanie shrugged. 'Why are you asking me?' She stalked past me and set the blocks down in her office.

I followed her still thinking out loud. 'Maybe he was rehearsing earlier. For the gala.'

'I've no idea, Tilly.' And then in a completely different tone she said to Marcus, 'How was it? Enjoy the view?'

I didn't bother listening to their conversation, too stung by her impatience. What was wrong with her?'Tilly! You can give me a hand here. We just need to move this lot.' She indicated a stack of boxes, each containing different make-up supplies, piled up on the floor next to her desk. 'Next week is going to be manic.'

She caught me looking at my watch.

'Going somewhere?'

She was snappy tonight.

'We're going for a drink. Marcus is coming.' I hoped the mention of his name would get her to come. Strangely she seemed to have a soft spot for him or at least she gave him the benefit of the doubt more readily than she did to most. 'Aren't you coming?'

'I think I'll give it a miss.' Her hands were busy smoothing one of the wigs onto a wooden block. 'I'm knackered.'

'Oh, come on Jeanie.' I'd heard that before. 'Just one drink.'

Once she'd got a glass in her hand, her favourite scotch on the rocks, she always perked up and would regale us with tales of her early days in provincial theatre with people who were now famous.

'No. Not tonight.'

'Sure?'

'Which bit of "no" am I not being clear about?'

I blushed, embarrassed in front of Marcus.

Glancing at her tight-lipped face, I decided to get on and sort out the brushes.

The others were waiting for me outside just beyond the stage door, and for once there was no sign of the usual small crowd of autograph hunters that perpetually gathered there. I could see why, immediately. While we'd been in the theatre several inches of snow had fallen and it was still coming down.

Closing my eyes, I lifted my face up, listening as the others talked around me. When a flake of snow gently kissed my eyelashes, I opened them and caught Marcus's eye. My heart gave a quick kick when he smiled and nodded, a small private exchange that only the two of us were aware of. 'It's like, inches thick,' said Leonie as I kicked at the layer of snow, grateful that I'd put on my sturdy biker boots on this morning.

'Isn't it lovely?' I said gazing down the unusually empty street. 'And so quiet.' I loved the way the snow deadened the perpetual sound of the city.

'So where, my darlings, shall we bless with our presence this eventide?' asked Philippe, spreading his arms wide like some nineteenth century impresario. He just needed a moustache to twirl and a pair of spats to complete the picture.

I caught Marcus trying to bite back a smile.

Standing on the edge of the circle, as the others all argued about the best place to go, I saw someone slip furtively out of the stage door. Without even glancing our way, she put her head down and scuttled off down the street in the opposite direction, leaving a solitary track of footprints in the virgin blanket of snow. Intrigued, I watched the disappearing figure. At the bottom of the lane, instead of turning towards Charing Cross station as she would normally do, she turned the opposite way. Where was Jeanie off to?

I caught sight of two familiar guys busy pushing a giant snowball down the street.

'Or we could build a snowman,' I said suddenly, when Dean, the senior props guy, gave me a wave. 'Come on, looks like they could do with some help.'

'Marvellous idea Tilly,' said Philippe with a fond roll of his eyes. 'You build while I get the hot chocolates in. These shoes are not built for manual work.'

'It is a great idea,' said Leonie loyally. 'I'm up for it.

Come on Fred.'

Fred turned to Marcus, who shrugged, but knew he was beaten when the other musicians and back stage crew all agreed that it was a great idea, and Philippe was despatched with another violinist to procure hot chocolate rations.

'Can we help?' shouted Leonie as she and I went rushing over, our feet sinking into the snow with delicious scrunches. Her voice bounced off the surrounding buildings highlighting the deadened sound around us.

'Sure,' said Dean and then looked at the ragtag group following us. His face broadened with a grin and one of those light-bulb expressions. 'How about we split into groups and make a snow orchestra?'

'Yay!' called Leonie.

There was a quick debate about how to fashion instruments using snow sculpture but with the usual ingenuity of their department, the two props guys came up with a far simpler solution and one of them rushed off back into the theatre to get supplies.

It was agreed we'd all work on different body parts and Leonie and I got head duty.

Rolling the snowball to start with was easy. A one-man job tracking along the wide street and cobbled court-yard, gathering up the fresh snow. As the ball got bigger it became a little harder and I stopped to catch my breath, looking over at Marcus who to my surprise had joined in, if not with alacrity, certainly willingly.

Casually dressed for a change, in dark jeans and a wool pea coat, he contrasted against the white backdrop. There was no doubting his masculine presence and I spotted a couple of the gay guys scoping him out and who could blame them? He wore black well, reminding me of a sleek, handsome jaguar. He'd weighed up the situation and had cornered a piece of territory where snow had drifted giving him a definite advantage and his snowball was growing significantly.

However, he was taking the job altogether too seriously. I quickly scooped up a handful of snow, patted it into shape and when his back was turned launched it his way and then ducked down, innocently pushing away at my snowball. It hit him square in the back and he looked around.

His eyes skated over me and I looked up and met his narrowed gaze with a guileless smile.

'Isn't it gorgeous? The quiet? The light?'

His mouth quirked. 'It is. Remarkably peaceful … long may it stay that way.' The look he shot me held a touch of mocking challenge and as soon as he turned away, I pitched another snowball his way which this time hit the back of his head. This time, when he whirled around, I didn't even try to pretend as he raised an amused eyebrow.

'I think you're slacking, Miss Hunter.' He looked at my puny mound of snow and then back at his work.

I grinned back at him and as I glanced down a snowball caught me in the chest.

When I looked back at him, smug triumph danced gleefully in his eyes. Light-hearted Marcus was a rather heart-stopping proposition and to hide the furious blush that suddenly seared my cheeks, I scooped up a handful of snow, quickly shaped it and returned fire. Before I saw whether it had hit him or not, I ducked down and scooped up a second, launched it, and had thrown a third, catching him right in the shoulder before he could respond, laughing at his startled expression.

'Right, this is war,' he called and ran over. Giggling at his pretend outrage, I turned to flee but he caught up and picking me up dumped me bottom first into a bank of snow that had drifted up against a small wall.

My hat came askew falling down over my eyes as I wriggled trying to get back up, gasping and laughing up at him.

For the briefest of seconds, my breath caught in my throat. Something flickered in his eyes.

To my left I heard Leonie squeal and saw that I'd encouraged the start of a pitched snowball battle among the backstage crew.

'Rat!' I cried.

'You started it,' he teased, straightening my hat and helping me up as snowballs whizzed past us.

'Who, me?' I batted my eyelashes at him. 'I don't know what you mean.'

'You're a menace Miss Hunter. Where'd you learn to fight dirty like that?'

'I grew up in Yorkshire remember. The playground in winter was a battleground. You learned the art of quick draw snowball pretty quickly.'

Eventually a truce was called and we started assembling what was rapidly becoming an army of snowmen. Marcus helped me lift my head onto his base both of us giggling wildly as half of mine fell away. We patted it back into shape.

'It doesn't look too bad,' I said stepping back.

'It's a bit on the skinny side,' said Fred, walking around it.

'Then it can be the new viola player, she's tiny,' suggested Guillaume from behind the snowman he was building with two other violinists.

The props guys had ingeniously brought down some black corrugated plastic piping which they threaded wire through to give them shape, and used them to give the snowmen arms which could hold instruments. Someone else had raided lost property and Leonie and another girl from Wardrobe were draping scarves and sticking on hats.

When Phillippe returned with a tray of hot chocolates, we'd assembled several snowmen and women and
the props guys had furnished them with instruments
made from bits of cardboard stolen from the recycling
pile outside one of the shops. They'd been cut into
shape and then the various details; the valve pistons of
trumpets, the strings of violins and the keys on the
clarinets drawn on in marker pen.

'Here you go, Tilly darling,' he handed me a steaming
cup. 'You look gorgeously flushed. Is everything alright
with you at the moment?'

'Fine,' I said. 'Thanks for this. There's nothing quite
like a hot chocolate in the snow. Makes me feel really
Christmassy.'

Now that our little snowy tableau was complete, we
stood in a convivial circle chatting as we drank our hot
drinks.

Philippe seemed surprisingly solicitous which was a
tad unnerving. Was he trying to impress Marcus, who
was standing next to me? He kept checking that I wasn't
too cold and being overly complimentary about my
skills as a make-up artist.

Surely his instincts weren't so off that he thought
Marcus was gay. Besides, Philippe had recently married
his much younger boyfriend.

'You alright to get home Tilly, darling?' asked Philippe when we finally started to say our goodbyes. I was the only one heading over the river. 'Do you want someone to grab you a cab?'

'I'm fine,' I said, smiling at him, slightly perplexed. We'd had plenty of late-night sessions before and he'd never worried. 'I'm going to get the tube from Charing Cross.'

'OK. Take care, sweetie. See you soon.'

'I can walk down with you,' volunteered Marcus.

'Don't worry I'll be fine. I do it all the time.'

'It's just one of my things.' He shrugged and fell in step with me as I started southwards. Our breath hissed out in puffs of steam in the cold night air, as we crunched along together.

'OK.' I could see that arguing with him would be a complete waste of time.

We headed down to the busy thoroughfare of the Strand towards the station.

'I enjoyed tonight. Backstage ... it was.' He nodded and his quiet admission warmed me just a little bit inside. He hadn't said much all evening and although it had been pleasant, a part of me wanted him to be impressed. This is what I did. This was the important part. I didn't want him to think I was a flake. That would have put him in the same category as my parents.

'Sorry I shoved you out of the way. You looked a bit ...'

He laughed. 'Yeah I had no idea it got quite so lively. Like Formula One in the pit stop. That was quite something.'

'We've practised quite a few times.'

'Has it gone wrong?'

'Has it ever.' I giggled at the memory. 'Quite spectacularly once. Thankfully in one of the early techs, technical rehearsals. Originally the change was only five seconds and we had another wig for him but we couldn't do it. After that, we tweaked the scene and redid the wig to add a couple of wild bits that we could just pin up and down for the scene.'

'Must be stressful with the guy timing it all.'

'The stage manager. It's fine, we've got two seconds' grace, it keeps us on the straight and narrow.'

'If you say so. I'm not sure I'd want someone breathing down my neck with a stop watch.'

I lifted one eyebrow and didn't say a word.

'I'm quite intrigued to know what happens, what with all the blood.'

'You ought to go out front and watch. It's quite a long one but you should see how it all comes together. Obviously, this show's finished but you could get a ticket for *Romeo and Juliet*.

'Ballet?'

'Don't be a big girl's blouse. It's not just about the dancing. You work there now, you should see how it all fits together.' For the first time, I felt his equal. Two professionals. No, perhaps not. Professionals were solicitors, barristers, accountants.

'Hmmm, I suppose so.'

'Or the gala performance, which is a selection of opera and ballet. It's a big charity thing. But the dress is Monday. That would probably be ideal.'

'Isn't it a bit short notice?'

So he knew that seats to watch a dress were hot tickets. He'd learnt something then.

'Jeanie likes you.' I stopped. That sounded rather horrid, as if I was trying to say I didn't but I ploughed on, hoping he hadn't spotted the quick pause. 'She'll get you tickets.'

As we arrived at Charing Cross, one of tomorrow morning's early editions on the late night news stand caught my eye, sending my pulse rate into overdrive. Crap, crap and more crap.

One of the redtops had the headline:

New role for Pietro D'Angelis, The Gardener
Italian Stallion, Big Voice, Big...

On the front of the paper that Jonno wrote for was a picture of Pietro naked and, despite the strategic blacked out bit, there was no doubt he was standing very proud. Pietro's worst nightmare. Even from here his pose suggested something pretty sordid.

Marcus caught sight of the headlines a second after me. His face tightened.

'Damn. I thought we put a lid on that sort of thing.' He tapped at his pocket as if searching for his phone. 'I'm going to have to make some calls.' He pulled his phone out. 'Goodnight Tilly.'

Without a backward glance, he turned and paced away through the snow, leaving me with my heart thumping painfully. Bloody, bloody, bloody hell.

Chapter 19

I burst into the flat clutching the newspaper, my cheeks glowing with cold and agitation.

'Felix,' I cried. 'Have you seen the papers?'

Felix looked everywhere but directly at me.

My heart somersaulted and I ploughed to a clumsy coltish halt. 'Felix?'

He hunched into the sofa, teeth gnawing at his lip.

Like the tumblers in a lock, falling one by one, realisation thudded into me.

'You didn't?'

Silence yawned between us. All I could hear was rushing in my ears.

'You promised me. You promised.'

I thrust the paper under Felix's nose stabbing at one particular line.

'How could you? Poor, poor Pietro. He must be distraught.'

Despite his olive skin, Felix's face paled and I could

see the pulse leaping in his temple. He didn't say anything. What could he say?

'Look! Look what it says! How could you? His picture, naked.' I shuddered. 'I know him. He's a granddad. He has a family. This is just awful.'

The paper quoted a source close to Pietro. Used a line verbatim. The exact words Pietro had used to me. Which I'd repeated to Felix. This was my fault.

'I'm sorry Tilly but Jonno kept saying he needed more. He kept hassling me. And he ...' Felix dropped his head in his hands. 'Sorry. This ...'

'I-I can't believe you. You said you hadn't told him. You lied to me.'

Felix shrugged. 'I knew it would come out. And Jonno, he's, he's the sort of guy that knows things ...'

'Like what? Knows things about you? Don't be ridiculous. You fiddle your expenses? You steal towels from hotels?'

'I ...' Felix looked panic stricken. 'He was going to tell you—'

I was too incensed to listen.

'After Katerina, you knew. You promised. You lied to me.'

I couldn't bear to look at him or even be near him. I walked out and slammed the door so hard it bounced open again hitting the wall behind, the knob smashing the plaster leaving a spider web of cracks creeping across the white painted wall. I took refuge in the spare room, and threw myself on the bed.

All I could think of was how Pietro must be feeling. Would he turn up tomorrow? How could I face him? My stomach turned over and over as I stared up at the ceiling long into the night.

At some point, I must have fallen asleep, and I woke the next morning to hear Felix knocking at the door.

'Tilly, please. Can we talk?'

What did we have to say? I couldn't forgive him this time. I buried my head under the pillow, hoping he'd go away.

'Tilly, please. I'm away tomorrow night, not back until Friday. Please Tils.'

Reluctantly I swung my legs off the bed and opened the door.

'Felix.' I stared at his haggard but hopeful face peering back at me through the narrow opening. 'I don't know what to say.'

'I messed up.' The words were accompanied by the familiar beseeching puppy dog plaintive look.

'You said that last time.' My unemotional words mirrored the numbness that had seeped its way into my body.

'Please Tilly, we can get over this.'

'Can we?' I asked hollowly.

He reached out his hands, the warm touch of his

fingers burning my ice-cold wrist and I stepped back.

'You used to laugh about the papers.' His brown eyes were earnest as he tried to give me a smile, as if jollying me along. 'Say they made stuff up. Tomorrow it will be fish and chip wrapping. People will forget. Please Tilly, don't stay mad at me. I promise I won't ever, ever do anything like this again. It's happened. We can't do anything about it now. It might not even have been me, you know. Jonno said there were rumours. The video was in circulation. Anyone could have, you know, at any point.'

Despair settled like a solid lump in my stomach. He really didn't get it. 'It wasn't anyone. It was us.'

Chapter 20

As I arrived at work I saw Jeanie snatch a newspaper away from Vince. The rest of the tabloids had taken up the story. There were pictures, stills from the film. What none of the stories revealed was why Pietro had done the films. No in true gossip style, they'd just laboured the point that he'd been a porn star in his youth, a raving sex maniac, who had slept his way to the top.

'You should be sympathising with him, not dribbling,' she snapped. 'The man's got a right to his privacy. It's ... it's,' she turned puce. 'Disgraceful,' she finally spat.

Vince folded the paper away, shame-faced. 'Sorry.'

'Whoever let the papers have the story and these pictures should be hung, drawn and quartered. Scum.' Jeanie's face twisted in fury.

A red flush raced up my cheeks, a lump lodging in my throat. She'd tear me limb from limb. I wanted to shrivel up and die right there and then. I felt just as sick now as I did last night when I spotted the head-lines.

'This is going to set a lion among the pigeons.'

'But our snow orchestra made the front page today,' I said, hoping to divert her. Heavy rain had denuded our little gang of props and diminished their shape, the arrangement of clumps of grey snow were all that remained of the heavy snowfall two nights ago.

I closed my eyes and when I opened them, I met Jeanie's intense scrutiny.

When my phone rang, I jumped. Christelle. Oh, damn.

'And you, are you going to use that phone or just keep pulling faces at it?' she growled.

Screwing up my face, I avoided meeting her eye. 'I'm supposed to be seeing my sister this afternoon. I double-booked myself. She's got the day off. We were going to have lunch and go shopping together.'

And I'd completely forgotten to phone her. My mind was somewhat occupied with other things.

Chapter 21

Those panda eyes turned my way as I rushed up to her.

'Did you enjoy it?' I bubbled. 'Wasn't Pietro amazing? So many curtain calls. The audience loved him. Did you enjoy the show?'

Christelle's silence almost felled me. With a sombre face, she merely nodded and a cold heavy lump settled in my stomach. I stared at her, my shoulders almost sagging under the disappointment of her disinterest. Determined not to cry, I lifted my chin firmly, pulling my mouth into a grim line and stared hard at her.

Then, I realised she was a touch dazed, as if she'd just stepped into brilliant sunshine and couldn't yet focus.

Marcus nudged me. 'I'll bill you later. You can give it back in your next lesson on Thursday.'

Had my sister's company been so unbearable? He nodded downwards.

Balled in Christelle's hand was a man's white hanky streaked with black mascara. The glassy look cleared, and her eyes lit up with an inner glow I'd never seen before. Stepping forward, she threw her arms around me. 'Tilly, it was wonderful,' she sobbed into my shoulder as she burst into tears. 'S-s-simply amazing.'

For a moment, uncertainty overwhelmed me.

She sighed. 'Stunning. Gorgeous. Sublime.'

'You really liked it,' I breathed.

'Oh Tilly, it was so wonderful,' she enthused. 'I can't believe you work here. You're so lucky. All this.' She waved her arm around at the magnificent building. 'It's amazing. You're amazing.' She stepped back and studied me before saying very quietly. 'I had no idea.'

'Marcus.' My head whipped around at the sound of Alison's brusque tone. 'Glad I caught you.'

'Any progress?' I heard her ask as I pretended to listen to Christelle now raving about the costumes.

'Not yet,' answered Marcus.

I strained to hear more.

'But the paper is adamant that the emails came from here.'

My heart sank like a stone to the soles of my feet. It had never occurred to me to ask Felix how he relayed the information to Jonno.

She was still buzzing half an hour later in Balthazar

where we'd retired for coffee and the most amazing mince pies. Just as well because I was lost in thought myself. Marcus had tactfully melted away before I'd had a chance to find out what he thought. It left an irritating question mark. Unfinished business. Had he enjoyed it?

Christelle, hemmed in around the tiny circular table, surrounded by my friends and colleagues, gaily talked away to Guillaume and Patrice, two members of the orchestra.

'Is that really your sister?' rasped Jeanie in my ear as she sipped an espresso.

'Mmm,' I replied.

'What happened? Thought you said she was a bit of a stiff.'

'She usually is,' I said, watching my sister as she tossed her glossy hair back, talking animatedly to Guillaume. 'We've been ... better.' Sadness tinged the moment. I didn't know that much about her as an adult. I'd never met any of her friends.

Shrugging, Jeanie eyed Christelle thoughtfully. 'She seems OK to me.'

I looked away from the concerned expression etched on her face, deliberately quashing the pinprick of guilt. I'd never asked my sister or parents to a performance but they wouldn't have come, would they?

Jeanie sucked in a sharp breath as if she'd just realised

the time. 'I've got to go. I'm late.'

'Late?' I queried but she was already out of her chair, the blush staining her cheeks, clashing with her red hair.

'See you tomorrow,' she said hurriedly and left.

Christelle sank into silence when we finally left the café and touched my arm.

'Thanks Tilly. Your friends are all so ...'

What? I realised I was dying to know what she thought.

'I had a lovely ... no a fantastic time. They're all so fascinating. Philippe's from the same part of Paris as Maman and he paints as well as plays the violin.'

He was also partial to the odd séance and owned a collection of antique Ouija boards but I didn't want to dampen her enthusiasm.

'He told me about his wedding. Sounded wonderful. They released fifty white doves.'

I looked at her. Deadly serious.

'Can you believe he wore white tie and tails? How dashing is that? Can't imagine many men would agree to that?'

Bless her.

'You should have seen the groom,' I said, biting my lip trying not to laugh at the expression on her face.

Her mouth dropped open.

'I don't suppose you get so much of that in chambers,'

I teased.

She giggled. 'God, no, Mr Hartington-Smyth would burst out of his pin stripes.' She sobered for a moment. 'What about Guillaume? Is he ...' she stumbled on the word, 'gay too?'

'Guillaume. No,' I couldn't resist, 'although he does live with Gary.'

Christelle's face fell – a lot further than I'd expected. Interesting. I took pity on her. 'Yes. Gary – the hamster.'

'He has a hamster. How sweet.'

Sweet? Owning a small furry rodent? Not to my mind but I could see that Christelle might have been impressed by his sexy French accent as well as the six-foot frame which showed to great advantage in a dinner suit. She didn't even know that he played violin with the touch of an angel and had the talent scout from the modelling agency around the corner panting into her espresso every morning.

When we said our goodbyes, with a proper cheek to cheek kiss, I felt something warm in my chest. Today had been quite a day.

Chapter 22

It was a surprise to receive a phone call from Christelle a few days later.

'Hey Christelle. How are you? Did you enjoy the other night?'

She giggled. She seemed to be doing a lot more of that these days.

'Yes, I had a lovely time thank you. Sorry to call you so early but I thought I'd better let you know straight away, so we can arrange how I get the presents to you.'

'Let me know what?'

'I've got to work this weekend. I've got a court appearance first thing on Monday and I have to interview a witness on Sunday.'

'Oh, right.' I wasn't quite sure why she felt the need to phone me and tell me first thing on a Thursday morning.

'Tilly!' She said in an accusing tone.

'What?'

'You've forgotten, haven't you?'

'Forgo ...' Oh pants. In a weak moment while we were watching the ice-skating at Somerset House, I'd agreed with her to travel to Yorkshire this weekend to see Mum and Dad. With everything that had been going on, it had slipped my mind. I sighed, acknowledging to myself that it had probably been a deliberate strategy. Classic Tilly avoidance tactics.

Felix had thankfully been away with work all week but he was due back this weekend. The week had been punctuated by apologetic texts and I was dreading his return. Suddenly the thought of being away from him and away from work sounded rather appealing. Although going to Yorkshire was possibly a bit drastic.

'Can't you change it?'

'No, it's taken weeks to get this guy to talk to me. He's a whistle-blower. I need him to make my case water-tight.'

'Whoa. Whoa. I can't go up on my own. Why don't we go another weekend? I'm sure Mum would rather see you ... both of us.'

Christelle sighed. 'Because you're free this weekend and I'm booked solid now until after Christmas.'

'Ah but the rota's change all the time. I need to check. I might need to work now.'

'No, you don't. I know for a fact.' That firm don't-mess-with-me tone probably put the fear of God into hapless jurors in court.

'Bloody hell, how?' In stark contrast my voice took on a plaintive wail.

'Guillaume told me.' She gave another one of those girlish and rather confounding giggles. 'And you told me you'd booked it.'

'Guillaume!' That explained a lot. Yesterday when I'd seen him, he'd had a decided sheepish tinge to his smile. 'Are you ... Seeing ... going out with him?'

It sounded so sixteen-year-old but it obviously worked for my sister who immediately said, 'Yes.'

'What? *Seeing* him, seeing him?'

'Tilly. Are you asking me if I'm sleeping with him?'

'Well now you come to mention it. No. I didn't dare. But are you?'

'I might be.' She giggled again.

'You only met him a week ago!' I sounded as stuffy as I'd once imagined her to be. It was a complete role reversal but I couldn't help myself. 'And why didn't I know?'

Chris's voice dropped to a whisper, 'Because, it's all been so ... and what if he didn't you know, feel the same way. I didn't want you to ... laugh.'

My starchy sister with free-spirited handsome, floppy-haired Guillaume. Who'd have thought it? A flood of shame washed over me. I was a crap sister. The least I could do for her was to go and visit our mother this weekend.

'OK, Chris – I'll go, if I absolutely have to. Although you know they'd far rather see you ...'

'Don't talk nonsense Tilly. I know things weren't great when you were a teenager but things have changed. It's you that stays away. You're the one that keeps your distance.'

That wasn't fair. 'No I don't,' I snapped. 'My hours are unsociable and we're usually so busy during holiday times.'

'Tilly, you're entitled to statutory holiday the same as everyone.'

Only Christelle would use the term statutory.

'You just choose not to go home. Don't blame work. It's your choice – and Mum and Dad make it worse because they're so wary of upsetting you. They'd love to see you but don't want to pressure you.'

I sighed. She was pushing buttons I didn't want pushing. If I didn't think too much about my parents, I didn't feel guilty. Rather than answer, I scuffed at the back of the chair with my booted foot.

'Tilly. You still there?'

'Yes Chris. I'll go. But you owe me. Big time.'

She didn't answer.

As soon as I put the phone down, having arranged for her to drop off the presents, reluctantly I went on line to work out the best way of getting home.

It didn't take long to research every form of transport north. Hell, who knew it was going to cost so much? It was almost cheaper to fly from Heathrow to Leeds. Thoroughly fed up by now, I sought diversion, checking my email for want of anything better to do. Redsman's latest email gave me a bit of a lift. In my last email to him, strictly business, I'd told him how much I was enjoying the adventures of forensic anthropologist, Tempe Brennan and had already bought the second in the series by Kathy Reichs.

To: Matilde@lmoc.co.uk
From: Redsman@hotmail.co.uk
Glad to hear you approved of my recommendation this time. Although I still think you could use a little education in the art of real football. Looks as if you're doomed to disappointment this weekend with two strikers on the bench.
R

To: Redsman@hotmail.co.uk
From: Matilde@lmoc.co.uk
Subject: Another disaster
I'm doomed to disappointment full stop. My weekend has just gone completely to pot. Just when I think things can't get any worse (and no we're not talking Arsenal's latest signing, what were

they thinking?) I have to go home.

I only want to go to Harrogate, not bloody Honolulu. The train is going to cost over £100 and National Express is fully booked on Saturday. I can't believe it's so expensive! I can't even book a seat on the 9.10 out of Kings Cross.

Tilly

I sat back and stared at the computer screen.

And now I was running late for my latest computer lesson. Damn, just when I thought I was starting to show Marcus that perhaps I wasn't as useless as he thought I was.

You'll never believe this. I'm going to Harrogate on Saturday. Would you like a lift?

Wow what were the chances of that? That would save me a fortune. When I was saving that much money, of course I accepted the lift. It was only after I said yes, gleefully thinking of all the things I could buy with the £100 I never had, that it occurred to me that perhaps I'd been a bit rash.

'You're late.' Marcus glared and rose from his desk. He slammed down his coffee mug, liquid slopping everywhere.

I stared at the quivering puddles on the surface. He seemed oblivious, his eyes burning with barely contained fury. I thought we'd moved on and come to some kind of détente but looking at him this morning, he'd got some bug up his butt.

I wasn't even that late. Surely he wasn't nervous about our meeting with Alison Kreufeld. It was me that was going to have to wing it when he unveiled the brilliant new stock taking system. I'd added a grand total of three items since our last session together.

'Sorry. Family trouble.' I stared distractedly at the mug with its football club emblem. Liverpool FC. Something shimmered in my brain and then I lost it as he spoke.

'Family trouble!' He spat the icy words.

'Oh yes,' I said gloomily. I still couldn't believe I'd agreed to go up to Yorkshire.

'Jesus Christ Tilly! You still don't get it, do you?'

I jumped at his vehemence. Something had really got his goat.

'Are you OK?' I asked realising as soon as I said it that he clearly wasn't.

'For fuck's sake woman. When are you going to start taking this seriously?'

'W-well ... I've got better. I've started inputting the products into the system.' Admittedly at a pace that could be outstripped by a three-legged tortoise but it was a start.

'What about the other things. Computer security. Taking any notice of that?'

Today his expression was even more grave than usual. Pissed off too. He paced up and down.

'Yes,' I squeaked. 'Mostly. Well, nearly.'

I stiffened, feeling the usual defensiveness creep into my body language as my brain started to process the earlier spark.

He glared even harder and wheeled to a stop. 'Your own personal security.'

With unexpected violence, he slammed his hand down on the desk, sending coffee drops all over the sleeve of his white shirt.

'If I were up to no good ... a serial killer ... a rapist ... do you know how easy it would be to track you down? Find you. Have you ever heard of Melody May?'

His sudden roar and show of emotion, so out of character, shocked me, even though I had absolutely no idea what he was talking about.

'9.10. This Saturday. You'll be at Kings Cross Station. You live in Clapham. Trewgowan Road. I'm guessing you'll probably leave the house at about 7.30 am to get there in time. Be extremely quiet then. No one around.'

He sneered still looking angry. I backed up until I hit the chair.

'What ... what do you mean?' And why was he so

bloody angry. The furious emotion pouring off him in waves made me feel wrong-footed and lost. This wasn't Marcus. Calm, logical, distant.

'I work here ... that doesn't mean I have or should have access to your personal details. I know it all because you told me.'

'I ...'

I stared again at the mug on the desk. Liverpool FC.

'Or ... you could just agree to a lift with ... A. COMPLETE. AND. UTTER. STRANGER.' His words reverberated around the small room.

He followed my gaze, the dawning of comprehension on my face. I looked at him.

'You're ...' Colour flooded my face as the significance of the mug hit me with the force of a punch to the head. It was suddenly bloody obvious. In fact, so obvious, now I knew, I could see my own denial. Part of my usual pattern, exactly as Christelle had pointed out, ignore things I didn't want to see. I squinted at the mug, desperately trying to recall all the emails I'd sent. What I'd written in them. What I'd inadvertently revealed.

'His Royal ITness, The Prince of Darkness,' he snarled with a tight unamused smile.

'Yes,' I said faintly, plopping down into the chair with a thud. He glared at me and I smiled nervously at him. 'That was at the beginning ... you've grown on me since then.'

'I couldn't give a stuff what you think of me. What bothers me is that you are so fucking clueless. I reeled you in, asking leading questions about where you lived, and you answered them like a bloody lamb to slaughter.'

'You knew all the time it was me,' I squeaked.

'Of course, I bloody did. Matilde@lmoc.co.uk isn't that difficult to work out. And Santa Baby, the little virus you unleashed. Let's face it, who else in the building would do that? From the day I arrived you've been a thorn in my bloody side. When are you going to grow up and stop flouncing around in your sexy little skirts and start taking anything apart from the theatre seriously?'

Had he said 'sexy little skirts' while insulting me? I didn't have time to analyse what he meant by that as he was still in full rant mode.

'No wonder I think you're flaky ... you are.' He roared the last two words, slamming his hands on the desk on either side of me.

I jumped up from the chair, putting my hand on his chest to push him back, feeling the warmth of his skin through the crisp white cotton and the solid muscle of his chest. Adrenaline fired through me, sending my heart crashing into my ribs and heat firing in my cheeks.

'How dare you?' I shouted back, shaking now. 'You know nothing about the theatre. You and your bloody

La Bohème. You don't have a soul. You're just a pompous stuffed shirt who wouldn't know how to let his hair down if he tried.'

We stood facing each other, his eyes flashing furiously. I couldn't look away. 'I'm not paid to let my hair down.' His face came closer, I could see the hazel flecks in his eyes and the thick dark lashes fringing them. 'I'm paid to do a good job. Protecting the infrastructure of this place from idiots wreaking havoc. Among them, *you*.'

'I might be an idiot,' I spat, taking in another angry breath, my chest feeling tight, as I held his gaze, 'when it comes to computers ... but at least I care about real things not bits of ... bits of ...' I flung my arm out towards his laptop just as he stepped closer and inadvertently grazed his hip.

'I care,' he snapped, stepping in again, so that my arm dropped around his hip, touching his ... his bottom. Our faces were so close, I could feel his breath.

'Yeah, right,' I snapped back, tipping my chin up to show I wasn't intimidated.

'I care ...' his voice dropped to an irritated husky whisper.

Suddenly I found myself mesmerised by his lips which were millimetres from mine and hypnotised by the change in timbre of his voice. I swallowed, feeling my stomach fall away. His nostrils flared and he dipped his head, the same second as I let out a sigh of capitulation.

I always thought angry kisses were the stuff of films and books. They never really happened, but oh boy did they. Did they ever?

Fury fuelled, we duelled for a minute, pressing our lips against each other, twisting as each of us tried to gain control. It was like no kiss I'd ever had. We were panting, our chests planted together and still it wasn't close enough. Then his tongue touched my lips and I opened my mouth, a zing firing through me, lighting up parts that had been in hibernation for way too long. There was nothing tentative or gentle about his mouth taking possession of mine but I eagerly kissed him back as if I couldn't get enough of him.

His hands snaked up my blouse and were making forays under my bra while mine had slid down the back of his trousers, clutching firm, gorgeous buttocks.

Thank God the phone rang because I seriously think that we'd either have spontaneously combusted or just got down and dirty right there on the desk.

Breathing heavily, Marcus snatched up the phone.

'Yes Alison. We'll be ... right there.'

He put the phone down and looked at me, his face grave and his lips pinched.

I looked away and concentrated on tucking my blouse back into my waistband.

'I'm ...' He blushed and waved his hand to express his incoherence.

'Me too.'

'Not very professional.'

'No.'

'Alison's expecting us.'

'Right. We'd better go then.' Shock had robbed me of the ability to say anything. What the hell had just happened? Sexual chemistry to the power of ten and the rest. It had never occurred to me for one minute that cool, detached Marcus could lose control quite like that. Or me for that matter. I sneaked a look at him but he was busy rounding up his pen and smart desk diary, the red in his cheeks receding.

There was a silence as we walked to the lift. Once inside, he surreptitiously tucked in his shirt.

We didn't say a word as the ancient lift ponderously rocked its way to the fifth floor.

As we got out, Marcus turned to me, a pulse jumping in his cheek.

'Just one thing. Those emails. I hope you realise now how open you left yourself. You should be grateful I haven't shared them with anyone else. Hopefully I've made my point.' He strode ahead towards Alison's office.

My heart clenched in sudden pain. All those emails. None of them had been real. Yeah, he'd certainly made his point. I pinched my lips and wiped my hand across my eyes, swallowing hard before following him.

Chapter 23

Despite the sexual blow up just minutes before, Alison seemed oblivious to the tension crackling between me and Marcus or his less than sartorial perfection. Throughout the meeting, I couldn't stop staring at the coffee stains on his shirt cuffs. Our communication was stilted, ultra-polite, waiting for each other to finish sentences and neither of us looked at each other once throughout the entire meeting.

He did most of the talking, going into so much detail about software programmes and coding that even Alison's shoulders started to droop. I could see what he was doing. The bastard. He was being deliberately nice. Purposefully deflecting any attention from my snail's pace progress with the new system. He might have even used the phrase, 'Tilly's doing a great job inputting all the information, which is a bit of a thankless task, as it's a tedious and repetitious job,' which made me sound a paragon of responsibility and diligence, when he knew damn well I'd done fuck all.

Thankfully Alison asked me to wait for a quick word at the end of the meeting, and Marcus left without a backward glance. I stared out of the window, tuning out their brief conversation as they said their goodbyes.

'I'm very pleased with the way you've worked with the IT department.' I jumped and turned. Alison stood in front of me, a smirk on her face. 'Actually, make that bloody incredulous.' She cornered her desk and perched on the edge, her arms folded. 'Mr Walker has been very positive about your willingness to work with him and how receptive to his ideas you've been. Well done, Tilly. I know you were reluctant,' she paused and gave me a wry, knowing smile, 'computers not being your thing but,' she nodded her head approvingly, 'you've shown an admirable maturity, which ... I'll be honest,' she leaned back and crossed her legs, with a short bark of laughter, 'I didn't think you would. I thought you'd faff and fanny about making excuses and being arsey and flighty about it. Your probation period's up in a couple of weeks, so let's have that stock management system up and running by the time we finish for Christmas. Sounds as if you're well on the way.'

I can't even remember what I said to her as I left, my mind was still on all those emails I'd sent to Marcus. I clock watched for the rest of the day, until it was time to go home and the minute I got back to the flat, like picking at a scab, I went back and re-read every one of the emails Marcus and I had exchanged.

Bugger. I sat back. I'd been an idiot. Marcus hadn't even been subtle about it.

You know what they say, you only sing when you're winning.
Camden? I live in Clapham, not quite so hipsterish.

Clapham? Posh bird then.

Clapham North, the less posh bit. Trewgowan Road, decidedly unposh.

He really hadn't had to work that hard.

Once I'd started, it was hard to stop reading and by the time I'd finished, I was left with a serious dilemma. I'd spent so much time pigeon holing Marcus, *the suit*, into the box I'd created for him, I'd missed the bits that shone out in his emails. He was funny, witty and irreverent but sensible and smart. It was like a sharp slap in the face.

Out of curiosity I did a quick google search on Melody May, the name that Marcus had tossed at me. It rang bells and when the BBC news site came up with a page from two years ago, I understood. She was a young woman who'd met and corresponded with a man online for several months. Being sensible and wary, she'd refused to meet him, but over the course of their digital friendship, using her emails, Facebook, Twitter and Instagram he'd stalked her profile, working out where she worked, where she lived and her daily routine. He'd broken into her flat and taken her hostage for three days before anyone had realised she was missing. It was only thanks to her flat-mate falling ill during a business trip and returning early that Melody had been rescued.

Oh, bugger again. Marcus had been rightfully angry. And then he'd gone and been nice in front of Alison. And I wasn't even going to think about that kiss. *That was another matter altogether.*

I started typing.

Hi Marcus
    You were right, I should have been more circum-spect in my emails. Thanks for saving my bacon with Alison today.

Nope, I deleted it. Go with the flow I told myself, type what comes into your head and then edit it.

Hi Marcus
    Gosh, feels funny typing your name. I wanted to apologise for being ungrateful today. You were right, I realise now I was being very careless. And

thanks for being so nice with Alison and covering for me.

And what was with that KISS!!!!!

I couldn't send that one.

~~Hi~~
~~You'll be pleased You were right, I've been a complete flake~~

~~Dear Marcus~~
~~Today has been a bit of a revelation, realising that you were~~

Dear Marcus

Today wasn't the best day. Thank you for caring enough to get so mad at me. I can see now that I've been a bit of an idiot. I'm sorry ... we still have to work together which is probably going to be a bit awkward, so I wanted to clear the air.

All the best
Tilly

It had taken me two hours to get to that point. It still wasn't perfect but...

The front door bell rang, sharp and shrill. Pushing aside my tablet, I jumped up to get it.

A glow of yellow bloomed through the frosted glass, the shape and colour sharpening as I neared the door. When I opened it a delivery woman handed me a dozen yellow roses saying, 'Someone loves you.'

I gave her a nod, trying not to snatch at the card tucked among the furled blooms.

As soon as I closed the door, I ripped open the envelope.

I was out of line today. I'm sorry. Redsman.

My eyesight blurred a little. Out of line for shouting at me or out of line for kissing me. And which was he sorry for?

I peered down at the card again. Redsman not Marcus. Suddenly it seemed easy, he was my e-male again.

To: Redsman@hotmail.co.uk
From: Matilde@lmoc.co.uk
Subject: Flowers

Gorgeous flowers have just turned up, with an apology. You didn't need to do that. You were probably right (not probably, you were right) and I hate admitting it, (and it might never happen again) but I might have been a tad flaky on the e-safety side. OK, totally flaky in this instance only.

Tilly

I wasn't going to add a kiss.

His email came back within seconds.

To: Matilde@lmoc.co.uk
From: Redsman@hotmail.co.uk
Subject: Flowers
    Have just picked myself up off the floor. Flaky or not, I shouldn't have lost my temper. Again, I'm genuinely sorry, it wasn't very professional. Must be the theatre rubbing off on me! I'm going over to the dark side.
    Can we just forget about today and start again?
    Marcus
P.S. Dare I say the offer of the lift still stands. I've got to go up to this conference anyway and I'd be glad of the company on the trip.

On paper, screen, whatever, it seemed we were back to normal but I couldn't help wondering when I saw him again, how easy it would be to forget that kiss.

Chapter 24

It was only as the tube rattled through the tunnels up to Baker Street, that doubts began to surface. Scrub that, they'd been circling like vultures since I'd woken up but I'd ignored them as I hurriedly stuffed things into my bag. What would we talk about? Did we mention that kiss? What if I bored the pants off him? What if he drove like a lunatic? What about that kiss? What if his car was held together with gaffer tape and string and we broke down and had to spend hours on the roadside waiting for the AA? No, that was ridiculous. This was Marcus.

And just what about that kiss?

I was pulling faces at the memory when a black Golf GTI pulled up. He must have thought I was a right idiot.

'Morning,' called Marcus through the open window. He wore another one of those dazzling white shirts but this must have been the casual version as it was open at the neck, revealing a dusting of hair at the bottom of the vee. My heart went thunk and I could almost taste the Sahara Desert in my mouth. All I could think of was the feel of his lips pressed against mine. A zing of lust hurtled downwards. I stared for a moment. It was as if every time I saw him, I forgot how utterly gorgeous he was.

'Hi,' I said suddenly very shy. What on earth was I going to talk to him about all the way up the M1?

'Tilly? Are you alright?'

I realised he'd said something and I hadn't responded.

'Are you going to get in or have you decided I am a serial killer?'

'Yes ... I mean no,' I finally managed to spit out.

'Stick your bag in the back. The boot's full of stuff.'

I opened the back door and hefted in my enormous holdall and skipped around to the front. Maybe this wouldn't be so nerve-racking after all.

'Can I say something before we set off?' Marcus turned to me. His face held the familiar grave, serious look.

'Can we forget the other day and work? Perhaps we could just be two football fans who read a lot.'

I relaxed into my seat. 'Thank you ... that sounds ... a good idea. And thank you so much for putting in a good word for me with Alison. I'm not sure I deserved it.'

'Hmm, you owe me then. Right.' His face lightened. 'Just the one bag?' he asked, looking pointedly at the huge holdall in the back seat as I strapped myself in, grateful for the heater blasting out hot air. No wonder he was only wearing a shirt, it was lovely and toasty in the car.

'Yes. Why?' Immediately I went on the defensive.

'Are you helping the costume department out? Going on tour?'

The minute I realised he was teasing, without a second thought I leaned towards him and poked him in the ribs. He smelt clean and fresh, his hair slightly damp, as if he'd just stepped out of the shower. Thank goodness for that spritz of perfume I'd put on just before I got off the tube. I hoped I smelt as good to him.

'Very funny. Don't tell me. You're one of the tooth-brush-and-clean-boxers-in-your-pocket brigade.'

'Not quite, but you have to agree that is quite a bag.'

'I prefer to be prepared. It might snow, so I needed another pair of boots, plus a pair of shoes in case my boots get wet, and another pair of boots which go with the other skirt I packed and I've got a waterproof coat in there but I wanted to wear a nice coat to travel in. And of course Christmas presents.'

'I get the picture.' Marcus shook his head, laughing but keeping his focus fixed on the road.

'And I've got books.'

'What? You're the travelling library now?'

'You can never have–'

'Too many books.' He nodded his head in wry agreement. 'Yes, I know but what about your e-reader?'

'Well yes but what if it breaks or the battery dies. So, I popped two books in. Just in case and then another one because it's on my to-be-read pile.'

There was a pause as he did the calculation. 'For two nights away, you've brought two coats, four pairs of shoes and boots and three books!'

'That's about it. If I was going up on the train, I promise you, I would have made do with one coat, two pairs of boots and two books.'

'Of course.' The dry long-suffering amusement in his deep voice sent a quiver through me.

'And,' I said with a flourish, 'I've brought supplies.'

'Oh God, you've brought several gallons of coffee in a thermos flask, foil-wrapped home-made sandwiches, a shovel and several tins of beans. Have you got your travel rug?'

I burst out laughing. 'I'd forgotten about that.'

Twisting to reach my bag in the back, I hauled out a Tesco carrier bag. 'I had no idea what you ate, so I bought a selection.'

Delving into the bag, I produced a bright red packet. 'Maltesers, old man's Werthers' Originals, Walkers crisps and wine gums. And Jelly Babies but they're mine.'

'Christ anything else? I'm travelling with Mary Poppins.'

'Of course, on the sweet front, I'm practically perfect in every way.'

'Apart from being an Arsenal supporter.'

I paused. It needed addressing. 'You know that is the only reason I responded to your first email. You threw down a challenge. Although,' my voice slowed as I remembered the pinch of sadness when I realised he hadn't been the friendly e-male correspondent I'd first thought. 'I realise now you were deliberately trying to reel me in.'

Marcus's ears turned bright red and his fingers gripped the steering wheel a bit tighter.

'Ah ...' For the first time ever I saw him look discomfited. 'I didn't mean what I said the other day. I meant to teach you a lesson but you were fun in the emails, a lot more approachable, it made a pleasant change. It was nice being liked for a change. I've come up against a lot of resistance since being at the London Met.'

A horrible tug of guilt made me turn to him.

'God, was it really that bad?'

He let out a self-deprecating laugh. 'No, I'm a big boy, but it did get a bit wearing in those first few weeks. I'd come in full of confidence knowing exactly what needed doing and suddenly no one wanted it doing.'

'Sorry.' I crossed my legs, trying to look nonchalant.

'It's OK,' he added, 'you didn't say anything *too* bad about me.'

'What, you're a mind reader now?'

'No, but the agonies contorting your face were too much to bear, so I thought I'd relieve you of that worry.'

'Very good of you,' I said, still unable to completely relax. We'd exchanged a lot in those emails.

'Well apart from calling me the Prince of Darkness, His Royal ITness. That was quite amusing.' He shot me a wicked look. 'Although I don't think you meant it to be amusing.'

'Serves you right for not saying anything.' I turned to look out of the window to hide some of my mortification. Thank God I'd not mentioned my hormones misbehaving every time he came onto the scene. That would have been so embarrassing.

He laid a hand on my forearm and tugged. I turned to face him, although it was his profile because he was the sort of driver that kept watching the road. 'I enjoyed our exchanges. You were funny. We enjoyed the same sort of books ... and how could I say anything. Especially not when you clearly hated me.'

'I didn't hate you!'

'Sorry bit strong, clearly dislike what I stand for. Although I quite like being His Royal ITness.'

His quick grin made me feel embarrassed and more than a bit ashamed.

'I might have changed my mind a bit. You don't seem quite so ... corporatey now.'

'Aw thanks. Nothing like damning with faint praise.'

'Well be honest, you thought I was some bohemian hippy chick.'

'Point taken, although ... to be fair,' he grinned, 'some are flakier than others, the jury's still out on Vince, but I have to admit now I understand more about what goes on ... well.'

'You think we're the bee's knees?' I teased.

'I wouldn't go quite that far, no you still drive me insane. I mean how difficult is it not to open an attachment with a ruddy great virus piggy backing it?'

'How was I to know it had a virus on it?'

'How were you to know it didn't?'

'Ok, you win that one. But no harm done.'

He rolled his eyes. 'There could have been though.'

'I am sorry and I learned my lesson. I'm getting quite good now ... you've got to admit.'

'Quite good? Tilly you've deleted that spreadsheet three times now.'

'See that's why the card index works so well, impossible to delete.' I grinned at him.

'I will get that system set up even if it kills me.'

'It might well–' My phone burst into song and Marcus raised an eyebrow.

'Snow Patrol? I had you down as a Carmina Burana girl.'

Laughing, I dug my phone out of my bag. 'That's so last week's ring tone.' I looked down at the screen. It was Felix.

My heart plummeted. He'd obviously come home to find my note. The last thing I wanted was him trying to make yet another grovelling apology and I didn't dare attempt a one-sided conversation in front of Marcus. I scowled at my phone.

Marcus looked amused. 'What's wrong? Bad news?'

'No. Nothing important.' I switched it off and slipped it into my pocket.

We'd been travelling for a couple of hours and I'd started to get fidgety. The time had passed easily, as we'd chatted about so many things including books and football.

'Want to stop?'

'Wouldn't mind,' I said trying to stretch my legs. 'You must be ready.'

'Yeah, if you're not in too much of a hurry to get home, we could come off the motorway and find somewhere a bit better than a service station.'

'I'm in no hurry to get home, I promise you.'

'You don't get on well with your family?'

I sighed. 'We're just completely different. My mother is French. Hence my name.' He still looked nonplussed.

'Not just French – Parisian.'

'Yes, I remember. Matilde sounds quite sexy when you say it with a French accent.'

'Doesn't everything. What other language can make my little cabbage sound sexy – ma petite chou?'

'So, cabbage face, what's wrong with your mother?'

I wheeled round and stared at him. He was certainly perceptive.

'She might be from Paris but there's not one cell of Latin blood in her, I'm pretty sure she was hatched from an ice cube tray.'

'Sounds chilly.'

'It was. She didn't want me to be a make-up artist.' I stared at the opposite carriageway barely registering the cars flashing past. 'The morning I got my GCSE results, all hell broke loose. I wanted to go to college to do hairdressing and make-up and they'd assumed I'd stay on in the sixth form and then go to university like my sister.'

No matter how many teenage strops, and I threw some humdingers, my parents were not for turning.

'What happened? You got there in the end.'

'Mmm,' I nodded. Those two years in the sixth form had not been endured stoically. I made my parents pay with small but satisfying rebellions – a taste for scruffy, vintage clothes, which infuriated my ultra-smart mother and full-scale hair warfare. Every couple of weeks I would arrive at the breakfast table sporting a different hair shade, combination of colours or a style more outrageous than the last.

'My parents insisted I went to university.'

'Didn't you enjoy it?'

'Yeah. OK, I loved it because I got involved in loads of student productions.' Which stood me in good stead. 'Maybe they were right after all,' I said with a burst of sudden realisation.

'What parents, being right?'

'OK, you don't need to rub it in.' I didn't want to think about it too closely. 'Oh, look Chatsworth House.' I pointed to one of the brown signs. 'I've always wanted to go there. I love Jane Austen, especially *Pride and Prejudice*. I think they filmed some of it there.'

Marcus shot me a look. 'Shall we visit now?'

'What *now*, now?'

'Is there any other type of now?'

Stepping out of the car, a fresh wind whipped at my curls tossing them into my face. It immediately felt colder than in London but after the stuffy warmth of the car, the chilly air with its scent of the moors was wonderfully invigorating. I took in an exaggerated breath.

'Hell, it's cold.' Marcus wrapped a stripy scarf round his neck twice. 'Are you sure this is a good idea? Maybe

I'll just stay in the car.'

'It's perfect. You're just not used to real temperatures. I love it.' And I meant it. Tugging my hat down past my ears, and hoping it wasn't too unflattering, I pulled on my favourite dark green leather gloves.

'Come on then Miss Burke.' Marcus bowed and offered an arm. 'Let me escort you and take a look at this house and see what all the fuss is about.'

'Bennett, in *Pride and Prejudice*, it was the Bennetts,' I said quite charmed by his unexpected willingness to get into the spirit of the visit.

'Begins with B. It'll do,' he muttered into his scarf.

I was quite happy to let him link his arm through mine, it seemed perfectly natural to play along. Being there made everything else seem a long way away. 'If I'm Miss Bennett, who are you then?'

'I'm the kindly uncle that takes Elizabeth to Derbyshire and gets to fish in the pond. Uncle Ted.'

I giggled. 'He wasn't called Uncle Ted. That's far too informal, he was Mister something or other. And how do you know about the Uncle and the fishing?'

'Call yourself an Austen fan?' Marcus gave me a wide-eyed look of mock horror and then scrunched his face up in a horrible grimace. 'Had to study it for GCSE English. I didn't get it then, not sure I will now.'

'It was Mr ...' I searched my memory. It was buried in there somewhere.

He tutted and shook his head. We carried on in companionable silence, our feet scrunching on the gravel.

'Do you want to visit the Christmas market?' Marcus nodded to the orderly lines of stalls and kiosks that lined the driveway. I looked at the deliberately bland expression on his face.

'I'd love to.' I grinned cheerily at him, enjoying the tiny wince he thought he'd hidden. 'But,' I nudged him, 'I think it would be torture for you and I'd rather get some fresh air. I don't miss being outdoors when I'm in London, but now we're here I want to make the most of it.'

He heaved an obvious sigh of relief. 'Phew. I remember you and shopping.'

'You got off lightly that day,' I teased.

Despite the cold wind there were plenty of walkers out, muffled up against the crisp wind, some with dogs and others in organised groups identifiable by the maps in the plastic wallets around their necks.

When we came to the first magnificent view of the house, we stopped.

It was so vast. Both of us stood quite awestruck, gazing at the imposing façade with countless windows.

'My God, it's huge.' I gazed up at the pale-yellow walls several stories high. 'No wonder Lizzy changed her mind about Mr Darcy.'

'Isn't it sacrilegious to say that?' asked Marcus. 'Didn't she marry for love?'

'Romantic as I think I am, I am also a realist.'

We rounded to the front of the house and wandered through the garden which was beautifully kept with perfectly trimmed hedges and shrubs. The fir trees had all been decked with lights and I could imagine when it was dark it would look magical. Everywhere there was something to see, intricate gardens here and in the distance statuesque trees and the classic Capability Brown parkland designed to lead your eye to some intricate folly.

We'd been walking for half an hour when we left the path to get a better view of the south side of the house. Marcus put out a hand to pull me up a grassy knoll and as I reached the top I tripped on a loose sod of earth and went catapulting into him. His arms went around me and we stood breathless for a moment with nowhere to look but into each other's eyes.

I didn't let go and neither did he. I sucked in a breath as if that would help me hold on to the moment. We stood motionless as if time had stopped. I was aware of my heart thudding in my chest and the breath caught in my lungs. My heart was hammering away and Marcus looked lost for a minute before he lifted his hand to brush the hair whipping around my face. His fingers slid along my cheekbone and I almost melted into a puddle. Without thinking I put my hand up and laid my fingers on his wrist.

He brought his other hand up to trace the outline of the diamond embossing the leather of my glove. There was a shadow in Marcus's eyes as he gave me a sad smile.

'What's the story with your fiancé? You don't talk about him.'

I blinked away sudden tears. Saying it out loud would make it real.

'It's over.'

He raised an eyebrow and I felt his touch on my ring.

'He. He's done something. I can't forgive him for. I thought I could, but I c-can't. I haven't told him yet.' I bit my lip as the tears slid down my face. 'I could happily kill him.'

I clenched my fists so tightly I could feel the leather of my gloves stretching over my knuckles. 'More than kill,' I said, the anger spilling over, my voice surging with venom. 'Dig his damn heart with a spoon and feed it to the rats. He's a big. Fat. Lying rat.' I spat the final words shuddering with the rage that slashed through me.

'Remind me not to cross you.'

Marcus's sudden attempt at humour punctured my anger and I burst into hot furious sobs.

His arms went around me and we stood for a moment. I didn't deserve his sympathy but I couldn't resist leaning into him and savouring the sense of being held. His soft scarf tickled my cheek, absorbing some of my tears.

I pulled away feeling a terrible fraud, almost tempted to confess everything to him.

'Don't tell me? He's having an affair.' A frown crossed his face making me wonder more about the ex-girlfriend who'd given him the tie.

I laughed bitterly. 'Felix would never have an affair. He's too ... Oh.' I heard the shrill cry of a hawk above us as everything else receded. 'Oh.'

That's what he'd been trying to tell me. *Jonno's the type of guy that knows things ... he was going to tell you.*

'Tilly?' Marcus's voice came from far away.

I blinked and looked at him. 'Yes,' I whispered, 'I think he is.'

Suddenly something barged into my side, knocking me away from Marcus and hot breath wheezed over my hand.

'Buster! Buster! Heel!'

An enormous Airedale terrier had appeared and was bounding around my knees, woofing in friendly greeting, his bearded face nuzzling into my hand.

'Buster. Here! Now!'

A small blonde woman came running over, almost

falling over her outsize green Hunter wellies. 'I'm so sorry. He's still a baby. Come here, you naughty boy.' She grabbed at his collar but he was still nudging at me.

'It's fine,' I smiled at her rubbing Buster's head, grateful for the distraction. The wiry curls felt soft and his head was warm under my cold fingers.

The woman finally managed to hook her fingers under his collar and pulled him away. 'This way you silly animal. What have I told you?' With twinkly-eyed apology she dragged the bouncing dog away.

'Mr Gardiner. Uncle Ted. He was called Mr Gardiner,' I suddenly said, shoving my hands into pockets and starting to walk again.

'So he was,' said Marcus nodding and falling into step beside me.

Chapter 25

The rain started just past Sheffield and a grey mist descended making driving conditions difficult. Passing lorries churned up the spray, spattering the windscreen with dirty water. The windscreen wipers slapped back and forth at full-speed clearing the streaky mess.

Even though I'd not lived with my parents for years and had my own flat, the minute I saw the familiar cooling towers of the power stations and the grassed over slag heaps, I felt as if I was coming home.

'You look as if you've changed your mind about going home,' observed Marcus, watching me eagerly pointing out landmarks on the Leeds-Harrogate road an hour later. We'd kept to strictly impersonal topics since we'd got back into the car.

'I am. I thought I was dreading it but it's still home. I don't know what to expect with my mother, I haven't been on my own with her for years. I always make sure

I come home when Christelle is going to be here.'

'I liked her.'

'Yeah. I thought you might. She's much more your type. The blue-eyed girl. I'm the flake.'

'Can we just move past that one? You could give me some credit for changing my mind.'

'Really?'

'I've seen you in action ... you've never let your parents see that side of you, have you?' Marcus drew in a breath.

'You've been talking to Christelle,' I accused him.

'No, but she hinted. It's almost as if you've deliberately kept them away. And let's face it – we're all monsters as teenagers. Perhaps you haven't moved on.'

I watched his hands, competent and steady on the steering wheel.

'What if your parents were only trying to make sure you kept all your options open. What if you'd changed your mind? Or didn't make it? You could have ended up working in "A Cut Above" or "Scissor Happy" in the back of beyond, doing blue rinse perms for a legion of pensioners rather than in the theatre.'

I scowled unhappily at him. 'I'm not good at forgiveness.'

'Tilly! Don't be silly ... sounds like that Black Lace single.' He burst into song. 'Tilly don't be a silly. Don't be a fool ...'

I slapped at his arm, trying not to laugh at the tuneless words. 'That's terrible.'

'Mmm.' He flashed a sheepish grin and then carried on. 'Seriously, I don't know your mother but if you haven't been home much since you were a teenager, you haven't had a chance to build a relationship with them as an adult. Christ.' He said the words with vehemence. 'I blush at some of the things I said to my mum when I was a teenager. Moody sod. I could sulk for days.'

I thought about what he'd said for a moment. Maybe he was right. I looked at him with gratitude. 'Thanks. You're turning into quite the agony uncle these days.'

'My pleasure. Now which way am I going?'

The landscape had changed and my heart lifted at the familiar sights that told me we were on the outskirts of Harrogate. Only five minutes from home.

When we pulled up outside the detached house, I turned to Marcus with a self-deprecating smile. 'Don't suppose you fancy coming in with me. Help me out.'

He was already out of the car hefting my overnight bag into his arms and heading towards the front door. 'Now, now Tilly. I thought we agreed. Positive thinking. If you go in with that attitude ...'

'I know. But they'll probably approve of you. You're a proper professional sort of person.' Although she probably wouldn't like him being surprised on her. My mother didn't do spontaneity.

Marcus shot me a shrewd glance. 'That why Felix

was so appealing?'

I flushed a brilliant red and wrinkled my nose at him at his unwelcome insight.

'Got a degree in armchair psychology, have we?' I asked.

Mum didn't bat an eyelid and Dad seemed rather delighted to have another man to talk to for a change.

'Mum, Dad, this is Marcus ... um ... er ... a work colleague. He was coming up for a conference thing on ...' I glanced at Marcus for reassurance but he just smiled, 'computery things.'

'Oh, at the Harrogate Conference Centre?' said Mum, brightly.

No, at the Outer Hebrides Conference Centre, he thought he'd just divert here for tea with you. I didn't say that because by that time, she and Marcus were well away debating the merits of conference centres they had been to.

'Don't suppose there's a chance of a cup of tea for our guest?'

Mum pursed her mouth and then turned back to Marcus. 'I'm so sorry, how rude. Can I make you a drink, a tea or a coffee? And I've just made a batch of mince pies.'

'Tea would be lovely, Mrs ...' he shot a quick look at me.

'Oh, call me Elise. Mrs Hunter sounds so stuffy. And a mince pie?'

'Oooh yum. You must try one,' I said. Hers were the best. When she'd arrived here all those years ago, she'd been determined to embrace every British tradition possible. Every year she made several batches of them, flatly refusing to have shop-bought ones in the house. 'Mum has this special secret recipe, she puts orange juice in the pastry and orange zest on top of the mince-meat.'

'Not so secret now then,' said Dad with a wink as he invited Marcus to call him Trevor.

I bit the inside of my cheek. This was such a far cry from Felix's one and only visit. Like a boisterous puppy, he'd been overfamiliar and bouncy calling my mum Mrs H and Dad Trev and putting his feet on the coffee table within the first hour of arriving. It hadn't gone down well.

Before I knew it, the three of them had segued seam-lessly into talking about cars of all things. Apparently, Mum was thinking of getting a VW golf.

Pottering about the kitchen, she ushered us into the chairs around the kitchen table, sliding hot mince pies onto plates for everyone.

'And what about petrol consumption?' Dad asked as I was still wondering why we weren't subjected to the formality of the lounge where guests were normally entertained.

Marcus gave him a caught-out-schoolboy smile. 'Depends on how you drive, to be honest.'

Mum laughed. 'Town driving. I'm no boy racer.'

'Not bad.'

I watched as the three of them chatted easily. With his good manners, good looks and a damn lovely smile, Marcus was house-trained. Parent friendly.

My mother was not however so normally friendly – full stop.

'Yes, I met her at the opera.' I tuned back into the conversation as Mum turned to me with a wide smile, handing me a cup of tea.

'How lovely that you invited Christelle, Tilly. She so enjoyed it.' Mum gave a wistful smile. 'It sounded wonderful. Didn't it Trevor? Did you enjoy it, Marcus?'

'Yes, more than I expected.' He threw me a conspiratorial wink. 'Tilly thinks I'm a complete Philistine, I'd never seen any opera before then, but I surprised myself. It's amazing when you see what goes on behind the scenes.'

'Yes, I can imagine it's quite an undertaking. And I hear it's a very beautiful theatre. I'd love to go one day.'

I raised my eyebrows at that one but didn't say anything.

'I knew they'd approve of you,' I said in a quiet undertone as I showed him to the front door.

'I suspect that's not necessarily a compliment.' Marcus's lips firmed and I immediately felt ungracious. 'Your parents weren't the least bit the way you described them. Your mother's a lovely woman. She's very proud of you and terrified of upsetting you.'

'Don't talk daft. But thank you for being nice to her. You've been ...' *Amazing? Lovely? Gorgeous?* 'You've been really kind to me. Especially today. I ... I'm really grateful. It's been a funny few weeks and that's an understatement. Thanks for the lift and ... everything else. You've really helped today.' Standing on the doorstep brought me level with him. 'In the car. Things you said ... it's been good.' Something flickered in the depths of his green eyes. 'Thank you,' I said, hoping that my heartfelt thanks were conveyed.

He smiled, which softened his whole face.

'It sounds as if you need to resolve a few things. Perhaps we can catch up next week. Maybe go out for a drink?'

'That would be. Yes. Lovely. I'd like that.' My tongue tripped over itself.

He smiled and laid a gentle barely-there kiss on my lips.

'See you soon,' he murmured.

I shut the door with a silly smile on my face.

It's funny the things you notice. There'd been no huge changes in the house, just tiny things; a new carpet in the downstairs toilet, virtually the same as the last one, blinds on the kitchen windows instead of the old curtains and the cushions that had been in the spare room were now in the lounge.

'What a lovely man,' observed my mother as I returned to the lounge. 'Nice of him to give you a lift.'

'He's just a colleague, Mum,' I said, turning to look at the photos on the mantelpiece. Dad had disappeared off to the study.

I picked up one of the pictures. The only one of me must have been taken when I was nineteen. My hair, much shorter then, had streaks of purple woven through it. I was heavily made-up with a sulky expression on my face, accentuated by a dark burgundy pout. I'd loved that lipstick at the time. There were some very recent pictures of Christelle and the cats.

She caught my stare. I shrugged, embarrassed that she might think I was jealous or something.

'It would be nice,' she said touching the picture of me, 'if we could have an up to date one of you.'

Typical, she had to get a dig in about how long it was since I'd last been home.

'Perhaps we could take some in the garden tomorrow.' She gave me a conspiratorial smile. 'That's not the best photo. Your hair looks so much prettier now. It's such a beautiful colour.'

'Not purple, you mean.' The defiance that crept into my voice was habitual and for a second I saw a shaft of pain sear across my mother's face.

'No,' she agreed quietly. 'Not purple.'

I avoided looking at her and instead traced the edge of one of the picture frames. 'This is lovely.' It was a watercolour of the moors at dusk, with the heather pictured in the foreground, a deep dusky pink among bracken greens. In the distance coming over the crest of the hill, two girls tumbled through the heather and the painter had captured their unfettered joy.

'Do you think so?' Her face lit up, a secretive smile hovered around her lips. 'It's Blubberhouses Moor. I ... er, by a local artist. It was exhibited at the art fair at the Valley Gardens last year.'

I fixed my attention on the painting. Blubberhouses. Every now and then I'd hear it mentioned on the radio. The road through there, high up on the moor, was often blocked by snow or an accident. The name usually eliciting some comment from the traffic reporter. Looking at the picture sparked Technicolor memories of unsullied happiness.

Family Sunday walks, crunching through the frost-covered bracken with puffs of steamy breath filling the air as we laboured up the hills. Chris and I, half-running to keep up with Dad's long strides on the downward trip homewards. In the winter our reward was lunch in a local pub, The Sun Inn with hot soup and Coca-Cola for me and Chris, a pint of Old Peculier for Dad and a half of Tetley's for Mum. In the summer, we'd picnic at Bolton Abbey, my sister and I racing over the famous stepping stones that straddled the river.

Happy memories. Suddenly they bubbled over like a stream bursting its banks, startling me. They flooded into my head and it was as if I were seeing a film of another me.

Mum laughing and retrieving one of our shoes that we'd dropped in the river. Mum unpacking the wicker hamper which was pretty rather than practical. It weighed a ton but I always insisted we should use it, with all its lovely china and place settings. Mum plaiting my hair to keep it out of my face so that I could see properly to get over the stones.

I glanced over at her and I could see the same woman in her face. A woman I'd forgotten existed. It made me feel slightly dizzy and disorientated for a second as if I was straddled between two different worlds.

That Mum had spent hours braiding and curling my hair for me, buying pretty ribbons and clips.

Regret splintered through me and I tensed at the almost physical pain. I remembered the day I had all my hair cut off, less than an hour after I was officially enrolled into the sixth form – coming in from the hairdressers and my mother's face when she'd looked up from the paperwork she was poring over.

'I think I'll take my bag upstairs,' I said, suddenly hit by an overwhelming sense of tiredness. I felt as if I'd been picked up and spat out by an emotional tornado, and all the feelings were still whirling about inside my head.

My bedroom was still unmistakably mine even though I'd not lived at home since I left to go to university. Things I'd have expected to have been thrown out were still there – an old rag doll, a theatre poster for *Peter Pan* and in the corner three shelves overflowing with books, volumes filling vertical and horizontal spaces. I knelt in front of it and traced the spines. All my childhood books. *The Chalet School* books, *Ballet Shoes*, an enormous selection of battered Enid Blyton's, and an eclectic mix of classics: *Anna Karenina, Brave New World, Keep the Aspidistra Flying, Testament of Youth.*

The battered copy of *Testament of Youth* beckoned to me and I pulled it from the shelf and stroked the dogeared front cover. A scene played in my head. Me putting the book back on the shelf in the bookshop, unable to afford it because I'd spent the last of my pocket money on make-up in Boots. I never said a word about wanting it but later that afternoon I found a paper bag left on my bed.

I lay down, curling up and opened it, the tatty cover and smoothed back the front page.

To my little bookworm,
A necessity not a luxury.
With all my love Maman.

My stomach cramped with regret and grief. If only I could flick back to the early pages of my life and start a chapter again. It was time I started acting like an adult and show my parents that I'd grown up ... at last.

Chapter 26

The Christmas tree lights had been turned on and they'd been set to a tasteful slow fade. No gaudy flashing in this house. But it was a lovely tree, set full centre in the bay window. I touched the fir branches, scanning the range of decorations. Although Christelle and I weren't at home, Mum had still put on all the childhood favourites, even the little mouse sleeping in a half walnut shell I'd made in primary school which was way past its best.

There was the broken glass decoration which I'd insisted one year we keep because it still looked pretty. I frowned. I would have expected Mum to have taken advantage of our absence this year to have a fully colour co-ordinated tree with matching decorations and chucked out the broken one.

A fire danced in the hearth, spitting slightly as it lapped at the fresh logs in the grate. Draped along the mantelpiece, already filled with cards, was a garland of cinnamon sticks and dried orange peel, the scent of which was carried on the warm air floating out into the room.

Mum was sitting curled up on the sofa, engrossed in a book. To my surprise, it was one of my favourites, Jill Mansell's *Staying at Daisy's*, – not something I'd have expected my scholarly mother to read but then hey, what did I really know about her?

Judging from her twitching lips and her absorption, she was clearly enjoying it.

'Hi Mum.' I felt shy and hesitant. 'Sorry I fell asleep.'

'I know, I did pop in but you looked so tired earlier I left you to it.'

She'd also covered me with a blanket and the thought of it brought a lump to my throat.

'M-mum.'

She laid her book down on the sofa beside her.

I stood awkwardly not knowing what to say.

She smiled. 'I'm just having a pre-dinner glass of wine. Your Dad's doing the cooking tonight.' She poured me a glass from the bottle of red at her elbow. 'I take it you're still not drinking white.'

'Oh, God no!' We exchanged a shared look of amused horror.

'Funny that.' She smiled and toasted me with her glass. 'I wonder how Christelle got off scot free.'

I sat down in the opposite sofa. Mum and I shared

an unusual affliction. We could drink anything except white wine, which bizarrely had a catastrophic effect on us. Instant inebriation. I think if it hadn't been for Mum, no one would have believed me.

'Marcus seemed nice.'

'Yes.' I couldn't help the heavy sigh that escaped. 'He's far too nice. Wish I'd met him before.'

'It's never too late, Tilly.' The timbre to her voice suggested that she was giving me a message.

I didn't want to think about Felix. Not then. There was something else I needed to do.

'Mum ...' My voice was suddenly rusty. It was harder than I'd thought it would be. 'I'm ... sorry ...' I couldn't get any further than that.

'Sweetheart,' her eyes glowed with the tears that welled in them but didn't slip over the edge. She wasn't that much of a push over.

'I'm ...' what else should I say? I'm sorry I've been a crap daughter. Sorry I've been a complete bitch to you and Christelle and Dad.

Suddenly she was beside me, her arm round me and I could feel the softness of her body as she hugged me. Inhaling her familiar fragrance, it brought back the rush of enveloping security that had been there when I was a small child. The 'there-there comfort' after a fall, the 'we're on your side' after a row with a friend and the 'you're the best' after a failure along with countless other hugs of support that before I was sixteen I'd valued.

'I've been so horrible.' Tears spilled onto my face, which was crap because I owed her an apology and here I was feeling sorry for myself and that was wrong. I didn't want her sympathy because it wasn't deserved.

'Tilly. You were never horrible.' Even now she was calm and reasonable which ratcheted up the guilt another notch. 'Just angry with us. It lasted such a long time.'

I bit my lip, forcing myself to say the words. 'You must have hated me.'

She shook her head with an amused smile. 'Mothers don't hate their children.' Her face brightened. 'We might not like them all the time but we always love them.'

I knew as she said it, she wasn't interested in recriminations. All I had to do was make amends.

'You know, no matter what, your father and I are always here for you. We are on your side. I know it might not have seemed that way when you were younger.' She laughed. 'God knows, I did wonder for a long time if I shouldn't just give in and let you do what you wanted ...'

'I'm glad you didn't. You were right.'

'Of course I was,' she said with a smug grin which once upon a time I would have taken huge offence at. Instead, I gave her a wry smile.

'University was a good thing, and I did learn more than just the academic bit. That life experience helped, without it I probably wouldn't be where I am now. If I'd just gone to the local college, I might not have ever seen the bigger picture, the wider world.'

'Oh, I know that,' she said hugging me, 'but at the time, part of me kept thinking it would serve you right if I did let you get on with it and then relish saying "I told you so" when you were working in a salon in Knaresborough with three children.'

We both giggled at the image.

'And now look at you.' Contentment radiated across her face. 'Top of your game. Working ...'

Her words broke a dam and I had to admit the truth.

'Mum ... I think I've made a terrible mistake. With Felix. It's all ...' it was suddenly so obvious, 'a sham. We never should have got engaged. He's my, *was* my best friend for so long. We're more like brother and sister.' I didn't need to go into more detail with my mother but for all my complaints about not having sex, I'd never felt one millionth of desire that one furious, passionate kiss from Marcus had elicited.

Mum didn't say anything, she just smiled serenely. 'I just want you to be happy. Whatever your decisions. You know we're incredibly proud of you.'

I stared at her, raising a disbelieving eyebrow.

'Tilly! Of course we are. You're working in one of

the most well-known theatres in the world, with international stars.'

'Really?' I couldn't resist asking again, just for the
reassurance.

'Truly and absolutely.' With each word, Mum dropped
a kiss on my head.

We sat in the small pool of light for another hour as
Mum asked questions about which stars I'd worked
with and what they were like. Did I meet Pavarotti
before he died? Was Pietro as much of a womaniser as
the papers claimed? And was his porn king label true
or made up by the newspapers?

I went to bed, after a dinner where Mum prompted
me to repeat all the same stories for Dad, feeling I'd
found a friend that I didn't know I'd lost.

Chapter 27

My journey home on the coach was enlivened by the text conversation I shared with Marcus. Mum had dropped me at the coach station in Leeds at ten that morning, laden down with an additional huge bag which contained two bulging stockings for Christelle and I and various Christmas treats including a Lindt Santa, mini Christmas Pud and mini Christmas cake each and a selection of Christmas decorations which apparently hadn't made it onto the home tree.

As I boarded the bus, turning to wave back at Mum who wore a big smile on her face, I realised I felt happier than I had for a long time. Setting into a window seat, I made sure I could still see her and waved.

She waited until the bus fired up its engine, the roar rattling through the seats and diesel fumes permeating down the aisle. We waved cheerfully as the bus lumbered out of the station heading towards the M1.

Reflecting on the weekend gave my conscience a sharp

jab. Time for a little honesty of my own. Felix and I needed to do some talking.

Time I faced up to things. It was over and had been for a long time. I realised now that Felix and I had been play acting about the wedding. No wonder we hadn't ever got around to doing anything about it.

At ten past ten my phone gave a strident beep.

Bored!

Marcus's text made me smile.

I'm on a coach, average age 103. You're bored????
Cat 5 cabling benefits?????
Sounds moderately interesting. (She lied)
What colour shoes are you wearing?
???
That's how bored I am.
Orange.
No one has orange shoes.
I do.
Really?
No not really.
What can you see out the window?
Motorway.
What book are you reading?

Ha! Latest Kathy Reichs … bought it yesterday. Your
fault you put it into my head.
Might borrow it from you.
You'll have a job it's on my Kindle.
We could swap Kindles.

Now that was an interesting thought. Swapping a
Kindle was akin to inviting someone into your house
to peruse your bookshelves, except I had public and
private bookshelves. On the Kindle, they were all one.

Long pause, prompted Marcus. *Illicit reading?*
Fifty Shades plus others.
Any good?
Not telling, you have to read it and come to your
own conclusions. Can't stand people making ill-
informed judgements based on what other people
say!
High horse. I like it.

The text marathon lasted until Watford Gap, when
Marcus announced that the battery on his fancy-does-
everything tablet phone was about to die.

See that's what fancy technology gets you! I crowed
back.

I didn't get a response.

The next hour passed slowly allowing the thoughts I'd rather have ignored to slowly rise to the surface.

Crossing the threshold almost knocked me flat, as reality hit with breath-stealing clarity. From the moment I stepped inside, it was as if everything came into sharp focus making me feel suddenly old beyond my years. I think they might have called it growing up.

My relationship with Felix was over. Sadness. Regret. Hollowness. None of them could alter the unshakeable realisation. We'd both be upset but he wasn't who I wanted to spend the rest of my life with. He wasn't right for me. Carrying on any longer would be unfair. I felt sick at the thought of having to sit down and tell him.

If I could I would have stayed on that coach for the return journey to Harrogate, except that would be running away again, not facing up to things and that was how I'd ended up in this mess in the first place.

Felix wouldn't be home for an hour or two, although he wasn't expecting me back until tomorrow. How would he take it? I knew he'd be upset. Now I'd made the decision I dreaded telling him. I just wanted it to be over. How long would it take us to untangle ourselves? We'd been together for five years. The flat was mine but I couldn't just throw him out. I didn't want to hurt him. Maybe we could stay friends. I laughed mirthlessly, that was a joke. We were more friends than anything else if the truth were told. I couldn't remember the last time we'd been intimate. Brotherly hugs, chaste pecks on the cheek or forehead were the sum total of our physical contact in recent months ... years. And no wonder I suspected he was having an affair.

The frequent nights away, the constant texts on his phone. Now the idea had seeded itself in my head, it felt obvious.

And I couldn't think about Marcus. Too soon. Too much. But that kiss haunted me along with the almost kiss at Chatsworth. The dizzying spell of his touch resonated even as I thought of it now.

As I walked towards the coat rack I stumbled, tripping over a pair of shoes. I stared down at them and froze. For a moment, it felt as if the world tilted from its axis, a kind of Dr Who moment where there was a rift in time or something. Even though my head was telling me something was wrong, I couldn't quite compute. Yellow mustard, crocodile-skin shag-me shoes.

Slowly I walked towards the bedroom, almost weighed down with an enormous sense of dread. That horrible sensation of knowing but you had to be sure.

Low voiced murmurs were coming from the room but still I pushed open the door.

They didn't notice me at first. Vince lay on his side smoothing back Felix's hair from his face, the gesture so tender it felt as if a hole had been torn in my gut. Felix lay on his back, smiling up at him, his hand stroking Vince's wrist. My stomach cramped at the overwhelming sense of togetherness of the two of them. Envy, jealousy and sadness balled together, a huge amorphous mass that sat on my lungs, making it almost impossible to suck in another breath.

I must have wheezed or something because suddenly Felix shot upright, clutching the sheet to his chest.

'Tilly!'

I couldn't move.

Vince moved more slowly, defiant and almost triumphant. He laid a hand on Felix's chest as if saying 'he's mine'.

Nausea rose in my throat and ignoring the beseeching desperate look on Felix's face, I wheeled and ran out of the room.

What a complete and utter idiot. How unbelievably stupid was I?

I'd always known Felix wasn't interested in other women. I winced at my stupid smug confidence. Suddenly Felix's recent absences, his anxiety to know where I was, when I'd be back, made an awful lot of sense.

I had to get out of there.

The lights in Jeanie's tiny terraced cottage were thankfully on as I walked up the narrow front garden to the front door. I couldn't quite remember the bus journey there, although I'd managed to miss the stop for her house and had to get off at the next one. Water dripped down my face, coiling down my curls and sliding down my neck. In my haste to escape I'd grabbed the most unsuitable coat, a velvet number which was now soaked through. As I stood there, my brain racing in circle after circle trying to get a foothold on sense, I knocked hard at the door, channelling some of my blistering sentiments.

Jeanie's face registered a rainbow of emotion, surprise, horror, shiftiness and then puzzlement.

'Tilly ... what ... oh my, come in. Come in.'

As I stumbled through the door, she was already peeling off my sodden coat.

'Sweetie, what's happened?'

I shook my head and started to laugh. 'I've been such an idiot! Felix ... he ...' I couldn't get the words out, a fresh gale of nervous laughter burst out again. 'He.'

Jeanie's face filled with consternation and confusion, as well it might, but suddenly I felt as if a huge weight had been lifted.

'Come on lovie, come inside.'

She led me into the lamp-lit lounge where sudden

warmth enveloped me, making me realise just how cold I was. Shaking my head, I sat down in the arm chair and then promptly burst into furious angry tears.

Eventually the storm quieted and I was able to breathe easily again.

'Sorry I'm getting everything all wet.'

'Don't be daft, the chair isn't made of sugar.' Her practical words were what I needed to hear. An anchor.

'Sorry to turn up out of the blue. You must think I'm mad.'

'It's fine.' Her body language as she half turned towards the sofa at the other side of the room made me realise there was someone else in there. I looked over and wanted to die of embarrassment.

'Hi.' Carlsten Kunde-Neimoth, the world's most famous tenor, gave me a half wave.

Jeanie gave me a half shrug and a 'what-can-you-do' type of smile.

My jaw dropped. 'Holy Moly May.' I pointed between the two of them. 'No!' My voice raised in wonderment. 'No!' My finger flicking backwards and forwards like a metronome. 'No! You two!'

Jeanie blushed brilliant scarlet, her hands lifted in agitated flutters.

'Wow! Didn't see that, at all. Jeanie! *You?* Seriously!'

Jeanie's mouth pursed tighter, until it resembled a turtle's backside. At that point I realised that maybe I ought to back off a bit, my surprise possibly bordering on rude.

'Sorry.' I straightened up. This was after all a super-star singer who commanded world-wide respect and my boss. Aw, hell both deserved a bit more...

'Gosh, this is a bit of a surprise. When did this ... all start?' I had a million other questions but didn't quite know where to begin. Jeanie shacking up with a man was a turn up but one of this stature ... I'd not seen it coming.

'Carl, why don't you go and rustle up some drinks?'

To my amazement, Mr Mega-Famous Opera Star got up and docilely trotted off to the kitchen, ducking his tall frame through the tiny doorway.

I stared at Jeanie.

'Long story ... but what about you? And don't use this as one of your usual ignore the things you don't want to talk about tactics.' She wagged a finger at me.

'I think you and Christelle are in flipping cahoots. She says that to me.'

'Because it's true.' She gave me a stern stare.

I shrugged. 'Sometimes it's easier that way.'

'Avoidance is all well and good but one day it bites you on the back.'

'Bottom,' I corrected automatically.

She raised one eyebrow. 'Your moods have been up and down like a meteorite. I'm not stupid you know.'

I smiled sadly. 'No, you're never that. That's me. I'm the stupid one.' I ducked my head into my hands. 'I've been so dumb.'

'Stop beating yourself up and tell me what's happened. I take it it's Felix and I'm guessing the silly bugger's not died or anything.'

'No!' I spat. I felt furious, but with myself. And jealous. Of what he had. It was so obvious and I'd been so blind. No, blind was too kind. I'd deceived myself. I'd known. How could I have not?

'Felix is gay.' I sounded disbelieving but from the look on Jeanie's face it wasn't exactly a revelation to her. 'You knew?'

'And you didn't.'

'Not ... really.'

She pulled a sceptical face. 'Really?'

Biting my lip, I tried to shy away from her piercing gaze.

'Tilly? Seriously? Never?'

'No,' my voice peaked into its highest octave, 'never.'

'Oh,' she sounded quite put out and puzzled. With a stretch, she extended her legs and gazed at a point on the other side of the room.

'Why ... did you?' I poked her to get her to look at me.

'Er, hello, yes. Given there are gay guys aplenty in our industry, my gaydar's well-tuned.' She lifted her shoulders. 'I just assumed he slid both ways and you were OK with it.'

My mouth dropped open. Whoa? Did I appear that liberal and bohemian? I didn't know whether to be flattered or appalled. Inside I was my parents' daughter in a lot of ways, where sex and morals were concerned conservative was my middle name.

I picked at my sleeve not wanting to look at her. 'But we were getting married,' I muttered, sounding petulant, not wanting to hear the facts. 'Why would he do that if he was … you know?' Now my brain felt full of cotton wool, so thick I couldn't wade through it.

'Because he's an idiot.' She was Boudicca in a warrior stance, her whole body language exuding belligerence. 'And you've both been sticking your head in the clouds.'

I started to object but she held up a hand. 'No, listen. Let's face it, you've been dragging your heels about organising the wedding. Most women are off trying on dresses faster than a mouse given a key to the cheese factory. Christ, when I got engaged, the very next day I was on the doorstep of Pronuptia an hour before it opened.' Her face was filled with disgust. 'Although, look how that turned out.'

I shrugged. 'That doesn't mean anything. We're a lot older than you were and it's different these days.'

'Tilly,' she drew out my name, adding a few syllables. 'Rubbish. Tell me that Felix's proposal wasn't a complete shock to you.'

I glared at her. 'OK, it wasn't what I was expecting when we went to West Wittering for the day.'

I thought back to the day he'd proposed. Running down the beach, larking about. It had been a glorious windy, sunny spring day and on a sudden whim we'd taken ourselves off to the coast in a hire car for the day. We'd eaten ice creams and paddled in the freezing cold water. A typical Felix day: spontaneous, fun, silly. I wanted to cry again at the memory. We'd been high on happiness that day. As he'd splashed me and then almost fallen over himself, dropping his socks in the water, he'd turned and tossed into the wind. 'Let's get married missus.'

We'd celebrated with fish and chips and a Fanta can ring pull ceremoniously slid onto my finger. Typically irreverent and silly, two friends having a lovely day together.

'Yes, it was,' I admitted, sighing, hating having to admit that she was right. 'It was a spur of the moment thing but that's what I liked. I mean like.' Jeanie simply raised her eyebrows at me. I gritted my teeth. 'Felix's spontaneity.'

'Honey, there's spontaneous and there's downright Walter Mitty. Felix falls into the latter category. I don't think you ever wanted to get married and I certainly don't think Felix does.'

'He did, once,' I persisted, suddenly wanting it to be true.

'The only person that wants to see Felix married is his mother.' Jeanie stared hard at me. 'It doesn't take a scientist to figure it out. They're both in denial. You said yourself she's desperate to organise a wedding. I wonder if she's not a bit *too* desperate.'

I sat for a minute, letting the truth sink in. Getting engaged had been a lifeline for both of us. I needed to replace the chasm left in my life from divorcing myself from my family and I could see it clearly now, he must have hoped I might fill the gap for his mother. Now it seemed so obvious. Hindsight is a wonderful thing.

'So,' asked ever pragmatic Jeanie, 'what happened today? Flamenco delicto?'

'Yes, I caught him in bed with ...' I couldn't do it. I couldn't tell her. It was bad enough that Felix was having an affair with another man but having an affair with one of my best friends. I couldn't bring myself to say Vince's name. His betrayal hurt. That sly look of triumph when he'd laid claim to Felix had stung.

He would expect me to tell Jeanie. Expect me to tell everyone to get their sympathy, thereby making him the victim.

And if I told Jeanie now, it would be out of spite.

I refused to stoop to that level. Vince would have to man up and be the one to tell people what he'd done.

Not me.

'I caught him in bed with another man.'

'Ouch ... I'm so sorry love ... but how do you feel?'

Her intent look made me smile. 'Relief.' I let out a half-laugh. 'Bizarre, isn't it? I should be heart-broken. Instead I'm angry with myself. That's the worst thing. I'm such an idiot. And then it's a relief because it explains so much. And ...' I couldn't tell her about my feelings for Marcus, they were still too new and precious to expose.

'Well you came to the right place.' Jeanie enfolded me in another uncharacteristic hug. 'We'll look after you.'

We talked quietly for another half hour as my emotions gradually subsided. Jeanie suggested I stay the night and worry about the practicalities in the morning.

'So now can I ask? How long's *this* been going on?'

Carlsten had obviously been diplomatically lurking on the other side of the door for some time because he chose that moment to come in with two glasses of steaming red wine, grinning from ear to ear.

'Gluwein for the ladies.' He handed one each to us before turning to Jeanie. 'Ah mein liebchen ... now the truth is out,' he teased, giving her an intimate look.

My mouth dropped. He was ... Women threw roses at his feet on stage, gorgeous celebrities partnered him on the red carpet and the paparazzi stalked him.

Now it all made sense and explained why there'd been no night off get-togethers recently.

'Seems a bit odd formally introducing you but, Tilly this is Carlsten, Carlsten this is my dear friend Tilly who you've seen before in the make-up room.'

'It is a pleasure to meet you properly. I've been feeling like Bluebeard in reverse, locked away, while she has her wicked way with me. Understandable.' He gave her a cheeky wink, 'she doesn't want to disappoint her other suitors.'

Jeanie choked on her wine.

'Understandable,' I said gravely. 'When there are legions of them.'

He nodded with a wicked grin. 'I was ready to fight them off.'

'Oh, stop it, you two.'

I could see she was blushing.

His superstar smile would have cheered me up but the affectionate beam that he surrounded Jeanie with lit a small glow of happiness in me. She deserved some happiness, lots of it. Her first marriage had been a miserable affair.

Clutching my lovely hot wine between my ice-cold fingers, I warmed through as I forced myself to listen to Carlsten's self-deprecating tale of how he'd finally sweet-talked Jeanie into agreeing to overlook the unfortunate accident of his birth, him being one of the male species, and risk going out with him for a drink. ('Not a date', she reminded him sternly, as he recounted that part of the story.)

'He wore me down,' said Jeanie with a sigh but the contented look in her eyes told otherwise.

'I wooed you,' twinkled Carlsten.

'Blackmailed me.' She shot him a reproachful look tinged with a touch of pride. 'We were in the wings. He,' she hissed dramatically, 'was supposed to be on stage and he whispered in my ear that he wouldn't go on unless I agreed to go for a liqueur after the performance that night.'

Carlsten chuckled. 'You should have seen her face. The curtain was starting to rise and still she was arguing with me.'

There was a tiny curve to Jeanie's pursed lips. 'I blame my downfall on Tia Maria. The man managed to pour three of them down my neck.' They shared a look.

The warmth of their affection touched me. Jeanie deserved to be happy. For all her cynicism, life was for sharing and I could see their contentment in each other's company.

'Well ladies, I have cooked a beautiful beef stroganoff. Tilly, you will join us.'

'Of course she will,' announced Jeanie before giving me an assessing look. 'You need to get dried off. I'll find you some things.'

'I've got my overnight bag ... I'd just come back from Harrogate, walked in the flat and then came straight back out. No clean knickers though.' Not that I cared.

Jeanie grinned. 'Typical, so you brought your washing with you. Go and have a hot bath. When you come down we'll eat. And then you can help us dress the Christmas tree.' She pointed to the fir tree propped against the wall.

A punch of sadness hit. I still hadn't got a tree. Now, I wasn't sure I'd even bother.

'I'm so–'

'Don't say another word. It's fine. You're always welcome. You know that. Now get your arse into gear. Dinner will be ready in half an hour and I tell you, lovely as he is, Carl gets cranky when his food has to wait and he cooks nearly as well as he sings.'

I couldn't resist teasing her. 'Good at anything else?'

'Never you mind young lady.'

Chapter 28

A wave of grief punched into me at the sight of the framed photo of me, Vince and Felix on the shelf in my cubby hole. The horrible dark sensation threatened to overwhelm me as I stared at the picture. All three of us beaming into the flash light, our arms around each other. I pulled it down from the shelf and held it in my hands. Felix, the tallest in the middle, his handsome features lit up with his usual vivacious smile. The life and soul of the party as always. Shiny-eyed and full of life, we looked as if we might burst out the print at any moment. We'd been to see some stand-up comedy in Leicester Square and as we stumbled out after closing time the shot had been snapped by a paparazzi waiting to snap some minor celebrity.

I stared at the picture. Now I could see it. The unwanted third on the end. *Me.*

With a twist of my mouth I chucked the picture in the bin.

It would have been easy to brood and pick over things but I still had the meeting with Alison Kreufeld looming.

Suddenly straightening, I slapped the desk. I was going to nail that job. In the next ten days, I was going to show AK that I was the best freaking make-up artist on the planet and the high priestess of stock control. No more Miss flaky pants with all the delaying tactics. I was going to apply myself with the tenacity of super glue and get every product we used onto the system, down to the last eyelash filament, cotton bud and light bulb. OK, maybe not light bulbs, they were the facilities department's responsibility. I'd also go the extra mile and create a full catalogue of all the wigs we had in storage. That would impress her. There would not be a single excuse for Alison Kreufeld not to give me the job. It was mine.

Thankfully, Vince had phoned in sick but despite burying myself in my job and impressing the hell out of myself by creating a half-decent spreadsheet to list all the wigs we had, the day dragged and when it finally came to going home, Jeanie had to force me to leave.

'Come on lovie.' She stood over me. 'You're always welcome at mine, but you have to speak to Felix. If you don't you'll keep putting it off and you're just going to be in this limbo. As soon as you've talked to him, you can start making decisions and sorting things out. It will make you feel a lot better.'

'I know,' I said, rolling my shoulders trying to alleviate the pinched muscles nipping at my neck as I finally pulled on my coat and switched off the desk lamp in my cubby hole.

The damp, drizzly walk home from the tube, instead of getting a bus, suited my mood perfectly. I think it might even have been trying to snow again, but the pathetic sleety attempt wasn't going to stick. I stood outside the flat for a few minutes, looking up at the light shining from the bedroom window. Felix was home. I dug in my bag for my key and headed up the stairs, my legs heavy as I took each reluctant step. The echo of my footsteps felt like portents of doom as I got closer to the front door.

I paused in the doorway of the bedroom, the last place I had wanted to confront him and waited. I wanted him to be the first to speak.

Felix turned slowly and it came as a shock to see that he looked perfectly normal. In my mind, I'd built him up to some fiend. No. Still Felix, although he seemed to have shrunk inwards. The bounce and exuberance of the jumpy Labrador puppy had gone. Instead it had been replaced by the weariness of a droopy old blood hound. Unhappiness was etched across his whole face from the dullness of his eyes through to the downward lines pulling at his mouth.

'Sorry Tilly,' he whispered.

I was transfixed by the tear that rolled down his face. He sank onto the bed and put his head in his hands, a picture of such abject misery that all the hate I thought I had evaporated. I had loved him.

I went and sat down next to him, thigh to thigh.

The air around us felt permeated with sadness, dampening the fury that had initially buoyed me up.

'You're wet.'

'Yes. It's raining. I walked home.' Anything to delay getting back.

'I'm sorry.'

'You already said that. I want to hate you.' As soon as I said the words I regretted the ugliness of them. Felix wasn't mean or malicious. He was Felix.

'Tilly. I didn't mean to ... it just.' His broken words were hoarse as his face crumpled. 'I never. I didn't mean to. I love you,' he turned his head to face me and I could see the pain etched in the shadows under his eyes, 'just not ... not ... I thought we could make a go of it. Then I met ...' I held up my hand. I didn't want him to say Vince's name. 'I love him.' He gave a breathless sob, tears running down his face. 'Honest to God. I tried not to. I kept breaking it off with him.'

I put my arm around his shaking shoulders and we sat in silence for a few minutes as I stared around the room. The skirting boards were thick with dust, the wardrobe had its plinth missing and the wall had a streak of coffee running down it. The neglect echoed our relationship; I'd done too little to address the flaws I knew had been there.

When Felix's sobs slowed, I spoke. 'I don't understand. Why pretend with me that you were ...'

'I wanted to be ... like Kev ... like the others ... and you ... you were so nice.'

'Nice!' I flinched. That hurt. Nice. 'Thanks.'

'You were lovely. Honestly. I mean, you always saw good in me. We were the mojito team. You always made me feel that I could be better than I was. I thought we'd be OK but then it just got harder and harder. I'd see ... other men and wonder. Vince knew. He knew the first time you introduced us. He kept on. That I wasn't being true to myself. That I was wrong not to embrace what I was. I didn't know then that he fancied me. Then we, when you weren't ... we couldn't help ourselves.' Felix coloured but his eyes lit up as if reliving the memory.

I came close to snapping, 'Of course you could,' but I held off. Maybe it was because I could remember so clearly the magical zing of attraction when I'd first seen Marcus, the excitement and pure sexual fizz – but it didn't mean you had to go and bloody act upon it.

I hadn't sneaked around behind anyone's back.

'How long's it been going on?' I asked, my voice dull

and heavy.

'We went out one night, ages ago,' he drew in a shuddery breath. 'I knew but I didn't do anything about it. Not for a long time. I promise.'

I raised an eyebrow.

'The first time we met up, we just kissed that time.' He shrugged as if the detail were immaterial. 'Then we agreed not to see each other again.' He put his head in his hands. 'It was so hard. I did try. But a few weeks ago, he came down to the hotel when I was away.'

I felt the mattress dip as he lifted his head.

'It was supposed to be … just the once. I'd never … I needed to know …' Sadness haunted every line of his face. I reached out and touched his hand and he folded his fingers around mine.

His mouth crumpled and his chin quivered. 'After that, he wouldn't leave me alone. Wouldn't let me finish it. I tried but it was too difficult.' Felix swallowed hard, his eyes glassy.

'I love him.' The simple unadorned words, devoid of his usual bounce and hyperbole, punched a hole in my heart.

'Really, really love him. And I … I've been living a lie all this time, pretending. And I'm sorry I pretended with you when you're …' A tear slipped down his face. 'My best friend.' He squeezed my hand back. 'You shouldn't be nice to me.' He hiccoughed back a sob and sucked in a breath.

'No, I shouldn't,' I said with a sad smile, looking at his familiar face. He lifted a hand and stroked away one of my tears.

'I'm sorry Tilly.'

We sat in silence as I tried to absorb what he'd been through. Seeing him like this almost made it easier somehow. It was sad for both of us.

'Have there been others ... other men?' It felt weird saying that.

'No. No. I told you ... he was ...' A dreamy smile lit his face. Jealousy, envy, mortification all warred to take the lead among my churning emotions. 'He was my first.'

He turned to me. 'I never meant ... that's a line from a song isn't it. I never meant to hurt you ...'

He dropped his head in his hands again. 'It's a mess, isn't it?'

I stood up slowly and turned to look at him.

'I need a drink.' Heading straight to the kitchen, I grabbed a beer from the fridge. He followed and by mutual assent we both sat at the kitchen table.

'So, what now?' I asked.

He shrugged. 'I guess you want me to move out.' My heart twisted. It seemed so final and abrupt.

I looked at his half-hopeful face.

'Or I could move into the spare room.'

'Seriously?' I felt numb, with no idea what was for the best. It seemed the wrong time to be making big decisions. 'I don't know Felix. I can't sleep in our ... that bed again.'

'Please Tilly. I don't want us to part like this. I still ... I love you. Just not the way you ...'

I held up a hand and sighed. 'Don't. Things haven't been right for a while.'

We exchanged resigned, sad smiles.

'You can stay ... but I'll go in the spare room. For the time being. But he can't come around here.'

Felix nodded. 'Fair enough.'

'What the hell are we going to tell your mother?'

He ducked his head into his hands and shuddered.

Chapter 29

Vince still hadn't turned up to work but the following day as I determinedly headed down to the basement store room, I swallowed. I'd been down here for a couple hours and my throat was dry and dusty. Very dry. I needed a coffee and it would be much quicker to scrounge one from the IT department than go all the way to the canteen.

Who was I kidding? I was desperate for an excuse to see him.

'Hello.' Marcus looked up from the innards of a computer he was working on. 'What brings you down here?' He glanced at my hands. 'No thumbscrews either.'

'I'm guessing stand-up comedian doesn't feature on your CV.'

'Ouch, I'm hurt.' His eyes crinkled with devilment. 'Do you know your face is covered in grey stuff?'

I rubbed it quickly. 'I've been rummaging through the basement cataloguing wigs. Thanks to you, I'm probably going to go down with some nasty disease of the lungs from inhaling all the dust. It's all your fault.'

'How d'you figure that?'

'Your bloomin' brilliant idea to catalogue everything that moves.'

'Ah.'

'Although, I've found a couple of wigs we can re-use, which will help Jeanie's budget. She's delighted.'

He raised an eyebrow, which made me glare at him.

'Are you going to say, told you so.'

'I wouldn't dare.' He gave me an easy grin.

'I also came to ask if you wanted to borrow the Kathy Reichs book, I finished it on the coach on the way back. Once you stopped with the texts.'

'Just keeping your technological skills up to date, although with that brick sending a text must be like inscribing a stone tablet.'

'Hello, whose battery on their brick outlasted your new-fangled touch screen?'

'That's because I've got all sorts of interesting apps running in the background which eat at the battery life. Like email.'

'Well now I know it's you, you don't have to email. You can text me.'

'Or I could WhatsApp? Tweet? Instagram?'

'Ha!' I said with the flourish of a musketeer outwitting a foe, 'but as a phone doesn't work without the battery, none of those are any good, so I'd say mine on the technological front is far superior. It does all the things it should and has battery left over.'

I folded my arms in triumph. 'Don't suppose you could spare me a coffee?'

'Ah, so that's why you're here.'

Did I imagine the quick look of disappointment as he disappeared before coming back with two mugs? I sniffed. It smelt divine.

'Would you consider doing deliveries to the top floor?'

'No,' he laughed, 'because I know exactly where you put your coffee.'

'You do?' From his reaction, it was unlikely, he seemed far too laid back and even a tad amused.

'Yes, Fred told me.'

'Told you what?' No, still too laid back.

'Just because the CD rom drawer might be just the right size for a large Costa cup, it doesn't mean you have to use it that way.'

My face fell. 'Bugger! What a traitor. I thought Fred was on my side.'

'I'm sure there's plenty more he omitted. So how are things after your trip home?'

'Ah.' He'd provided the perfect opportunity to tell him about Felix but for some reason I hesitated. Would he repeat his offer of a drink?

'You haven't fallen out with your mum already, have you? Not after all my prime advice.'

I laughed along with his teasing. A welcome release of tension. 'I thought you meant with Felix.'

'Oh.' Suddenly the inside of the computer seemed terribly fascinating.

'He *is* having an affair.' The words popped out terribly matter of fact.

Marcus's head popped up, shock on his face quickly followed by concern.

'It was only when you suggested it, I even considered it. And now everyone keeps asking me "didn't I know?". Why does everyone ask that? Should I have done?' My words tumbled out full of bitterness. 'Or is it a subliminal thing, everyone assumes you must have known but you were in denial.'

'Whoa.' He held up both hands as if trying to stop the runaway freight train of admission. Now I'd started though I couldn't seem to stop talking.

'Yes,' I said with a note of despair. 'Not only an affair. But. With. Another. Man.'

Marcus's eyebrows shot up.

'Yes, that's right. A man.' My words continued, staccato-like bullets firing into gravel, spitting up with venom. 'What a mug? How stupid am I?' I pulled a face.

Marcus sat back. 'And you didn't know?'

'No,' I wailed. 'Although everyone else seems to think it was obvious. Why would I be engaged to him if I knew?'

'Fair point.'

'Except Jeanie seemed to assume I did know and was cool with it.'

'Some people are.'

'And some people aren't!' I glared at him and then slumped in my seat.

'And you had no idea ... I mean.' He winced. 'Sorry.'

'If I had, I wouldn't have spent a small fortune on push up bras, sensual bath oils and new lighting.'

Marcus seemed to be trying to hide his amusement but he wasn't doing a very good job, the dimple in his right cheek was a dead giveaway.

'Don't you dare laugh,' I warned him. 'It's so embarrassing ... trying to seduce your own boyfriend.' I groaned at the memories. 'Dance of the seven veils. Revealing cleavage. No wonder he was never interested. You're going to laugh ... I can tell.'

He swallowed. 'I'm trying hard ... I'm sorry ...' he sniggered. 'It's ... just ... you are ... well it's hard to imagine any man turning you down.'

'Well Felix managed,' I said with a sulky pout, folding my arms even though his words gave me a definite frisson.

And then we both burst out laughing at the ridiculousness of it.

'It's not funny,' I said, trying to catch my breath before going off into another peal of giggles. 'It's embarrassing.'

'What happens now?'

I puffed out my cheeks and slowly let the air out. 'I've let him stay. I feel so stupid but I can't throw him out. It's kind of my own fault for never seeing it. And the worst thing is, it *is* my own fault. I can see it so clearly now. I've been such an idiot. Really immature. Blaming everyone else for stuff.'

'I have to say you're a nicer person than most.'

I shrugged. 'We've been friends for so long.' I shook my head. 'I just feel so dumb.' At least it made me angry. 'And ugly.'

'Ugly?' He sounded astounded.

'Inside ... all cross, resentful ... nasty.' My hands clenched in and out. 'I hate it,' I burst out.

He stared intently at me. 'You are most definitely not ugly, inside or out.'

The air buzzed with undercurrents and yet we were both so still, focused on each other as if there was an invisible thread between us, drawing us in. When I took a step forward he was already doing the same and we met half way, to stand for a full thirty seconds just looking at each other. Excitement and anticipation fizzed, as if I were perched on the edge of something momentous. Slowly we moved into the kiss, inching forward as if to prolong a moment that I felt sure would be fixed in my memory forever.

Sometimes you just know something is right, even when things are in turmoil, you just know. The certainty clicked as soon as our mouths touched. We settled into a slow, thorough exploration, lips and tongues teasing with the tentative steps of a first dance.

Eventually I calmed and just stood in the circle of Marcus's arms enjoying the warmth of his chest through the fine cotton of his shirt. He smelt delicious and I could feel the steady beat, the beat of his heart under my cheek. His arms around my back held me fast and I wanted to stay there for ever. Nothing untoward could happen while I stood here. Marcus was as safe and steady as a lighthouse beaming out to sea. A safe harbour. Bizarrely, the very thing I'd fought so hard against.

His chin rested on top of my head, reminding me of the comfort he'd offered when we were at Chatsworth. Only this time I gave into the temptation to nuzzle in the smooth, musky scented skin of his neck. As I did, his hold tightened for a second as if he were trying to do the right thing and then with a groan, his lips found mine again.

It was a soothing kiss, restrained but with the promise of more.

He pulled back and stroked my cheekbone.

'Sorry, maybe I shouldn't have done that, it's not exactly great timing but ...' he gave me a very direct look, '*I* find you very attractive.'

That look hit the spot and my knees wobbled as my heart jumped with an extra beat.

I opened my mouth but nothing came out. My cheeks had fired up with a distinct blush, I could feel the redness seeping along the cheekbones.

'Cliché, but when you finish, would you like to go get a drink, a meal?'

'I'd love that.' I gave him a very grateful and slightly shy smile. 'This looks rubbish though doesn't it? The fiancé isn't even cold in his grave ... or whatever.'

Marcus put his head to one side. 'Tilly, I couldn't give a stuff about him. From the minute you backed out from under the table flashing those delectable pert cheeks of yours, in the flimsiest pants I've ever seen, and I have it on very good authority that you have a fine selection, which has further fuelled the very inappropriate thoughts about how I might punish you next time you have a computer mishap.'

'Oh,' I squeaked, surprised by the sudden widening of his pupils.

'Come on, the chemistry has been building for a while.'

'I-I wasn't sure you'd noticed. I thought it was just

me feeling ...' I stopped talking quickly.

'I was trying to keep my distance because I knew you were engaged.' With a naughty grin, he added, 'Sorry but all bets are off now.'

'Right.' Suddenly I felt rather breathless and flustered, the sardonic twist of his mouth suggesting he had something in mind. I wasn't used to being chased.

'That's us corporate marauders I'm afraid. We don't waste time, we go straight in after what we want.' Lowering his voice, his eyes darkened and I felt a frisson of desire. It had been one heck of a long time since someone had me feel all woman but he was doing quite nicely.

'What time do you finish?'

'About six, where shall I meet you?'

'Why don't I come and collect you, I've got to go and see the ladies in the costume department.' He gave a heavy sigh.

I grinned happily. 'What've they done? Surely nothing worse than me?'

'No one else is as bad as you.'

When I got back to the department, no one seemed to have noticed how long I'd been gone. I decided to type up the notes I'd taken down in the storeroom. To be honest I wanted to hug the secret of the blossoming feelings for Marcus to myself, and savour the early excitement and that tentative fizz of sexual attraction and the delicious feeling of being wanted and desired.

Once I'd managed to update the Excel spreadsheet, feeling rather pleased that I had managed without messing it up, I popped into Jeanie's office.

'You OK?' she asked.

'Yeah. I'm getting there.'

The clock ticked with stubborn slowness all afternoon, but I diligently tapped away at the computer.

By the time Marcus appeared most of the department had drifted out into the early evening gloom and I had input every item into the new system.

'Sorry, that took longer than I expected,' he said.

'See, I'm not the worst.'

'It's an extremely close competition; I wouldn't feel too confident if I were you.'

His smile robbed the words of any offence.

'You ready?' he asked.

'Yes, and I've got news.'

'What's that?'

I left the cubby hole and crossed the room to the row of pegs where I kept my coat, smiling to myself as I imagined his reaction when I told him I'd finished the project and nearly finished cataloguing the wigs.

As I shrugged into my coat, I saw Marcus lean down under my work station.

'What's Vince done to upset you?' he asked, pulling the picture of me, Felix and Vince out of my bin.

'Both of them,' I said taking the picture out of his hands. 'Felix.'

I stabbed my finger at Felix in the middle of the picture.

'That's Felix?' His voice pitched at the end.

I felt a chill, not so much at the tone of puzzlement in his voice but his sudden absolute stillness. It was as if he were frightened to move a muscle in case it brought everything around him crashing down.

He followed my finger with his, tracing a line bisecting the picture where Felix stood between me and Vince.

'Oh God. You know, don't you?' For a minute, there was a rushing in my ears and I could barely focus.

The acute anguish on Marcus's face told me everything I needed to know.

I peered around even though I knew everyone else had either left for the day or gone down to the make-up room.

'The man Felix is having an affair with is Vince,' I hissed in a fierce whisper. 'You mustn't tell anyone.'

'But ...' An anguished expression flashed across his face. 'I saw them.'

I closed my eyes, tensing in sudden understanding. 'When?'

He grimaced. 'The night after the gala performance.

There were a few of us outside the stage door. Philippe, Guillaume, Leonie. Vince came out of the theatre and ran straight over. I ...' Marcus's shoulders hunched. 'I remember because it was such a passionate kiss in full view. And no one else said anything but there was an odd atmosphere, but I didn't think too much of it.'

'Oh God, they all know.' I bent over, clutching my stomach as the physical pain of betrayal sliced deep, followed by a sense of utter mortification. It explained Leonie's recent coolness towards Vince and Philippe's concern that night. 'I need a drink.'

Wariness crossed Marcus's face. He probably wasn't sure what to do with an emotional female. He was well to be wary. I needed a very large drink.

I didn't give him much choice to do anything. Grabbing my coat and like a destroyer on course for its mission, I ploughed past him, warrior queen hell bent on drowning my sorrows and dragged him straight to the Marquis of Anglesey.

Chapter 30

'I'm going to ssshhtab him in the eye ... no, both eyes. Rip his balls off ... shorry.'

Marcus winced. 'Pin them up on the top of the roof thingummy ... and tha's just Felix and jest for starters. I'm gonna burn all his suits ... and ties ... and shoes and CDs. One big bonfire ... in the road 'cos we don't have a garden.' I reared up from my slumped position and pointed a wobbly finger at Marcus. He'd scrunched his forehead up in worry. 'You shink I'm pissed, doncha?' My head seemed to have decided it belonged to a Thunderbird puppet, wobbling dangerously as I worked hard to keep it upright. Gravity had other ideas.

I tried hard to think what the point I was making was? It had gone.

'You shink I'm talking bollocks, doncha?' I nodded sagely. 'I'm talking bollocks.' I picked up my newly replenished wine glass which wavered unnervingly, the light refracting from the glass like the warning signal of a lighthouse. Far too late. 'More wine, vicar?' I toasted Marcus, who clearly regretted getting me a fourth glass. 'My round nexsht time.'

I tried to smile winsomely at him which is pretty difficult to do when all the muscles in your face seem to have gone on their own side trip. He had that don't-you-think-you've-had-enough look on his face.

'Even when you're looking all disapprovy and superior, you've got a *very* lovely face. You know that? *Lovely* eyes. Those Slavic cheekbones. Bet all the girls in that banky place you worked before ... geddit, banky wanky place, bet they all fancied you, didn't they? You're alright ... when you're not being a stiff. You're looking all disapproving.' I giggled. 'I said that already, didn't I?'

'You did Tilly.'

'I did, didn't I?' I took another heady slurp of wine. 'Bloody lovely.' My head span. Shit, I needed to get a grip. Act sober. I sat up straight and focused on his face. Bloody hell, his eyes were gorgeous.

'D'you know? You've got bloody lovely eyes.'

'You said that earlier.' Was he taking the piss?

'Did I?'

'Yes.' He was being all amenable and patronising.

I waved my hands in frantic denial. 'I mean they're very handsome ... on a purely observatory level. Not that it means I fanshy you or anything. I'm just obser-vating.' I tried to focus on his face. 'No, don't fanshy you at all. Not my type ...' As I said it I felt myself crumple. I gave a mocking, self-effacing, mirthless laugh. 'My type. Ha! Tha's funny, isn't it. My type. Blokes who fancy other blokes ... not me. I bet you don't even fancy me, do you?'

He was laughing at me now, not even trying to hide it.

'Donchoo laugh at me.' I stabbed a belligerent finger his way except it missed and I ended up stabbing the upholstered bench seat behind him.

He grabbed my hand and kissed the palm, his eyes dancing with amusement. 'You've got a very short memory.'

'You think you're soooo smooth, donchooo.' My head seemed really heavy. I remembered the earlier kiss. 'Smooth and a good kisser. Excepshhhhunally good kisser. D'you kiss all the girls like that? You're good. Really good.' I narrowed my gaze at him. 'Loads of practice probly.'

He grinned. 'I am smooth and you are completely plastered.'

I tried to call on all my dignity. I might have been a slightly bit tipsy but I wasn't so bad. Not really, although the room had taken on a slightly odd angle. I closed my eyes for a second. No! Whoa! That was much worse. I opened them again, which was hard work and focused on Marcus's face. Except it kept swimming in and out of focus. How did he do that? Cool trick.

'D'you do that ...' It was like being in a goldfish bowel ... even bowl, except goldfish weren't that good looking. He seriously was fit. 'How d'you ...' I squinted but his face kept moving, his lips here and then gone. The more I stared at them, the more I wanted to kiss them. They were bloody lovely. Who knew that lips could look so lovely and be sooo magnetic? I could feel the pull towards them, or maybe that was just me. My head drooped and I had to haul it up again. Yup the lips still looked lush. The eyes, green still, yup they looked sort of...

Oh, hell my eyes had closed again and my head felt very wobbly.

'Tilly?'

'Mmmm.' My eyes didn't want to play anymore. Shame 'cos he was a sight for ... for eyes.

'Tilly?'

The room had started spinning and his face was withdrawing down a tunnel but boy he smelled yummy. I sniffed and discovered I was nose to neck. Warm gorgeous smelling skin.

I kissed that lovely slightly bristled skin, just under that strong firm chin. Delicious. I put the tip of my tongue out to taste. Saltiness. Bristles. Inhaled deeply as I felt his arms go around me.

'Tilly.' I could feel him trying to hold me up and

everything was like spaghetti. 'Tilly, you can't be this much of a lightweight. You've only had four glasses of wine. You can't be this,' he paused and I felt his hold tighten, 'this drunk.'

I blinked at him. 'Drunk? Me? Nooo.' I blinked again. 'Maybe. As a skunk.' With a smile, I sank into his arms. He was bloody lovely.

'Come on, Tilly.' Marcus's voice had that dinner lady tone. Authoritative but kind.

I fought my way into my coat, which suddenly felt as if I was trying to dress an octopus. How come I had so many arms? How come they didn't work so well?

He wrapped my silk scarf around my neck, one time too many instead of looping through itself to look nice and attempted to pull me to my feet.

'Did I finishsh my drink?' I asked, trying to go back to the table.

'No, but you've had enough.'

'Only two,' I said in a very Joyce Grenfell voice, waving the appropriate number of fingers at him. 'Only two. Only two. Only two.' My pitch got higher and louder with each repetition. It sounded rather sing songy and nice. To add to it I did a little wiggly dance which ended badly because I barged into a table slopping pints everywhere.

'Oops sorry.' I gave the three chaps at the table a wide smile and a little wave.

Marcus wrapped an arm around me and guided me to the door. I don't know why he thought he needed to, I was just fine.

As we stepped out of the pub slap bang onto the busy pavement, I paused, halted by the kaleidoscope of colours, smells and sounds, there was nowhere quite like Covent Garden on a crisp winter's evening. Tourists bustled past. Black cabs rumbled by. Everywhere there was life and energy. It was all rather jolly. I smiled up into Marcus's face. He had that indulgent, patient look which quite frankly I didn't expect at all from a go getter, jet-setter like him. Was he a jet-setter? Maybe I got that bit wrong?

'Do you go far in a jet?' I asked. The words weren't quite right but I couldn't figure out why not.

'What?'

'Jest tetting? Do you?' I swayed on the spot. I grabbed his arm for extra support. 'Whoa who moved the pavement?'

Hanging on to me with one arm, I watched as he hailed a cab. Despite there being lots of other people around us trying to do the same, the cab stopped for him.

'You're a dark lord, aren't you?'

'What?' Even perplexed, he had a sexy look on his face. Lovely shaped eyebrows over those green eyes.

'Or is that lord of dark arts? Summoning cabs out

of the darkness? Am I in cahoots with the devil?'

'Tilly. Shut up.' Despite the words, they were said gently and punctuated with a small kiss on the top of my head as he pulled me against him and for a moment I relished the smell and feel of him, the steady rise and fall of his chest. Dark arts lord or not, I felt very safe and comfortable and then suddenly I felt myself slipping through his arms, the blackness of drunken oblivion calling.

Chapter 31

Someone had opened a mine shaft in my head, little hammers tap tapping away with reverberating frequency. Why had I still not learnt my lesson? Vodka, gin, even red wine, I can knock back with reckless abandon but I knew what white wine did to me.

What a bloody mess. Everyone at work knew. And I'd let Felix stay. They would think I was an idiot.

I turned to nestle into the mattress, back into sleep but no such luck, it felt hard and unyielding, not like my nice soft mattress at home. Alarm bells rang. Not my bed. Oh shit. Definitely not my bed. Not my bedroom. Not my home.

A quick rattle through my memory files only produced a few vague facts. I'd left work with Marcus. I'd got slaughtered with Marcus. I left the pub with Marcus. I got in a cab with Marcus.

The horrible sick feeling twisting in my stomach wasn't anything to do with my hangover. Classy Tilly.

Really classy. I peeled open my tired, gritty eyes, blinking, and raised myself on my elbows. The room swam in and out of focus for a moment.

Purple hyacinth curtains, pine door opposite, the noisy rattle of the radiator and the gasping wheezy flush of the toilet right next door. I flopped back against the pillows. Thank God for that. Jeanie's spare room.

'Morning.' Jeanie's overly cheerful voice penetrated my doze. She stood beside the bed in a paisley dressing gown, her trademark red and pink hair almost standing on end as if she'd had a fright in the night and to my eternal gratitude, bearing a cup of tea in one hand and a fizzing glass of clear liquid in the other.

'Alka Seltzer, young lady.' She waited until I eased myself to a sitting position and shoved it into my hand. 'Drink.'

'Mean,' I croaked. She knew I hated the stuff and had taken advantage of my semi-conscious state but I forgave her because she'd brought piping hot tea. I welcomed the scald down my throat which chased away the hideous chalky slimy taste.

'Oh, lord,' I groaned.

'That's one way of putting it.' She perched on the bed. 'Do you remember anything about last night?'

'Sort of,' I hedged. There were an awful lot of black holes.

'That's a no then.' She knew me and my spotty memory. 'You were completely smashed when Marcus brought you back last night.'

I pushed tangled hair from my face. Oh dear God, yes. Marcus. It was all dribbling back in horrible Technicolor vividness.

'He seemed to find it quite amusing. Although that was probably because you kept telling me how handsome he was and what lovely green eyes he had.'

'Oh God, I didn't.'

'Oh God, you did.'

I dropped my head into my hands, mortification burning streaks across my cheeks.

'You didn't want him to go. Begged him to stay.' An amused smile hovered just short of a smirk around her lips.

I winced, remembering looping my arms around his neck and smiling stupidly at him.

I groaned. 'It's not funny. Did I make a complete dick of myself?'

'That's about the size of it.'

I took another scalding sip of tea. 'What must he think of me?'

'Actually, he was rather gentlemanly about it.'

I shot her a suspicious glance. She was being far too nice. Jeanie didn't do nice.

'What did he say?'

'Not much, just said you were very upset. He did mention that you were an exceptionally cheap date and that he'd never seen anyone get quite so drunk, quite so quickly.' She was laughing at me now. 'Clearly you didn't bother enchanting him about your little problem with white wine before he offered to buy you a drink.'

'Clearly,' I said, not the least bit amused by her obvious delight in my chagrin. 'I should have told you.' I gave a mirthless laugh. 'Everyone else knew. It's Vince.'

'Vince?'

'Him and Felix.'

'Vince!' Her outraged squawk as she leapt off the bed made me jump. 'Vince! The stupid, stupid, stupid …'

I tried to hold back the tell-tale hitch in my breath.

'Oh, my poor girl,' she said before adding in a vicious tone. 'The toad! Wait till I get my hands on him.'

'You and me both,' I sniffed with a half laugh.

'How could he? The conniving lying little shit. Bloody men. They're all the same.'

I smiled at her disgust. 'Even Carlsten.'

'He's still on his best behaviour. Prohibition. We'll see. But what are we going to do about you?'

'Probation,' I corrected automatically. At least some good had come out of all this. I'd nailed the new computer system in time for my meeting with Alison.

'I could sack the little git.' Her face told another story.

We both knew she didn't mean it.

'On what grounds? Is there a policy on nicking someone else's boyfriend?'

'I could find something.'

'Thanks Jeanie, I was worried about telling you.' Her hand closed over mine and we lapsed into silence.

'Hmm. We need breakfast. Bacon butties. I can't think on an empty stomach and you need food inside you, any paler and we'll be calling Ghostbusters. Get dressed. I'll see you in the kitchen.'

Jeanie's unconditional sympathy made me feel a lot better about going to work and facing Vince.

I told her the full sorry tale as we sat at her kitchen table, chomping on thick doorsteps of bread and slices of bacon glistening with grease.

Jeanie chewed ferociously on her butty as I told her who else knew.

'What's the plan? The N.O.'

'N.O.?'

'Nodus operandi ... surely you know that with all those detective books you read.'

'It's Latin and its modus operandi.'

'Are you sure?' Jeanie seemed unconvinced. 'If you say so.'

I gave up, there was no point arguing with her, besides we had more important things to discuss. 'I haven't got a blinking clue. Half of me wants to go in all guns blazing, rip the shit out of him and tell him I'm never ever, ever going to talk to him again. The other half wants to pretend there's nothing wrong.' My face crumpled. 'I just want everything to go back to how it was before.' I burst into tears. 'V-vince and F-felix.' I lay my head on the table.

'Aw, hon.' She stroked my arm. 'I don't know what to say.'

'I feel as if my whole world's been ripped apart. Everyone knew but me ... and you. They all must have thought I was such a berk. Why didn't anyone tell me?'

There was relative calm in the studio with only a couple of other people working quietly. And there at the other side of the room was Vince. He looked up as I walked in.

The room went very still and suddenly filled with quiet confident fury, I stalked over to him.

Vince froze, as wary as a gazelle scenting danger and ready to spring away at any second, as if he knew something very serious was afoot.

'Tilly ...' he held his hands out.

I stepped backwards, feeling sick but holding my head high.

Swallowing hard, his Adam's apple danced, as if he were trying to summon up the words. I could almost see him trying to work out his strategy. Choose the right words. To do what? Apologise? Explain?

A beseeching, pain-filled expression crossed his face. 'Tilly,' he appealed, his hands outstretched.

'Don't you dare,' I spat. 'Don't you make out you're the victim here.'

I had to get out of here. I couldn't bear it but as I turned and spotted my work area, and the half-finished wig, resolve appeared from nowhere. No walking out. No dramatic huffs. I had a job to do. A professional job. Personal life had to stay outside. I wouldn't lose what was important to me.

I forced myself to turn back to him and say in a quiet, calm voice, 'Vince. I'm very upset.' I lifted my chin, pulling on every last shred of dignity. 'I don't wish to discuss this at work.'

He pouted. 'Well everyone's sided with you. Philippe and Leonie are refusing to speak to me.'

'And you wonder why?' I asked quietly.

'I bet you've got Jeanie on your side, too.'

I shook my head. 'Grow up Vince. There are no sides. You should look to your own conscience. Friends don't do ... this to each other.'

Turning my back on him, I returned to my work area and picked up the Juliet wig. I wouldn't put it down or do anything else until I'd finished making the last ringlet. And I would not look up at Vince again, or at least until I'd done three.

The second ringlet in, I caught him in my peripheral vision tiptoeing into Jeanie's office. He wasn't tip-toeing but he might as well have been, from the furtive hunch of his shoulders and the slow circumnavigation of the room to get there. Through the glass windows I could see him talking with great agitation to her. Hands flying faster than a sign language interpreter.

A small part of me, the not very nice bit at all, was pleased to see that her face exhibited nothing but disgust. I couldn't tell what she said but from the cowed expression on his face and the speed at which he scurried back to his desk, he'd got short shrift.

I settled into a pattern and had completed the back of the wig when Jeanie swept out of the office, irritation wrinkling her forehead. The minute she'd gone, Vince scuttled out, clutching his mobile phone. No prizes for guessing who he was going to phone.

'I brought you this.' Like a benign genie, Marcus appeared and handed me a cup of coffee. I almost melted with gratitude as I inhaled the glorious smell.

'Oh, thank you,' I took it from him and wrapped both hands around the cup, savouring the heat. 'I think I love y–.' As soon as the words spilled out I wanted to pull them back, especially as I was looking him full in the face at the time.

His face softened, laughter lurking in his smile and then something else, a steadiness in his gaze, which had me stuttering for breath.

'You're not so bad yourself.' He sat down on the bench. 'How are you feeling this morning?'

'Not great.' I grimaced at him, luckily still feeling too rough to be too embarrassed about what I'd just said.

'How's the head?' His mouth quirked at one side but he managed to keep his expression grave. 'You went for it last night.'

'It's OK.' I winced. 'Sorry I should have warned you about the wine thing.'

'Yeah, what is that all about? I've heard of cheap dates but that was bargain basement.'

'It only happens with white wine,' I said with indignation. Yet another thing I'd never live down. He must have thought I was a complete nut job. 'My mum's the same. I normally never touch it.'

'Except when you want to get completely bladdered.'

'Mmm, not my greatest idea.'

Marcus smiled. 'I don't know, it had its compensations.'

I put my hands over my face. 'I don't remember a lot of it ...' And I certainly wasn't going to tell him the bits I did.

'It's alright. I can fill you in.' The half-amused smile on his face held a hint of challenge. 'Apparently, you think I'm gorgeous and I've got two really lovely eyes but you don't fancy me. So, that's OK then. Although you do think I'm an exceptionally good kisser.'

I choked on my coffee. Had I used the word 'fancy'? How old was I?

'Anyway, I'm glad we've cleared all that up, I wondered if you *did* fancy going to the match on Saturday. Arsenal, Liverpool. Three o'clock kick off at The Emirates. I've got two tickets.'

I couldn't decide whether to scowl at him or take it in good spirits. 'You're kidding.'

'Just a thought.'

'God I'd love to ... do you know I've ... you do, I told you before. Wow. That would be so fantastic.' Those tickets had to be like gold dust.

'Great. Maybe dinner afterwards.'

'Y-yes that would be ... that would be. Very good.' Tickets to see Arsenal and dinner. A date with Marcus. I wanted to bounce in my seat but I managed to contain myself as we made the arrangements to meet before he disappeared out of the door.

Woo hoo. Then I bounced up and down in my chair, with a quick spin thrown in for good measure. I let out a squeal, the make-up room was empty. Maybe not. My ears just registered the tell-tale squeak of the door. A shadow appeared on my desk, indicating someone was behind me.

'You're back aren't you?' I said.

''Fraid so. I just had one more thing to say.'

I kept my back to him, trying to be nonchalant.

'Just one more thing.' He leant down and brushed my neck with his lips, a whisper of a kiss and then said very softly. 'Just because you don't fancy me, doesn't mean I don't fancy you.'

By the time I'd summoned my wits to turn around, he'd gone, leaving my pulse doing the light fandango.

Chapter 32

'Football!' Jeanie shook her head with obvious disapproval and topped up my red wine. As she stretched out on her sofa, tipping her face towards the fire crackling in the fireplace, she added, 'I can't imagine anything worse.'

'Have you ever been?' I sat opposite her in what I'd come to think of as my chair, the little green velvet cushion nestled just in the small of my aching back.

'No.'

'So how do you know? You might enjoy it.'

She lowered her wine glass. 'I've never been eaten by a lion but I'm sure I wouldn't like that.'

'That is so random.'

'At this time of night, and after a day as long as today, it's all I've got.'

We were both knackered after a particularly gruelling shift. Vince hadn't turned up today, calling in sick again. Despite the extra workload, it had been a huge relief.

Well, to me anyway. Jeanie probably could have done without having to re-allocate the team to ensure that everyone got on stage on time.

I still harboured the urge to murder him. Funny that I could forgive Felix but not Vince. Yesterday the day had limped by, not helped by my hangover which helpfully turned into an all-day affair. A sleepless night had followed where my thoughts vacillated between hope and anticipation. They veered towards Marcus and depression and deep disappointment whenever I thought of Vince and Felix. Where my wildly fluctuating emotions were concerned, becoming a nun seemed an excellent life choice. I'd retreated to Jeanie's, unable to bear another confrontation with Felix or the confirmation that I was an even bigger mug by agreeing to let him stay. I ought to have asked him to leave but I didn't have the energy.

'What do you wear to a football match?'

'Clothes?'

'I meant you. Miss kitten heels.'

'Well ... obviously I won't wear them.' But what would I wear? The days of going to see Leeds United with my dad in a big woolly pom-pom hat and a stripy scarf in a Paddington duffle coat were long gone. 'I'm just hoping it won't snow. The forecast says it might next week.'

We lapsed into silence.

'You can borrow my North Face jacket. That'll keep you warm.'

I'd also look as puffed up as the Michelin man ... but then again there was a lot to be said for being warm. Marcus had seen me plenty of times before, my sensible side pointed out. The vain, altogether more-in-charge side of me pointed out, it was a first date. I owed it to myself to look my best.

'I wish you hadn't asked that question.' I grumbled, knowing I was about to face another sleepless night.

Wrapped up in a large moss green velvet scarf, Jeanie's North Face coat, dark green skinny jeans (fresh from H&M that morning), a pair of brogue lace up ankle boots, and an Arsenal beanie hat, I waited for Marcus to turn up, hoping that I looked suitably chic but not out of place in the football crowd. We'd arranged to meet on the junction of two streets, just around the corner from the stadium. Already the streets were thronging with good natured groups all heading to the game. I hopped up and down on the spot, as if I was cold but in truth I couldn't keep still. I hadn't been to a real game in years and I'd forgotten the atmosphere. The feeling of community as we all swarmed towards the ground. That indefinable sense of belonging. Sharing smiles and chatter with complete strangers who all had the same goal. The smell of beer and burgers.

Little kids skipping along beside their dads, in matching scarves and hats. The towering walls of the stadium, making you bristle with nerves like a nervous army about to storm the castle.

I caught sight of Marcus before he saw me and took the time to watch him as he strode my way. How was it possible that he looked even hotter than usual? The jeans helped. They definitely helped. A couple of girls gave him a second and third look and who could blame them. A black leather jacket emphasised his broad shoulders, narrowing down to highlight lean hips and those long legs. Definite eye candy. I couldn't help but smile, he was mouth-watering.

'Tilly.' He greeted me with a peck on the cheek. 'Looking forward to the game?'

I nodded, momentarily lost for words, as he smiled down at me. Perfect white teeth in a movie star grin. They needed to slap a health warning on him. This man will make your heart beat faster than is medically good for you.

'Should be a good one. I brought hankies for you.'

'Why, so I can mop up your tears when my boys trounce you?'

He nudged me in the ribs. 'Yeah right.'

Suddenly I stopped. No hat. No scarf. He could have been supporting anyone. It didn't bode well. 'Marcus?'

'Yes.' He sounded wary.

'Which end are we in?'

He laughed. 'You're OK. I've got a mate who's an Arsenal season ticket holder. We're at the home end. It's me that has to keep my gob shut.'

'That'll be a challenge then.'

We exchanged silly banter all the way into the grounds and up to our seats which were so high up I felt almost dizzy.

'It's as bad as Drury Lane, although there's a wee bit more leg room here.'

'Trust you to compare it to a theatre.'

'At least I don't call half time the interval!' I reminded him.

He laughed.

Flirty banter was the order of the day. There was no awkwardness between us, no shyness or being on best behaviour. It was a bit difficult to be shy around someone who was mercilessly rude about your favourite player, likening him to a donkey with three wooden legs, or muttering abuse about the keeper who took a couple of brilliant saves. We both disagreed with the ref's decisions, although not in tandem.

It felt good to be surrounded by all that straight forward, no nonsense, say it how you feel it testosterone. I remembered his early emails. Car chases. And smiled.

'What are you smirking about? It's still nil nil.'

'Nothing,' I said continuing to smile.

With a mischievous grin, he pulled off my hat, sending my hair spiralling all over the place. Whatever he planned to do or say never happened as it was one of those moments when everything stalled and we just stared at each other. 'I love your hair.' He stroked a section from my face and then used it to pull me gently towards him.

We were so absorbed in the kiss we barely registered the sudden roar of the crowd as around us everyone surged to their feet.

'I think someone might have scored and we missed it,' I finally murmured when I managed to come up for air, feeling dazed and very thoroughly kissed. A plastic cup bounced off Marcus's head and a voice jeered, 'Get a room.'

He tucked my hand into his and we sat more decorously for the rest of the match.

When the next goal was scored, I leapt to my feet, screaming along with the rest of the crowd. For obvious reasons Marcus didn't join in.

When we spilled out of the stadium as part of the happy, celebratory crowd, it was dark. A good-natured throng of people poured out all heading towards the tube station. I held Marcus's hand tightly in the crush.

'Come on.' He tugged me down a side street which was still busy but here there was room to walk along the pavement instead of on the road.

I was starting to feel chilled right through to the bone.

'You're looking a little blue around the edges.'

'My feet are frozen.'

'My place is only a ten-minute walk and I did promise you dinner.'

'Is that a man ten-minute walk or a real ten-minute walk?'

'What's the difference?'

'My dad's idea of a ten-minute walk is often a good half hour.'

'No, it's really only ten minutes.'

'Then lead on Macduff.' And I was nosy. I was dying to see what his place was like. I was guessing that it would be neat and organised, all shiny surfaces like his office at work. Probably not to my taste at all.

'Can I correct you there, it's actually "*Lay on Macduff*".'

'And you're loving that, aren't you?' Payback for all the grief I'd given him about not knowing about opera.

He grinned at me. 'Yes.'

He lived in a mansion block, which I wasn't expecting.

'I thought you'd live in one of those glass and steel jobs, testament to the god of all things contemporary,' I said as we went through a lovely old stained-glass door onto a black and white tiled floor and up a flight of stairs with beautiful wrought iron tracery and brass banisters.

'I thought about it, came close to buying a place in Canary Wharf ... but my parents live out in Watford.'

'You've got parents.' Stupid, of course he had parents. He squeezed my hand which he hadn't let go of, even when he opened the main front door downstairs. He had a sister too, he'd told me all about her on our trip up north.

'Yes, I see them every couple of weeks and it's only a forty-five-minute drive. Which is why I chose this place.'

We climbed a second flight of stairs before stopping outside his door.

'Come in.' He tugged me inside.

The warmth hit us. 'Bliss,' I said, taking off my beanie hat and shaking my hair free.

'Here, let me take your coat.' He peeled the coat from my shoulders and then while my arms were anchored to my sides, he paused and leant in for a kiss before pushing the coat down. Neither of us paid any attention as it dropped to the floor. His kisses were rapidly becoming addictive and like a pair of dancers we already seemed to know exactly how to slot together. His tongue teased my lips and I opened my mouth and felt all my senses flare as he deepened the kiss.

With a gentle beguiling thoroughness, he explored

my mouth, taking charge with a delicious authority. It had been so long since I'd felt wanted, that this thoroughly male attentiveness stirred desires that had been left untouched for quite a while. There was no doubt about it – Marcus was all man.

When he drew away I almost pulled him back again but his lazy smile promised so much, I felt a warm pang of feminine satisfaction. The heated glow in his eyes made me feel rather smug.

'You OK?'

'Just about.' I rubbed my lips and must have looked a little dazed. I blushed, had I really said that out loud? I wasn't used to the effect of his kisses. I felt a bit light headed and dreamy.

Lean hipped and long legged in well-fitting jeans, he seemed completely comfortable in his own space and those kisses full of simmering lust had lit a slow burn. At the same time, the proprietary kiss on the boundary of his territory made me feel as if he'd taken charge of me. I was the guest, here to be looked after. With sudden insight, I realised just how exhausting daily life with Felix had been. Always having to be the sensible one, making the financial decisions, making sure the bills were paid and the insurance sorted, it had been like looking after a child. Felix had no sense of responsibility for anything. At first it had felt great, no pressure to do the right thing but after a while it had palled.

God, he and Vince were going to be a disaster together.

'Can I get you a drink? White w ... no not white wine. Red? Can you drink red? Vodka? Gin? A beer?'

I grinned. 'I can drink anything just not white wine.' I followed him through the hallway from which several doors opened. He went into a surprisingly big kitchen with a centre island.

'Wow, this is nice. You could almost fit my whole flat in this kitchen.'

'Benefits of a City salary.'

Floor to ceiling glass-paned cabinets filled one wall, ranged on either side of a brick chimney breast in which sat a large stainless steel double oven with five gas burners.

'Have a seat while I get you a drink.' He nodded to one of two bar stools on the far side of the island.

'Thanks,' I hauled myself up onto one of them, leaning my elbows on the walnut wood top.

'I've got a nice bottle of Barolo.' From a single width rack, between the wall of kitchen units and the brick chimney breast, he pulled out a bottle.

'That would be lovely.' And it would; I knew very little about wine but Pietro loved a good Barolo and he could afford expensive wine.

'Good, I'm cooking Italian, so that will go down perfectly.'

'You're cooking?' I thought of Felix's idea of cooking.

Lots of mess, too much seasoning and vast quantities of pasta.

'Don't look so worried.'

I looked up and shook my head. 'I'm fine.'

'Don't worry; no one's ever died from my cooking.' He grinned. 'Well, not yet anyway.'

'You can cook then?' I asked responding to his teasing.

'They don't call me Jamie Oliver Walker for nothing. Wait till you've tried my pomodoro y prosciutto pasta.' He kissed his fingers and lapsed into an atrocious Italian accent.

'Sounds lovely ... what is it?'

'Bella pasta, mama mia, vino rosso. Oregano.'

In response, I said, '*Un bel di vedremo levarsi un fil di fumo sull'estremo confin del mare. E poi la nave appare.*'

His face fell. 'Are you fluent?'

With an insouciant shrug, I added, '*Come un mosca prigionera l'ali batte il piccolo cuor!*'

'One thing I've never mastered. A foreign language. I always feel a bit of a dick when I go to another country and before I've even attempted a word, they speak to you in perfect English.'

I turned away, squeezing my lips together.

'Say some more, it sounds ...' He raised his eyebrows signalling the rest of the sentence.

In a deliberately husky voice, I said. '*Che gelida manina! Se la rasci riscaldar. Cercar che giova? Al buio*

*non si trova. Ma per fortuna – e una notte di luna, e qui
la luna l'abbiamo vicina.'*

'So, what did you say ... or can't you tell me?' He
waggled his eyebrows with exaggerated lasciviousness.

I pretended to think about it for a moment and then
said with a completely straight face, 'Your tiny hand is
frozen! Let me warm it into life in mine. Why look
while the murky darkness lingers? But by good fortune
tonight the moon is bright and up here the moon is
our closest of neighbours.'

He swiped at me with a tea towel. 'Opera ... I presume.'

'You mean you didn't recognise it?' I giggled to myself.
'It's from your favourite,' I paused and raised my
eyebrows at him. *'La Bohème?'*

'Very funny.' He hooked the tea towel around the
back of my neck and pulled me in close for another
lingering kiss.

'I'm going to take you to see it one day.' Although
the words came out without thought, as soon as I said
them, his serious expression made my heart miss a beat.

'I'll hold you to that,' he said softly. 'I suspect I shall
be getting to know an awful lot more about opera. So,'
he relinquished me, turning back to open a bottle of
wine, 'do you speak Italian or just lyrics?'

'Just lyrics,' I laughed. 'Sorry, you hear it so often,
you start singing along. Obviously not in front of the
likes of Carlsten and Pietro and the English translation

is up on the screens for the audience. Me and Vince always used to ...' I faltered.

'I have to admit, I don't get it,' Marcus gave me a gentle smile, his unspoken sympathy making my heart jump. 'But I'm willing to give it a go. You can educate me.'

Sudden tears sprang to my eyes. It was possibly the nicest thing he could have offered to do.

'Tilly.' He put down the bottle. 'I'd forgotten about Vince and Felix.'

'No, it's not them. It's just so nice of you to want to learn about it.' I gave him a tremulous smile. 'To tell you the truth, I much prefer ballet. Music wise, opera wouldn't be my first choice. Too much of a bus man's holiday. I'd rather go and watch the Foo Fighters or the Imagine Dragons.'

'I remember ... Snow Patrol.'

We talked music and our favourite bands and I watched as he moved around the room with economic efficiency, pouring two glasses of red wine and handing me mine. With quiet grace, he pulled out onions, switched on a music system which filled the room with the Stereophonics and unselfconsciously chopped, fried and stirred without making any further conversation. I found it enormously soothing and a mark of his quiet confidence. Felix would have filled the silence with inane commentary, as if silence were some kind of failure. Marcus glanced over occasionally with a nod or a smile, tapping in time to the beat and occasionally joining in with the raspy lyrics of the band. His voice wasn't bad ... and I had heard the best in the world but I enjoyed seeing him like this, relaxed and at home in his own space.

Sipping red wine and watching him, I felt safe and totally at home. The bottle of wine slowly emptied as conversation ran smooth and sure. I hadn't even seen the rest of his flat but it didn't seem to matter. Cocooned in the kitchen with the smell of tomatoes and onions, music washing over me with Marcus's presence felt right. No drama, no frenetic activity, just quiet contentment. It felt like home, my parents' home – the secure, normal upbringing that for so long I'd fought and reacted against.

Once he slipped the dish into the oven and set the timer, it suddenly went very quiet.

I swallowed. The air sizzled between us, anticipation, nerves and a sort of awareness, as if we both realised that something big depended on the next step.

He took my hand and led me through to the lounge, putting on lamps as he went so that the room was bathed in low watt glow.

Tapping our glasses gently together, Marcus faced me on the sofa, our knees touching.

'Tilly, there's enough chemistry between us to blow

this place sky high.' He took an inward breath and let out a long sigh, pinching his lips.

'Chemistry, drama, high emotion ...' he paused. 'That's not me. It's all a bit mind-blowing. It's not what I'm used to.'

Bemusement shadowed his face. 'And even as I say this, I can't believe I am. I've never felt this strongly about anyone. You remind me of an angry kitten spitting at every turn, and yet you're so passionate about what you do, engaged with your life, your job and friends all intertwine. It's alien and yet I feel like a boy with his nose pressed up against the glass wanting in.'

My heart skipped and hopped. I chewed my lip and held his steady, serious gaze. His eyes crinkled at the edges with a reluctant smile. I think that meant that he liked me.

'I came into the job, deeply cynical, convinced you were all unreliable, artistic types, undisciplined, casual and I wanted to disapprove, but then I saw another side.'

'Oh,' I said, hoping he'd seen something positive. 'Is that a good side?' I took a delaying sip of wine. 'Why did you join the LMOC if you felt that way?'

'It wasn't a conscious, career decision.' He screwed up his mouth. 'More running away. I had a great job with a bank. I loved it. City culture. Lads. Alpha male. Man eat man. Didn't bother me. I had fun, earned loads of money, worked hard. High octane job. Everyone was the same. Even the women.' He laughed without mirth, his mouth turning down in disgust. 'Sophie. My girl-friend. She fitted right in. Worked on the trading floor. She asked me out. We were together for a couple of years, I thought it was serious or as serious as any City relationship can be. We spent most of our time out. Meals out. Nights in bars. Brunch out. In hindsight, it was all very superficial.'

'Is that the tie girlfriend?' I asked.

He nodded and continued. 'Apparently, my boss made a bet with another colleague. Whether either of them could get her to sleep with them while I was going out with her.' He took a long swallow and I could see the disgust in the way that his shoulders suddenly sprang up towards his ears. 'Typical testosterone competitive shitty behaviour that was fairly normal where I worked. Thing is she heard about it ... and being equally compet-itive, she slept with a completely different colleague to piss them off.'

'Really?' That sounded beyond shallow.

Marcus nudged my knee with his hand in a half-hearted reprimand at my levity, but I'd made him smile.

'I thought I loved her. That's probably what made it worse, when I realised I didn't care either way. It shocked me. That kind of indifference. That's when I knew I had to get out of that environment. I resigned immediately. The job came up at LMOC. It seemed a handy stopgap until I found something better and I took it because it was as far removed from the city as possible.'

'Even though we're all artistic losers.'

'Well,' he smiled gently, 'not all of you. For you I could make an exception.'

I raised an eyebrow.

Shyly I looked down at my knees, inside my heart bursting. If there was ever a line to get a girl into bed, he'd just delivered it. He could accept me as I was. If I wasn't already half in love with him, that declaration pushed me over the edge. He touched my face and I dared look at him again. It was there again, that half amused and semi-serious expression. I felt his thumb graze my cheek and my heart went all silly again, beating about with over-excited flutterings. I couldn't tear my gaze away from his.

Somehow, like magnets, we drew together until the kiss became inevitable. I sank into it and pulled him back with me lying prone on the sofa, revelling in the feel of the heaviness of his body, his lips roving over mine. I heard him groan my name and then the kiss deepened, setting light to all my nerve endings. Talk about a divine kisser. I pulled back slightly to take a breath and giggled.

'What are you laughing about?' Marcus whispered in my ear, nibbling his way down my neck.

'You are an exceptionally good kisser.'

'I believe you said that before. You're not so bad yourself.'

He stroked my face, tracing the contour of my cheekbone. 'You know that day you did mine and Fred's make-up.' His finger glided across my forehead and down to follow my eyebrow. 'Just watching you with him, turned me inside out. Then, Christ, when it was my turn, your hands on my face, your whole attention focused.' A wicked smile sharpened the planes of his face. 'Very erotic. I had to think some very serious thoughts and pray very hard that you didn't look down.' With that, he ducked his head and his lips traced their way along my jawline, as his hand slipped lower down my body, just skimming the edge of my breast, with a teasing pass, down onto my waist where it rested on my hip.

Our bodies pressed closer and my hands roved down his back, feeling the muscles toned and firm beneath my fingers. I strained against him, as if I couldn't get enough of him. Rasping breath punctured the air. How I wanted him and so delicious that it was reciprocated. Passion dazed me and I savoured the kisses, feeling my heart open and bloom with desire. I felt drunk with the headiness of being desired and like a shaft of brilliant sunlight it brought a piercing awareness. I wasn't a teenager diving in for the thrill anymore, unheeding of the consequences, ignoring the whisper of sense. I wanted more this time. Not living from moment to moment.

With fierce regret, I forced myself to slow down and pull back. This time I wanted to get it right. Make conscious decisions instead of going with the flow. With perfect synchronicity, Marcus responded, resting his forehead on mine, his breath coming in soft puffs. I glowed in smug triumph, it was good to know I affected him as much as he affected me. We stayed like that for at least a minute, catching ourselves, our heartbeats slowing to normal and it felt peaceful and easy.

'Tilly, will you come to bed with me?'

He wore the familiar and utterly endearing grave expression. This felt grown up. Decisive. I was making a choice instead of falling into something.

Chapter 33

Warm skin, musky scent. I inhaled. I'd forgotten the joy of being curled up with another body, my head resting on a shoulder and hearing the steady beat of another heart. Marcus's hand idly stroked my bottom. We were woozy and cosy under his duvet in the aftermath of sex. Serious, steady sex. So different from the jokey, half-hearted fumbles when Felix had made the effort. Now it all made sense.

Marcus made love with an intensity and thoroughness that made a girl feel there was nothing else in the world but her. I felt warmed to the core by his thoughtful attention and now he seemed happy to lie interlinked, nestling in the afterglow, quiet but without retreating.

'Got any Italian for me now?' he asked, shifting slightly so that we faced each other. With one bedside lamp lit, it cast enough light for me to see the gentle amusement on his face.

'*Oh! sventata, sventata! La chiave della stanza dove l'ho lasciata?*'

'Let me guess,' he stroked my back, pulling me closer. 'Stunning, stunning. The man is an amazing lover, let no one say otherwise.'

I fluttered my eyelashes at him. 'Wow, that's pretty close.' I let him have his smug moment for a beat before adding, 'Oh dear! How thoughtless of me. Where can I have left the key for my room?'

He hauled me to him for a kiss. If it was supposed to be punishment, I'd take it every time.

Eventually, we pulled apart.

'Will you stay the night?'

'I should text Jeanie, let her know I'm safe.'

'That's a yes then.'

I nodded and kissed him.

'Are you up with the lark or do you prefer to sleep in?'

'You're kidding right? With my job, I quite often don't finish work until after eleven and then we go out. A night bird and ...' I wrinkled my nose at him, 'I'm absolutely dreadful in the mornings.'

'Oh, dear that makes two of us. I have to set two alarms. One the early morning warning and then the real one, which I absolutely have to get up for.'

'Heaven help us then. I won't be getting a cup of tea in bed from you then ...'

'We'll have to get one of those tea-making things that grannies have. What did they call them?'

'Goblin Teasmade. My granny had one.'

'That's it.'

'Do they still make them?' I asked out loud, while pondering the 'we'll'. I rather liked the sound of that. It was also a sort of solid stick-in-the-mudness that was a long way from Felix's reckless spontaneity that had once seemed so attractive. Look where that had got me.

OK, so maybe I was going straight from one man to the next but I'd not spent any time thinking about where things might go with Marcus. Now I was here, the rightness of it all felt right – two jigsaw pieces that were meant to fit together.

'We can look on eBay.'

'Look for what?'

'A tea making thingy.'

'Oh,' I giggled, still thinking of jigsaws and my stomach gurgled.

'Still hungry?' asked Marcus with a wicked lift of his eyebrows. 'My you've quite an appetite.'

'You haven't fed me yet!' I said with indignation.

Marcus pulled me closer, hooking a leg through mine so that I was pressed against him, my face up against the warm smooth skin of his neck. His hand gently circling along the hairline on the back of my neck. I buried my nose in the warm skin just between his shoulder and neck and savoured the lingering scent of aftershave and the more potent top-note of male.

I rubbed a hand over the hip bone that was closest, skimming down and back in a rhythmic stroke, just wisping across the top of his thigh with feather tip fingers feeling the coarser hair there.

His hips moved in answer and I could feel him stirring. Lips moved along my hairline and a hand cupped my breast, fingers with an unerring aim going straight for the bull's-eye.

'Mmm.'

My stomach interrupted again.

Marcus's hand slipped down and patted my belly. 'You're not going to be one of those high maintenance chicks always demanding food, are you?' he whispered, nipping my earlobe. I wriggled decadently against him. Skin on skin. It was such a delicious feeling.

'Tilly, if you don't stop that right now, I won't ... ooh'

We had to order Indian take-away because the pasta dish was burnt to ruination.

'Football good, was it?' Jeanie had a teasing grin on her face as I walked into the make-up studio the following day wearing a white shirt that belonged to Marcus and the same skinny jeans as yesterday.

'Very, Arsenal won two nil.' We'd watched *Match of the Day* curled up in bed together with a cup of tea, which he had to get out of bed and go and make because I still qualified as a guest. Although I made it up to him and had to leave him there as he didn't work on Sundays. The office functions, HR, PR, Accounts and IT, usually worked nine to five hours.

'Excellent. Marcus enjoy the game?'

I chose to ignore her obvious innuendo. 'Not so much as he's a Liverpool supporter.'

I glanced over at the empty cubicle. 'Vince not in again?'

'Food poisoning apparently. Still throwing up.'

We had a rule that no one could return to work after a stomach bug for at least forty-eight hours after the last episode of sickness or diarrhoea. 'Handy.'

'Not for us it isn't. Can you give Carol a call and see if she might be able to come in and do an extra couple of hours for us?'

Even with Carol who could come in, we were still rushed off our feet. Although she could help with the chorus, Vince's absence meant that we had two extra principals to get made up in the usual amount of time. Thankfully I could round up Pietro early who had a mortal fear of being late so always arrived at the theatre in plenty of time.

I found him in the canteen slurping black weak tea, talking to Guillaume and Philippe.

'Pietro.'

'Tilly,' he answered, mocking my aren't-I-glad-to-see-you voice.

I ignored Philippe, who was desperately trying to catch my eye.

'OK, I need a favour. Is there any chance you can come up to the make-up room early so that I can get you done? We're a man down.'

'What do you think gentlemen?' Pietro pushed back his shoulders, immediately the regal king addressing his subjects. 'Shall I help the damsel in distress?'

I put my hands on my hips and tilted my head.

Guillaume nodded with unusual alacrity. I eyed him, a vague notion popping into my head. He caught my steady stare and blushed, his gaze sliding away. Hmm, interesting.

Philippe chuckled. 'Given that she could deepen your wrinkles, give you an extra chin or two and no doubt paint in a bald spot and receding hairline, I think it would be perspicacious to bow to the lady's wishes.'

'Perspicacious indeed, Philippe.' I shot him a disdainful look.

'As it's you, dear Tilly, I shall come directly.' Pietro rose to his feet and nodded, 'Gentlemen. I bid you adieu.'

'Tilly! Wait.' Philippe jumped to his feet. 'Can I have a word?'

I shrugged. 'I'm ...'

Ignoring my obvious reluctance, he pulled me to one side. 'I'm so sorry. Jeanie told me. I didn't know what to do. You know Vince, nothing lasts with him. I saw them together once.'

'Tilly, I need you.' Pietro insinuated himself between us. I could have kissed him. I was mad at Philippe and I'd forgive him eventually but I still felt a fool that so many people had known.

'Thanks, Pietro. I owe you.' We stepped into the lift together.

'No, Tilly. I owe you. You were very discreet after I told you about. Well you know.'

My heart banged uncomfortably in my rib cage.

I wanted to die of shame.

I couldn't bring myself to say a word and smiled stiffly. At least I didn't have to worry any more about Felix getting me into trouble selling any more stories.

Chapter 34

'Bloody HR. They want to see me now, Tilly. I'm supposed to be seeing Anna Bridgeman, the new understudy for Juliet in twenty minutes. At three-thirty. Can you meet her instead and take some photos and measurements? It would be great if we could use the same wigs for her but I think her hairline is a lot lower than Brigitte's.' Jeanie thrust a notebook at me. 'And have you seen the weather, it's bloody starting snowing.'

'Really?' I raced to the window. Sure enough there were a few white flakes twisting and turning in the sky. 'It won't settle,' I said sighing.

'Good,' said Jeanie, 'that's the last thing I need today.'

'Is everything OK?' I wondered if Vince's recent absences might have raised a few questions. He'd reappeared this morning looking very hale and hearty for someone who'd been laid up with food poisoning all weekend.

'No idea. I've just been summoned,' she emphasised the word with an irreverent shake of her head. 'Probably more new policies. Honestly, as if I give a toss about our equality policy or health and safety. I just want to get on and do my job.'

Her mouth turned down. 'Bloody inconsistent. I have better things to do with my time. And keep an eye on Vince. I don't want him sloping off anywhere.' She turned around and gave him a pointed look.

I wondered if it might have anything to do with the assistant head of department job. It was only five days until my probation meeting with Alison. Five days to Christmas Eve. And I still didn't have a clue what I was doing for Christmas. And although I didn't have to go to Judith's, the prospect of being on my own suddenly felt a little daunting.

In the event, Jeanie returned well before Anna turned up. She walked through the door, wild-haired, her face flushed. Stiff-legged and carefully placed, her motion reminded me of an unwilling puppet being forced into action.

'Tilly, you need to go up to HR.'

'What? Now?'

'Yes.' Her monotone voice held no emotion but I could see her jaw tensing.

I shot a glance over at Vince, who looked up with avaricious curiosity. Jeanie gave her head a slight shake.

Fear trickled down my spine.

'Am I in trouble?'

'You need to go up there now.' Before she could turn her head away, I caught sight of unshed tears pooling in her lower lashes.

I took the stairs two at a time, ignoring the painful beat of my heart which protested at my rapid strides.

The HR department was nestled under the eaves and much overlooked in the building. The HR Director, Marsha Munro, met me, looking distinctly uncomfortable. In her spacious office, along with Alison Kreufeld, two men sat at a round table, the Chief Executive, Julian Spencer and ... Marcus.

That made my step falter. What was *he* doing here? Surely if they were making me redundant it wouldn't involve him. Maybe he was here to talk about the training he'd been giving me. He'd said they were looking at rolling it out company wide. But he didn't meet my eyes, instead he seemed totally impassive. A far cry from the teasing laughing man I'd kissed goodbye yesterday morning.

'Miss Hunter,' Marsha began with great formality. 'Take a seat.'

I sat opposite the four of them, my eyes darting to the window behind them.

Outside the snowflakes were bigger now, coming thick and fast, turning the sky to an oppressive grey. Today there was nothing magical about them, they felt like harbingers of doom. I shivered, wishing my imagination could take a break for once.

Chapter 35

I let myself into the flat.

Felix was there, a pile of clothes in his hands. Relief flashed on his face almost as if he thought I'd come to rescue him from the washing.

'Tilly! Come and see what I've bought today.' He dropped the pile of clothes and pulled me towards the lounge. I didn't have the energy to resist.

'Look.' He waved his hand in a courtly gesture.

On the other side of the room, leaning against the wall was the saddest, scrawniest Christmas tree I'd ever seen.

'I just knew you'd want me to rescue him and give him a good home.' Felix beamed at me as if none of the last few days had happened. It was so typical of him, I let out a small half-huffed out laugh. He never let anything keep him down for long.

He grabbed the tree and held it upright. 'Not the prettiest but ... I thought we could decorate it together, like old times. We can still be friends, can't we? And you love Christmas. And I don't want to spoil it for you. And you could still come with me to Mum's.'

I stared at the spindly branches, some barely covered with needles and the trunk which leaned too far to the left and the grubby wall behind it. It looked lost and lonely. An outcast just like me.

'I've lost my job,' I blurted out.

'What?' He straightened up, dropping the tree back against the wall.

I sucked in a breath, loathe to say it because saying it out loud made it too real.

'I-I,' I swallowed back the sob. 'T-they suspended me.'

'You? But why? Not because of Vince. That's ridiculous. It's outside of work. They can't fire you because I'm ... I'm with Vince, can they?'

'No, they can't.' My hands shook as he grabbed them and towed me to the sofa. 'But they can if they think you've been selling stories to the tabloids.' I sank into the seat, feeling my pulse banging in my temple as I stared at his hand holding mine. The dark hair flopped forward. He was a grown up, he shouldn't have floppy hair. I freed my hand, pulling away from him. 'They have evidence. That it was me.' I still couldn't get my head round that.

'Who have?'

'The management. The computer people.' I kicked my heel back at the sofa leg. 'Who cares? I've been suspended. Because of gross misconduct. Me. They think *I* sold stories to the tabloids.'

'But you ... can't you tell them?'

'Tell them what?'

He shrugged. 'That it wasn't you?'

There was no sense of contrition on his face. He really didn't get it.

'Felix.' I shook my head sadly, knowing that he would never understand and I had invested badly, oh so badly, in him. 'It makes no difference, I shouldn't have told you.'

'What are you going to do?'

For a second the room spun and I couldn't say a word because I had absolutely no idea. Without my job, I had nothing.

'Tilly?'

I suddenly realised I was wet through. Almost catatonic, I walked out of the lounge, dimly aware of Felix repeating my name, shedding clothes as I went before locking myself in the bathroom.

Finally feeling warm again after a lobster skin inducing shower, I'd managed to half dress when he banged on the door.

'Tilly, it's your phone.' Through the frosted glass, I

could see him waving my mobile.

'Oh, for God's sake,' I muttered and cracked the door open and stuck my hand out to grab it and then slammed the door shut again.

Christelle's words were tumbling out as I put the phone to my ear. 'Tilly, oh my God, are you OK? Guillaume told me … you'd been escorted from the building. What's happened? Why did they do that? What have you done? Have you been suspended?'

Being a legal eagle she would know what that meant. Know that being escorted from one's place of work boded badly. It hit me all over again just how much trouble I was in. The anger I felt at Felix had been a welcome distraction.

My breath hitched and an involuntary sob escaped. A second one followed in quick succession and another, and another.

'Tilly?'

I sank onto the toilet seat. I couldn't hold it back anymore and for the first time I began to cry in earnest.

'Tilly!' My sister's voice called out but like a swimmer being swept away, the riptide of emotion held me fast and I couldn't stop the sobs shuddering through my body.

'I-I'm s-sorry … it's j-just …' I sucked in air, trying to talk but now I'd started I couldn't stop and the sobs overwhelmed me. 'M-my job. It's … g-gone.'

I broke down and began to weep even more. I slid off the toilet seat onto the floor and hunched against the wall, trying to make myself as small as possible. I put the phone down on the floor and wept into my hands.

When I finally spluttered to a halt, my eyelids sore, tired and puffy, I sat on the floor, the cold of the tiles seeping into my numb bottom.

'Tilly.' I heard Christelle's urgent tones. 'Talk to me.'

Snatching up the phone, I whispered, 'You're still there?' She'd stayed on the line all this time.

'Of course I am, where did you think I'd be?' Her clipped, matter of fact response, made me smile. Typical Christelle in one way, but totally unexpected in another. There was no of course about it, I couldn't think of anyone else who would have waited on the line for so long.

'Now tell me what's happened.'

Between unladylike sniffs, blowing my nose on toilet paper, I told her the whole sorry tale. The letter, Vince and Felix. I omitted the detail of Marcus, I couldn't bear to reveal that.

She listened without interrupting, apart from making a few encouraging noises. I finally ground to a halt and lapsed into silence. My head on my knees, eyes closed as if that might keep the world at bay.

'Did you do it?'

'No I didn't but Felix ...'

'That's not what you're being accused of. Did you sell the information to a tabloid newspaper?'

'No.'

'Ergo there can't be any evidence that you did. What is the evidence?'

'They said emails but I never sent any emails to anyone. Well not on purpose–' Surely the virus thing couldn't have anything to do with it.

'As your legal representative, I'd be very interested in seeing this evidence.'

'My what?'

'Tilly, I am an expert in employment law. A barrister at one of the top chambers in London. Barracuda. A barracuda you hear. Not my words I hasten to add, but we are going to fight this. We are so going to get your job back.' The way she said it made it sound as if she was the heavyweight champion of the world. 'And they are going dooooowwwwn.' I let out a startled giggle. 'Nobody messes with my sister. Now go pack a bag.'

'What?'

'I'll be there in twenty minutes. You're coming to stay with me.'

Chapter 36

Christelle giggled as Guillaume reached around her to snag something from the wok on the hob where she was busily rustling up a fragrant stir fry. Garlic, ginger and Chinese five spice perfumed the air, waking up my appetite. I hadn't eaten all day.

He leaned in and tugged at the strap of her Kath Kidston pinny saying something a little too loudly in her ear. (Only Christelle would wear an apron in the kitchen.) She giggled again and pushed him away play-fully.

I scowled. Guillaume had obviously forgotten that I could understand every word of the sweet nothings he kept murmuring to her – although, there was nothing sweet about the last one.

That was the problem with Christelle's ultra-svelte apartment, I'd discovered in the last twenty-four hours. Escaping the love birds and their early mating rituals was impossible.

Christelle's palatial pad was beautiful, the last word in deluxe; smart bathroom fittings, granite topped kitchen with shiny surfaces and posh appliances and a vast lounge dotted with not two but three cream sofas. My tatty little flat didn't compare at all, although I could get used to everything working properly. The whole place was a testament to open-plan living and since Guillaume's arrival, it had been difficult to avoid their enthusiasm for one another. And I was being a miserable, depressed, horrible old cow. How could I possibly begrudge Christelle her obvious happiness, especially not when she'd been so brilliant since she'd come like an avenging angel and scooped me up.

As soon as she'd brought me back here, battling through the snowy roads in her Volkswagen Golf, she'd got me settled into the spare room, insisted on making me eat hot soup with crusty rolls and a very runny brie and then sat down with an official looking notepad and cross examined me in great detail. Her first question had been brutal. 'Did you send those emails?'

I almost burst with frustration. 'Of course, I didn't. I thought you'd believe me.'

'It's not a question of whether I believe you or not. Sometimes I must defend people I know are lying through their teeth, but if that's what they've told me, I have to go with it. Ergo, I must ask the question. It doesn't matter whether I believe you or not.'

I nodded as if that made complete sense. Was 'ergo' a legal technical term or just a Christelle type of word?

'Do you do that a lot?' The concept of defending people even if you knew they were guilty seemed totally alien to me.

'Yes, it's part of the job.'

'Oh.' I sat back. That just sounded wrong. 'Really?' I asked wanting confirmation that what she said was true. 'Do you ever get people off that you know are guilty?'

'Yes, Tilly.' She swept her hair back in exasperation.

'Oh.' It was as if a pin had pricked a balloon. My perception of her professional, upper level career changed in that instant. At least my job was honest. We transported people to a make-believe world but those audiences were willing participants, volunteering to suspend belief the minute they paid for the tickets.

By eleven o'clock I was exhausted but Christelle pronounced herself delighted with our progress. It didn't feel like progress to me but she was adamant she now had a strategy. It all hinged on the evidence they had. She'd drafted a letter which was so full of legalese and demands for her client, that I was pretty sure it would put the fear of God into the HR Director. My sister, I liked saying that, made Godzilla look tame.

'OK, we'll call it a night. And tomorrow I'll have a letter couriered over.' She pulled her chair round next to mine and nudged up to me, leaning against me, shoulder to shoulder. 'We're going to fight this. And you can stay here as long as you want.' I heard her draw in a quick breath. 'I ... would you think about staying for Christmas? We could have Christmas Day together. If you haven't got any other plans. You know. Then it might be, you know, nice.'

More pesky tears welled up at her sudden diffidence. I leaned back into her. 'I'd love to. That would be lovely. The two of us. We could even try and skype Mum and Dad.'

'Yes.' She beamed at me. 'With bucks fizz. Toast them. And bagels and cream cheese for breakfast. And a proper Christmas dinner. Queen's speech and everything.'

'You have to promise me one thing,' I said. 'Actually, make that two things. We get to watch Dr Who and ...'

'What?' she asked looking wary.

'No chestnut stuffing!'

Despite her reassurances, that I mustn't be despondent, it didn't stop me waking early the following morning with the horrible realisation that I wouldn't be going to work that day or for the foreseeable future. It was highly unlikely that they'd hold a disciplinary panel before Christmas or until at least the New Year.

Without work or being able to contact anyone there, I felt isolated and lonely in this strange part of London that I didn't have the nerve to venture out in. When I looked out of the window, the snow had melted away in the night, leaving no trace. With a horrible thought, I wondered if my job might do the same. Christelle left for work the next morning leaving me with a key, so I could come and go but it was as if all the confidence had been sucked out of me. I didn't want to leave the safety of her flat.

Instead I'd spent the day brooding over the fabulous views of the Thames which could be seen from two sides of the bank of windows that lined the apartment and torturing myself by re-reading the old emails on my Kindle.

Marcus. He should have been on the stage. What an actor. He'd made me believe him. Saturday night had felt so real and I felt physically sick, each time I realised again that he'd been setting me up. He hadn't meant a word of what was said that night. And why was I even surprised by that. I so clearly wasn't his type. It wasn't even as if he ever intended to stay at the LMOC. He'd be back with the professional, corporate types probably now that his *investigation* was over.

Despite the pain that reading them gave me, I couldn't bring myself to delete his emails. Perhaps I'd keep them as a salutary reminder of my complete and utter stupidity.

'Dinner will be ready in fifteen minutes, Tilly. Can you lay the table, please?'

I rose without answering and crossed to the cutlery drawer. Guillaume shot me a horrified look. I couldn't help laughing. Christelle had asked me in French.

'I-I'm sorry,' he stuttered.

I smirked and said dryly, 'It's OK – I'm getting used to it.'

He blushed, obviously thinking of all the suggestions he'd made in the last half hour.

Christelle, with her back to us, tightened the bow of the floral pinny, her shoulders shaking with suppressed laughter. Guillaume looked nervously at her and then back at me. As well he might, he had obviously had a fascination with the damn apron.

I felt slightly awkward now that the three of us were sitting at the table. Did Guillaume know what I'd been accused of? Were people talking about me at work? Whispering and wondering? Christelle had already warned me that I shouldn't bring it up. The suspension letter had made it clear that the allegations were confidential.

Guillaume gave Christelle a look, she shook her head slightly but he shook his.

'Tilly, no one believes it you know.'

Christelle put her hands over her ears, saying 'La-la-la-la-la.' Guillaume smiled.

'That's what I love about her, everything by the book.' He winked at me as my sister blushed. Love eh? That had been quick.

'Tell me about ...' I winked back at him. 'But in this instance, I wouldn't swap her for the world.'

'Aw, Tilly.' Christelle reached over and grabbed my hand and gave it a squeeze.

'You're not supposed to be listening,' I said with a teasing smile.

'I know and you two are not supposed to be talking about this but it's very useful to have someone on the inside.'

Guillaume raised one Gallic eyebrow. 'I have other uses you know.'

'I know,' she replied with a sultry look.

'Excuse me,' I interrupted.

'Sorry.' Guillaume's irrepressible grin suggested he was anything but. 'But everyone is talking about it, saying they can't believe you would do anything wrong. You are held in very high regard. Philippe is suggesting we all go out on strike. Jeanie, she is very cross. Even Vince is subdued. I think they all miss you, already. There is a nasty tension in the air. Everyone has also heard what Vince has done. Most people are disgusted with him. Vince and Felix.'

'Really? How?'

'Jeanie and he had a flaming row in the canteen.

Most people heard it. She was furious with him.
Avoided him all day, told Philippe she could hardly bear
to look at Vince. Then Vince caught her at lunchtime.
Made the mistake of asking her to forgive him. It was
akin to watching a volcano erupt. Her face,' he winced,
'turned bright red and then kaboom ... she exploded.
Everyone knows now.'

Talking about them all gave me a sharp pain in my
chest. God I missed it all. What would I do if I never
got to go back? Christelle must have caught the flash
of pain that crossed my face. She leaned over and put
her hand on my wrist. 'Don't give up. You have to stay
positive. They would have received my letter today.' She
gave a self-satisfied smile. 'That would have put the
shits up them. They won't be expecting that you've
called in the big guns.'

'What do you mean?'

'I sent it on the firm's headed paper.' Her smile was
as smug as a cat who'd swallowed the entire contents
of a dairy.

'Is that good?' I'd never heard of the company she
worked for but then I was hardly likely to.

'Anyone in employment law will have heard of us.'
She cited some of the high-profile cases of CEOs and
MDs who'd successfully sued their employers for
millions for unfair dismissal, breach of contract and
sexual discrimination.

'Wow. I didn't realise.'

'Yeah, this is slightly different, in those cases, they wanted to see justice done. You want your job back. So, we have to prove that they are wrong. They should provide the evidence. Until they do, we can't do anything.'

'But what evidence have they got? I never sent any emails to the paper. I swear I didn't.'

'Then, it's up to them to prove that you did. We need to see those emails.'

Where are you? Need to speak to you urgently. Meet me at 5.30pm at the Costa at Waterloo Station.

Jeanie's text at 6.30 on Thursday morning startled me from sleep.

Her text posed a dilemma. Did I tell Christelle? Or not tell her. It was breaking the rules. The HR letter made it clear that I wasn't to discuss anything with other colleagues. Although I'd decided, after listening to Christelle say she defended wrong 'uns, that the law was decidedly murky.

'You're up early,' remarked Christelle, as I wandered into her kitchen. In a slim fitting black dress accessorised with turquoise beads and cropped cashmere cardigan, she epitomised elegance. The scarf I'd bought her was so going to look gorgeous with that outfit.

'Did I wake you? I'm due in Chambers early because

I've got a pre-trial meeting with the defendant's solicitor. Pain in the arse because we've been over everything. We're going to lose. The man's an idiot and so is his client. And then,' she brightened, 'we can start thinking about Christmas.' With a piece of toast hanging out of her mouth and darting about the kitchen loading papers into a soft leather briefcase, I decided it was probably best not to bother her about the text.

'And you mustn't worry. I've had another look at the paperwork. And that laughable confidentiality agreement, which they've introduced well and truly after the horse has bolted.'

She grabbed a notepad and waved it at me.

'Sage and onion stuffing or sausage meat? Or I suppose I could try and find the Jamie Oliver recipe.'

'What?'

'I'm making my shopping list. I thought we could go shopping later this week. I'll try and leave early one night.'

'Christelle, it's Christmas Eve the day after tomorrow.'

'Well, I'll,' she wrinkled her nose. 'I'll swing it somehow. Not tonight, maybe tomorrow.'

Her excitement made me smile. Enough with the brooding. It wasn't going to get my job back. I had to shake off this lethargic lassitude. It wasn't me at all. Suddenly I knew exactly how I was going to fill the hours before I met Jeanie.

Chapter 37

By twelve o'clock I was well into my stride. I'd been to Clapham to my flat, collected Mum's bag of goodies which had been forgotten in all the drama of the last few days and done a marathon round of shopping in Sainsbury's on the way back to Christelle's. My enthusiasm had over-taken the ratio of hands to bags which meant that I had to hail a cab to transport everything back and my fingers had only just recovered from the grooves cut into them by the heavy plastic bags.

I'd made the driver stop outside a local greengrocer and although he wasn't keen, I persuaded him to help me stuff a Christmas tree in the back of the cab, the top doubled over to fit, shedding needles everywhere. It took several trips in the lift to get everything up to Christelle's ninth floor apartment and by the time I'd got the last load in, I almost collapsed in a heap.

Now, with Michael Buble's Christmas CD blasting

out, I'd lined up all my ingredients, *Blue Peter* style, with everything weighed out in little dishes. That was the joy of Christelle's kitchen, she had loads of stuff. A proper blender, measuring jugs, pastry cutters, a real pastry brush and a cooker that worked. I'd set her iPad up on the counter and had found the special Jamie Oliver stuffing recipe, thankfully I'd remembered most of the ingredients, even the sage leaves, when I was shopping. It was a family favourite that we'd adopted after watching a Christmas cookery programme.

My first batch of mince pies were already in the oven and I'd guestimated the amount of orange juice I'd used in the pastry but I was hopeful they'd taste as good as Mum's. I'd put grated orange zest on the top of the mince-meat before sealing each pie, just the way she did and had even painstakingly cut tiny holly leaves to decorate the top, which she didn't do. I quickly realised why. I got bored trying to roll tiny berries and decided that the holly leaves glistening with beaten egg were quite fancy enough, thank you. The second batch would have to go unadorned. Life was too short.

I flopped onto one of the cream leather sofas with a cup of tea and ran through my mental check list admiring the view. Today was one of those crisp frosty days with the deepest blue cloudless sky and the view from the picture windows spread out in the brilliant sunshine.

Despite being close to zero outside, inside it was lovely and toasty. No drafty windows and half-hearted radiators here. Although the apartment was a touch too modern for my taste, I realised everything being properly maintained, cared for and looked after was far more comfortable to live with. With a sense of shame, I thought about my flat and my laissez-faire attitude to it, realising that all the things I'd got so used to, could be improved and repaired. I'd fallen into a rut, accepting things as they were.

The thought splintered in a thousand directions as it dawned on me, I could move. Sell the flat and buy another one. Or rather I could, if I got my job back. I had enough equity to put down a big enough deposit to take out a small mortgage. It suddenly seemed the grown up, sensible thing to do.

Finishing my tea, I put down the cup on a coaster and sat up. Once all this job business was resolved, I'd put the flat up for sale. Decision made, I felt much more positive. And now I'd had a brief rest, I had work to do. Jumping to my feet, I went and sorted through Mum's huge bag, which proved a revelation. She'd packed Christmas. There were two separate parcels of decorations, including tinsel, silver for Christelle, gold for me and a selection of familiar family decorations, as well as some new ones. With the added collection I'd bought that morning, the tree was going to be well laden.

There were also several wrapped presents for each of us and two stockings. I rubbed my finger over the sequinned M on one of them. We'd had them forever. I couldn't remember a time when they weren't hung with great ceremony on our doorknobs before we went to bed on Christmas Eve.

With a pang, I thought of home and the family celebrations we had, our particular traditions. Bucks fizz for breakfast, the neighbours in for champagne cocktails, Dad wearing his elf apron in charge of the turkey and Mum's hopeless attempts at lighting the Christmas pudding.

I was going to make sure that Christelle and I had a Christmas of our own to remember.

Putting up the tree proved the more problematic element of my perfect sisters' Christmas mission. I cursed. I really wanted it all to be done by the time Christelle walked through the door after work. I'd bought extra decorations in the supermarket and two strings of fairy lights but hadn't thought how I was going to get the blasted tree up.

Ransacking her cupboards didn't help. I didn't think my sister would be too pleased if I used her biggest saucepan and I'd still need something inside it to anchor the tree. And then I spotted the parasol outside on the balcony. The base would be perfect.

Almost perfect I discovered, but with a bit of shaving

and planing with a very sharp knife and building a fine sweat, I managed to ram the trunk into the parasol base. It's amazing what you can do with a bit of determination and I did use Christelle's oldest Sabatier knife.

Rush hour had hit big time and Waterloo still thronged with people and noise but after being holed up in Christelle's calm, quiet flat, the busy atmosphere felt as if I'd come out of hibernation. I'd achieved a lot today and feeling a little bit brighter, I lengthened my stride and weaved around the people, my skirt flouncing. Yes, I felt a lot more like me. It would be good to see Jeanie and I hoped that she might have some good news.

Taking an appreciative sniff of my cappuccino I took a good look around the coffee bar. No sign of her yet.

Scanning the tables I missed him the first time but with magnetic power, my gaze was drawn back to a table in the far corner where familiar green eyes watched me. Ridiculously I still looked around to see if there was any sign of Jeanie.

I flushed, searing heat racing over my body like hot sand, my legs suddenly wobbly. The rush of emotion, so confused and fierce made me freeze. Shit, I didn't want to see him. I had nothing to say to him. All I could remember was that horrible scene with him, Marsha and Julian all staring at me, united accusation radiating from their stilted body language.

In sudden panic, I wheeled round. I had to get away before everything overwhelmed me. Before I got to the door he caught up with me, stumbling over chair legs and bags in his haste. He insinuated himself between me and the door, blocking my way and put a hand on my arm.

I shook it off and took a step back, scowling at him. 'Where's Jeanie? Did you make her text me?'

'No, I asked her to help because we both wanted to help.'

'Help?' I snarled. 'Yeah right. What do you want Marcus?'

'What do you think I want?' he asked, irritation sharpening his words.

'I haven't got a bloody clue.'

'I want to help you.'

'Bit late, isn't it?' I narrowed my eyes, unaccountably annoyed by the calm, unemotional expression on his face. 'I didn't see you jumping to help the other day.'

'Why don't you come and sit down?'

'I don't think we've got anything to say,' I said, pushing him aside.

'For God's sake, Tilly.' He grabbed my arm, his touch angry and then let go, chastened when I gave him a look of icy fury. 'Grow up. It wasn't personal.' Mutinously I stared at him. Suited and still bloody gorgeous. My heart fluttered, the traitorous bugger. I really wanted to hate him. I did hate him, it was just my body had other stupid ideas.

'Easy for you to say. It felt extremely personal when they took *my* job away and ...' *And after I slept with you.* It hurt to think about being curled up in bed with him, instead I stared down at the steam curling out of my coffee lid. It didn't help. Images tumbled in my head. His hands stroking my skin. The heavy weight of his leg over mine. The heat of his breath on my neck.

My stomach cramped in pain as I tensed, fighting to keep the memories in check. I couldn't do this, not with him. My voice came out small and defeated as I looked up at him and said, 'Please leave me alone.'

'I can't do that.' He reached for me again but I moved my hand out of reach, my jaw clamping tight. He had no right to touch me. Not again.

'Leave me alone, Marcus. You got what you wanted. You found your leak. Pretended you were interested. I don't know what you're doing now but I'm–'

'I'm trying to help you for Pete's sake,' he hissed, his cheeks reddening.

Some small part of me was delighted I'd got a rise out of him.

'Why?' I said as rudely as I could. 'Guilty conscience?'

'Just sit down and give me five minutes. What have you got to lose?'

I stood and weighed it up for a minute.

'Please.' His expression was guarded now.

'OK.'

I followed him back to the table in the corner and sat down in my coat, making it clear that I wouldn't be there for long.

I played with my coffee cup, anything to avoid looking at his face.

'Something's not right. I don't believe you sent those emails.'

'Funny, you didn't mention that in the meeting,' I muttered, still toying with the cardboard sleeve on the cup, the familiar sense of utter helplessness rising.

Frustration touched his face.

'Look I'm trying here. Trying to make sense of it. I shouldn't even be here. I could lose ...'

'Lose your job?' I flung the words at him. How dare he? I sat up straight, pointing at him. 'You sat there,' I relished the words as I spat them at him, 'and said nothing while they accused me of sending emails to a paper. You said I'd sent them.' I clutched my coffee cup, seriously considering throwing it at him now.

'What the hell was I supposed to do?' His words tumbled out. 'And I didn't say you'd sent them. I said they came from your account. There's a difference. Unfortunately, it counts as evidence. Damning evidence as far as the board is concerned. There's an email trail from your account to a national newspaper. That's incontrovertible evidence.'

'Well you can stick your incontrovertible,' I raised my hands in exaggerated finger speech marks, '*evidence*, because I didn't send those emails, but clearly while you were keeping me otherwise occupied, someone else decided I had been.'

'I beg your pardon?' He stiffened.

'You heard me. I'm not completely stupid. Actually, I am! Completely bloody stupid. You were investigating the leaks. Funny that you magically found the answers that weekend. Is fucking someone part of the snoop's charter?' I hurled the words at him, making it as ugly as I could. 'Is that why you slept with me?'

He crunched up his coffee cup in his hands, the cardboard crackling and coffee spilling over his fingers.

'Thanks a bunch. You've got a high opinion of me. Is that really what you think? What you think of me?'

I shrugged, lifting my chin and ignoring the horrid mean feeling inside me. 'I'd say the evidence is incontrovertible. You oversaw the investigation. Presumably you knew what was going on, while we were at the football and ... a-afterwards.' My voice cracked but I kept my chin held high as I gave him an icy glare.

His jaw tightened, the pulse in his neck twitching but he managed to keep his voice cold and controlled. 'That wasn't the case at all. The security consultant's report went direct to the Chief Exec as well as me.' I hadn't realised it would hurt quite so much when he didn't deny that they'd been digging while I was with him.

He carried on, 'And as I said, the evidence was there.' Finishing his sentence, he put both elbows on the table, his case laid out, all reasonable and logical.

I shot him a disdainful look as I took a sip of coffee before saying dismissively, 'So you keep saying.'

'Jesus Christ Tilly,' he erupted, his Adam's apple working furiously, 'Stop being so fucking melodramatic. This isn't getting us anywhere. I contacted you because I don't think you did it. No,' he hissed, slamming both hands on the table. 'I know you didn't do it but if we're going to clear your name, you're going to have to bloody talk to me and stop sniping at me. I was as blind-sided by that meeting as you were. You didn't do it. OK.'

I drew back in my seat, shocked by his outburst, unsure what to say.

'You don't believe I did it? Big of you.'

He took in a breath, a touch of regret haunting his expression. 'It's not a question of believing. I know you didn't do it.'

'And how did you come to that conclusion, Sherlock?'

He went very still and held my gaze. 'Because it's completely out of character. You ... you wouldn't do something like that.'

The husky timbre of his voice made me feel things

I didn't want to feel. 'It doesn't help though does it? You said they've got evidence.' I straightened up, determined to keep things professional.

He hadn't got the same memo; when he leaned over and touched my forearm, his eyes intense, and said softly, 'Yes, but if you didn't send those emails, some else did,' I had to fight against the growing warmth in my chest. I couldn't afford to let him touch me again. His job came first and he wasn't that scrupulous about making sure he got results.

'Well duh, Sherlock,' I sneered. 'I think I might have already deduced that.'

His mouth firmed but he got the message. 'We have to prove someone else sent those emails, using your account.'

I screwed up my face, and shook my head. 'Easier said than done. I'm guessing if they'd handily signed their name on the emails coming from me that someone might have picked that up.'

Marcus's mouth twisted in a wry smile. 'Unfortunately, the paper isn't being very forthcoming. Protecting their sources.'

'I bet they are.' I let out a thoughtful sigh. 'I might as well tell you. It was probably Felix.'

I flinched under Marcus's cool assessing gaze. 'Remember I told you I couldn't forgive him. He sold the picture of Katerina. There were other stories as well.

His friend's brother is a reporter.' I bit my lip. 'It never occurred to me. I guess he used my email account.'

'That makes sense.'

'Why do you say that?'

'Because whoever was doing it, deleted the emails from the sent box. Trying to hide their tracks or make sure you didn't see them, but the security consultants we used found them all on the email provider's server.'

'Still doesn't help, though.' I felt more hopeless than ever. 'Felix could have used his laptop when I wasn't around. My password and log in came up automatically in the webmail.'

Marcus frowned and rubbed at his forehead. 'He could have been emailing while you were somewhere else.'

I didn't follow.

'If we pull off the times that the emails were sent and work out where you were, we could find you an alibi. Do you keep … of course you don't.'

'What?'

'I was going to say an electronic calendar. We could have shared it and I could cross reference the two.'

'Ha! I've got something better. Remember this,' I rummaged in my handbag, 'funny little book.' I opened my diary to point to the week to view page, filled with scribbles. 'They have dates in. You use this thing called a pen, and write in it. Odd concept, I'm sure, but it worked for hundreds of years. Ever heard of a chap called Samuel Pepys. Oh, I forgot. We've had this conversation before. And you scoffed at handy little black book.'

I flicked through the pages. Dress rehearsal. Christelle lunch. Poker night.

Marcus pulled back his sleeve, with a quick peek at his watch. 'I need to get back to work.' He almost sounded regretful. 'But we need to go through every date. I've got a list of all the emails sent which we can cross reference with your diary.'

'I'm not sure that's a good idea.'

Half of me wanted that more than anything else and the other half, protected by a strong sense of self-preservation thought it was a really, really bad idea.

'Tilly, do you want your job back?'

I did, more than anything.

'I tell you what.' I couldn't see him on my own, I needed distance. Keep it impersonal. 'Come round to my sister's. I'm staying there for now.' I gave him a challenging look. 'She's a barrister.'

'Yes, I know. She mentioned it.'

'Did she mention she specialises, luckily for me, in employment law.'

'No, I assumed she was ... I guess a criminal barrister.' He gave an approving nod. 'But employment that's good. Very good.'

'Yes. She's going to represent me at the hearing. I think she'll want to be involved. She'll need to see this *evidence.*'

His mouth twisted. 'Are you sure that's a good idea?'

'Don't worry about your job.' I stood up and pushed my coffee away in disgust. 'I'll make sure Christelle doesn't tell anyone. Let me speak to her and I'll send you a text later.'

'You've got my number.'

'Yes,' I snapped. He'd given it to me when we'd arranged to meet to travel up to Yorkshire.

As I went to walk away, Marcus grabbed my wrist. His touch on my forearm gentled and I think his thumb gave one tiny stroke of my inner wrist.

'I'm not worried about my job. I'm worried about losing any leverage I've got on being on the inside. Access to information. The emails.'

Chapter 38

I was back at the flat well before Christelle who'd texted to say she was on her way home which gave me time to switch on the lights on the tree and the second set I'd arranged rather artistically, if I said so myself, in an outsize vase on one of the side tables. When she walked through the door, tea lights burned in votive glasses on the coffee table and the flat smelled of cinnamon and spice from the mulled wine I was heating gently on the stove, a last-minute inspiration after I'd walked past Marks and Spencer at the station where they were handing out free samples in tiny plastic glasses.

'Honey, I'm h ...' her voice died away as she walked into the lounge. 'Oh my God Tilly,' she let out an excited squeal. 'This is gorgeous!'

She stood in front of the tree and clapped her hands. 'Wow! You've been busy.'

'Come through to the kitchen and I'll get you a drink.'

'Won't say no to that, something smells gorgeous.'

She took the steaming glass of red wine and she took a deep sniff.

'Mmm, lovely. And here was I worrying that you'd be brooding on your own today.'

'I did plenty of that, I promise you but ... well, you've been so brilliant, I wanted to say thank you.'

'You didn't need to do that. It's lovely to have you here.' She winced. 'Even under the circumstances.'

'Ah, I have news on that.'

I explained about Jeanie's text and my meeting with Marcus.

'I hope it's OK, I suggested he came round this evening. At eight.'

I'd decided on the tube journey on the way back, that with Christelle at my side, I could cope with seeing Marcus. She would know what to do with his information.

'No, way! That's fantastic. He's the IT guy.' She paused. 'Hang on, the guy I sat next to at the opera.'

'Yes,' I said, wondering whether I ought to say any more about him. *Oh and by the way, also the guy I fell for big time, slept with and then he sold me down the river.*

Christelle did a little happy dance, making me pleased I hadn't said that out loud.

'That is seriously good news.' She did another hip shimmy around the kitchen table. 'I can't believe our luck. A witness that turns. Brilliant. This will weaken their case.'

'At the moment Chris, I thought you said there isn't a case, it's just a hearing.'

'And if you believe that, you'll be hung out to dry. And don't call me Chris.'

'How about Elle?' I said, feeling a tightening in my stomach at her words. I had so much to lose, I needed any information Marcus could give us.

'Now that I could live with. Like Elle from *Legally Blonde*. Chris sounds too masculine. I like being a girl.' She tossed her hair over her shoulders with an exaggerated pout, making me smile. There were sides to my sister I was discovering all the time.

My hands shook as I lifted them to open the front door. From the moment Marcus's deep voice had echoed over the tinny intercom, butterflies had been dancing erratically in my stomach.

'Come in,' I said, determined to keep things strictly formal. He'd ambushed me earlier, but now I felt composed and calm. Did I hell! But I was determined to appear impassive and indifferent to him. Without offering to take his coat, I led him into the open plan lounge to where Christelle sat at the dining table with a foolscap notepad. I wanted to smile; in a pool of light deliberately staged she appeared terrifyingly efficient.

'Marcus, my sister Christelle. You met at the opera.'

She rose and offered her hand, inclining her head with a regal nod. I bit back a smile, which faded quickly when Marcus completely unfazed, shook her hand and said, 'Nice to see you again. I think you might still have my handkerchief.'

Christelle pursed her lips. 'Thank you for coming this evening. I understand from Tilly you might have some information for us.'

Marcus looked at her and then me, a quizzical expression on his face.

'Look, I'm here because I want to help Tilly. Can we cut the power play? We're all on the same side.'

Christelle's face broke into a rueful grin. 'Busted. OK. Let's start again. Thanks for coming. Do you want a drink?'

Starting afresh, with a round of coffees at the breakfast bar, Marcus opened his laptop and sat next to me at the kitchen table, pulling his chair up close to mine so that we could both see the computer screen. I tried to keep my distance but his familiar scent had my stomach in knots. He seemed oblivious but I did wonder when he took in a deep breath before opening a spreadsheet on the screen. He'd clearly been busy, although the odd figures in the series of columns meant nothing to me.

He pointed to the screen. 'I've transcribed all the

dates and times of each email sent from Tilly's account to the paper here. I thought we could go through each one and try and match them to where Tilly was at the time.' He turned to me, a ghost of a smile on his face. 'Got your diary?'

'Yes,' I muttered, opening it up.

'Here we go, first one this year. November 22nd.'

I flicked through the pages of my diary. 'What time?'

'6.30pm.'

'Bugger. I was at a training workshop on prosthetics in the morning but at the theatre for a late shift.'

'OK, how about November 24th in the afternoon?'

'Normal day at work. Could have been any of us.'

'Can you remember it, anyone acting strangely? Secretively? Using the computer?'

I consulted my diary in the vain hope that it might spark some small memory. 'That was after the virus.'

'Don't mention the virus in the hearing, whatever you do,' Christelle butted in. 'That's probably another sack-able offence.' She shot a warning look Marcus's way.

As far as she was concerned, hanky-lending with-standing, the jury was still out.

The harder I thought the more evasive the memories became. I shook my head, trying to remember anyone being on the computer. Often, all I'd written in my diary was the time of my shift and the name of the production.

'Don't worry.' He laid a hand on my forearm which I tried to ignore but I noticed quick curiosity in Christelle's eyes. I shook his hand off.

Christelle bristled beside me. 'Can we stick to the facts?' Marcus ignored her and picked up my diary again.

'Plenty more. We'll find something. We only need one. November 30th, 9.00pm.'

'Home. Alone.'

As we worked through the list, my spirits began to sink. On every single occasion that an email had been sent, it could have feasibly been me.

'I don't believe it. Seriously?' Every single time I was without an alibi. At home on my own. Not even Felix was at home.

After a while I laid my head down on the table.

'This is hopeless. Not one single date.'

'Can we double check?' Christelle pulled the laptop towards her. She clearly didn't trust Marcus to read and cross reference the information thoroughly enough.

'I'd be glad if you did, a second look would be most welcome. I would hate to miss anything.' Although he'd tried to rein in the sarcasm, I could tell my sister was irritating the hell out of him.

'Marcus ...' I wanted to appreciate his persistence but we had gone through every date. 'This is hopeless.'

'Don't give up,' his voice had softened.

'We're not,' snapped Christelle. 'But this isn't helping. You're making Tilly feel worse. Are you sure there isn't another way of proving her innocence?'

Tears pricked my eyes. I didn't want to be always crying.

'Look you guys, can we call a truce for the moment? Christelle, I know you want to leave no stone unturned but Marcus does genuinely want to help.'

Christelle's mouth firmed in a mutinous line before softening.

'Sorry, suspicious minds. A hazard of the job. Witnesses usually have a hidden agenda, or a motive for helping.'

'Come on let's take a break and clear our heads for a while.'

Christelle pulled a half full bottle of Rioja from the side. 'Want any?'

Marcus and I both nodded and she poured us a glass each.

'Is there anything in the fact that Tilly was always alone when the emails were sent?'

Marcus frowned taking an appreciative glug of wine. 'What – you think someone was deliberately framing her knowing she didn't have an alibi?'

'No! You've been watching too much *CSI*. I meant if Tilly was alone at home, where was Felix? With Vince? Did Felix know your passwords?'

'Unfortunately, he did,' I answered Christelle, keeping an eye on Marcus who tipped his head sideways as if lost in thought. 'You know how rubbish I am with computers. He set his laptop up so that I could check my emails at home.'

Marcus stood up and started to pace up and down around the table. 'If Felix wasn't at home, he'd have his laptop with him, presumably?'

Christelle straightened. 'So, you couldn't email anyone.'

Marcus pulled a face. 'It's not the strongest argument and how do you prove it?'

They were both barking up the wrong tree. 'Sorry guys, I could still email because I use my tablet when Felix's not around.'

Christelle chewed the end of her pen and scrunched up her face. 'Damn.'

'*CSI Southampton*!' Marcus threw himself back in the stool in front of his laptop.

'What?' Christelle exchanged a quick look with me.

'It's an in joke,' I said stiffly.

Marcus had opened his emails and was scrolling through.

'Bingo!' He turned the laptop screen to face me and Christelle came to stand behind my shoulder.

To: Matilde@lmoc.co.uk

From: Redsman@hotmail.co.uk
Subject: High Fidelity
    I'm glad you're enjoying it. One of my favourites.
And also a great film.
    Have you seen it? Not often you can say that,
when they abandon a perfectly good English
setting. Can't understand that? Why didn't they
leave the record shop in England? In fact, why do
film and TV companies have to fiddle with settings?
The Office? Life on Mars? Have we made an English
Friends? Mates? CSI - Southampton? Thankfully
High Fidelity survived. I'd recommend it if you
haven't seen it. One of those rare films that translates well from a book.
    R

I turned to him. 'I don't get it.'
    'Look at the date. Look at the time.'
    'Who's Redsman?' asked Christelle, peering at the
email.
    Marcus and I ignored her.
    'I get that,' I said, pointing to the day and date. 'The
same day and around the same time as the email to
the paper. How does that help? It just shows I was
online.'
    'Yes but,' he scrolled through the spreadsheet and
pointed to a series of numbers and dots, which could

have been the Enigma code for all I knew, 'these are IP addresses.'

'What addresses?'

'Internet Protocol,' he looked at me and smiled. 'When you connect a device to the internet, it pinpoints your location using an IP address. If the emails were being sent from different devices in different places, they'd be using different IP addresses. So, if someone was using your email account at the same time, the IP address would be different. Which means if you were at home sending this, you couldn't be in two places at once.'

'Excuse me,' Christelle interrupted again. 'But who is Redsman?'

I turned to Marcus, bouncing in my seat.

Christelle insinuated herself between us. 'Will one of you tell me who the hell Redsman is?'

'It's–'

'I am.'

Christelle stepped back, veiled amusement dancing about her mouth.

'You are.'

'It's a long story,' I said quickly avoiding looking at both of them and craning towards the screen. 'You mean … this proves I didn't send them.'

Christelle smiled and I understood the Barracuda references.

Marcus vacillated for a second. 'It doesn't prove it categorically. You could have been using either of the devices.'

'It's enough,' said Christelle, with authority, looking rather smug suddenly.

'It is?' I asked still not daring to believe that this might be it.

'It's about the balance of probability. The chances of your own device against the probability that someone else was using your log in on another device, would be enough.' She picked up her notepad and scribbled furiously before she gave a slow calculating smile. 'It gives us a very strong case.'

'But I still have to do the whole disciplinary panel thing.'

Christelle nodded. 'However, you are allowed to call witnesses and provide your own evidence.' She gave Marcus a telling look. 'And if one of their witnesses stands up for you, it will help no end.'

'Not a problem,' said Marcus picking up his wine glass and giving me a searching look over the rim.

'What about in my letter?' She tapped her notepad with her pen. 'Can I say that you have provided this evidence?'

'I think it will be sufficient, if you ask them leading questions about the IP addresses which were used, rather than say I came to you.' Marcus's tone was firm.

'They'll have to come to me to verify the information and I can confirm it.'

I lifted my chin, fighting against the lump settling in my throat. He was hardly going to jeopardise his own position. Not for me. Any stupid thoughts that he'd come to my rescue were cast aside in a swift, brutal guillotine slice of a reality check. It left a hollow, bleak sensation swirling in my chest.

'Right, I'm going to work up my notes.' Oblivious to my leaden pain, she scribbled a couple of lines on her pad. 'Marcus, can I have your phone number, in case I have any technical questions? I need to do some work. I'm going to type all this up and put it in a letter, telling them that new evidence suggests that someone else sent those emails and ask them to check the IP addresses. I'll have it couriered over first thing in the morning. I'll leave you two to it.' With a stern frown my way, which suggested I might have some explaining to do, she picked up her papers. She rubbed at her eyes which were slightly shadowed. It was late and she'd already had a full day in court. 'This is going to help but ... ' she and Marcus exchanged a guarded look.

'What?' I asked, fighting hard against threatening tears. 'Tell me. I'm not a five-year-old.'

'They could still hold out. Say you didn't observe proper security measures, leaving yourself open to this sort of thing.'

Marcus winced.

I lifted my shoulders and stuck my chin up, determined not to let either of them see how close I was to losing it. 'Then, there's not a lot I can do about that but at least I can prove that I didn't send those emails. I didn't go to the paper. I didn't do what they accused me of. I know I was an idiot. And if they sack me for it, that would be fair enough. But I couldn't bear it if they still believe that I would sell stories to a newspaper. There's every chance they decide to make an example of me.' I turned towards Marcus, keeping my face blank. 'You did try to tell me. All that computer security stuff.'

'Yes, but there could be a case to argue, you weren't expected to be computer literate in your role. That—'

'That's an excuse and you know it. At the end of the day, I have to take responsibility.' I let out a half-laugh. 'Exactly like Alison Kreufeld said.'

And now I completely understood what she meant. In this mess, I only had one person to blame. Myself. And I would have to live with the consequences. My sister could help me sort the practicalities out such as ensuring I received any references I needed but I realised in a moment of clarity that there was every chance I wouldn't get my job back. If I could at least clear my name, I stood a chance. There'd be other jobs, not as wonderful perhaps, but I had skill and experience, I would get another job.

I got up and moved around to Christelle's bar stool and gave her a hug. 'Thanks, Christelle. I really appreciate this. I ... I love you.' I was not going to break down. Not now. I'd held it together all evening. I could manage a bit longer.

In the dim light, I caught the tell-tale sheen of tears and she paused for a moment and then hugged me back.

'It's my absolute pleasure. I'm looking forward to it. We're going to nail them. I'll see you in the morning.'

Christelle touched my face. 'I love you too.' We'd never ever said it to each other before.

'Goodnight. Night Marcus.'

She headed to the small study room where she often worked at home.

'You OK?'

I nodded. He looked tired too.

'I will be. I just wish it was all over.' I picked up my wine.

'It will be soon. Your sister's rather fearsome. I can imagine her letter will stir things up.'

'I hope so.' I sighed heavily but inside I wasn't so sure. Picking up my wine glass I walked over to the window. Outside the lights of the city twinkled like crystals dancing in the wind. Giant holly leaves lighting up a sky-scraper in Canary Wharf and a six-pointed star adorning another building.

Marcus came to stand behind me and I ached to lean back into him. I wished I could turn the clock back but I knew that too much had changed. He was all business. It was his job to unearth the facts. I guessed he was keen to get to the bottom of things.

'Everyone knows it wasn't you. Philippe was threatening to set up a picket line today. Jeanie has already told them they're being ridiculous. And whatever your sister put in her letter certainly put the wind up them. You didn't do it.' He put down his wine glass on the wooden coffee table. The tea lights had long since flickered out.

I moved away from him, putting distance between us so that I didn't cave in and reach for him and make a complete tit of myself.

'Let's hope they believe you. After all it would mean you got it wrong the first time.' His mouth tightened. 'Don't worry. I will make it clear, that technically, it was virtually impossible for you to have sent those emails.'

'Thank you,' I said stiffly. 'I appreciate it.'

With a quick twist of his wrist, he glanced at his watch. 'No problem. I'd better be off. If you … need anything. You've got my mobile.' He might as well have offered me his business card at the end of a meeting.

'Thanks. I'll be OK.' I gave a cool smile. 'I've got Christelle on my side.'

It hurt when he gave an indifferent shrug. My

instincts had been right. Whatever I'd felt for him was one-sided. Maybe there hadn't been an ulterior motive for taking me out that Saturday but he'd clearly realised the same as me; that it wasn't meant to be. We were two very different people. I would always be one of the creative, prone to flights of fancy types of people while he would always be the professional, corporate man who dealt in facts and reality.

Chapter 39

The radio tuned to *Heart FM* filled the silence, with every other song a Christmas one. I sang along to Wizard, George Michael, Mariah Carey and Bing Crosby as I washed up the breakfast cups. For once I didn't mind being on my own. Before I'd always had the theatre to go to. Now it was just quiet all the time. I missed the camaraderie of my theatre friends. The teasing. The colour. The thunderous applause. The melodic soaring of voices. But after a night of soul-searching, pre-empted by a good old cry, I'd realised while I was unlikely to keep my job, there would be others.

Waking up, I felt calmer, like a small boat bobbing in a wide ocean after a storm. Even Alison had said I was a talented make-up artist. With a wry smile, as I emptied the washing up bowl, I realised how far I'd come. Some might say I'd grown up. They'd probably be right. I'd even planned my day to keep myself busy.

Once I'd finished tidying up here, I was going to go over to the flat, pack a few more things to bring back to Christelle's and make a list of things to do to smarten the place up before meeting her this evening for the first event of the Hunter sisters' Christmas calendar.

Christelle phoned as I was wrapping her silk scarf, confident that she was going to love it, as well as the leather business card holder embossed with a C and the DVD of *Legally Blonde*. Sadly, the T-shirt with the words *You can't scare me, my sister's a legal eagle* which I'd ordered from the internet, wouldn't make it in time for Christmas but picturing her face when it did, made me smile.

'They want to see you.' She sounded full of glee. 'Today. ASAP.'

'But it's Christmas Eve.'

'Yup, they obviously want to sort things out quickly.'

I didn't need to ask who *they* were.

'And that's good?'

'Technically yes.'

'What about not technically?'

'Let's go with the positives. They said they have new evidence. It must be good ... otherwise they'd follow procedure and convene a disciplinary panel. Can you meet me at the stage door in an hour's time?'

'Sure.' Nerves shimmered in the pit of my stomach.

I just wanted to know one way or the other whether I'd get my job back. I also wanted to know why Marcus hadn't been in touch. Was that good or bad?

I dressed with care. If I was going into battle I wanted to look the part. Christelle's professional armour of black must have rubbed off, because I found myself pulling on a little-worn tailored black dress which just skimmed my knees. I looked good in it, but not me.

I shook my head at my reflection in Christelle's full length mirror, another reminder of my half-hearted homemaking. In the flat I'd have to stand on the loo seat in the bathroom to get a view of my bottom half. Why had I never got around to buying a proper mirror? I took another appraising look at myself. I needed to be me. I added high heeled red suede ankle boots and a matching cherry red shrug and a red beret. That was more me. Battle ready, I left the flat gripping my vintage 50's crocodile handbag like a lifebelt.

I could have spent the whole journey second guessing what they might say, what might happen and I refused to let this damn episode take any more head space. Instead I focused on all the things I wanted to do in the next six months. Tart up the flat. Put it on the market. Look for a new job. Maybe invite Mum and Dad down to stay. Get them tickets for something at the Met.

And then the lift at Covent Garden deposited me at

the top of the station and the stage door was a ten-minute walk.

Nerves shimmered. Christelle was already there and waiting for me.

'You OK?'

I nodded, not trusting my voice to work. My legs were shaking as I signed the visitors' book.

'Don't worry Tilly.' She led the way into the lift. 'The fact that they want to see you now, is good. It means that the situation has changed.' She paused. 'Although, you ... you need to be clear in your mind what you want the outcome to be.'

'What do you mean?'

'Sometimes when they suspend someone, admitting that they're wrong can be quite tricky. Organisations can get very funny about setting the wrong sort of precedent.'

'What are you saying?'

'They might want to pay you off. Don't worry; they'll agree to give you references. Compensation but ... they might not give you your job back. I'm just warning you. Preparing you.'

'Don't worry. I realised that. I want references. That's the most important thing.'

She shook her head and was about to say something but the lift doors drew open and there was no time to say anything. Alison Kreufeld lurked outside as if she were waiting for me and before Marsha's secretary could reach me, she nodded at me and winked.

'This way please, Miss Hunter,' said the secretary, side-stepping Alison who trailed after us.

Marsha and the Chief Executive were sitting at the same round table as we were ushered in to the room. I didn't know if I was relieved or disappointed that Marcus wasn't present. Where was he? And what had he said to them? Presumably they'd spoken to him after receiving Christelle's letter. I guessed he was still the company man. Had he told them that he'd contacted me?

'Good afternoon and thank you for coming so promptly.'

'Good afternoon. This is my legal representative, Christelle Hunter.' Spending time with my sister had rubbed off. Despite my churning stomach on a warp speed spin, I was pleased how together and professional I sounded.

'Ah yes,' the Chief Executive's voice sounded strained. 'You've been most diligent on behalf of your client.' I don't think he meant it as a compliment.

'Thank you.' Christelle's crisp acceptance made me smile as his mouth tightened. She had no intention of making this easy for anyone.

Marsha exchanged a look with Julian, part exasperation and part impatience.

'Miss Hunter, Tilly. Since we last saw you, we have received new information which completely exonerates your name and makes it clear that you had absolutely nothing to do with the emails that were sent.'

Under the table Christelle nudged my foot with hers, I could feel her leg jumping up and down.

'We wish to make an unreserved apology and would like to reinstate you in your position with immediate effect. You can return to work as soon as you'd like to.'

Christelle opened her mouth.

Marsha intercepted holding up her hand. 'Tilly, we know that this whole business must have caused you terrible distress and we,' she shot the Chief Executive a dirty look, 'would like to make some reparation. Your work has always been exemplary and in fact some of the performers have been quite vociferous in their support of you. Our Artistic Director, Ms Kreufeld has been most insistent that we should make an internal appointment and on her recommendation, we have therefore decided to promote you to Assistant Department Head with a significant pay rise on a permanent contract.'

Stunned, I sat there vaguely aware of Christelle talking about paperwork and revised contracts.

'If we could have a moment.' Christelle nudged me, rising from her seat and inclining her head. I followed her out of the room.

'Are you OK with this?' she asked.

'Are you kidding?' I asked, my legs so shaky they could barely hold me up, even though I wanted to jump up and down and squeal. 'Absolutely.'

'We could still play hard ball.' She winked.

'No, this is,' I threw my arms around her, jittery with emotion, 'just perfect. Thank you so much. I don't know what I'd have done without you.'

'Neither do I,' she said with a cocky grin, returning the hug.

'No, seriously. You have been amazing.'

'Only because I completely believed in you. You're amazing.'

We returned to the room and in a complete daze, my hands trembling, I signed something which Christelle sanctioned.

As the meeting drew to a close, I finally managed to gather my wits about me. 'Can I ask what evidence did you find?' I was dying to know how Marcus backed me up.

Marsha smiled grimly. 'We had a full confession from another member of the team. He said he'd been deliberately using your account so that he wouldn't get found out. He resigned immediately.'

'What?' I asked throwing a stunned look at Christelle who appeared equally surprised.

'Vince Redmond.'

'I can't believe it.' I said for the 95th million time as I sat in Jeanie's office. Christelle, brimming with triumph, had beetled off to collect a turkey crown from Marks, having discovered that for all my Christmas preparations, I'd completely forgotten the smaller matter of a turkey.

'Vince confessed.'

'Hmm.' Jeanie seemed very grumpy.

'He must have listened to his conscience after all.'

Jeanie scowled.

I nudged her in the ribs. 'Go on, don't you think he deserves a smidgeon of credit.'

'Tilly!' With a sudden jerk, she shoved a pile of papers into her bin. 'He didn't confess out of the goodness of his heart.'

'Well why did he then?'

I could see her weighing things up before a decided smirk crossed her face. 'Marcus persuaded him it was the right thing to do.'

'Marcus?'

'Yes.' Her sudden grin was positively evil. 'Let's say he put Vince in an impossible position.'

'What did he do?'

'He rounded up a few witnesses, Philippe, Pietro, Guillaume, Carol, myself and explained that he had evidence that could be vilified—'

'Verified.'

'That too. To prove that you couldn't have sent the emails at the time you had and he waffled on about IDs and two places at once. Then he went and stood in front of Vince and said, "I know it was you. And I can prove it, it will just take a few days, but it's inevitable. In the meantime, Tilly's going to be worrying all through Christmas about the job that she adores." He looked round at everyone and said. "We don't want that, do we?" Vince went very red. And then Marcus whispered very loudly, "Or I could just beat you to a pulp."'

'He did what?' I laced my fingers together tightly to hide the surge of electricity tingling through my veins, like jitterbugs.

'Very masterful, he was.'

'Blimey and what ... Vince just confessed?'

'He blustered a bit and then he and Marcus left the room. That was this morning.'

'Where's Marcus now?'

'He said he had some shopping to do.'

By five o'clock I was just putting the finishing touches to my lengthy list of improvements to the flat after wandering around through the silent rooms with a notebook and pen, trying to avoid the memories of all that Felix and I had shared. I'd packed some extra clothes ready to go to Christelle's – we were going to sing carols in Trafalgar Square at seven, before returning to her flat for Prosecco cocktails – when the door-bell rang.

When I opened my door, there was no one there but a large box sitting in the doorway.

There was no delivery note or anything – just my name written on the top. It was too big to carry back upstairs, so I sat down on the cold concrete step buffeted by the winter wind.

Peeling back the cardboard, I looked down into the box, swiping at my hair which was being blown over my face. All I could see was a large flat rectangle of pale grey opaque plastic. What on earth was it? Putting my hands into the box, I slipped each one down on either side of the plastic to pull whatever it was out. My fingers on one side touched the cold glaze of china and a handle, the other side was solid. I grasped the thing and slid it out of the box and pulled the unwieldy object onto my knees, starting to smile as I realised what it was.

A piece of paper with my name on it caught in the wind and I had to snatch at it.

My heart thumping, I unfolded the paper.

Happy Christmas
Mx

A thousand butterflies took flight in my stomach as I studied it, before laughing out loud. The squat, Bakelite Goblin Teasmade was the ugliest present anyone had ever sent me.

'Is it the best present or the worst?'

Peering up through my windswept hair I saw Marcus looming over me.

I slowly stood up, carefully placing it on the step trying to school my features, while a thousand hopeful thoughts raced through my head.

'Where on earth did you find it?' I asked, still unable to believe he was really here.

'On the internet, but I had to drive to Croydon to pick it up. That's why I wasn't at work earlier.' He was watching me closely and I realised I hadn't answered his question.

I stared back down at the teasmade in thoughtful silence.

Marcus waited as I struggled to find the words.

'That depends ...' My voice shook. I wanted to be calm and not give anything away but it was so difficult when he was standing there looking utterly gorgeous in one of his usual suits, with that familiar serious expression highlighting every feature of his face, narrowed green eyes searching mine and his hair standing in uncharacteristic little tufts as if he'd been running his hands through it.

'It ... It depends on,' I took in a sharp breath and then deciding what the hell, finished quickly with, '... on who's drinking the tea with me.'

We stared at each other for a moment. My heart fizzed with longing at the expression on his face.

'I ... I hoped it might be ...' for one adorable moment which made my chest tighten, he sounded terribly unsure.

I took in another breath, holding onto it so tightly it almost hurt waiting for him to finish.

'... me?' The questioning note made my insides turn liquid but still I held out.

'What's changed? You ... you said you didn't want Christelle to let anyone know you had helped find the evidence. I thought you'd washed your hands of me.'

The lines around his lips, which I couldn't peel my hungry gaze from, tightened as if in pain.

'I had to appear impartial. I didn't want there to be any room for anyone to question the evidence or my motives.' The hurried words were forceful and almost panicky. 'Make sure no one could accuse me of being emotionally involved.'

My heart bumped in my chest. 'Emotionally involved?' My fingers curled over my thumbs as if I were clutching them to keep myself grounded even though the rest of me seemed to be preparing to float away.

Marcus lifted a tentative hand and I watched as he

lifted it towards me to stroke away one of the curls dancing in the wind across my face. The tip of his finger just trailed across my cheek and I was a goner. The gesture just got to me, I could hardly speak but there were still so many questions and I daren't assume anything. I waited.

'Yes. Despite everything I thought when I started, I couldn't help myself. You and everyone else there are all bloody useless with computers and drive me insane with your completely crap disregard for technology, but I've never worked anywhere where people who are so,' he held out his hands in a gesture of frustration, 'bonkers, ridiculous, crazy, idiotic, dramatic, weird work together so seamlessly. It's some huge Luddite machine that magically slots together, the orchestra, the costumes, the actors, the lighting crew. On the night, it's some incredible miracle.

'And you,' he took my face between his hands. 'You are amazing. I've seen hundreds of workaholics, wedded to the job, letting it define them, dominate their waking hours but not adding anything to them. With you, you live for the job and embrace it with such passion and joy. You bound with energy and positivity. I envy that. I've never come across it before. Not for glory or for promotions or money. Just because you love what you do.' His eyes blazed with an emotion that hit me, almost stopping my heart as he lowered his voice, 'I've never met anyone quite like you. I fell in love with work again and ...'

I think my face must have said quite a bit because with a sudden movement, he hauled me into his arms and planted his lips on mine with determined possession, his hand cradling my head in a move that I found unbearably sexy. The electric, tentative touch of his tongue, a gentle contrast to the firm pressure of his mouth made my knees almost buckle and forget we were standing on the doorstep in full view of the street. We'd kissed before but this was a whole new ball game, a set your soul on fire, desperate imprint of skin on skin filled with searing intensity. Completely intoxicating. I was lost. Oh man. Everything was soft, gentle and so, so moreish. His tongue teased mine and my whole system went on red alert, nerve endings firing up to full throttle.

When he released my lips, he smoothed my face and took my hand and led me towards the front door. 'I'm most definitely emotionally involved. You made me feel things that I didn't believe in. Like love.'

'Oh,' I said in a very small voice.

'Do you think you could feel anything for a corporate bod masquerading as the Prince of Darkness?'

'I think I might be able to manage that.' I smiled at him. 'You never know. I might even go over to the dark side and master this technology business.'

With an unromantic snort, he said, 'Steady on. I don't think I'm ready for that. I wouldn't want to think I'm redundant already.'

A naughty smile sprang to my lips. 'I'm sure there are other things you could teach me.'

'Shall we get that teasmade installed?' There was a suggestive twinkle in his eye that made me laugh.

'New euphemism?' Reluctantly, I pulled a rueful face. 'Slight problem, I'm supposed to be meeting Christelle in two hours in Trafalgar Square.'

Marcus gave me a very wicked smile. 'That's OK, I asked Guillaume to keep her occupied. We're meeting them at eight.'

'In that case, let's take this baby for a trial run. And then I'll let you know how it measures up in the Christmas present stakes.'

Epilogue

Wrapped up against the wind with Marcus's arm around my shoulders, I looked up towards the very top of the Christmas tree to the star, lit up and shining like a brilliant beacon, and noticed the first flakes of snow starting to fall. Around us voices joined in with the choir singing *Silent Night*, the notes rising and falling, carried by the flurries of air swirling around us. The magical atmosphere of community and happiness brought a sudden rush of contentment and tears of joy filled my eyes.

Even though my cheeks were chilled by the faint spray drifting across from the fountain spot-lit with coloured lights, inside a special warmth filled me, radiating sheer bliss. Next to me Christelle, bundled in a cashmere scarf and bobble, caught my eye and smiled, her bright red lipstick etching her mouth in a serene smile. She winked before turning to mouth something to Guillaume who gave a small give-away start and pulled her closer to him.

I nodded upwards and her gaze followed mine and then, with a mutual smile, we both lifted our faces up to the sky waiting for our angel kisses. Smiling to myself, I snuggled into Marcus who responded by turning me round and putting both arms around me, pulling me closer into his body. A tingle raced through me, sparked by recent memories of his touch. His lips traced a path down from my forehead, kissing the tip of my nose before planting themselves with a searing kiss on my mouth.

This was shaping up to be one of the best Christmases ever although Marcus's present was as yet un-tested. We'd been somewhat pre-occupied by other things, involving unwrapping each other's layers, literally and figuratively speaking.

Distracted by a sudden thought, I pulled back and gnawed at my lip. He'd gone all the way to Croydon to buy the perfect present and I hadn't got him anything. If only I'd got him those cufflinks.

I realised he was looking down into my face, his handsome face softened with a tender look that made me want to pull him close and keep him there forever. Reliable and steady, serious and grave by turns, he was everything that I could ever wish for and hadn't known I wanted. Suddenly my words came back to me, 'The best presents are things you didn't know you wanted but you love them.' There was one thing that I could give him, to seal this perfect moment. I grabbed the tail ends of his scarf and tugged, before standing on tip-toe to whisper, 'I love you.'